BISON
BOOKS

Season's End

A NOVEL

Tom Grimes

UNIVERSITY OF NEBRASKA PRESS
LINCOLN AND LONDON

∞ The paper in this book meets the minimum requirements of American National Standard for Information Sciences—Permanence of Paper for Printed Library Materials, ANSI Z39.48-1984.

First Bison Books printing: 1996
Most recent printing indicated by the last digit below:
10   9   8   7   6   5   4   3   2   1

Library of Congress Cataloging-in-Publication Data
Grimes, Tom, 1954–
Season's end: a novel / Tom Grimes.
p.   cm.
ISBN 0-8032-7067-4 (pbk.: alk. paper)
1. Celebrities—Fiction.   I. Title.
[PS3557.R489985S4   1996]
813'.54—dc20
96-7732   CIP

Reprinted from the original 1992 edition by Little, Brown and Company, Boston.

for Frank Conroy

Acknowledgments

THE AUTHOR wishes to thank the New York Mets for their assistance and generosity, in particular Frank Cashen, Al Harazin, Joe McIlvaine, Jean Coen, Dr. Alan Lans, Dr. James Parkes, Mike Cubbage, and Howard Johnson. Thanks also to James Michener and the Copernicus Society for their generous support. And much love and thanks to Jody and Charlie.

BOOK I

I celebrate myself, and sing myself,
And what I assume you shall assume,
For every atom belonging to me as good belongs to you.

— *Walt Whitman*
"Song of Myself"

One

A WORD OF ADVICE: Don't appear on the cover of *Sports Illustrated* when you're twenty-one.

Although I had been the leading hitter in the minor leagues for two consecutive seasons — despite the fact that I suffered a three-week stretch during which my bat did not once touch a pitch — I knew that the real reason I had been brought up to the majors was to replace a dead man. Ted Monday, the former left fielder, died while grilling a steak in his yard. Thirty-three, in perfect health, an athlete; yet he died for no apparent physical reason. There had been no heart attack, no stroke, no cancer, no overdose. His body just stopped being a live thing. He had been a baseball player. He went out like one. He died on the Fourth of July with a Budweiser in his hand.

The big-league coaches wanted to get a look at me. They said I was the best pure singles hitter they had ever seen. (But this is only three men talking.) I'm a righty, and they suggested that I learn to drop my right shoulder as I made contact with the ball. That way, they said, I'd hit home runs, loft the ball into the blue-collar sections of the stadium, far past the corporate boxes and first-row baseline seats reserved for visiting celebrities, up into the celestial realm of stardom and product-endorsement contracts. But first I'd have to put a little weight on, add some beef to my 160-pound frame.

"Drink some beer once in a while," Lunch (as in "out to") Molloy said. He was a flatulent, rhino-shaped man with a nose that looked like a fresh fig hanging from the center of his eyebrows. His purpose on the team, as I saw it, was to imitate the figure of the imperturbable batting coach, ever unruffled.

"I do," I said. "Every day."

"Then why are you so skinny?"

"I don't eat."

"Then drink some more."

The team hired a special batting instructor to accelerate (so they hoped) my development. He was a Hall of Famer, a former golden boy in the game: viceless, unselfish, leader by example; anonymous during the off-season, married to a U.S. president's niece. He was, quite possibly, the greatest hitter the game had ever seen, and he'd sacrificed a week of fishing and flown in from his island retreat in order to stand behind me at the plate, spit into the mud, and earn $75,000.

"Naw, not like that," he said, after I'd fouled off a slider. The dirt at his feet was pitted with wads of slimy tobacco.

I drove the next pitch, a curveball up and in around my hands, into the opposite field. Clean single.

"Now that's better. What did you do that time?"

"I hit the ball fair."

"No. You waited. Wait on the ball. Don't be afraid to wait."

The pitcher served up a mediocre fastball and I took him downtown with it, ripping the pitch into the left centerfield alley, my power lane.

"You're not waitin'," he shouted, then hawked into the mud.

"I jumped all over the pitch. When I get a mediocre fastball I'm supposed to jump all over it."

"Not until after you've waited. Wait! Then jump all over the pitch."

A change-up that read Hit Me! in capital letters ambled toward the plate. I waited, expecting the pitch to move in and out like a change-up should, shimmy a little, loop and dive like a paper airplane. But it just glided by slowly, on a straight line, and I developed sort of a dumb interest in it, as if it were a tropical fish cruising along in a pet shop tank. The ball made a muffled thud, like a kid punching his pillow, when it hit the catcher's mitt. Strike.

"Now you're waitin' on the ball." *Pthupp!*

The next day a local sports columnist wrote that he had "witnessed some of the secret knowledge of the game changing hands."

My owner, Edmond Perlmutter Percy, called me up to his suite of offices a few hours before I was to play my first game in the majors. He said that he wanted to make clear to me his attitude toward the game so that I, as one of his "boys," would reflect it, both on and off the field. From his wheelchair he spoke to me in the blustery, forgetful manner of senile tycoons, as portrayed by ham actors in bad Hollywood movies.

"The American public expects ballplayers to be moral, clean-living, symbolic young men. The game is played on grass, expensive mats of sod. Two dollars a square foot to be exact. I have the seats painted candy-apple red every year. This place costs me money. Don't scrape your cleats on the locker room floor. That's porcelain tile. Pick up your feet!" He paused for a coughing fit, then resumed. "The American public expects ballplayers to be —"

A short, white-haired attendant in a blue suit leaned over and whispered into the magnate's ear, then was waved away. Mr. Percy looked at me again.

"As your owner, I expect that you will do nothing to tarnish the reputation of this ballclub, or this hallowed sport. If you have any homosexual tendencies, or plan to marry interracially, I order you to repress the aforementioned desires until such time as you have been long forgotten by the American viewing audience. The way you act influences the possible heterosexuality of young American boys. Don't let me hear that you like to wear dresses!"

At this point, he fell asleep. The assistant, who had been as solemn as a pallbearer throughout, motioned to me to remain seated. He woke the ancient industrialist and handed him two pills and a Dixie cup filled with water. Mr. Percy then signaled that he wished to have his wheelchair turned so that he could look out of the window at his stadium, the silent sun-swept lawn, the pseudomystical aura of the diamond. His assistant gripped the handles of the chair, but Mr. Percy shooed him away again. He wanted *me* to chauffeur him. When we both could see the field, he reached over his shoulder, placing one hand on mine. His skin felt like a crisp new dollar bill.

"I expect great things of you," he said. "I sense it. I can sense great things in the making. This ability made me rich."

This and his father's steel mill fortune.

"Let's you and I never talk about money, boy. You just go out there and do great things. Promise me you and I will never talk about money. Don't even think about it. You'll become obsessed. Let me worry about money. At your age money will only disrupt your life, jade you, turn you into a self-hating cynic. You're not ready for money yet."

"How old were you when you inherited your father's fortune?"

"I admire your forthrightness. I was nineteen. But I was already rich, so the money didn't disrupt my life. So forget comparing yourself to me. It won't get you anywhere."

Mr. Percy was silent for a moment. Then he gestured toward the field. "Revere this game," he said. "Revere it. This game reveals in incomprehensible ways the awesome sublimity of profitable things. It's an expression of our collective national spirit. This game . . . is our religion."

"What did we have before the game?"

"God."

Mr. Percy spun his chair around quickly, on his own steam. "Remember one thing," he said. "Do not allow yourself to fall prey to sexual envy of blacks. Overlook their natural endowments. Avert your eyes in the locker room. Play with them on the field, but avert your eyes in the locker room. Avert them!"

I went four for four that night and got the gamer (not then a statistic) against the defending world champions. We played before a crowd of desperate and wishful fans, people I felt I knew, was bound to by grief and fear, my poor boy's blood: the lonely souls who sit in the upper decks waiting for a winner, the generous and embracing spirit of a pennant-bound club to latch on to. My teammates, men I'd known for only a few days, congratulated me, yet managed to ignore me at the same time. This sort of behavior is common on ballclubs. Players don't like to get too close to anyone. You never know how long the other guy is staying. That you may be the one who isn't going to be around, you don't even think about. In the minors I would dress next to someone for half the season; the next day he'd be gone without a word — moved up, down, traded, released. One time dead. Expendable, as interchangeable as auto parts, our popularity fluctuating with the whims of the fans and the press, ballplayers tend to be self-concerned, narcissistic types, stalked by both the void of anonymity and the specter of unfulfilled promise.

Three names hovered in the air that somber autumn: Messersmith, McNally, Saigon. Nineteen seventy-five. Old orders were toppling. A revolutionary and dispiriting sense of compromise, of defeat, was descending on the republic, an uneasiness in the land where gleaming new automobiles stretched from horizon to smog-clotted horizon. An evil malaise. And I was twenty-one, and playing a child's game.

Two

NUMBERS: somehow they're connected to death, our ruminations on the final and the infinite. They describe for us, in an incontestable way, the invisible and ineluctable limits of the game. We are points on a straight line, creatures haunted by vanishing points and horizons, dumb to the round wonder of the world.

The best ballplayer I ever saw was George O'Kane, bean-pole thin and an arm like a cannon. In the minors, before I was summoned by Mr. Percy, we played the outfield together, that sun-warmed pasture seemingly safe from the random violence of cities and infields, and shared the same room on the road. He was from Peekskill, New York, a small industrial town in the southeast part of the state planted at the foot of the Catskill Mountains, seventy miles above the Oz-like city to the south. Two years older than me, he had been born in 1952 the day the first thermonuclear bomb was detonated at Enewetak and was named All-City the day John Kennedy was assassinated, his beginnings linked, in the random bingo-logic of history, with cataclysm and early death. Six two, 150 pounds, he ran like a purse snatcher, hit with a sneaky, almost phantom power (he swore it was all a matter of bat speed and pussy juice, refusing to wash his hands after he'd made love to his girlfriend the morning of a game, rubbing down his bat with an unwashed pair of her panties when we were on the road), and reacted, for a period of time, to every event formal or extraordinary by honking the word "moosecock" at bewildered and humorless standersby, using the expression with an illogical, jack-in-the-box style of surprise, an almost phonetic, Road-Runneresque catchall, something birdlike and animated at the center of his being that couldn't express itself in normal speech.

"Oh-oh say can you see . . ."

"Moosecock!"

Numbers warp when they reach the light-speed of myth. The closure of statistics yields to the open-endedness of legend, straight lines curl into circles, and the entropy of cardinal numbers with their test-your-strength-and-win-the-Kewpie-doll fluctuations bends toward the groundless bedrock of zero.

I once saw him throw a ball from dead center to home, flat-footed.

We are ballplayers. We accept the ineffable and get on with the game.

"What are you, sick?"

We were on some deserted community diamond, George's Malibu, unwashed since 1968, parked on the grass behind the backstop, a cooler full of beer on the backseat amid bats, gloves, cleats, and mud. We had the day off, courtesy of our minor league coach, Houston Slaught, who said if he threw up any more from watching us play he'd have to turn in his stomach lining for some American Tourister luggage. So, George and I, far from love and home, took off into the great, sleeping, sun-stunned midwestern countryside, the earth, in that drought year, as dense, hot, and parched as a pizza stone.

I was standing in the batter's box, that invisible coffin, taking practice cuts at spitballs — scudding, slow-moving pitches that sail in on a clothesline, then, a foot in front of the plate, fall through a trapdoor in space, taking some going-down elevator-shaft plunge before recovering their sense of forward motion — when George stepped off the mound and walked toward me.

"You can't *see* the ball," he said. "You feel it." He looked at me momentarily, sizing me up. "You need weed."

Gok (short for George O'Kane, a prehistoric acronym, some caveman handle suited to our more primitive selves) and I went through a period of massive marijuana abuse, an obsession brief but deep. A publisher's daughter was a kidnapped urban guerrilla, Nixon an addlepated drunk talking to portraits in the halls of the White House, and bourbon-stoked senators were still talking winnable wars while kids brought up on "Bonanza" and Pop-Tarts went around spouting Mao. It was a strange time. A lot of people did drugs to get by; others thought of them as a charge card to enlightenment. George and I were ballplayers. We smoked pot to hit fastballs.

The grass had been the color of Georgia clay, flowerpot red with bamboo-smooth stems. George's portable tape deck was leaning against the backstop, Bob Marley cranking out some initiation rite-of-passage top-forty hit. We passed the joint between us: the pot cleared out canyons in my skull, my brain opening like some river-carved canal in the earth.

"Moosecock. Enough dope. Get in the box."

"I don't wanna hit."

"Get in the box or I'll shit in your locker."

"The ball has a face."

"Get in the box."

George had a heater that crossed the plate at triple-digit speed, his entire body one inverted, K-shaped coil at the midpoint of his motion — major league velocity and the control of a wino, his only chance for pitching immortality contingent upon an enlargement of the strike zone to Green Giant proportions.

"You almost took my head off!"

"Bite me."

The next pitch glided in with a cartoon slowness, the drug letting out the waistline of time, seconds doing rubber-band stretches. A lost-in-space weightlessness flowed through me as I saw the ball stop and hover, still as a hummingbird, over the plate, while I, insubstantial as a movie image, slashed and chopped at it like some amphetamine-crazed samurai.

"Moosecock! Hit the ball!"

A screamer rushed toward me, the ball bursting into a great, swollen pumpkin that I swung at in self-defense and popped over the backstop.

"Better. You know what your problem is?"

"Fear of authority?"

"You're not high enough."

We prepped another joint, George rolling the stick with cowboy confidence, plastic sandwich bag held between his teeth while he removed a few buds from the pouch then sprinkled them as finely as a spice into the tongue-dampened paper he held in his other hand. We sat with our shoulders pressing up against the backstop, knees drawn in, and passed the joint between us, the ritual itself calming, calling up in me some long-lost village pleasure, some Paleolithic sense of contentment.

"We don't share anymore," I said. "Everybody has this 'It's mine' fixation. I think that's why we like to go out and eat Chinese. It's the whole let's-try-seventeen-different-dishes approach to the meal. Materialism overlaps with community. We feel linked to our nomadic, cave-dwelling past. Pitchers of beer are good. That's a sharing. Bumming a cigarette. 'You want to smoke a joint?' Very good. Excellent. Totally egalitarian, in the best sense of the word."

I looked out at the field, its white, regimental baselines opening out to embrace the cow-pasture expanse of the outfield, and realized that I had been talking for nine centuries. I stared at the green range and it soon began to vibrate, a microscopic, blade-ruffling shiver running through it until it finally began to rise, the entire field levitating like some B-movie UFO. I was a ballplayer, used to sublime events, acts tinged with magic. I watched the hovering diamond, a pagan icon, some floating Druid altar, and was unamazed.

"You know, I think it would be impossible to die in an on-deck circle."

"Moosecock. Get up and hit."

I think what drew George and me to each other was a polar magnetism, some opposites-attract bonding. Where I was ruminative, an alchemist working with the sly metal of stats, ever conscious of the long-shot immortality that dwells in numbers (even

as they defeat us), George crashed into outfield walls, swung at
pitches three feet over his head, and goosed first basemen before
breaking into his Road Runner scramble for the bag at second.
An ad-libbed sense of spontaneity drove him, some electrical current of improvisation oblivious to cries of restraint. If he entered
a barroom bathroom wearing jeans and a polo shirt, he emerged
naked and wrapped head-to-toe in toilet paper, a schlock-movie
mummy limping across the cool surface of the gummy indoor-
outdoor carpeting, pecker extended like a flagpole. Where I but-
toned my shirt to the collar and polished my cleats before every
game, George had to be told to bathe. If I didn't want to die,
George didn't know he could.

"You wanna hit, close your eyes when you swing."

An inexplicable sense of grace infused my play that blissful
year in the minors. It was free of the loop-the-loop vicissitudes of
slumps and streaks. Five sixty-eight, .432. Combined, George and
I batted 1.000, committed zero errors. Yin-and-yang perfection.
Neither of us that fleeting year struck out to end an inning, neither
of us hit into a game-ending double play. Some potion, some elixir
of immortality coursed through our veins, and it fed the infallibility of our gloves, sang the genius of our rosin-dusted bats.

"Don't look."

I hoisted the bat handle even with my right shoulder, then
clung to it as if it were some lifeline thrown down from heaven,
the ground dropping out from under my feet the instant I closed
my eyes. I waited to feel the pitch approach the plate, listened for
the ball's whispering speed, sniffed the air for the blossoming
scent of leather and sweat. I sensed at first a radar blip, a dime-
sized comet streaking across the face of a black screen. Then saw,
as if a shutter lens had opened — somewhere, not quite on the
world, not quite in my mind — a four-color, 3-D object, its stitching flashing by like the ties in a set of roller-coaster tracks, its
speed eating up air, mushrooming now like some nuclear cloud,
its phantom heat passing through me like X rays. So I swung.

I heard the echoless, gunshot report of ball meeting bat, an
instantaneous, firecracker marriage. I opened my eyes and saw the
ball winging on a bullet-straight line. No arc, just the wicked

single-mindedness of a missile. When it reached the outfield it struck the metal cap of a supporting post in the chest-high chain-link fence, tearing the cap off, and making the entire fence begin to rattle like a thousand sets of keys.

"Moosecock."

"Good dope."

"I didn't think it was shittin' possible," Crotch Daniels, our batting coach, said, the day George and I returned, "but we did it. We produced an entire generation of shitheads. Williams is trying to hit with his eyes closed." He moved away at that moving-sidewalk pace of managers, lost in some fugue of gum chewing and waking sleep.

"Moley," George said, "get your dick out of your ass and throw the ball."

Moley, one of our minor league relief pitchers, pinched the tip of his tongue with his pitching fingers, raised them and adjusted his cap by its bill, paused on the way down to slip the tip of his index finger deep into one nostril, touched his fingers to the left breast of his shirt, then fingered the ball deep inside the pocket of his glove.

"Don't look at him. Look at me," George said, bat cocked, feet twenty-four inches apart, knees slightly bowed, heels alternately lifting and tapping the batter's box surface in some body-focusing, Mexican hat dance movement. "Watch" — *crack!* — "my eyes." The ball dropped behind the 397 mark.

Gary Bump, our second-squad catcher, tossed Moley a new ball without leaving his crouch. "Yeah. Watch his eyes and tell him you love him."

George drove a shin-high pitch veering away from the plate into right field. His eyes were still fixed on me when I looked back at him. "See?"

Slap! This one landed in the short porch in left, a 309-foot dream for right-handed pull hitters, of which George was one. *Thwap!* Alley in left center. George closed his eyes and snored. *Clack!* Clean single.

Gary Bump signaled to Moley to come in off the mound.

"I think I'd bat a thousand if I was on acid," I said.

"Moosecock. Don't think."

George was called up to the majors the last month of the season, our parent club overwhelmed by a veritable mutiny of injuries both actual and feigned, arrogant rookies and bored-stiff elder statesmen giving in to a collective piss-on-it attitude, twenty-three games to go and forty-five out of first place.

While George was driving north he stopped to empty his bladder and noticed that his urine was as foamy as warm cream soda. Two weeks into his stretch in the majors, he called me. "Every time I take a piss the shit has more head on it than Piels."

Thirteen games, forty-four at bats: six home runs, eighteen runs batted in, two triples, nineteen doubles, seventeen singles, forty-two runs scored, no errors. A brief, historically unprecedented stint of perfection, a phantom immortality, flashbulb hot, then cold as stone.

George died with a week to go in the season, his kidneys disintegrating like a worn-out sponge. Some natural degenerative tic bred in the bone, moving too quickly for the iron horse of technology, too stealthily for the untrained eye.

I rented a black suit, size thirty-eight, black shoes, size eleven, and drove seven hundred miles to carry an eighty-four-inch capsule down ten steps with five teammates, the end line of numbers reached only after the straps had lowered the box its last, fleeting inches.

I played the final three games of the season in the minors, going oh for eleven. No runs, no hits, no errors — no chance to make one. A ghost.

Three

MY ARRIVAL in the majors was the turning point of the
team's season that year; at least, it was according to the press. I
was the team's magic, they said. I was linked to divine powers —
in print. Heady stuff, calling for a willed suspension of disbelief
in one's tabloid incarnation. Nevertheless, we won thirty-eight
out of forty-five during a stretch of hazy, infernal days when the
temperature stayed in the high nineties well into the toxic summer
twilights. In September we were even better. Talk of a huge contract coming my way appeared in a sportswriter's column. The
sum would make me the highest-paid player in the club's history,
according to the article. This was news to me, and news that did
not endear me to my new teammates. Trade gossip suddenly listed
me among the five men in the game known as "untouchables."
The fate of the franchise, critics said, hinged on my career.

In spite of this, I still had to go out and play. I grew used to
the silence surrounding my locker. Each day before a game I
pulled on my bright colors, smeared streaks of lampblack underneath my eyes, and checked my form in a full-length mirror before
the harsh stares of my teammates. Some days, with the sun warming me as I stood in the verdant expanse of left field, I felt as if
the game were being played in another dimension, somehow out
of body, beyond time. In the tomblike dugout, though, I sat at
the far end of the bench and stared silently out at the field, seeing

only the cold mechanics of the game, its illicit thrills, the symmetrical pointlessness of it. When I came to bat I stepped into the box and, ignoring the taunts of opposing catchers, set myself, then remained deathly still, bat cocked, waiting . . . until I could deliver another wordless, arcing drive into the expanse of inexorable sky.

On road trips I roomed alone, followed through hotel lobbies and franchised eateries by the doubly refracted aura of my new celebrity, my vertiginous public self.

When the season ended we were one game out of first, and I was hitting .444, a mysterious, somehow deathly triumvirate of numbers. And ineligible for the batting crown because I was fifty at bats short of the minimum number to qualify. It was as if, in a way, I hadn't been there, hadn't existed. The last time I came to the plate that season I felt as if my bat had been transformed into something insubstantial, a ghost of its former, normally tangible self. I swung at the first pitch, a knuckleball. By virtue of its practically spineless nature — the ball only rotates a quarter of a revolution during its trip from the mound to the plate — the pitch has a tendency, when it's thrown correctly, to assume the flight pattern of a bumblebee, a thing prone to random loops and dodges. I expected to see the ball leap off my bat. I knew I had hit it, had made contact. I *saw* the ball smack the thick end of my bat. And yet, somehow, it appeared behind me in the catcher's mitt, a squat leather shield the size of a trash can cover. I did a sensory check of my surroundings. My name and number were glowing in transistorized letters on the face of the electronic scoreboard, a stock market accounting of my presence, the ticker tape proof of my being. I remembered hearing — or believed I remembered hearing — my name spoken by the ballpark's announcer as I stepped to the plate, a disembodied, metallic voice, megaphone flat. But it now seemed as if I could have been some aural poltergeist, blown to bits by the stiffness of the breeze. I could picture myself in the on-deck circle, the batboy wishing me luck, then stepping into the batter's box, the blossoming green plain spreading out before me like a silk fan. But what substance was there in these movie-screen images? Who knows if the world closes up shop behind us after each passing instant? What if our presence is illuminated by nothing more than the rote of memory? I called time and stepped out of the box.

"Sucker kind of moves on you, don't it?" Dork Cooper, the opposing catcher, was looking up at me through his mask, bovine impassivity concealing his decade-deep knowledge of the game. To him, the warp and woof of magic was nothing more than a slight rotation of the fingers, the caress of a red cotton stitch.

In the air I could smell the vinegarish aroma of sauerkraut, the musty fragrance of ballpark beer. I tapped one cleat with the head of my bat and watched as clumped earth broke apart and fell scattershot to the ground. As I stepped back into the box, several voices in the stands cried out, "Get one, Mike," their admonitions rising plaintively above the restless white noise of the crowd. Empirically, I could determine that I was at bat, could bring a fraction of certainty to my presence there. Ball, bat, players, fans. Earth. The totems of the phenomenal world. I touched the outside edge of the plate with the tip of my stick. But when the creature with the duck-billed forehead and whiskered walruslike face began to pretzel-twist himself out on the mound, sixty feet six inches appeared to shrink like some Hitchcockian reverse-zoom trick played with filmic space. The pitcher seemed to be winding up only inches from the plate. When he came forward he released a non-asymptotic curveball, a projectile that seemed to be ungoverned by the laws of motion. The ball floated several feet beyond the first-base line, moving mothlike one moment, hovering like a helicopter the next. Then it slipped back inside its representative, statistically measured skin and blew by me, landing, untouched by my cut at it, in the oiled center of the catcher's mitt. It was as if the ball occupied some transcendental plane of space, a new layer of the universe revealed by the advent of the slider.

"Steee-rike two."

The third pitch was a rising fastball that screamed down from the mound with dive-bomber abandon before suddenly planing upward. As it climbed toward the vanishing point of triple-digit speed, the ball punctured some unseeable black hole ten feet in front of the plate, then reemerged half an instant later in Dork Cooper's mitt.

"You're out, bonehead. Season's over," Cooper said.

The crowd was laundry-detergent-commercial bright when I turned away from the plate, the sweep of primary colors disorienting in the brilliant September sunlight, cubes of color topped with home-team caps and dark glasses. As I headed toward the dugout, I became aware of the fact that my Game of the Week at-bat image had gone out to 30 million viewers, the plane of my existence reduced to the two-dimensional, coast-to-coast peephole of television. I thought for a moment that my reality was held together by the magnetic pull of the crowd's enthusiasm, by the aura of the game itself. I was no more than a projection of the collective imagination of the faithful, the phantom and spindly helix that unites the ineffable with the world of flesh. Making contact was like getting a piece of the untouchable. Hitting safely was like seeing the face of God.

Batter's box, field, stadium, space. I was a ballplayer. I was paid to delineate the borders of the transcendental and the unseen.

But in the end, my summer heroics were illusory. When I looked at my final stats the day after the season ended, I felt as if I were reading the estate tax return of a dead man, a life summed up in numbers, inarticulate but haunting. Stories of my silence and the arctic timbre surrounding my locker were suppressed by Mr. Percy, and the country's leading sportswriter canonized me in his syndicated Sunday column the day the playoffs began. "His abilities," he wrote, comparing me to Mickey Mantle, "threaten the dimensions of the game."

My picture appeared on magazine covers. Perhaps it was those headshots, all those guillotined images of myself in which I seemed to be dead but smiling, that made me ask myself: What *are* the dimensions of the game?

Four

I COME FROM NOWHERE and everywhere. I was raised by bewildered parents ineptly passing down their values, both pinched and generous, to my brother and me. We lived with unspectacular style and hopes (except for my own) and a grudging acceptance of one another in a shingled row house rooted at the edge of a noxious city, and watched a lot of TV. From the tube I learned much of what I know of the republic — its shallow history, its boom-or-bust egomania, the unlivable glory of its myths.

My father, who rode an elevated train two hours each day to and from his office through a borough of windowless tenements, their insides gutted by fire — the skeletons of vanquished dreams — wished aloud in front of the TV set that we lived in Mayberry, North Carolina. There he would be the unarmed sheriff, the safety and, at times, the destiny of the town resting in his hands. His evenings would be passed strumming his guitar on the front porch, while Aunt Bea, whose function as the maternal presence in the home spared my father the sexual complexity of a wife, baked. Or else there was the off-screen interlude of romantic rapture with Helen Crump, virgin schoolmarm; unseen, the sexual aura of the relationship was kept alive implicitly, innocently — American sex, middle class. Sponsored by Campbell's soup. Never, though, were Andy's omnipotence and wisdom more evident than when coping with a problem of Opie's, his son. A widower, Andy seemed at times to have birthed the boy himself, or carved him out of the trunk of a tree and breathed life into the boy's inanimate body (when in fact the matrix was a producer-generated model of acceptable family symmetry, tested before pre-view audiences in Seattle and other hybrid cities). In lieu of such Zeus-like powers, I believe, my father would have settled for just a bit of Eliot Ness's flinty, mortal authority. If just once he could have shouted, "Rico! Youngblood! Book 'em," much of the frus-tration of his being an underpaid office manager would have been defeated. To strike back, to be in control of his own life — if only once — instead of spending Saturdays with a Time-Life home-repair manual in one hand, the other clutching the slimy, canta-loupe-shaped float inside the malfunctioning toilet tank, his only assistance coming from his lazy, daydreaming, mechanically dis-inclined older son, who stood behind him heel-deep in water, swinging a monkey wrench at imaginary fastballs.

My mother was indifferent to evening television, its fantasies unmatched to hers during the early sixties. But she sat there with us anyway, smoking Newports, her feet tucked under her legs as she curled up on the couch by herself. I'd get up during the night and she'd be there, still wearing leopard-skin stretch pants and a pullover sweater. Wide awake, chain-smoking, watching the late late show at three A.M.

"What are you doing up?"

"Go back to bed."

"What are you watching?"

Then she'd fill me in. Characters, situations, plot twists, deaths. The rise and fall of various stars careers. "He did nothing after this." Or, "This was his one big role." And finally, "Look at his eyes. Did you ever see blue eyes like that?"

My mother never made it any secret that she was in love with Paul Newman.

My younger brother, Bennie, who had once spelled camel, c-a-m-o-o-l, and another time volunteered the explanation that interracial marriages between blacks and whites produced an is-sue we then called Puerto Rican, was, as far as the rest of us were concerned, a step above an idiot. And though he had passed (barely) all his subjects and earned the right to be promoted, a desiccated old nun suggested to my parents that Bennie would benefit from repeating second grade. (We're going back to basics, Coach said after every sloppy loss.) A suggestion from one so close to God and the Pope (was my mother wedded to Christ?) could be nothing but infallible in my parents' opinion, and so Bennie was left back by consensus (excluding his own vote), stripped of his temporal identity, stigmatized and suddenly friendless, his grammar school years a cycle of fallow encouragement and easy reproach. He found solace and company (voyeuristically) in the seemingly attainable respect, if not glory, given to dutiful minor men — the Joe Fridays, the paramedics and the fire fighters, the uncorrupted civil servants of the republic. Bennie spoke aloud from his dreams some nights in the bedroom we shared. He wished that he would grow up to be a veterinarian, able to tend the wounds and pains of helpless animals. In the dark he spoke words of comfort to the dumb and the afflicted.

I identified with Superman. But I wanted to know more about his secret mortal life in the Standish Arms Hotel. I wanted to live in a hotel when I grew up. I felt there was something cosmopolitan about it, that it was the apex of civility and class, that living there would grant me anonymity, a feeling of finally being at ease in the world, comfortable, at last, with my own transience. I wanted the show to delve into Superman's childhood in Smallville, probe his adolescent pains, or reveal the autobiographical novel locked in Clark Kent's desk drawer. I wanted the show to explore the decline of his super powers in old age, his doubts, his longing for home, the loneliness of his exile, his alienation caused by powers that extended far beyond those of mortal men. I wanted to see how Superman would manage dying.

We each had our secret dreams. I wanted to be a ballplayer. All the usual reasons: fame, glory, the company of mannish boys, those puerile heroes oblivious of death. The immortality granted to legends.

Let's talk symmetry.

Field, foul lines, ball, bat, men. Rules. Arbiters of those rules. Records. The relentless measure of history. The inviolability of our numbered and statistical lives.

The first time I ever touched a hardball was when my father brought one home from the old Polo Grounds. It had been sliced foul off the bat of a minor player, was a bit of dust in the game, and my father had reached up and miraculously caught it bare-handed. Grass-smudged and chafed, one red cotton suture split; I was fascinated and thrilled by the parabolic loops the spinning stitches described. The mystery behind the ball's apparent use-lessness, the awe I felt in its presence connected me, at the age of seven, to the world of men. I took the ball up to my room and set it on my dresser, and for a long time I simply looked at it. The ball assumed its place in my private mythology along with the uniforms of civil servants, the sexual aura of worn and faded blue jeans, the wonder of cowboy boots, the wordless amazement and terror caused in me by guns.

I found it a terrifying and strange place, the masculine world, governed by unspoken codes and wild boys running in packs like wolves. A world pulsating with the promise of violent death. I lived in fear. The only time I was disconnected from that fear was when I'd get a hit. A clean single stops time. Bat meets ball, time freezes, hovers, the ball leaps past the infield, time starts again. Unprovable theory, of course, but absolutely true. Texas leaguers, their sublime arcs over infields a beautiful and comforting illusion (even if we all know we're free-falling in a straight Einsteinian line), are less suspenseful. A good clean rip between the shortstop and third. Boom. Stasis. Peace. Stopped time.

Of course, this is *all* illusion.

Timelessness. A baseball game could — *could* — go on for-ever. An inning could be played in eight minutes or an hour. One of the teams might never be forced to relinquish its at-bat status, surrender its upness. A team could score endlessly, never make an out, the side might never be retired. Forever, infinitely, without end. The illusions of the game.

I had always been, except for that single minor league season with George, a streak hitter. I marked the talismans of my streaks with a single-minded attentiveness. History, weather, quotidian events; the tides, international despair, the alignment of the planets — all these things, I believed, influenced my streaks. The universe turned in relation to me. No more, no less.

My slump began the year after George's death, on April 29, the day Saigon fell. My average in the early spring, carried over from the season before, had climbed back to, then remained, as steady as a healthy heartbeat, at .432. That number suddenly spooked me, marked me in some way, I felt, for an early death. Then out of nowhere, I stopped hitting, couldn't hit a pitch. At one point during the slump, after about two weeks, I began to believe that I would never hit the ball again. I had done something, committed some unforgivable sin, been indifferent to everything but my place in the game perhaps, and the gods had stripped me of my powers. It wasn't my stance, my hands weren't dropping when I swung, my concentration wasn't affected by personal troubles. The ball was simply refusing to let me hit it, even as much as foul it off. I paid no attention to the minor cuts, strains, dislocations, blisters, even the pain that moved from my right shoulder to my neck and back; I had learned to play with pain ages ago. To me these minor afflictions weren't causes but omens, signs put up to remind me of my mortality, my fallibility, the arc of my talent. When I healed it meant that I had been forgiven. (By what deity I was never quite certain. TV maybe.)

The slump ended on Memorial Day, early in the afternoon when my shadow was short, almost nonexistent. I began hitting again. I hit twenty-three singles in a row, each on the first pitch thrown. The feat went down in the record books. My average climbed over .400 again. I hit safely in every game through the Fourth of July, when Mr. Percy called me up to the majors. The places changed, the faces and the names, as did the anonymity of my efforts. Everything, in other words, except the streak. That continued, in blossoming tension, throughout the hazy summer days and long, smoky twilights. At one point I hit so many consecutive and nearly identical singles, each seemingly possessed by a Zen-like aura of repetition, that at the plate, I am told, I seemed to be more in a state of meditation than concerned with taking signs from the third-base coach, or the runner on second. Opposing pitchers swore that I hit the ball with my eyes closed. Finally, the concept of average began to be replaced (at least in my mind) with the possibility of achieving the terrifying and unknown, the infinite and eternal, the perfect. There were times during that streak when I believed I would bat 1.000. There were days when I believed I wouldn't ever die.

Five

IT SEEMS that ballplayers' lives attain some sort of dumb resonance only after accumulating the dust of time. We depend on yellowing newsprint and record books to tell us who we were.

I won the Rookie of the Year award and Mr. Percy offered me a six-year contract that would pay me $45,000 per year, plus several penurious incentive bonuses (win triple crown — three times — receive American-made automobile) — in other words, more money than I had ever seen, or had expected to see, in my life. At least bunched together over the space of so few years. Hammer, my agent, called to advise me against signing.

"Let me share two names with you. Messersmith. McNally. Ring a bell?"

"Nothing's been decided. I can't wait on some arbitrary decision."

"You'll get more, just wait. Do you see me getting anxious?"

"I wish I could see you, period. I call your office and you're unavailable because you're out on your boat negotiating palimony settlements in rock star divorce cases."

"This is not my boy. Be patient. We're closing in on them. This is peanuts they're offering."

"The most money I ever made in my life is two hundred dollars a week. This ain't peanuts in my book."

"I hear you. And I'm here to protect you from yourself.

Middle-class white kid makes it big. Feelings of guilt. Loss of 'one of the guys' status. Overcompensates with modesty. Underrates self-worth."

"They took a chance on me."

"Sexual guilt. Abhors self before figures of paternal authority. This is not the image we want to create. With your talent, in two years we could be selling people electronic equipment, after-shave, vans that look like moon vehicles. There are endorsement deals with corporate entities and million-dollar-a-minute advertisers out there waiting for us. But we don't cash in if you don't create viewer need. I saw you interviewed on TV the other night. Since when are you Marcel Marceau?"

"What the hell is 'viewer need'?"

"The viewers desire to know you, their need to. Why? A: To feel good about themselves because you, whom they have come to like and respect through the ubiquitousness of your electronic image, are taking the time to talk to them. You are visiting them in their homes, advising them — as friends — to buy a superior product, one that you purportedly use."

"This is a sick mind you're working with."

"B: Extension of A. Emulation. Believe it or not, there is no age restriction in this category. Men in their fifties, research shows, imaginatively emulate ballplayers. Their heroic, death-defying virility."

"What research?"

"C: Pathological extension of B. Obsessive identification lead-ing to jealous rivalry. Feelings of impotence, despair, and the need to impress a girlfriend — always an imaginary figure, idealized in the extreme — or simply the folks back home. Impress with a vengeance, I may add. Homicidal in the late stages. Hating your image no longer enough. Fragmentation of self-image. Attempts to contact you, fails, self-worth sinks below zero, buys gun. Need I go on?"

"Where do you get your information? That's what I'd like to know."

"I seek out theories, I read into popular culture. What is it telling us? What obsesses the mind of mass man? Is there such a thing? And, if so, how much disposable income does he spend annually? I don't believe or disbelieve. I withhold judgment. I weigh and sort. I am open to all lines of information. Can I share something with you? I read the *Enquirer*."

Hammer was in China negotiating a title bout for another of his clients, Po "The Ninja Warrior" Kam Fong, the Chinese heavyweight contender, when Mr. Percy called me to his offices to sign a contract.

"Who has given you everything you've asked for?" Mr. Percy said, opening the meeting.

"I haven't asked for anything."

"Nevertheless. You know what this contract says, in terms of dollars. Do you know what it means, though, in terms of virtue, self-sacrifice, loyalty? You can prove you do by signing it."

"My agent says it's not enough money."

"Your agent's a thug."

"He says I should walk for anything less than triple your offer."

"Disloyal. A fluke. Flash in the pan. An agitator! I'll pin these labels to your name so fast if you don't sign that you won't know whether to shit or wind your watch! By the time you're twenty-four you'll be forgotten, ancient history, a freak. You won't make a team playing in the Appalachian League!"

"You're unconvincing when you're bluffing."

"A wiseguy to boot. I've spoken to the other owners about you. You're talented, but your image stinks. All those singles. You think people come to ballparks to see some clown hit singles? They want home runs! Fans pay to see home run hitters, strikeout kings, giants! I'm not going to shell out good money for you to go out and hit singles. When we tell you to drop your shoulder to hit more home runs, goddammit, you drop your back shoulder!"

"I'd strike out more. I'd be trying to be something I'm not."

"You'd be signed to a six-year contract. Why is it the rookies are always the idealistic ones? Do you all belong to some sort of club, or something?"

"I'd like to discuss this with my wife."

"Just what Gehrig would have done! That's what I like to hear. Hark back, son. Hark back to the heroic figures of yesteryear."

"How much did Lou Gehrig make a year?"

"You can only hark back mythically. This is 1975. There's a recession going on. Forty-five thousand. Final offer."

Six

BARBARA AND I came from the same neighborhood, were brought up in similar row houses by similar sets of parents, worked summers and after school in various shops along the same street, knew many of the same kids. I was walking along Jamaica Avenue one afternoon when I saw her through the plate glass window of Mason's. She was dusting greeting cards and wearing blue knee socks and a tartan plaid school uniform skirt. She had straight brown hair that hung to her waist. Unaware of me standing behind her outside the glass, she became — unfortunately for her, for us — a creature as fantastic and illusory to me as Daisy was to poor shirt-crazed Gatsby. Years later, only when Barbara was asleep some hours after we had been through yet another hurtful and irrevocable argument was she restored to that figure of innocence in my eyes. Only at those times, in dawn's sullen light, was I able to tell her I was sorry, to feel amazement, remorse, and regret, and admit to myself that Barbara was not all I said she was, but more than I could any longer see.

But this was more toward the end of it with us, a time when millions were being paid to lifetime losing pitchers and utility infielders with no more than one good season recently behind them. At the beginning we still had each other.

"What did Mr. Percy say?"

"That I hit singles. That's worth forty-five thousand per year. If I did what they asked and hit homers, I'd be worth triple."

"What about Hammer? What does he think?"

"Hammer's in limbo. Why I can't reach the man who bought the first cordless telephone, I don't know."

Barbara and I thought over Mr. Percy's offer as the leaves surrounding our rented house in the Northeast seemed to burst into flame, first bright deep orange, reds like the skins of apples, finally cinnamon as they dropped to the ground. I was afraid not to sign the contract. I told myself, in my most paranoid moments — those center-of-the-universe fantasies when you believe everyone, everything, hinges on your move, your decision — that I would be vilified by players and fans alike if I thumbed my nose at Mr. Percy's offer, which was, for the time — a very brief time — an above-average, perhaps even generous salary for a barely seasoned rookie. He'd dump me on the open market and there wouldn't be any takers. I saw myself playing semipro ball, a has-been at twenty-two. If I took the $45,000 for six years I'd be a certified ballplayer, my existence finally validated.

Then, too, there was the matter of my guilt. I'm superstitious. Not in the I've-lived-another-life-and-have-friends-from-the-Middle-Ages-who-still-visit-me way. I suffer from a Catholic sense of karma, in which all action comes back in the form of retribution.

"What should we do?" I asked.

Barbara was sitting on the seat beside me in our old Nova, the heap I had bought while I was in college, its shocks as useless as rusted pogo sticks. We were on our way to her sister's house for Thanksgiving dinner, a snug A-frame, gabled and peaked, very New Englandy, chestnuts lying in the leaf-filled driveway, golden light spilling from the porch window like hosannas. Inside, there would be the smell of nutmeg and rosemary, the harvest colors of the meal, the shouting of children, their nasal pleas and delights.

"Well, what do you want to do?"

I thought this over for a few minutes. I realized that for all the scholarships I had mulled over and accepted, and how much thought I gave to signing with a pro team, I was, at bottom, quite indifferent to my own life. I never thought of what I wanted, but simply of what would be best for my game, how best to preserve a gift that was mine, yet somehow separate from me as well.

"I want to play," I said. "I don't care if I get rich or not, I just want the details cleared out of the way."

"I want a house with seven bathrooms."

"Don't start."

"I want gutters that get stuffed with leaves, and I want to be able to call a man named Mr. Chaney to come and clean them out."

"I'm not laughing."

"I want nannies for the children, and I want to ride around in a big limousine toying with the idea of seducing the driver while I cross and uncross my legs and my stockings make that whoosh-whoosh sound."

"Barb."

"Sign the contract."

I was on the phone to Mr. Percy's office first thing the next morning, Hammer, of course, being unavailable. I told one of the lawyers that I wanted to come in and sign my contract. He said that he would have to get back to me, then hung up. They kept me waiting three weeks, my subsequent and increasingly anxious calls to Lee Wheeler, the general manager, going unreturned until one night at three-thirty. The telephone rang and I rolled over in bed and answered it. It was the lawyer I had originally spoken to. Mr. Percy would see me himself, he said.

"It's three-thirty in the morning."

"You were the first thing on my list. I like to get in early when the office is quiet. Be here at ten."

Mr. Percy looked as if he had died and was being animated by some expensive, tax-deductible electronic device. He'd been painted to seem lifelike by a cosmetician kept on staff, Mr. Percy existing now only as a symbol, the dead revolutionary leader kept alive by innuendo and press blackout. His last act before death, though, had been stinginess. He'd cut his offer by $500.

"You said forty-five thousand dollars. This contract reads forty-four five."

"I've suffered financial reversals since the initial offer was made."

"You're talking to someone who hasn't had the means yet to suffer financial reversals. I agreed to forty-five."

"Can't do it," he said.

"We're talking about a lousy five hundred dollars a year."

"The figure is forty-four five, son."

"Five hundred dollars, you'd keep your self-respect."

"I don't have any self-respect. I have money. Now sign or get out."

I had to close my eyes in order to focus on my disbelief. When I opened them I saw the field. Mute and deserted under the slate-colored December sky, the diamond seemed to me an idiotic place haunted by manufactured defeats and trumped-up victories, the turf of egocentric and insane men. I wanted to be playing in other, unmoneyed realms. But as that wasn't possible, I grabbed the gold-plated mechanical pen that one of Mr. Percy's aides held out for me, signed my name, then tossed the pen down onto Mr. Percy's desk. He laughed at my play-acting.

"Good boy," he said.

Once out of his office, I told myself to forget the incident. It was only $500 and the bluster of an old tycoon. What I should have told myself to do was run.

Seven

LUNAR CYCLE. A seven-day free-fall facilitated by the clench of uterine muscle and flow of alkaline fluids. One ball, 500,000 bats. Unfertilized, no prettier than a salmon egg, she still drives us nuts. Half a million schoolboys brush their hair and race to get to her door first, begging, "Love me." One is anointed, the rest shrivel and die. Inside, outside, the process seems to be pretty much the same.

Barbara missed her period shortly after Memorial Day. "I think I'm pregnant," she said.

We had thrown away our contraceptives, the pills and the coils, the creams and the jellies. This was shortly after the fall of Saigon, deep into the puzzling barrenness of my springtime slump. I had lost George the preceding fall, was still in the minors, and had turned twenty-one. My youth fell away from me like the bottom of a rocket, the great hulking carcass of years jettisoned as I drifted off into the orbit of the professional world. Barbara had a job she didn't like, was too restless for college, and was suddenly parentless, her father having died at an early age of cancer midway through Barbara's high school years, her mother killed minutes after leaving the house one morning. Victim of a hit-and-run, she had said, "See you tonight." When Barbara answered the phone at work later that morning, she learned that, at nineteen, she had been separated from her mother by eternity. She found herself adrift in the shallow river of adulthood, a world in which one seems to stay anchored only by ritual, one's sense of free-floating anxiety kept at bay by responsibility and work, or by having someone to love. Devastated by her mother's death, Barbara chose not to show it most of the time, and when she did, I was too dumb or absentminded to notice. But there was a subtle intensification of our need for each other. Away at college, I thought it was merely the result of long periods of separation. That Barbara was lost I did not, at the time, completely understand. Being lost, then, wasn't a concept I had encountered, much less felt. I was a ballplayer. In some ways I was still looked upon as a child, though my stature in the world increased, I was to discover over the years, with the size of my contract. I had my handle, my role: left fielder, .400 hitter, breadwinner, demigod. But Barbara, high-school-educated young wife, found the key to her completion ground down over and over again to the same question.

"Have you thought about having a baby?" my mother said. A relentless organizer, she was driven by some ravenous need for a middle-class, connect-the-dots sense of pattern. She had asked Barbara the question at Sunday dinner, the preceding fall. Barbara and I were barely six months out of the marital starting gate. The end of my first season in the minors was only a month behind us at the time, and an uncertain winter lay ahead. I was rolling into the second and final year of my first pro contract. A twenty-year-old minor league phenom, I could be washed up at twenty-one — injury, collapse of concentration, outplayed, dead. Barbara still had the postnuptial jitters, a what-have-I-done-with-my-life type of anxiety common to many brides. Then, too, there was the abyss of our youth. Between us we had a combined forty years' worth of immaturity and ignorance. After viewing thirty-one thousand hours of television, our minds and souls were tempered by the flash-fire resolutions of police shows and domestic dramas, ad jingles and coffee commercials. If the problem couldn't be solved in thirty minutes, we didn't know how to deal with it. A potential for child-warping misguidance was stitched into us, its power great enough to lobotomize the innate genius of an Einstein. That my mother didn't see, or simply overlooked this did not surprise me. A single-minded and manipulative attentiveness to her brood governed the majority of her advice-filled waking hours. To her, there were only three events in life: weddings, christenings, and wakes. Every other minute was downtime.

"Actually, I've had a vasectomy," I said, trying to deflect the remark. I wanted to avoid getting into a toe-to-toe with my mother on baby-spawning grounds. Her logic was easy enough to shoot down, but her torture-chamber persistence was mind numbing. I was trying to spare Barbara this Chinese water torture tactic of my mother's, the same question asked sixty thousand times. My mother viewed Barbara as the weak link in my armor. She wanted a grandchild, and my don't-bother-me indifference to her wishes set up an emotional "objective correlative" to irresistible force meets immovable object.

"No wonder you can't think straight," my father said, joining the conversation without setting down his knife and fork, having honed, over the years, his slice, shovel, and chew mechanics down to the flawless motion found in Cy Young Award winners. He ate with an implacable deliberation.

My father's remark drew a chuckle from my younger brother, Bennie. "What are you laughing at?" I said. "I'm your older brother, your idol." It was true. In spite of years of cursory acknowledgment, assorted juvenile tortures, and my colonial domination of our shared bedroom, Bennie worshiped me. Slightly spastic, unhip, shy, Bennie excelled in wood shop, and on weekends helped my father rake leaves and patch cracks in plaster. The handwork and paternal apprenticeship provided him with the warmth of identity, the security of hair-tousling approval — things I ran from, yet ran to in my own way, my fathers clipped from the book of myths. "That's it," I said. "No autographed balls for you." Even this drew a laugh from Bennie, every mock reproof a shorthand love. Meanwhile, as I had hoped, my mother stewed at the head of the table over the lost thrust of her procreative diatribe.

"One day you'll wish you had listened," she said.

"No, I won't."

" 'Spermicide. Kills on contact,' " I said, reading off the tube's label. "I don't know if I like the sound of this." It was months before the dinner with my parents, months before George's death. Barbara and I were in bed, our clothes scattered about the floor with a Hollywood logic, underwear and socks forming a trail through the dense underbrush of lust. The cries of kids playing ball in the field below floated up on the rebounding waves of June sunshine, punctuating the whispers of our lovemaking. Barbara was sitting up, lubing her new diaphragm, a dough-colored circle of rubber the size of a silver-dollar pancake, the edge of it rolled so that what you had in effect was a loop with a concave belly of impenetrable elastic, a sperm-tailored trampoline.

"You don't have any choice. You want to go back to wearing a plastic sandwich bag?"

Barbara had tried the pill. But the intermittent nausea, periods of mild dejection, and ten extra pounds of water she carried seemed a poor compromise. And after a checkup revealed her blood pressure to be abnormally high, she was taken off the contraceptive by her physician. An IUD came next, a two-thousand-year-old remedy pioneered by Turkish traders. The profit-goaded merchants inserted pebbles into the uteri of their camels before embarking on long, horny, desert treks, "Down boy," I suppose, not good enough when dealing with a thousand-pound dromedary brandishing a boner the size of a nightstick. Barbara's device was made of die-molded plastic. It had been inserted by her seventy-year-old gynecologist, the nearly blind old coot a great comfort to Barbara whenever she had to climb into the bucket seat and stirrups and be inspected like a mine shaft. Barbara experienced sharp, gut-spiking pains after the insertion, and then, as they faded, her menstrual cramps turned up a notch during her next period. One day they were bad enough to lay her up in bed, a sore lower back and no relief. Nylon threads hung from her uterus so that she could check on the device's whereabouts. Then, one morning, she sat down to empty her bladder and the thing flew out with her water like a kernel of corn popping in a heated aluminum pan.

"Thank God," she said.

"What next?"

Neither of us wanted to return to the genital mitten. Even with a plastic devil's head and fibrous dreadlocks for intrauterine tickling, the pleasure was still definitely second rate.

"Coitus interruptus?" I suggested. "Some sort of sexual balk where I pull out in midthrust and fire a million little baby-bearing guppies into our percale sheets?"

"I don't think so."

We were in a diner, a twenty-four-hour-a-day food emporium that catered to a clientele of used car salesmen, lunch-hour secretaries, medical technologists, and couples from the room-by-the-hour motel two doors down the strip.

"What do you think they use?" I said, pointing out one couple. The man was in his late thirties, metallic, blue-black hair, cream-colored V-neck sweater, a cobweb of gold chains around his neck. The woman: early thirties, Ming the Merciless nails painted fire-engine red, brass-colored earrings as long as door knockers, meticulously coiffed hair, and a dress as tight as a nylon stocking pulled over the head of a mugger.

"Oral sex."

Dr. Dispingaitis discussed vaginal spermicides with us. "These work about ninety percent of the time," he said, "if you go with the foam."

"What happens the other ten percent?"

"You get a new tax deduction."

I looked at Barbara. "What do you think? Maybe we should look at a kid as a write-off."

"People used to look at them as investments," our fading gynecologist added, his right hand trembling, the collar of his starched, white examining-room coat standing up off his shoulders and threatening to swallow him whole. "Before Social Security, that is."

"Ten percent is awfully high," Barbara said.

"I agree," he said.

"Besides," I said to Barbara, "are you going to want to squirt a snowball-sized wad of Gillette foamy up inside you every time we make love? Where's the spontaneity?"

"Spontaneity is parenthood," Dr. D. said.

Foam was out.

"Diaphragms are almost one hundred percent safe," he said, "especially if you use them with jelly."

"I don't know if I like the idea of my sperm being napalmed," I said, as I watched Barbara fold the rubber pancake in two and insert it.

"You didn't think you were killing them all through high school when you whacked off on a pillow?"

"That was different. I looked at them like stray cats. They were out there in the world. You know. Somehow they'd get along and survive."

The diaphragm worked. But I began to feel that it turned Barbara into something of a sexual stewardess, her precoital trips to the bathroom to lube and insert a bit like a come-fly-with-us piece of customer service: my whim, her work.

"I need a baby," I said.

"What?"

"We have to have a child."

The announcement stunned Barbara, delivered, as it was, from the coin-dropping end of a gas station pay phone by a slump-crazed outfielder hip deep in confusion and miles from home. It was spring and I wasn't hitting. My deduction: the universe was doomed. That the sun hadn't dropped from the sky and fried the earth like a cracked egg I attributed to the power of television programming — no apocalypses without network approval.

"I think you should calm down and tell me what's going on," Barbara said.

So I did. Saigon had fallen, my best friend was a worm-festering corpse, I was sending 500,000 sperm to their death every night I wasn't playing on the road, and I hadn't hit a pitch in three weeks. History, mortality, and the conundrum of sexual freedom were conspiring to see to it that my bat didn't touch a pitch.

"You don't think it could just be good sliders?" Barbara said.

"Absolutely not."

"So what are you saying?"

"The game wants offspring."

To heal wounds, to keep abreast of death's tireless pace, to pacify my selfish soul: yes, all these things. I returned home at the beginning of Memorial Day weekend for an eleven-game home stand during which we, as a team, could recover from the lonely wins on the road, and forget the confidence- and possibly destiny-shattering defeats. Ballplayers are fragile and not long on perspective. We assume our privilege automatically; it has been doled out to us since birth. Open spaces, clean bright uniforms, the praise of civic-minded elders and adoring minions. Off in some dark brown corner, a voice may be asking, "Who are these cretins?" Maybe something nastier. But we are ballplayers. We are oblivious to the pleas and wants of the unblessed billions.

"Well, I don't know if I'm ready to have a baby," Barbara said.

"How can you not be ready? We go through spermicide like other people go through Crest."

"I mean psychologically."

"Forget it," I said, as I pushed her back on the couch. "That's all in your head."

"The diaphragm goes in."

"Come on. Be a sport."

"In."

Later, with my head on Barbara's chest, her hand stroking me with a distracted, almost automatic tenderness, I slowed down and listened.

"I don't know if we're emotionally ready for a baby," she said, her voice washing over me with the unforced ease of wisdom. "We've only been married twelve months. What if we outgrow each other? We're only twenty-one. And you don't even know where you'll be in a year." So. The unsayable was sayable. Worse: it was true. The nightmare of impermanence. The way we create ourselves out of the detritus of loss. All true. Or, perhaps, these were simply postcoital ruminations. "It's not fair to the child. I mean, we can't have a baby just because you're not hitting."

I caught a breath in my lungs, held it a moment, then let it go as if I were releasing a bird to flight. "You're right," I said.

"I'm glad you think so."

"I always think better after I come."

"I know."

The next day Lynn Pike, the opposing pitcher, came in with a temple-high fastball that ruffled my eyebrows, and before my teammates could pull me off him I had my bicuspids sunk half an inch deep into the trunk of his throwing arm.

"Jesus H. Christ, Williams!" Houston Slaught shouted. He kicked his office door like a Rockette, the steel slab shaking the cinderblock foundations of its frame as it slammed shut. "You kick a guy in the balls, you don't bite his fucking arm! You want to bite people, go play hockey. Jesus!"

"Sorry, Coach."

He dropped into his foam-padded swivel chair and reached for the desk drawer. His hand reappeared with a plastic Maalox bottle, which he shook, uncapped, held to his lips, then sucked on like an infant with a pacifier.

"Stomach problems, Coach?"

He lowered the container and glared at me, a don't-push-your-luck scowl mastered by working-stiff fathers and men whose business has no truck with the feminine world. "Williams," he said, exchanging the intestine-coating antacid for a bottle of Kentucky bourbon the color of polished maple, "sometimes your sheer stupidity is miraculous." He poured three fingers of the mash into a bar-style glass, then knocked back the shot with one, robot-stiff movement. Seeming to forget I existed, he let his diaphragm drop-kick a duodenum-clearing belch up through the mucus-plastered canal of his throat. "Ah," he said, then capped the bottle and set it on the corner of his desk. "Now. What, may I ask, is your fucking problem?"

This was a man who had played his first baseball game without a glove, I had been told. A Depression kid who haunted snowy St. Louis street corners and roasted mickeys on the ends of two-foot-long twigs. He had been shipped off to Normandy in 1944, and there caught a piece of white-hot metal just above his right knee. A catcher, he lost some quickness in his ability to come up throwing out of his behind-the-plate crouch. Nevertheless, he worked his leg back into serviceability with the help of isometric therapy, weight training, and a Red Cross nurse whom he married in the tradition of Hollywood war heroes. Twice an All-Star, he rebounded from the death of his first child by leukemia to lead the league in games played, at bats, and doubles. He and his wife adopted a Korean orphan after that war, then had three more children before the end of his playing career. He understood slumps, distractions, personal problems. I assumed he would understand the metaphysics of my hitlessness.

"I miss O'Kane."

Caught off guard, experience teaching him to expect tales of girlfriend troubles, past humiliations by opposing pitchers, or the simple presence of bone-deep meanness, he paused for a moment before answering. "I know," he said.

Neither of us spoke for several moments. And because he didn't immediately launch into a pep talk laced with platitudes, I trusted him with my grief.

"I feel like I should have a baby," I said.

"That doesn't get O'Kane back."

"No, but it evens things up a bit."

He nodded, and I could see in his eyes that he had gone the distance with his own death-bred demons at one time in his life. But he didn't reduce his response to anecdote. "What's your wife say?"

"That we shouldn't start a family just because I'm in a slump."

"That's good advice. She could have said worse things."

"Like what?"

" 'Okay.' "

We talked about my stance at the plate, how opposing teams were pitching me high and tight or low and inside to test the quickness of my bat. Being a disciple of Ted Williams's theories on hitting, Houston Slaught felt that my swing was too level. "You should be uppercutting more," he said. "How do you think a scrawny guy like Williams hit five hundred and twenty-one homers? You hit a few out of the park and you'll see them start pitching you differently. You'll see some respect." Then he was quiet for a moment. He leaned back in his chair and put his right hand to his face, middle and index fingers tapping his cheekbone lightly. His thumb was hooked underneath his chin, and his ring and pinky fingers hid the sight of his slightly chapped lips. "You angry?" he said from behind his hand, his eyes swiveling to meet mine only after he had laid the question down as gracefully as a good bunt.

"Yes."

He nodded almost imperceptibly, then looked away from me. His eyes fixed on the scratched, cluttered face of his desk, as if what he had to say was something almost to be ashamed of, too intimate to be delivered eye to eye. "Funny thing about people close to you dying," he said. "You never get used to it. And you never get over it."

I was fined $100 for biting Lynn Pike and I went over to the visitors' locker room to apologize to him. He was sitting on a straight-backed metal chair in the trainer's office, the team physician lacing his upper arm with black thread and a crescent-shaped needle. "I'm sorry about what happened. I don't know . . . uh, I don't know what to say." I shrugged. "I'm sorry."

"Why don't you eat shit and die."

I let Lynn Pike glare at me for a moment, accepting his hate in a sort of eye-for-an-eye exchange for his stitches.

"You bit a pitcher?"

"It was only a little bite."

Barbara, anxious for summer, was working in our garden when I got home. She was wearing a pair of cutoffs and one of my old tank tops. On her feet were high-top Keds and floppy orange socks. When she stood up, her kneecaps muddy as a schoolgirl's, I was stunned by her effortless, uncoaxed beauty. It was there in the line of each thigh, the delicacy of her arms, the fineness of her unblemished hands: an untutored gorgeousness, innocent as spring. Another brute fact carrying no less weight than George's death or Lynn Pike's hate. Ball. Bat. Beauty. Grave. A universe composed of absolute and discrete facts.

"Let's go to bed," I said, grabbing Barbara's hand.

"Wait, I want to hear about the biting." And so she followed. . . . "So you bit him?"

The sun was cool and round as an orange beyond our bedroom window, unmaking its own light with a stinging slowness, its unhurried beauty matched by us only in the slow glory of our love-making and the arc of long, high fly balls.

"It wasn't just because he threw at me."

"Well, what else was it?"

There was O'Kane's death, my barren streak at the plate. Barbara's uncertainties about our future, the tentative life I was given by my contract, the vast promise and dread of tomorrow. The ground seemed to be continually vanishing beneath my feet. One moment I would be walking along, my cleats biting snugly into the solid back of infield dirt, the next the ground would be falling away from me like a rock dropped from the top of a skyscraper. The closer I tried to get to the nucleus of my confusion, the more it changed shape on me. It was as if my emotions, even the specter of my own being, obeyed the laws of quantum physics. "Everything," I said, letting my body fall into a head-to-toe slump. We were quiet for a moment. Then I felt Barbara's hand stroking my side as if she were comforting a frightened animal. Our clothes were heaped on the floor at the foot of the bed. The garden was uneven and sprawling, a jumble of roots, vines, and stalks. The dream of a rectangular plot — neat as a grave — had given way to an effusive cramming and adding, the freshly turned edges of it billowing like the soft flanks of a cloud. A fan of the things-don't-always-add-up school of thought, Barbara felt that baseball — with its ravenous appetite for numbers, the day's box scores stacked on top of one another in local papers like obituaries — had in some way warped me. I needed to know final scores, had to sift and tally, then determine where everything ranked in the history of the game. Barbara was comfortable with the chaotic and the opaque. So instead of being asked what did I mean by "everything," I received the raindrop-soft plucking of her lips along the bony shell of my ribs. The grace and mercy of silence.

The next day I struck out five times.

"Look," Houston Slaught said, "why don't you sit this one out." We were playing a twinight doubleheader. The thought of sitting out the second game filled me with an illicit sense of relief. But instinct, or what had been woven into me so completely from childhood on that it now passed for instinct, told me not to give in, to press harder.

"I don't think so," I said.

"All right. You're benched."

"Maybe he's right," Barbara said. "It doesn't sound like he did it to be mean." Houston Slaught had simply shrugged when I looked at him. Then he turned away, rested his forearms on the dugout railing, and stared out at the field. Around me there was the conspicuous chatter of eavesdroppers and embarrassed stand-ersby, teammates who had been within earshot of the conversation and now wanted to distance themselves from the intimacy and shame of the moment. "I mean, he did give you the option of saying you'd like to sit out the game. I think that showed consideration."

I wasn't in the mood for a generous assessment of others. The team had won both games of the doubleheader, and twelve in a row going back to mid-May. A crop of new pitching — two curveballers and one seventeen-year-old from Lake Park, Georgia, who tossed a ninety-plus fastball — some infield adjustments, and a bit of dumb luck had yielded a .667 winning percentage over the course of the spring. Even George's replacement, Otis Armstrong, was holding his own in center field, getting on base five out of every ten tries in the leadoff position. Collectively, we were in a groove, perched atop the division by six games. But my pride had been hurt. Natural reaction: fuck "collectively."

Instead of answering Barbara, I raised a can of beer to my lips, relegating Houston Slaught's "consideration" to the lowly realm of the so-what and the despised.

"Come on. Don't sulk about it," she said.

I got up from the kitchen chair to take another beer from the refrigerator. Barbara was well aware of the kamikaze pace of my brooding and drinking bouts, headlong plunges into thick-tongued self-pity and the comforts of tunnel vision, walls, and numbness.

"Nothing I say is going to help, right?"

"Check."

"Right. In that case, grab me a beer."

We spent the night at the kitchen table, talking. Barbara filled the ashtray with butt ends and ashes, each new cigarette lit to meet the excitement of a freshly recovered remembrance. We marveled at how long we had been together — a fleeting five years — and breathed life into dead memories with the vigor of our longing. Time turned its magnifying glass on the puniness of my slump, and my troubles fizzled like a carpenter ant caught in a pinpoint of light by a wicked schoolboy. When the sky turned purple, we got into our bruised, dust-ringed Nova and drove out into Owney Ackerman's pasture to watch the sun rise. I was still sipping on a cold beer when the first bloom of orange pooled on the horizon.

"Day game," I said. "Not pretty."

"Maybe you should get some sleep."

"I think the game wants me drunk."

"What about your coach?"

"I just want to say I apologize, H.S." I was standing in the doorway of Houston Slaught's office, duffel bag hanging from one hand, dark shades perched on the bridge of my nose. Houston Slaught looked up from his scouting report sheets, the stunned glaze of annoyance on his kisser. It was a benefit-of-the-doubt nod to my apparent idiocy, a sense of restraint that barred any hasty exhibitions of full-blown wrath. "Benching me yesterday. Sheer wisdom. In fact, if we were Muslim, I'd be salaaming you at this very minute."

"Williams, are you on that wacko weed again?"

"Absolutely not, H.S. It's Sunday. I'm in a state of grace."

In the top of the first, I stood with my glove raised above my head like an Olympic torch then saw the ball smack the ground ten feet to my left.

"No problem," I said to Otis Armstrong, after he retrieved the ball and stopped the runner from going to third.

"Are you all right, man?"

"No sweat. It was the sun."

"Man, it's fucking overcast as shit."

"That makes it even trickier."

"Nice grab, Williams," Houston Slaught said as I clomped into the dugout, a mixed look of boredom and executive disgust on his face.

"It's a game of inches, H.S. I was in the vicinity."

"You're an outfielder, Williams, not a patrol car. Catch the goddamned ball."

"Absolutely, Mein Führer."

My first at bat I asked the ump if I could see the ball. When he obliged, I rubbed it on my shirt, along the spine of my bat, then brought it close to my face, looked it eye to eye, and said, "Walla, walla, walla."

"Williams, what in pissation are you doing?" It was Delbert Lamston, catcher for the Arroyos, Malcolm X glasses and the body of a tree trunk.

"I'm giving the ball my scent."

"Can I have the ball, please," Spike Marshall shouted from the foot of the mound.

"Williams, we don't need you chanting to the ball," Don Harris, the umpire, said. "Would you please turn it over to Lamston?"

"Anything you say, D.H."

I hit the first pitch into my own dugout, a liner that ricocheted off the back wall as Tip Peters and Gary Bump fell over onto their sides in order to get out of its way, cries of "Shit!" and "Moron!" issuing from the long blue trench like the bleating of pissed-off sheep.

"Contact," I said. (To myself, of course.)

I hit the next ball into the dirt beside the plate and it trickled foul. On the third pitch I was called out on strikes.

"What was that?" Houston Slaught said, when I returned to the dugout.

"Progress."

In the fourth I came to the plate with two men on and the game knotted at double zero. "Can I —"

"No."

I drove the first pitch down to the leftfield bleachers, singing Irving Berlin's "What'll I Do?" from the moment I stepped into the batter's box until the instant the ball drifted foul. Then I hit into a triple play.

"I'm definitely happy with this, H.S."

In the seventh I swung with my eyes closed, attacking each pitch like a ginseng-starved Bruce Lee, martial artistry and linebacker intensity yielding a drive deep into center field. When I opened my eyes I saw Ronnie Petit digging for the warning track, then snagging the ball over his left shoulder.

"Do you know what in the shit you're doing?" Houston Slaught said.

"No."

"Good. Keep doing it."

"The game wants me playing with abandon," I said to Barbara. My bag still hanging from my shoulders, I dug into the refrigerator for a beer, took one out, and opened it, not even stopping to kiss Barbara or say hello.

"You're a little wired."

"My bat touched the ball for the first time in three weeks. You should be able to run an air conditioner off me." I recapped my chanting, ball fondling, Kung Fu trips to the plate, as I walked in and out of rooms, emptying my bag in one of them, then sliding into the bedroom and changing into a new set of clothes for no apparent reason. The rush of exhaustion and near breakthroughs was goosing my synaptic gaps, squeezing off neurons like a high-speed retractable arm capping bottles. When I came back into the kitchen, Barbara had one elbow on the table and a supporting fist mushed into her left cheek. "I have a theory," I said.

"I don't think I want to know."

"We need to drive."

When the speedometer needle hit fifty-five I felt like some mental runoff valve had been spun open in my cerebellum. As we planed up the smooth palm of a back-country two-lane, then banked north into a green sea of cornstalks and soybean shrubs, the speed of the passing world eased into a step-for-step pace with my own internal clock. I reached into the glove compartment, retrieved a Stones tape, slipped it into the cassette deck, and cranked the volume up to mad-dash decibels, the flat-out, heedless plunge of American wanderlust kicking my emotional gears into overdrive with the first ringing of a chord toothy enough to cut metal. After several high-octane moments the succoring boon of speed gave way to the madness of open spaces. I felt a frontier craving, some sort of Klondike delirium coursing through my blood. Every capillary in my body felt perched to stand up and scream, "Floor it!" The land was opening out around me. The mania of plainsmen and ballplayers had been and still was fed by it. The sheer, indifferent screen of borderless horizon seemed to contain both the promise of immortality and the bank-on-it certainty of babbling, spit-covered depravity. The nearly obscene fertility of the vast expanse had led the fortunate to see the face of God, and left the rest behind to stumble around knee-deep in cowshit, succumbing on Saturday nights to an unmeasured barnyard lust. This was an unchiseled place, far from the worked, maniacal clutter of cities. It nurtured the visions of the rapacious and the blessed. Here, anything was possible.

"Can we just stop and sit?" I asked Barbara.

"I thought you wanted to drive."

"I need to feel things being still."

"Are you okay?"

"No."

I pulled into an unfenced tractor road and cut the engine. Around us, the corn stood in hushed, expectant rows, as upright and attentive as the members of a choir. The white noise of the insect world pulsed, a cone of sound clenching and unclenching with the deft genius of a heartbeat. There was an inextinguishable vibration given off by the physical clarity of the place, a faint, tuning-fork quiver. The dusky light was as soft as the fur of a cat, and time seemed to slow like some great locomotive as the ticking of the engine faded to silence. I closed my eyes for a moment. The rhythmic calm of simple breathing stroked me like small waves until I felt something I hadn't for a long, long time: peace. The ground once again opened up beneath me and I was falling — but it was all right. I had shed the gravity of flesh.

Then Barbara's hand was on my arm, touching lightly, and the falling slowed as I opened my eyes and went to her, time lashed to the slow and deliberate freedom of my movements. Later, there was some question as to who unbuttoned the other first. Later.

But in the feathery silk of heather-colored light, there was only the delicious lentitude of abandon, the fever of eternal time.

Before it was dark, Barbara was carrying our child, and the next day, Memorial Day, I went three for four beneath the gaze of a beneficent sun. The thronging of the afternoon crowd, murmurous as a river, floated upward, all the gravity of the grave extinguished as we celebrated the ease and warmth of the game. And then, at some point at which time seemed to stop, the game pausing to hold us in the embrace of eternity, it seemed as if we hovered above the fields of our collective past, and blessed with our lightness and momentary grace the memories of our congenerous dead.

Eight

HAMMER RESURFACED shortly after I had been to see Mr. Percy, solo. While Barbara and I were tying popcorn and Cupid-shaped cherubs to the branches of our Christmas tree, the telephone rang. Hammer was back from his African junket, he said, to make me a rich boy. "I have news to share," he said.

"Where have you been? What were you promoting in Africa? The Rolling Stones play the banks of the Congo, live on closed-circuit satellite. Jagger as the Marlow of rock 'n' roll."

"I detect animosity, the backlash of abandonment, the defensive posturing of the orphan, in your voice. A regrettable turn of events in our relationship. I apologize. Couldn't be helped. Some backwater junta decided they wanted a PR man to smooth things over until the rigged election. You understand."

I didn't say so.

"I'm trying to reestablish our connection, that bone-deep affability and warmth we've always shared, by way of an explanation here. I'm transmitting apologies and regrets long distance via a WATS line. Come on, lighten up. How's Barbara?"

"Larger."

"My warmest holiday wishes to her."

"Cut the crap. Why the sudden interest in my career?"

"You've heard the decision."

"About what? Christmas is postponed due to slow retail sales?"

"Don't overdevelop your sarcasm yet. That's a midcareer move, something we'll want to zoom in on after you've suffered a few nationally leaked, behind-the-scenes setbacks, a contract dispute, a libel suit, reckless and career-wrecking drug abuse. Sarcasm is 1980. You've got a few years. The news, which you obviously haven't yet heard because — I was teasing you — it hasn't gone network, has just flashed across my cable monitor, and I can report telephone confirmation by a mole I have on the scene. Repeat, this information is checked and confirmed."

"Are you an agent or Deep Throat? What are you talking about?"

"Seitz voted Messersmith and McNally free men. The reserve clause is dead. Salaries are going to skyrocket. Let Percy pay you the lowest permissible salary for the coming year. So what. Take the twenty percent pay cut, it only amounts to thirty-four hundred a year. We can manage; funds are available. You and I are talking long-term partnership. Already the endorsement contracts are piling up on my desk like sweepstakes offers. In two years we'll arbitrate. How big a raise would you like? Pick a number. Already it boggles the mind. I don't even want to mention the salary range. I don't even want to think about it."

Hammer seemed to be salivating on the other end of the line.

"But I have to say it. I have to hear this figure out loud. Can I say it?" Pause. "Four million for six years if you let me negotiate a long-term deal now."

There was a spooky silence, as if Hammer had talked himself into a heart attack. I knew that what I was going to say would either kill him or revive him.

"I signed for forty-five."

There was a deep-sea silence in my right ear. I looked across the room at Barbara and covered the telephone's mouthpiece with the palm of my left hand. "I think he's in a state of shock. He says he could've gotten me four million."

"Yeah, right. Ask him where he was when you needed him. Ward Cleaver would have been there."

Probably an unarguable fact. I put my ear back to the receiver.

"How many years for?" Hammer muttered into the line, his voice thick-tongued, shocked, his very syntactical bearings yanked out from under him.

"Six." Noncomprehension. More silence. "Look, I would have had to have stayed with them anyway," I said.

Hammer, pulling himself together, or perhaps operating on some sort of somnambulistic form of automatic pilot, instinctively asked *how* I was to be paid.

"In currency. Most likely by check. I know it's an unusual arrangement, but they conceded."

"Checks," he whispered. "W-2s, withholding, taxable income. Where were you brought up, Disneyland? What about salary deferral, amortization, tax shelters, perks? What about cars, condos, bridge loans for offshore corporations? What about good old-fashioned cash under the table?"

"I'm sorry."

"Are you getting it in marks or yen?"

"What?"

"Your paycheck," he said, lacing the words with enough contempt to make audible the unuttered "dummy" that I knew capped the sentence in the recesses of Hammer's figure-clouded mind. A moment's silence. "You didn't?" he said.

"I did."

"I don't believe it. You're getting dollars." And then Hammer, his thoughts turned inward, muttered to himself, "The schmuck's getting dollars." Then silence followed melancholy click.

An unshakable restlessness afflicts me during the off-season. My life feels incomplete, wasted, never more so than during that first year. I began counting the events that made up my day — meals, chores, bill paying, TV. When they were all accounted for I knew that I could put that day away, then go on to the next one. Just like working out arithmetic problems. I was in limbo, waiting for the season to begin, for the shroud of winter to lift, for our child to be born. I couldn't shake the feeling that my life was on hold, interrupted by matters that did not concern me. And I began to wonder if my feeling of incompleteness, or neurotic restlessness, was simply the effect of the mass of information we receive each day. That mass of information that I was now contracted to be a part of.

You'd be surprised how inconspicuous one can be, yet still be the Rookie of the Year. The incorporeity of the role amazed me, in a deflating way. I didn't want celebrity, yet I felt cheated, unsatisfied with myself in some vague way, as if I was inconsequential, when it seemingly passed me by that winter. To compensate for the lack of notice I received on the streets, I went out and bought a pair of sunglasses to hide my unrecognized eyes. The shades created, for me at least, some illusion of fame. I wore them while I drove. I wore them in dark bars and underground parking lots. And sometimes, when it was late and I'd had too many drinks and was feeling sloppy and sorry for myself, I'd slip them on and wander through the darkened, silent house, singing "Georgia" with the mental soundtrack of Ray Charles and the Raylettes.

I spent money, too. Gobs of it. Tons of it. Money I didn't have.

"I'd like a stereo." I was standing inside a paneled room that was windowless and stuffy as a bunker, first in line for a post-Xmas, pre–President's Day, one-time-only, storewide sale. It was a mall shop catering to electronics freaks, a tiny place squeezed in between a housewares outlet and a massage and transcendental meditation parlor. A salesman, wired for the kill, intercepted me like a missile the instant I stepped through the door.

"What kind?"

I thought for a moment. "Big. Loud." I wanted something that erased the memory of the hi-fi/television combo we had at home when I was a kid, its tinny sound ringing in my head like a coin dropped into a blind man's cup. "Expensive."

"Is money an object?"

"No."

He led me through a maze of amplifiers, cassette decks, turntables, and speakers, at one point sending out for coffee and eggs for both of us while we pored over catalogs and discussed watts per channel, separation of sound, and potential eardrum damage.

"Okay, look. I think I know what you want. I'm gonna level with you. This tuner, it's the best. It's the most expensive, but it's the best. If you want to argue, we can stop talking. I would sell you this speaker and go to my grave with a clean conscience. You see what I'm saying?"

"I'll take it. Turntable?"

"Anything with a belt. This model, this is fine. It's the best, so you're systemwide compatible. Speakers." He said the word as if it were an ancient mystery, something tinged with adoration-demanding qualities. "Speakers are like brides. Be sure you want 'em before you say 'I do.' " The pair he showed me were the size of milk crates and had a bass line that sounded like a velvet hammer was thumping my eardrums.

"I think louder."

"How loud?"

"If I'm on the road, I want to be able to hear them from home."

"Yeah? What do you do?"

"I'm a baseball player."

He nodded, once, slowly, then took me into . . . "the room." Standing in the corners, erect as cadets, were two five-foot-high columns, their black mesh faces emblazoned with silver thunderbolt logos. "I'm going to say this, and I'm going to say this once: Listen." He hit a few control panel buttons, tapped into a channel, and the speakers crackled to life like electricity in the air tearing apart just before a summer storm cracks the sky wide open. A moment later, the two of us were assaulted by a tornado of sound, the experience weirdly thrilling, as if I'd ceased to exist as anything human and was simply a state of consciousness spinning around inside the music. After a few minutes, he cut the power, and the sound faded as if the entire world had died. "Well?"

"I'll take four."

"Can we afford this?" Barbara said, as I bear-hugged the last of the boxes and carried it into our small living room.

"Of course. I've got the contract, the reserve clause is dead, and Hammer's lining up endorsement deals right now. Relax."

The next day I received a memo from Hammer, a sober note strangely unlike his other communications in that it was somberly straightforward, stripped of the clamor of his previous hype, and virtually intelligible. It read, "If you want to act like a lobotomy patient every time you're interviewed, these are the kinds of product endorsement contracts you can expect to receive. My advice to you is to take the offer. No others are forthcoming. Attached you will find a bill for my services." The endorsement contract was with a hair-restorer company called Nouveau Root; Hammer's bill was for 20 percent of my first year's salary.

A week later, in spite of the fact that I had yet to receive a nickel's worth of my 1976 income, the IRS sent me a letter stating that my estimated tax payments for 1975 were unpaid and overdue. The bill, including penalties and interest, was for $179,031.24.

Immediately I wanted to be back in high school, playing ball on the lumpy field behind the windowless brick gymnasium, riding home on the bus on spring evenings after practice feeling loose and tired, the dinner my mother had cooked waiting for me at home, even as I glided passively through the winding streets of our town, staring out at the walnut-sized buds forming on the trees and the city's skyline, partially obscured by a toxic purple haze, floating like a mirage in the desert, just beyond the slim black line that was the polluted river. I felt like a new bride, a virgin who had just been carried across the threshold into a world governed by obsessive and insane men. I wanted — I needed — someone on my side. I turned, as I could at the time, to Barbara.

"Ignore Hammer's bill, forget the hair commercial, and go see an accountant about the IRS bill." She was standing by the window in the baby's room, hanging Donald Duck curtains. Her bell-shaped maternity blouse billowed out around her midsection like a gown of Anna Karenina's.

"Why don't you think I should do the hair restorer commercial? It could be the down payment money on that place we want."

"We'll get the money some other way."

"I could get a paper route."

"I don't like the idea of you promoting fountain-of-youth products. It's a scam."

"I'm suddenly shameless in the face of bankruptcy."

"These guys are dishonest."

"Of course. They're businessmen."

I called the number of the accountant's office which Barbara's brother-in-law gave me and asked for the man I was to speak with by name. I was put on hold. Then a man who introduced himself as Arthur Lotski picked up the phone at the other end of the line and told me to send my tax information to the office, marked to his attention.

"I'm supposed to deal with Sam Doniger," I said.

Solemnly, in pretentiously measured beats, Lotski said, "Mr. Doniger is being phased out of the business. I'm taking over his clients."

"Why's that?"

"Mr. Doniger moved on two months ago."

"He's gone?"

"Physically, yes."

"But I need to talk to him."

"Mr. Doniger's dead."

"But this is important."

There was a brief silence, then I was given curt instructions to send in my wage data and wait for a call from his secretary to set up an appointment.

"I think I made a big mistake," I said to Barbara.

"What?"

"I think I've just made the man who's going to do my tax returns hate me."

I telephoned the hair restorer people and told them that I couldn't accept their generous offer, as my recent journey to see a faith healer had miraculously produced a sudden budding on my scalp and if I appeared in their commercial we would both become liable for charges of fraud. I received a dunning letter from Hammer, no call for an appointment from Lotski's office, then, surprisingly, an unexpected summons from Lunch Molloy, our batting coach.

Lunch was calling long distance to tell me to report to spring training twenty pounds heavier than the season before. "You're being moved to the fifth spot in the order," he said.

"I'm a singles hitter. I'm not the guy you want batting fifth. What gives?"

"Orders."

"From who?"

"The peanut vendor. From who. Who else?"

"I'm not your number-five hitter. Fifth is for guys built like fire hydrants, stumpy little third basemen with basketballs for asses. Not me."

"The powers that be say it is you this year."

"You want a twenty, twenty-five home run guy, someone who connects with the ball once a week and deposits it in the leftfield bleachers. I hit singles. Fragments. Epiphanies. Pauses. You know?"

Lunch cleared his throat. "Yeah, well, that may be true." I pictured him sitting in his Florida living room, a beer on the Formica-topped end table beside his chintz-covered couch, the stack of *TV Guides* on the coffee table beside his cotton-socked foot. He was half watching an afternoon movie while he spoke to me, dreaming an old coach's dream, indifferent to the present, sailing, instead, over the terrain of his past. "But this year you're expected to hit home runs."

"That'll ruin my game. Would you ask Reggie Jackson to hit singles?"

"We don't own Reggie Jackson," Lunch said, matter-of-factly. "Just put on the requested weight, and let us worry about your game. We get paid for it, you know."

Just let *us* worry about *your* game.

Eating was easily accommodated into my regimen of anxious boredom, weight lifting, and restless depression. The more I ate, the hungrier I became. Barbara and I would eat dinner late in the evening, by midnight I was up again, my head moving cranelike just inside the refrigerator door, scanning perishables, while my hands busily scooped up leftover legs of chicken, deck-of-card-sized stacks of cold cuts, hanks of cold spaghetti. Triple-decker sandwiches became my passion, their malleability a source of deranged personal excitement and experimentation for me. The comfort of their quintessence — the bedrock of sliced fresh bread — freed me to create with abandon, secure in the knowledge that no matter what I slapped between the slices — combinations of turkey, tomatoes, gorgonzola, and bacon; roast beef, coleslaw, and chicken livers; ham, salami, tongue, and onion; any psychotic Jewish-deli combination imaginable — I would always wind up with a "sandwich." I was belching nonstop, my stomach turning like the inside of a hot-air dryer from indigestion, when I went to see Lotski.

He was a bird-faced man in his early thirties. He wore a dark blue suit, oversized glasses, a school ring the size of a pigeon egg, and a Bicentennial pin on the wide lapel of his jacket. His movements consisted mainly of reverent, priestlike nods and slow, show-your-cards flourishes of the hands when he was making a point. He was solemn, for my sake it seemed, when he laid out the pages of my sinful financial history. I felt that he was offering his ear to me, his power to forgive, as if he expected me to unburden my financially guilt-wracked soul. "Bless me, father, for I have sinned. I have coveted my privacy and turned down an endorsement contract. I did not itemize my deductions, and I thought about filling out the 1040EZ short form." Lotski then began to explain — in looping, head-spinning accountantese — why the IRS had contacted me.

"You see, your team reported a two-hundred-and-sixty-seven-thousand-dollar payroll disbursement on their 1975 corporate return, which they filed at the end of October. The figure turned up next to your name."

"I haven't received any money yet. That salary is spread out over the next six years, and I don't receive a check for any part of it until spring training opens next month. I hadn't even signed in October!"

"Be that as it may. They most likely assumed that you would, and entered it on their ledgers. Let me put it as simply as I can. Last year you were a promising rookie. Now you're a year older, a step slower. By getting you onto their books last year, they are allowed to claim you as a depreciation, like an aged piece of machinery, this year. Their tax savings will equal roughly forty percent of your salary this and every year of your contract. Have a bad year and they can write off practically your entire salary as a loss, a bad investment, something which produced no return on the capital they originally invested. The tax laws are structured so that the worse you play, the more you're worth to them. Follow?"

I followed. Two hundred and sixty-seven thousand for six years. Mr. Percy had even known I would sign for the $500-a-year pay cut. King takes pawn. Check.

"I can amortize your income going back over five years," Lotski said. "That will substantially reduce this tax bill. And I believe I can have the interest and penalty rescinded. But you're going to have to expect your cash flow to be tight for a year or so. Don't count on any major expenditures for a while."

I wanted the off-season angst purged from my soul by days spent sprinting across green outfields under the warm clutch of a subtropical sun. I wanted the snap and tone restored to my muscles by exercise and salt air, my spirit lifted from its funk by the sandlot ease of spring training games. I wanted to reconnect myself with the die-hard fans, the out-of-step souls who lurk in delapidated citrus-league ballparks in late winter and watch the game with a sun-dazed disinterest and goodwill. More than anything, I wanted baseball to be unimportant once more. Unanalyzed by critics, unjudged by employers, the game once again pure, unsullied by the hands of television producers, programmers, tax lawyers, and arbitrators. Obviously, I wanted too much.

I left Barbara, boarding a Florida-bound 747 dreaming just these boyish, naive thoughts, and showed up at camp, my face beaming like a goosed choirboy's, on the first morning of spring training. All I wanted to do was play baseball. When I tried to get in, I found the place was locked up tight.

Nine

WOMEN TEND to grieve silently, accept their suffering, and carry on. They are cyclical, like the gospels and washing machines. Men, on the other hand, despair and get ugly. Quit their jobs and drunkenly watch afternoon movies sprawled on a Barcalounger, clad only in graying underwear and three-day stubble. Perhaps this is related to our flash-in-the-pan orgasmic nature. Who knows?

It was just this sort of embittered sulking that characterized the beginnings of the lockout negotiations. Screaming, threats, humiliations: a hundred-year-old tug-of-war, by turns rancorous and fraught with inarticulate love, the squabbling and machinations between the players and owners heated up by the microwave-quick powers of TV and headline news. I felt a desire for a soul-numbing drunk that first morning, something to free me of my restlessness and carry me light-years away from the spirit-poisoning maneuverings of the lockout. I picked up a twelve-pack of beer, went back to the motel room that I was paying for out of my own pocket, and sat in an armchair staring out at the sun-swept beach till thinking seemed futile enough to drive me to television.

I was watching a John Garfield movie when the phone rang. I had been trying intermittently to reach Barbara in order to tell her not to worry, that everything was all right, then to begin sobbing long distance. When I heard the first ring, I thought: She heard about the lockout on the news. Knowing my proclivity to despair, my aversion to an it-will-all-work-out-everything's-going-to-be-fine sort of levelheadedness when there were objects to be hurled, walls to be punched, and profanities to be shouted, she had called instantly.

"Hello."

"Williams. It's Cap." My manager, Cap Carver, a walking ironing board of a man who kicked dirt at umpires, lived the life of an alcoholic monk, and would, it seemed, push a baby carriage down a flight of stairs if he was in a hurry and it was in his way. For Cap, a remorseless, hermetic soul, managing a baseball team seemed to be an alternative to homicide. "We'd like to see you down at the stadium offices."

"The stadium's locked, Cap."

"Look —"

Mr. Percy's voice was suddenly on the line, distant and cajoling, sounding like some fairy-tale enchanter speaking from the bottom of a well. (He had a penchant for speaker phones.) "Mike, I'd just like you to come down here and explain this whole thing to me," he said.

"I thought you paid lawyers an exorbitant amount of money to do that for you."

"Lawyers couldn't find water if they were standing next to a faucet. I want to know what you think, Mike. You're a bright boy." I wanted to say, "Yeah, I'm bright. I know that forty-five thousand less five hundred is forty-four five." But I felt the tongue-biting grip of reason, and so I just sat and listened in silence.

"Listen, Mike. I'd just like you to do me this favor. I'm not an unreasonable man. If the men have something to talk about, I'm willing to listen." He paused for a moment, then said, "I think you'd be a good spokesman for them."

"They hate me."

"Because you're smarter than them."

There was a spidery silence. "I really think you should talk to your people," I said.

"Why are you setting up this opposing-camps attitude?"

"Mr. Percy —"

"Do you really think I want to see the end of baseball?" he asked, cutting me off. "Just come and talk to me."

"I'm right in the middle of drinking away my despair here."

"So, we'll have a drink together. I'm buying." Then he paused before adding, with a hint of the businesslike edge, the happy cowboy hard sell, trimmed from his voice, "In case you didn't know, I've been ill for most of the winter."

By this time I was sitting forward in my chair, the receiver pressed to my right ear. The fingers of my left hand were rubbing my forehead, as if their steady massage could erase my ambivalence and suspicions. The beer had softened my brain pan, and knowing whether I was resisting him intelligently, or reacting with paranoia, seemed beyond my capacities at the moment. This is your employer, the man who has given you your career, a voice in my head said. How can you deny him? I felt myself falling into one of those funks where I surrendered all rational belief in my own worth and, instead, became certain that if it were not for a paternal savior like Mr. Percy, my existence would mean nothing. I could hear him waiting for my answer, breathing lightly at the other end of the line. Then, at the instant I was balanced like a coin standing on edge, he very quietly said, "Well?" I don't think he was surprised when, with duly noted resignation, I exhaled and said, "All right."

"Thank you for coming, Mike." Mr. Percy leaned forward and put his frail, almost disfigured hand on my knee. He had arthritis and the hand was gnarled, the back of it sticking up like a hump, his fingers bent down and inward like the roots of a tree clawing the earth. We were seated across from each other in armchairs. Cap Carver paced back and forth, as impatient as an usher at a wake. He had a cigarette clamped between the fingers of one hand, and he seemed to focus all of his thoughts and buried anger on it. Lunch Molloy was sitting in a corner chair, staring wide eyed into space and chewing bubble gum with the obliviousness of a roadside heifer. "Let me ask you something," Mr. Percy said in a priestly voice. In his ministerial black suit and white shirt, he looked like an early nineteenth-century technocrat — stern as a barber's strop and dry and dead as a December leaf. "Have you spoken to any of the other men yet?"

"I haven't seen any of them. We were due here only yesterday."

"How about your roommate?"

"Number one, we don't have any rooms. I'm paying for mine out of my own pocket. And number two, as far as I know, Oscar Rife hasn't shown up yet."

"Rife. That rabble-rouser! He holds out every year. Of course he's not here yet. Carver, change Mike's roommate. I don't want him rooming with Rife."

"Lunch, change his room," Cap said, not breaking his slow stride. Lunch nodded sleepily, his jaws keeping up a steady chewing motion.

"Now Mike, I want you to tell me what this is all about."

"You don't know?"

"I told you, I've been ill. Very ill. I wouldn't be here today if I hadn't been informed of what was going on at the last minute."

"You don't know about our room reservations being canceled, the threats not to pay us if we don't start playing by April first?"

"Threats? Mike, I'm a businessman. And, in my anonymous way, a great philanthropist. Why do I need to bother with threats? If some of the others want to threaten, that's their business. I don't make a nickel on this team, and if I sold it tomorrow my accounting staff would get down on their knees and kiss my feet. And if — Cap, is that true? Did he have to go find a room on his own?"

"I don't know."

"Well, if it is, we'll take care of it, Mike. You'll be reimbursed for every cent. Just keep the receipts. Now, I'm in the dark here, and you have to help me out."

This wasn't what I had heard. The winter grapevine had leaked the news that Mr. Percy had covertly led the owners' fight against free agency. They were trying to reverse the decision made by Peter Seitz the preceding December, which had put an end to the reserve clause, essentially freeing players after six years in the majors. Players were no longer bound to their owners in perpetuity.

It was revolution. It was the end of history, they said. And so they took the matter to the U.S. District Court in Kansas City in the hope that there some cattle baron's grandson would restore their version of sanity and feudal authority to the business. They wanted to lasso the runaway horror of employees with rights and drag the whole mess back into the nineteenth century. The outcome did not look good for the owners as spring training neared, and so when we showed up for work, they locked us out.

"Tell me something, Mike," Mr. Percy said. "Are you unhappy?"

"No."

"I'd say that a young man of — how old are you?"

"Twenty-two. One year older than last year. I've depreciated a bit. Remember?"

Mr. Percy simulated a seamless bit of mock senility and let my reference to his convoluted and tax-dodging — though perfectly legal — style of bookkeeping go unnoticed.

"That's a very young age for someone to be making the kind of money you're making," he said.

This was true. In the course of a year I had leapfrogged from working-stiff wages to a handsome, junior executive's salary. Nothing princely, just good, solid, middle-management compensation, a level of net income that buys a suburban home with putting-green-smooth lawns, sprinkler systems, and electric garage doors; station wagons with laminated wood-grain side-panels; and a seven-figure life insurance policy. My salary outstripped my father's, and he had put in my lifetime plus one year at his job, his Cold War beginnings a time of men in gray suits and felt hats, a period of Hathaway shirts, stubby, filterless cigarettes, and no inflation. And nowhere on my father's horizon did there loom any hope of free agency, of kingly endowment. Merely the thin cushion of a pension, pin money for a doddering time of rhythmic sighs and soul-deep distraction, a decade of wearing pant waists at nearly midchest and walking the sun- and sand-swept sidewalks of subtropical cities in white patent leather shoes — waiting. So what was I to say? That I was entitled to the money, even more money? That my salary was league average but

I was above average, gifted, the instrument of some by turns heroic and pointless skill that had forever lifted me above the rank of clock puncher?

Guilt and reason, though, are incompatible, like drinking and driving. A doomed enterprise governed by slow reflexes and overreactions. The words began to drip off the tip of my tongue. "It is generous, but —"

"So you're not unhappy?"

"No, but —"

"I don't see your agent hovering, now that you might need him. He's taken his money and run, hasn't he?"

"Mr. Percy, the point of the disagreement is —"

"I'm here, though, Mike. Aren't I? I'm here. And do you know who will be here after all the thugs and agents and arbitrators clear out of our game? We will. I'll be here because, Mike . . . I love this game. And you, you'll be here because you love it, too. And because you can play it the way fans love to see it played." His Capraesque grandstanding was coming at me too fast, everything good from puppies to terminal-disease-curing home runs filling my chest with a naive and sentimental desire to do good. (I'd obviously been drinking way too much.) Kitsch tears welled up in my eyes, my soul full of alleluias, greeting-card goodness ringing through me until I said, "I know. I want to play. But —"

"So you're happy, then?"

"Yes, I'm happy when —"

"Then, Mike, that's good enough for me. I'm going to call the other owners and get this season started. I've never heard of such lollygagging in my life." An aide, blue-suited, and polished as a White House wineglass, appeared and escorted Mr. Percy to his wheelchair. As I stood, Mr. Percy reached out and took my hand. "Walk with me," he said, as a second man, moving with the somber demeanor of an undertaker, walked ahead of us to the polished mahogany doors. Their brass handles gleamed with the servant-buffed brightness of aristocracy. I walked slowly, taking here-comes-the-bride-sized steps in order to stay beside Mr. Percy's wheelchair. The man ahead of us took hold of both handles at once, turned them, then moved forward, just inches ahead of

Mr. Percy and myself. As we stepped through the parting doors there was a sudden bath of flashbulb light, and the fishing-line whirr of cameras automatically advancing film, shutters clicking away with the chittering industry of insects. Microphones the size of torchlamps clustered in front of my face as the firefight rhythm of questions began. "Did you cut a deal, how much are you making, when are you going to start, what if the other players don't?" All of the inquiries fired at me in one babbling volley. I wondered why these people were here. Was Mr. Percy's every action subjected to scrutiny by the media? Why had they been allowed to enter the building?

Beside me, a thicket of microphones reached down toward Mr. Percy, and the wizened industrialist quickly eased into his ministerial role, the microphones recording his words for dissemination among the faithful and the jaded. Unlike me, he was comfortable in the secular pulpit. Speaking into microphones did not seem to make him question his own beliefs, shake the foundation of his being. He ignored the questions put to him and simply said, "My boy here is happy and he wants to play baseball. And dammit, if that other riffraff isn't satisfied with the terms we're offering, let them go out and start their own league. Let them worry about squeezing out a profit."

I heard the nearly inaudible scratching of reporters' pencils racing over pocket calculator–sized notepads, as I tried to disengage my hand from Mr. Percy's. Flanking me on my right, Cap Carver stared straight ahead, his eyes seemingly focused on some blank patch of space. Cap answered questions with the curt, toneless manner of a presidential secretary having a bad day, all corporate formality and harried irritation, and summed up his feelings in one final remark. "We're ready to open this camp anytime they're ready to stop whining and play," he said. Then he made his way through the mob of journalists.

Strangers who dealt with me on a first-name basis pressed in and began tossing out questions with stream-of-consciousness ease. Any hint of silence on my part would be a sign of guilt, arrogance, or condescension. "Are you going to play, Mike?"

"What about the Players Association, Mike?" "Are you saying that you accept the reserve clause?" "Don't you feel like a scab, Mike?" I felt compelled to make my way through their questions, if only to avoid being misunderstood and loathed. I tried to answer each question in the order that I heard it, but my replies were interrupted and overlapped by new questions. In reaction to this, my responses developed their own staccato, and qualifying, pace. The words themselves seemed divorced from all sense of meaning. They were connected, by that point, only to the feverish buzz of the news-hungry mob. "Yes, I'm going to play, no, I'm not saying that, yes, but I want to, no." A fractal conversation, veering toward unintelligibility, laced with variable and explosive meanings. A wave of no-comment anger crested in me, an embittered, caged-animal animosity. I felt Mr. Percy squeeze my hand even more tightly. When I looked down at him, he smiled, an abundant meanness — yet only a glimmer of satisfaction — sculpting the line of his thin, corpse-white lips, his shrunken figure awash in the monkeyhouse clamor of the spectacle.

By one o'clock I was back in my motel room, confused, angry, and bitter over what had happened — though I couldn't exactly say what had indeed occurred. It was as if the entire scene had been silent footage of some nuclear explosion, all lyrical mushroom-cap fury with no real effects. I was wondering if it was possible for there to be no fallout in the wake of the event when the phone rang.

"Hi. How ya do-ing?" in a syrupy drip of a voice, all honey and silk. It was Hammer.

"I'm getting dollars, remember?" The beer had worn off and I was beginning to get a headache.

"We'll fix the salary thing," he said. Hammer had a way of totally eradicating all former disagreements and disputes. He lived strictly in the present, a perpetually blossoming state of let-bygones-be-bygones, some discrete and yet continuous beam of affection and corporate intimacy leaking from every pore and hair follicle.

"Are you going to get me paid in Monopoly money?"

Hammer chortled. Then turned, for a moment, deeply paternal. "I want you not to worry," he said.

"I'm not worried."

"Brave front. Love to see it. Which is by the way and, in fact, exactly, why I am calling."

"I've been traded."

"That wouldn't be such a bad thing."

"Mr. Percy called you and he wants his money back."

"Can I tell you something? You should pray for that to happen."

"I've already spent the money. I can't pray for that to happen."

"Listen to me. Poor people spend money. It leaves their hands, it becomes an irrecoverable object. Money, below a certain income level, is a non-Proustian thing —"

"I'm getting Proust now?"

"I've never read, but I grasp the concept. Loss and recovery. A fifteen-to-thirty-year sliding-scale depreciation of the past. I get it. I grasp it. Can I share an insight with you? Proust was writing for accountants. Anyway, spending. Spent. These are words you need to strike from your vocabulary. Think of it like potty training. Your vocabulary is infantile, strictly a below-twenty-thousand-a-year-income-level vernacular. Words like 'spent' are feces; you drop them everywhere. You paint with them like a two-year-old. Can I share something with you? It's time to toilet-train your tongue."

"The drug you're on sounds great." I dropped into the vinyl-covered armchair by the sliding doors.

Hammer dug deep into his chubby, cellulite-ribbed throat and delivered up another woolly chuckle, though one less unself-consciously felt. It was a staged, this-is-only-a-dramatization, look-at-what-a-good-sport-I-am neon sign of a laugh. Always the self-promoter, even when he was flattering me — particularly when he was flattering me. Then guillotine finish and rebound. "Dry sense of humor," he said. "I love it. Anyway, fronts" — the man a master of dismissive and off-the-cuff segue — "fronts is why I'm calling. Masks. Personas."

"I'm not doing it."

"You've already done it."

"I'm still not doing it."

"You don't even know what I'm asking."

"I like it that way."

"All I'm saying is meet me."

"No."

"I'll talk, you listen."

"No."

"I have footage," he said, "dot, dot, dot." It was a cryptic threat, a conversation-stopping, watch-me-pull-a-rabbit-out-of-my-hat bargaining ploy that he knew — Hammer somehow always knew — would break the momentum of my rejection.

"I haven't been to bed with anyone but my wife."

"Sex scandals are strictly minor league, a bit of naughty glitz to sugarcoat the game. They have no more than a wham-bam-thank-you-ma'am effect on the public's information-gathering erogenous zones. I'm talking ugly, or great potential for. Since when do you see owners without me?"

"You mean, outside of the time I had to sign my contract by myself?"

"That was an act-of-God-clause circumstance. Strictly beyond my control."

"You forgot."

"I didn't, I remembered. Only it was too late."

"How do you know I saw Percy?"

"Attribute it either to my Godlike powers of omniscience, or someone owed me a favor. Take your pick. All-knowingness aside, I've seen a sneak preview, a let's-go-to-the-videotape hatchet job of your so-called press conference."

"I never agreed to any press conference."

"Which is why you shouldn't as much as buy a hot dog anywhere near a stadium unless you check with me first."

"I can never find you."

"Forget that. That's all in your own head. Listen to me. Your parent company is a newsmongering cyclops. People with what you might call a salary-driven bias have done a cut-and-paste job

on you, but good. Said video collage is to be beamed out to the
jealous and rhetoric-swayed public at six this evening. Can I share
something with you? You don't come across as a labor leader."

I realized what Hammer was talking about. No matter what I
had said, the only coherent message that the medium would deliver to the millions was that I was, as he himself had put it, Mr.
Percy's boy. "Can we sue?" I said.

"So young and already so litigious. Civil court as the voice in
the whirlwind, an entire baby-boom generation of tantrum-
throwing Jobs. I augur bad things for the future. Answer to your
question: Anybody can sue anybody. Winning. Winning is a key
and often overlooked factor in attorney-contested matters. Can
you win? Maybe. Defamation of character? A possibility, a curveball high and outside. As your agent and attorney, I would have
to advise nyet. That's why I'm saying: See me. A little brainstorming session, some ground-rules blueprint type of conversation in
case we have to rebut, which I'm thinking we should."

"No."

"Strictly a no-strings-attached fifty-minute hour. I have the
tape. I'm fifteen minutes from your motel. A chat."

"Absolutely not."

"Hi, come on in." Hammer was in a baseline-wide-pinstripe
suit, his tie the size of a folded dinner napkin. On his feet were
black suede platform shoes. A late seventies fashion felon. Quiana
shirt, and Little Miss Muppet crescents of hair over the ears.

We were in the office of Phil "Trip" Pareles, Media Consul-
tant — an associate of Hammer's. It was a smoked-glass-and-
black-Formica cube with piped-in air and a Quaalude-slow
perspective on the traffic oozing through the grid of city streets
below, a canyon-deep abyss filled with harsh, grimy capillaries of
color.

"Have a seat," Hammer said. "So, first thing — you've got
personality." Hammer sliced the air with his index finger. "We'll
get rid of it."

"I like my personality. It's one of the things I can afford."

"Clogs the screen image. Gotta go. But, not to sweat a thing.

Understood?" Again his hands moved, in unison now, a Moses-like parting motion, some *Dominus vobiscum,* go-in-peace gesture, assuaging, wandlike. Then he was quiet for a moment, studying me. "I can see you looking at me."

"Maybe that's because I'm looking at you."

"I see it."

"I'm six inches away."

"I'm *aware* of you looking at me. That's bad. Major video faux pas. Leads to all manner of egregious televisual projections, personality and character being the two main and no-no type things I'm thinking of. Character. Bad word. What do you think of, by way of association, when I say the word 'character'?"

"Cartoon."

"Wrong. Way off base. Flaw. Characters have flaws. Therefore, for you to be perceived as ideal, you can't have character. Character is a pre-TV mode of being. Absolutely World War II. Sometimes, and I'm opening myself up to you on a level of intimacy that might be considered uncorporate, but I feel strongly about our working relationship, sapling state that it's in, so I feel I can tell you this — you want to know something? — I have an overwhelming desire to be a 1940s black-and-white movie."

"Just run the tape, please."

"All right."

Hammer removed a Beta cassette from a thin cardboard sleeve and walked across the gray shag carpeting to a cockpit-sized control panel, a dark altar made of black, injection-molded plastic and luminous, pocket watch–sized gauge faces. Reading-level needles tick-tocked back and forth, in some cases, like the finger of a metronome. Others remained as erect and motionless as a cadet at attention. Above the panel, the faces of twelve television sets, each tuned to a different channel, leapt randomly from image to image. It seemed as if the image-kernels burst into new image-kernels every three seconds. It was a successive and yet seemingly inexhaustible process of metamorphosis, spooky in its apparent endlessness. At first the sudden bursting of the image made the experience feel something like watching video popcorn. But then

I began to feel as if I could detect a discrete yet continuous rhythm, as if I were in the presence of some eternal, pointillistic being.

"I have to admit it," Hammer said. "I love the umbilical pull of the tube. There's a sense of wordless well-being I feel in its presence. I guess it's what a battery must feel like when it's recharging. It's my belief that we're all reincarnated as television images. Sort of a video pantheism. If I could come back as a pencil cup on 'The Mary Tyler Moore Show,' I'd be happy." The two of us stared at the tube in dumb unison, a generation-deep hypnosis overtaking our conscious thoughts. "You know," Hammer said, breaking the silence, "when I sleep I surround myself with half a dozen glowing TVs. Very Tibetan, don't you think?"

Hammer pressed the VCR's "play" button and the twelve-eyed beast went blank for an instant. There was some chainsaw static as the sound came on, lightning-bolt waves of diagonal interference, then the smooth inertia of sprocket-driven image. The doors to Mr. Percy's office parted with the slow pomp of majesty. The camera recording the event was picking up the backs of journalists' heads, the scene marked by the informal urgency that tinged presidential announcements with their special veneer of power. When the two of us appeared in the doorway, I was walking beside Mr. Percy in his wheelchair, holding his hand like a dutiful son picking his father up after a long hospital stay. A percussion of microphones knocking against hard surfaces, and the eruptions of sound technicians coughing into their sleeves boomed into the aural foreground of the tape. The camera did several funhouse zooms. Then the tape slipped into a groove of edited material. As Mr. Percy and I moved into the hallway, an announcer read voice-over copy: "Last year's Rookie of the Year, Mike Williams, met with his owner, Edmond Perlmutter Percy, this morning, in the hopes of leading his teammates back into the ballpark."

"I never said that."

But on screen, words poured from my mouth like spewing, media-generated carbon monoxide, the surgical editing of the tape nearly invisible. "Yes, I want to play ball," I said on tape, my

name spelled out beneath the image of my chin in unserifed white
typeface.

"I was saying yes to another question," I said to Hammer,
who, engaged in the talking-head version of me babbling away
on the screen, ignored me.

"I am happy," my on-screen voice said, my answers connected
to questions that were being tossed into the air like confetti, jour-
nalistic fungoes looping out of every corner of the long, imperial
hallway.

"You see what you're doing?" Hammer said. "You see?" There
was a look of candid insistence on my face. "You look to believable to be believable. You look so honest people are going to have
to distrust you."

The tape jump-cut from me to Mr. Percy. On screen, he had
swollen to Lionel Barrymore proportions, a captain of industry
marked by Dickensian tics and flourishes. The fossilized near-skel-
eton that he was behind closed doors had seemingly rejuvenated
itself for the cameras by an act of will. "My boy here is happy
and he wants to play baseball," he said, appearing at once to be
firm, protective, paternal, and wise. There was a sense of conviction in his voice that seemed driven by the force of immeasurable
wealth. "If that other riffraff isn't satisfied . . . ," he continued.

"He's great," Hammer said, "he's really great," speaking over
Mr. Percy's words, which, in the late twentieth century, were almost moving in their lack of public equivocation. The mantle of
authority had collapsed, and I understood that beyond Mr.
Percy's visual performance, Hammer was responding to the sentimental and naive nostalgia evoked by Mr. Percy's implacable
self-assurance. As a nation, we were ripe for a benevolent dictator,
someone who was a combination of Father Christmas and Wyatt
Earp. Mr. Percy was not it, but his imperious and commanding
presence augured the coming of such a figure.

There was a final, surrealistic cut-and-splice amended to the
tape. "Are you willing to go back to work and give up free
agency?" a voice said. The question seemed to issue from some
audio porthole, a shouted dockside plea coming not from the

room on the screen but a loop of studio-prepared tape. I did not remember the question's even being asked. "Yes," my mouth said. It was nearly seamless, but it was still obvious to me that my response had been pulled out of context and grafted onto an appended question, some videotape surgeon inserting a blip of fabricated copy into the corpus of the tape.

"They doctored that," I said.

"Of course," Hammer answered, satisfied with himself for appearing self-assured and convincing. I thought that perhaps a bit of Mr. Percy's hubris had rubbed off on him, and I marveled at the speed with which he moved toward emulation. I watched him watch the end of the tape, then turned my eyes back to one of the sets when the announcer's voice began to deliver the coda. "And so, with the public angered and some of their own teammates turning against them, the question remains as to when the majority of the ballplayers will suspend their walkout and allow the season to get under way." Then the screens went blank and Hammer zapped them with a hand-held remote control button. The atmosphere seemed to suddenly vanish, the imageless sanctum at once as sterile as a bell jar.

"We're not on strike," I said. "They locked us out." I noticed that I was raising my voice. "How can they air that?"

"Your owner owns half a network and sixty-three independent television stations across the country. I think they'll slip it in somewhere."

"But it's not true. It's an out-and-out lie."

"It's a 'mistake.' At eleven o'clock they'll fess up and issue a correction, a little sidestepping legal maneuver dropped in during the segue from low-priority news to sports and weather."

"This thing is going on the air?"

"The copy we have is a little rough, but basically — to answer your question — yes."

"I'm going to look like a Hitler supporter at the Nuremberg trials."

Hammer slipped behind the desk and into the cupped palm of his upholstered chair. "It's not a pretty picture, I agree. That's why I called. We can do things."

"You have people killed?"

"Another press conference. Video rebuttal."

"I'm not going back in front of the cameras."

"You have no choice."

"I'm not doing it."

"I'm not suggesting this. You look like you've scabbed out on the entire organized Players Association — solo. It's six hundred and twenty-three to one. If I don't corral you into producing some rage-assuaging countermaneuvers, I could be an accessory to a crime. Your peers will stomp you to death in front of sixty-six thousand fans on Bat Day. This is not a let's-run-it-up-the-flagpole, brainstorming-session piece of gray-matter detritus here. This is bona fide panic. You have got to go on TV."

"Last time — no."

Ten

"ISN'T THIS GREAT?" Hammer and I were on the beach. It was late that same afternoon, hours after I had allowed him to convince me that the insanity of trying to expose the sham of the morning's press conference by holding one of my own was actually sane and logical, perhaps due to the nature of its own insanity. A jerry-built dais banked with microphones had been set up along a strip of sand-abutting pavement. Technicians unspooled heavy lengths of cable and connected mobile power generators to a video projector that had been placed in front of the dais. A sports bar–sized screen stood behind the dais where I would be sitting. There was a Felliniesque starkness and absurdity to the scene. The spare, sun-brightened beach, the press conference clutter. It was a clash of natural elements and technological litter, the entire milieu dreamed up by Hammer, after a quick call to his astrologer.

"Initially, I wanted to preempt the six o'clock news," Hammer said, "but then I felt we should take a wait-and-see approach — especially since FCC regulations would probably not look kindly on rebutting a TV news story before the story is actually broadcast. Be that as it may, I still feel that doing nothing is absolutely and totally beyond any categorical definition of right. A boo-boo, big time. So, out of compromise comes — Why be modest? I'm Ivy League — genius."

He gestured toward the makeshift set. His plan was for me to hold my press conference *during* the six o'clock news.

"You get the whole news-conference-within-a-news-conference layering effect? The which-is-reality slash which-is-illusion modern theater aspect of it? People watching you on television watching yourself on television. Personally, I think we'll have our greatest success if half our audience is stoned."

Hammer guided me toward a looming Winnebago that was parked in a lot several yards from the dais. "We should talk a little strategy," he said. "Number one: Don't appear to be thinking seriously while you're on camera. Thinking has a negative video connotation, very Dostoevskian. You look perturbed, people will think you're Raskolnikov. How do you avoid this? Simple: Don't think."

He led me through an ant colony scrabble of pedestrian traffic as he spoke. Audio technicians wearing droopy corduroy jeans and Li'l Abner work boots, and graying men of indistinct age, the aroma of dead tobacco corkscrewing in the air around them, worked with huge, caisson-sized pieces of equipment. Monitors and generators sprouted long black wires, and the men setting them up worked at a union-protected pace.

"Where are we going?" I said.

"Just over here." He pointed to the motel-sized mobile home.

"Who's getting the bill for this, by the way?"

Hammer laughed. I was beginning to discover that the size of the laugh was always in direct proportion to the size of the bill — which was, of course, never discussed. "Mike," he said, "we're friends," his voice conveying surprise that I even asked, as well as mock reassurance. He patted me on the back. Five figures, I thought. No question.

"I don't have a cent."

"You shouldn't be getting yourself worked up about this type of thing. It could be very performance deflating."

"Tap city, I mean it."

"Mike, you're rich. You're loaded with megabuck marketing potential — baseball cards, peanut butter commercials, school lunchbox licensing deals. Your earnings potential is unlimited.

You're just in a position where you don't have any money yet."

We stopped outside the door of the Winnebago. The sign on it said Makeup.

"Let me ask you something personal," Hammer said. "Are you committed to facial hair?"

"I don't like this already."

"Very Oakland A's, very early seventies. This is 1976. It's a cusp period. We're not in an either/or mode of dress at the moment. You've got leisure suits and bangle bracelets out there. Elvis is weighing in at two-forty. Suddenly chinos and penny loafers are nostalgia-laden icons. It's a very schizoid time to be picking out a wardrobe." Hammer opened the Winnebago's door, then stopped and held me in check for a moment with a single upright finger. "The Democrats could get back into the White House this year, so thinking a blue-collar look might be all right. Then again, you've got inflation, which could spawn a whole conservative-backlash type of movement, so you could go prep school look, too. It's a very coin-toss type of dilemma at the moment," he said. "After you."

I stepped inside the vehicle. It was a suburban covered wagon that got four miles to the gallon, a rolling living room/dining room/kitchenette with climate control and the option of taking a shower while the driver was being chased for a speeding ticket. The front of the cab had two orthopedic-looking bucket seats and a dash as long as a rubdown table. There were crushed Styrofoam cups and crumpled, stepped-on newspapers lying on the floor. The main part of the vehicle — a warped fusion of garden apartment architecture and city transit–style bleakness — looked like a hooker's closet on acid. Portable clothing racks crammed with kaleidoscopic paisleys and sequined, palette-bending, neon-bright solids were shoved up against opposite windows, blocking out most of the late afternoon sun. A makeshift vanity littered with crinkled tissues, lipstick cylinders, marshmallow-sized wads of cotton, eyelash brushes and Visine bottles stood just beyond the wardrobe. At the far end of the den was a sturdy chair. It was supported by a thick metal stump rooted to the floor by a halo of bolts. There was a hair-drying cone the size of an astronaut's helmet attached to a swivel arm above it. A mad doctor's assortment of instruments — crimping irons, scissors, shears, scalpels, razors, a Dark Ages torture chamber array of tonsorial devices — lay in front of the chair on a mirrored table. A door opened at the back of the trailer and a figure stepped out into the dim light.

"Mike," Hammer said, "this is Gordon. Gordon, this is Mike."

Gordon was wearing a peach-colored halter, white culottes, and sensible shoes. He had long, mouse-brown hair that curled up at the ends, riotous black eyebrows, and the grunge of two-day stubble on his cheeks. In his right hand was a smoldering nonfiltered cigarillo. Your basic, everyday transvestite — a culturally disorienting combination of John Garfield and the girl next door.

"You call me down here for this — to trim cotton candy?" Gordon said, his cigar ash bursting into dandruff-sized flakes as he waved a dismissive hand at my hairline.

Hammer placed a calming hand on my forearm. "Not to take it personally," he said. "It's the hormone injections."

"I don't think I want to surrender any hair to a person under stress."

"Just a trim. It'll be fine."

Hammer went over to Gordon and, in a whisper, began, I imagined, to placate him. Or her. I was willing to entertain suggestions. Gordon was histrionically shrill for a moment, then seemed to acquiesce. Hammer looked over at me and motioned to the chair. Grudgingly, I took a seat, and Gordon's reflection appeared in the mirror in front of me.

"What are we doing?" he said.

"How about a Mohawk?"

"Honey, if I moussed this baby hair, you'd look like a unicorn." He tugged on a few strands and I heard one snap.

"Hey."

Hammer cut in. "I think we just want to be going in the direction of nondescript," he said. "Something pluralistic. Something vague." He paused for a moment, distilling his thoughts, weighing and sorting them into zip code–directed batches, then said, "Can you give him a haircut without any ideological implications to it?"

"Tell me, honey," Gordon said to me, "did you do anything wrong?"

"No."

"What then?"

"Stupid."

"Then turn around, face the mirror, and shut up."

Gordon wrapped a damp hot towel around my face and neck. "This'll give you a nice glow on camera," he said. "You ever see the skin on girls from Seattle? Like cream. You know why? No sun. Wetness, no sun — cheeks like a tushy." Gordon's fingers began massaging my scalp. This was to encourage circulation, he said, a wake-up call to all those protein-sucking follicles, which were, in my case, gross underachievers. His fingers probed the cavity of skull at the top of my spinal cord and a Valium-like drowsiness spread over my limbs. My skeletal self seemed to dissolve. I was becoming one with the vinyl chair, devolving, melting, deliquescing into some premammalian being — protozoic, single celled, Gumby-like. Then the massaging ceased and there was a twittering of scissors above my head. After a few minutes, Gordon peeled the towel away from my face. The cool air was a tonic, reviving me. I opened my eyes and saw Gordon approaching my lips with his scissors. "Let's get rid of this ratty thing under your nose. Okay?" He trimmed my mustache, then applied a lighter-than-air cream to my face and scraped it off with a straight razor. My face was as smooth and taut as the skin of an apple.

"Perfect," Hammer said when I opened my eyes again. "Totally amorphous."

"Thanks for the haircut," I said, stepping out of the chair.

Gordon looked at me. He had a new cigar in his mouth and the flame of his BIC lighter was reaching for the tip of it. "Anytime," he said.

"If you ever swing about forty percent closer to the other gender, give me a call."

"What's wrong with right now?"

"Sorry. Ballplayer and faithful husband," I said.

"So are most of my tricks, sweetie."

As Hammer and I stepped out of the Winnebago, his assistant rushed over to us. She was an amazingly tall brunette wearing a gray business suit and black fuck-me pumps. An androgynous sex object, she was a combination of Playmate of the Month and Henry Fonda. There was something Amazonian about her, some steroid-fed hugeness. "You're running late," she said to Hammer. "You'd better get this show on the road if you want to make a six o'clock start."

"We're coming right now."

She turned and walked away from us, and a confused sort of lust rose up in me. I didn't know whether I wanted to make love with her, or go one-on-one in a half-court game.

"We'll talk theory as we walk," Hammer said, tugging at my sleeve. "First of all, look amused. Glow. Pretend you're watching some old home movies. Two: Keep a half smile on your face at all times. I want your arms on the table when you're sitting down. Why? This sends out a signal: I have nothing to hide. Follow? On second thought, use one hand — your left hand — use your left hand to support your chin. Not a bored schoolkid's look, just something bemused, casual. Think leisure wear. Three, and I can't emphasize this strongly enough: Be porous. Porosity. A fill-in-the-blank type quality. This is key. Let the audience make you up. You want an image, think colander." We were near the dais. "Okay. Go take a seat. And remember: Exude malleability. Better yet: Exude nonbeing."

There was a cluster of sportswriters seated in front of the dais, basically a long folding table draped with Fourth of July colors. Their molded plastic chairs were pulled into neat, tight rows, most of the seats huddled in front of the bouquet of microphones standing in the center of the table. As I walked behind the dais and took a seat, the huge TV screen looming up behind me as dusk descended, I was immediately tattooed with questions.

"Were you traded, Mike?"

"No."

"Renegotiate a larger contract?"

"I wish."

This show of self-deprecation drew a laugh from the audience. Hammer stood on the sidelines, nodding in encouragement.

"What about your earlier press conference. Are you happy with that?"

"Why the haircut and shave?" another voice shouted.

It took me several moments to realize that my press conference was in progress. I had expected some sort of scene one, take one cue, but instead it was simply happening. I was "live." No longer a mere swamp thing, I was something ethereal, a tripartite creature made up of body, soul, and image. Hammer wanted me to appear extremely natural, which in itself sounded extremely unnatural. "Be colloquial," he had said. "Don't be afraid to drop in a few 'uhs' and 'you knows.' Remember, your grass-roots fans are beer drinkers, guys who own push mowers and used cars, women whose jeans are getting a little too tight for the midriff blouse look anymore, but they wear them anyway, desperately clinging to their youth. These are people who live on layaway plans and buy snow tires on sale at eight o'clock in the morning in February, waiting in line to be first."

Hammer's sociology reached, at times, warped and perhaps unwittingly misanthropic extremes. Nevertheless, he remained insistent upon the use of the colloquial. There was also one other scripted ploy that he had dreamed up. "You need a deflector," he'd said. "A buffer. Some figure to mitigate the professional and careerist edge that, no offense, you exude. I mean, you should. You're a ballplayer. Am I right?" To soften this edge, Hammer came up with the idea of having a freckle-faced ten-year-old interrupt the proceedings to ask me for my autograph.

"He'll be wearing a T-shirt and shorts," Hammer had said, thinking out loud earlier that day in Pareles's office, his friend's secretary recording his remarks in a bristling shorthand. "But he should definitely not be blond. We want to stay away from the obvious and, on purely multicultural grounds, the unmistakably Aryan. Go sandy blond. Something natural. Something devoid of historical connotation."

"This sounds incredibly sophomoric and cloying," I said.

"Of course it's sophomoric and cloying — it's television."

Hammer booked a local child actor, a veteran of innocuous, off-brand commercial shoots and mail-order catalog modeling. "The kid's got a great surprised and uh-oh look," he said, "which is what we want. He's blind to the urgency and the social implications of the spectacle. He interrupts, then gets scared when he realizes there's a whole audience staring at him. This is where he does his oh, shit look. You placate him — on camera — and tell him to sit on your lap."

"On my lap?"

"He's your sidekick, your 'cohost,' your mascot. He signifies your innocence." I stared at Hammer blankly. "Let me put it another way," he said, then went into an explanation of the tidal pull of nostalgia and the fundamentals of marketing. The audience, over dinners of boxed macaroni, meat loaf, franks and beans, or tuna casserole — the patchwork staples of midweek clock punchers — would link the boy with me; or, more critically, me with the boy. This would be my shield against charges of egotism, greed, and union-driven malice. The video mise-en-scène being beamed out to the masses would restate my love for the game, for its endemic, wholly American innocence. The image that people would carry away with them, the one that would linger in their mind's eyes, would link me, in a positive way, with our collective sandlot past, that place of scraped knees and puppy loves, of high-pitched cries of delight and a tribal, comic-strip sense of community. The myth of childhood, Hammer said, would be our media-image trump card, our nod to a prepubescent oneness. I would be, forever after, he said, fondly linked to memories of seemingly eternal summer days, the magic of snow-brightened, almost deliciously interminable Christmas Eve nights.

"All from one kid?"

"They'll get it, they'll get it," Hammer assured me. "And you know what the beauty part is? They won't even know they're getting it."

The boy was not due to appear for several minutes, which allowed me time to address the writers and to make a statement. I looked down at the prepared copy that was taped to the table directly in front of me. Cue cards with identical copy in boldface leaned — hidden from the cameras — against the clump of microphones on the table.

"I'm supposed to read from this prepared speech here," I said, reading exactly what was written in the prepared speech, "but I think I'll just wing it." We'll give them the illusion of spontaneity, Hammer had said. "The event that took place this morning, and which we'll be looking at on this screen behind me in just a moment, first of all wasn't a press conference. Looking around, I see that some of you were there this morning. Well, maybe you were told that there was going to be a press conference, I wasn't." Someone interrupted at this point, as Hammer had predicted, and asked, "Then why were you there?" Still reading from the cue cards, I said, "I was there at the personal request of Mr. Percy. I went simply out of a sense of courtesy when he called."

"Why did he call?"

"He said he wanted a player's opinion on the lockout. He asked me if I'd come talk to him. I said I preferred not to, but when he asked me to as a personal favor, I agreed. Now that does not in any way mean that I am sympathetic to management's desire to reverse the reserve clause decision that was made by Peter Seitz in December. I am a player, not an owner, and my heart and my allegiance lie with the six hundred other players in the two leagues."

"How do you know the morning press conference is going to be shown?" a voice said.

This was not in the script. Hammer had warned me about deviating from the planned pacing and strategy that he had worked out. He had tutored me on how to field random questions. "If the question's aggressive, something like 'Do you feel guilty about making so much money?' say, 'That's a good question. Can we come back to that in a moment?' The moment never coming, of course. And for general questions, like 'How can you be sure the reserve clause decision won't damage baseball?' simply say, 'I think that's obvious.' It's a meaningless statement which confuses the issue enough to imply a sense of complex meaning. You get my drift?" So, as the question that was asked seemed to fit into this latent-aggressive mode, I said, "I think that's obvious," which stunned even the news-hungry hounds long enough for me to retrack the direction of the show. (It was a show, after all.)

"I just want to say," I read off the next card, "that I consider myself fortunate to be playing baseball, and that my prime concern is for the fans. I think we owe it to them to settle the business of baseball and to get out on the field and begin playing."

That was the end of my statement. Hammer had timed it so that the end of it would dovetail with the broadcast of the morning press conference. To cover our bases, Hammer had even scheduled our event to run behind the broadcast so that a taped version of the news could be shown, if necessary. Once I'd finished speaking, the questions began ringing like Christmas bells again. My pat answer to every question was to be, 'I'd like to hold that for another time. Right now I simply want to clarify any misunderstandings about this morning."

It was at this point, while I was being asked if I considered myself separate from or superior to the other players, that the freckled kid arrived. With rehearsed tentativeness, he approached me and said, "Are you Mike Williams?" I turned my attention from the press to him and, hesitating a moment, as instructed, said, "Yes."

"Then would you sign my glove?"

I paused, following Hammer's orders to the letter, then said, "Uh, sure."

I reached out and took the glove from the kid, politely turning to the scribes as I did. "Excuse me," I said. A nod to courtesy. "Do you have a pen?" I asked, turning back to the boy. He shook his head. "You don't have a pen? What kind of autograph hound are you?" I turned back to the writers and, drawing them into the conspiracy with innocence, asked, "Can I borrow a pen for a minute?" Several were offered and I took one, then looked back at the boy, who was staring at the mob of journalists with his patented look of sudden awareness and dumb fright. Seeing this, I said, "Do you want to sit down?" The boy, nodding warily, his cornered animal's eyes still fixed on the corps of press hounds,

edged closer to me. He put his hand out and I took it in mine.
"It's okay," I said. "Don't sweat it." He looked at me and I lifted
him, seating him on my lap like a dime store Santa Claus. The
image was complete. I was father, friend, average guy, secular
saint. The scribes were respectfully silent. "You comfortable?" I
asked. The boy nodded.

At that moment, the screen behind me burst into animated life.
I glanced over my shoulder and saw the doors of Mr. Percy's
office beginning to swing open. "Let's watch this thing, okay?" I
said. And together, as insidiously scripted, we did. As I sat there,
the boy on my knee, I saw myself on screen, my hand in Mr.
Percy's, that wheelchair-bound icon of progress, power, and
wealth, his face deeply lined, his skin as white as refined flour,
and realized that I was Mr. Percy's myth. My words were impalpable, destined to fade from memory. Everything that was said
would be forgotten. What would linger was the picture of me
standing beside the shriveled autocrat, my hand held tightly by
his. What Mr. Percy had achieved no effort of mine could undo.
I was his freckle-faced boy, his mythic and absolving counter-
point.

The press conference on the air ended, and I corrected state-
ments that had been distorted. The image of myself as Mr. Percy's
puppet blazed in my mind, and I found that I was burning with
a need to speak. On the sidelines, Hammer was making throat-
slitting motions, and mouthing the word "Cut." By the time I left
the beach and began driving back to the motel along the seabound
boulevard, I had gone on record as saying that I was not happy
with my contract, that I had been bullied into signing it, that I
deserved to be paid more, that I was used as a tax deduction, and
that I would win the batting crown that year. In other words, I
offended everyone connected with the game. I overlooked the fact
that, in spite of all we had recently been, we were still a nation
of children, our dream of innocence supported by our breadbasket
wealth. But I was a ballplayer. It was not my place to criticize.
The corn-fed New World had been transformed, long before I
arrived into Bunyanesque fable, something inviolable, God-given,
and eternal. My role was simply to embody our frontier-bred

dream of pastoral glory, to mime another cycle in the pageant of the game.

I reached across the car seat and dug into the six-pack I had picked up at a convenience store. A dusky calm was seeping into the streets after the long, sun-stunned afternoon. Ahead of me, the sky was the color of a blood orange. Alone, driving along a highway bounded by the vast horizon of the sea, drinking a beer — even this mundane act made me into something of an icon. Our myth-spawning past invested our least heroic gestures with intimations of stalwart grandeur. Perhaps it was the scale of the place, the raw sweep of the continent. We are narcissistic and self-deifying, and what I had done that evening was sully our collective myth with logic, statistics, and a discussion of wealth. For this, I would not be forgiven. Not when I had turned my back on the irrecoverable past, and tainted, with the bluntness of my words, the sentimental dream of a hallowed and unvanquished world.

Eleven

SOME MYTHS can take their toll. Anyone cannot be anything; the genetic shuffle won't allow it. And then there's luck. Like prime-time TV shows, some of us wind up in a primo, Thursday-night comedy-slot lineup and jump to the top of the charts, our phantom success totally unconnected to content, our place in the game the roll-the-dice-let's-see-what-happens result of some caffeine-crazed network executive. Others, by chance, get Friday night at nine-thirty, a time of backseat love and major drug abuse, the only ones home and tuned in the addicts of some grim corporate diversion — basketball, hockey, nighttime baseball. Luck, in some cases, can be as good as talent; maybe better, because you can't betray it.

Barbara was mopping the floor when I phoned, drunk.

"Why didn't you call earlier?"

"I did call earlier. I called sixty-seven thousand times. Why didn't you answer?"

"Because I was stuck in the snow."

I didn't want to ask where, on what errand, because I knew by the irritated tone in Barbara's voice that it would turn out to be something Mike-generated, some for-me thing she was doing, assuming, with a subtly accreting grudgingness, the subservient role of helper, administrative assistant, unemployed spouse. After a dozen beers, I was too filled with a guilt-fueled cowardice —

drunk, tank-top-clad husband calling pregnant, snowbound wife — to step into the marital batter's box and take a chin-high verbal fastball. "Are you all right?"

"It was snow, not a rapist."

"You seem a little testy. What's wrong?"

"Nothing. I'll be fine." In other words, I'll be fine, no help from you. "What were all those television appearances? And that kid."

"He was the myth of childhood."

"What?"

I gave Barbara a nutshell synopsis of my day: encounter with Mr. Percy, the early drinking, the sad, hallucinatory history of my entire Felliniesque afternoon.

"Hammer thinks we sent out so many conflicting signals that the whole thing will turn out to be a media-image wash, entirely forgotten ten seconds after the tube is turned off. He also feels that the presidential primaries should detract from any heat I'd have to take."

"Well, that's nice of them."

There was a long, penitential silence. I pictured Barbara duck-walking across the snow-blanketed driveway to the back door of our house in the Northeast, plastic supermarket bags dangling from each hand, winded by the time she reaches for her keys. And under her shirt her plum-colored nipples and striped belly, a thin dark line running up the center of it as if our child had run a finger along its inside, leaving a faint trace the color of a bruise.

"You don't sound too happy."

"I'm thirty pounds overweight, the baby's late, I look like Baby Huey, and I haven't had a beer in eight months. Would you be happy?"

"Don't get upset."

"I'm not upset." The next silence seemed to go on for a lifetime. "I should go to bed," Barbara said. "I'll speak to you tomorrow."

"All right."

"Good night."

I cleared my throat, opened my mouth, and the breath caught in my throat. Finally, it broke free and I said, "Night." I kept the receiver to my ear until I heard a steady, impenetrable silence, then set it down, stood up, and went to the window. Beyond the terrace the lights of the marina beamed like the voices of choirboys. I was living in a motel, able (with the help of elevators) to leap tall buildings in a single bound. A uniformed crusader, a demigod capable of creating the ball-and-bat magic that thrilled the millions. On bubble gum cards I stood, arms akimbo, my bright uniform colors seemingly the work of immortal wizards, straddling the world. Superman.

Dividing lines are often invisible, moving deeply into the realm of the transparent the closer you get to home.

Unlike Barbara's parents, my own insisted that I go to college, my father fighting off pro scouts as if they were peyote-crazed Comanches attacking the frontier homestead.

"They're offering a thirty-thousand-dollar signing bonus," I argued, after I had been approached, on the sly, by a National League club. This was 1970, my senior year in high school. Gas was 28 cents a gallon, Levis $4.98 a pair. A new VW cost two grand, a house in the neighborhood under twenty-five. At seventeen I could have my mortgage paid off and a new car, or else I could take required courses and ten electives over the next four years and hope to be selected in the college draft. "That's thirty thousand just for signing my name on a piece of paper," I said.

The scout, Bernie Papy, was an exiled Cuban who, he told me himself, had been Castro's pitching coach back in the forties, before the revolutionary gave up the imperialistic pastime — rivalries, division winners, champions — turning down a pro contract in the process. He had tracked me down to the ice cream parlor where I worked for a strict, elderly German couple three evenings a week after school. I was wiping down the stainless steel wainscoting behind the grill with a solution of white vinegar and hot water when I heard a voice at the counter say, "So, is the tuna salad good?"

I turned and saw Bernie Papy's dark brown face and jet black hair. "Yeah," I said. He was wearing white pants, white shoes, a guayabera shirt with an embroidered breast pocket, and a trench coat that he hung on one of the coatracks. He looked like Philip Marlowe in the tropics, and definitely stood out among the double-knit trousers and brown Thom McCann shoes of the neighborhood. He sat at the counter with his elbows on the blond wood, thumbs supporting his chin, leathery hands pressed together prayer-style. The tips of his index fingers pinched the brown bulb of his nose.

"Gimme the tuna salad on rye toast with lettuce and extra mayo, and a vanilla shake, extra sweet."

I brushed some grease onto two slices of rye bread and set them on the grill, then topped them with square iron weights. Bernie Papy watched me, one palm supporting his chin now, the fingers of his other hand tapping the counter. He, Mrs. Jergens, and I were the only people in the lunchroom. A stinging October rain had kept the semiregulars indoors. I held a stainless canister to the mouth of the vanilla syrup pump and depressed the handle twice. Two thick streams of syrup the color of varnish shot into the container.

"It's okay," he said. "Keep going."

I looked at him, then glanced at Mrs. Jergens, a three-hundred-pound woman with calves as large as phone poles, grayish stumps bloated with water. She was seated in the booth she occupied every evening from five until eight, while Mr. Jergens was home taking a nap. Her tiny feet, shod in white nursing shoes, were propped up on the green vinyl bench on the opposite side of her table, her roost cluttered with knitting, the daily crossword puzzle, pill bottles, and an empty ice cream soda glass.

"That's gonna cost you another dime," she said, her powdery second chin quivering as she spoke. She looked over the tops of her reading specs, which sat halfway down the bridge of her nose like some Victorian accountant's.

Bernie Papy turned his head and looked at her. "Do you charge extra for toasting the bread, too?"

"If you don't like it, you can leave."

Bernie Papy stared at Mrs. Jergens a moment longer, then turned to me. "Gimme four more squirts," he said.

"Your teeth'll fall out on the counter."

"Don't worry about it." He turned to Mrs. Jergens again. "I'll pay the twenty cents," he said. Then he looked back at me. "And go easy on the milk. I got a sensitive stomach."

I added four blasts of syrup to the container, topped it with milk, then clipped the canister into the silver-and-green blender and turned it on. I flipped the toast, sliced a pickle on the butcher block slab abutting the refrigerated section of the work counter, laid the frog-colored fingers on a plate, and removed the toast from the grill. The gob of tuna was just hitting the bread when I heard, "Not so much. Take some off of there." Mrs. Jergens's voice hit me like a fastball in the back of the neck. I looked up and stared at the steel wall in front of me, a blue-collar rage fueling my nearly criminal impulses. All I had was the blind face of the wall to help defuse them.

"I'll pay," Bernie Papy said, his voice a frustration-assuaging grace descending upon me. I turned and looked at him. "Go ahead, kid. Load it up."

"Michael, you charge him double," Mrs. Jergens said, scolding me. As I carried the sandwich to Bernie Papy, she mouthed the words "I don't like him" behind his back.

I set his plate down in front of him, turned and unhooked the milk shake canister from the blender, put a glass into a stainless steel base, filled it halfway, then put the glass and the canister on the counter next to his plate. He nodded at me as I left his drink for him. "Nice catch Robinson made today, huh? Stole a double from Bench."

"I didn't see the game. School."

He nodded. "Too bad, good series." I thought this was pointless chatter and was about to find some work to do when he said, "So, Curt Flood. You believe this guy? Making ninety thousand a year, goes and challenges the reserve clause. Kinda anti-American, don't you think?" An odd question, I thought. Not exactly How about this weather? But it was 1970. Nixon was calling for law and order from the White House. The war in Nam was grinding on. Riots had shared the summer news with ball scores, an empire-crumbling frenzy jump-starting the engines of destruction in various cities across the country, a madness brought on by final hours and last hopes.

"Guy's got a right to his opinion," I said.

"Yeah, everybody's got a right. Everybody's gotta put their three cents in — inflation. I think it's the war. Nobody listens anymore. Everybody just yells." He took a bite of his sandwich. "No reserve clause. Night baseball. Next year, the Series at night. Can you believe that? Freezing, after dark."

"Pretty strange," I said.

"Strange? It's insanity."

"Michael, don't you have work to do?" Mrs. Jergens said, scowling.

I refilled napkin dispensers so I could work around Papy.

"This tuna's good. What do you do to it?"

"Use cheap mayonnaise."

"That must be it."

He talked baseball, tossing out bits of history, lore, and esoteric knowledge — hitting tips, trade secrets, stars' salaries. My ears were more sensitive than a stethoscope. Then the rain let up, a few customers came in, and I had to make up their orders. Bernie Papy asked for a check, left a ten under the lip of his plate, and was gone when I looked for him a moment later.

I didn't see him again for two days. When I walked through the gate in the chain-link fence that surrounded our high school ball field, he was standing there, this time with a porkpie hat clapped to his skull. We had just played the final game of our fall season, a tune-up for the city playoffs. I had gone three for four and thrown a man out at home from the corner in left. Not a bad outing.

"You're Mike Williams?" he said, feigning surprise. "I was sent up here to look at you." He motioned to his car. "Come on. Get in. I'll give you a ride home." He handed me his card, then walked around the front of his car and opened the door on the driver's side. "Get in," he said. There must have been a cross cast to my expression, the anger of the duped and the newly enlightened. "All right, so I didn't just come in for a tuna sandwich. Sue me. In the meantime, you want a ride?"

Bernie Papy had gotten my name from Al Damm, a neighbor-hood father and pressman by trade, who had coached me in Babe Ruth League and followed and reported on the careers of local talent. The hierarchy of professional scouting was as layered as any other intelligence-gathering organization. Pharmacists, in-surance salesmen, part-time security guards — the voiceless and the overlooked who still clung to the sweet fire of the game. At the grass-roots level it is all instinct, nose, and outsized hope, the cruel, parsing dissection of talent that takes place the closer you get to the majors still several levels removed.

"You have any idea how many guys don't make it?" Bernie Papy said. The car seat was cluttered with cellophane wrappers, notebooks, racing forms, *Sports Illustrated*s, gloves, a thermos. While he held the wheel with one hand, his other picked its way through the tangle like a squirrel rooting around for a nut in high grass. He released a guttural sigh when he snagged, then with-drew, a half-foot-long cigar the color of a dead leaf. "I mean even just to the level you're at," he said.

"What level am I at?"

"The pros want you. One in ten thousand — one in a hundred thousand — ever hear that. Then you know how many make it in the minors?"

"No."

"One in a hundred. You know how many top, can't-miss pros-pects make it in the pros? One in twenty. I've been in the business for thirty years, I've had, tops, half a dozen guys stick. You ever stop to consider that you've got practically no chance whatsoever to make it to the pros, let alone excel there?"

"No."

"Good. Then you've got a shot." He looked out at the strange streets around him. "Hey, you know where we're going here?"

I directed Bernie Papy through the narrow, car-clogged streets of the neighborhood, blue-collar enclaves ten minutes outside the city, evening falling there in late autumn and all through the grim winters with the weight of lost hope. There was a sameness to the houses. Brick-faced, shingled, attached in block-long rows, the light hovering in each window seeming to announce a private sorrow, some naked longing, the rote of mortality woven into the skeletons of the homes with tongue-and-groove precision. A territorial bleakness was built into the landscape, and the exits for escape were unmarked. By the time I got out of Bernie Papy's car, I had a thirty-thousand-dollar ticket out.

"No," my father said.

"Why not?"

"Because you'll have nothing to fall back on."

I had made my first Little League team by default, trying out at the behest of a friend, Patrick Dyer, who was subsequently cut. For eight years I was applauded at Communion breakfasts and Knights of Columbus brunches, help-yourself buffets held in school basements, catered by graying, thick-necked men in faded suits and military caps. In high school the occasions were marked by assemblymen and city council nominees. Once even the mayor breezed through, patting my back as he looked through me and hurried by in a bath of flashbulb light. My mother clipped newsprint histories of my adolescent heroics and pasted them in a leather-bound scrapbook. In our finished basement — built by my father on weekends and winter evenings with President's Day sale paneling and off-price cellotex ceiling kits — there was a tawdry shrine to my achievements. Gold-plated trophies of batters in midswing were set on shelves in a lighted glass case against one wall, my adolescence already the stuff of museums, the dust of the past. I had been told that I would have my pick of schools, choice of girls, share of glory, that I would have my way with the world. So, unfamiliar with the language of defeat and tentative progress, I had no idea what my father was talking about.

"Why should I need anything to fall back on?"

"So you don't have to clean bathrooms when you don't make the pros."

"Who says I'm not going to make it?"

"No one."

"Then why are you saying I won't?"

"I'm not."

"Then why can't I sign the contract?"

"Because you'll have nothing to fall back on if you do."

"Are we going to go in circles till I give in?"

"Yes."

My father once bear-hugged our refrigerator and carried it to the curb as trash, had cleaned out a wasps' nest under the eaves of our house with his bare hands. He twisted rusted steel bolts until their tiny faces screamed help and they pirouetted out of their holes like dervishes. A brute tenacity drove him, his will as single-minded and implacable as a vise. Our conversation Ping-Ponged back and forth across the kitchen table, my mother a silent spectator, the breadth of it ranging from the reasonable to the petty, from threats to weeping. My father played a steady baseline game, returning my every volley, while I charged the net wildly.

"College ball sucks."

"Then you should be a top draft pick."

"I'll miss all that time in the minors."

"Some distance will do you good."

"This is a good offer."

"Others might be better."

Finally, I gave in. My father had, during my high school years, taken a strong interest in my career. It was a chance for him to be listened to, heeded, to feel wise and, in some way, powerful. He was adamant about and protective of my career. He took Bernie Papy's number from me and called his airport motel room, then diplomatically explained the decision, thanked Bernie for the club's interest, and told him that I would be accepting a scholarship. We would apprise him of my collegiate whereabouts within a few months. The entire phone call was one long thank-you letter.

"He says good luck," my father said when he hung up.

"He's being polite."

"He thinks you made the right decision."

"What would he know?"

I sulked, then accepted my fate with an adolescent's discontent and entered college the following September. Barbara graduated that same summer and took a clerical job at a local, poorly regarded hospital. We had grown up less than a mile away from

each other. Our parents' houses were virtually the same, except
that ours was attached on only one side, was closer to the park
and the huge, three-story houses that bordered it, and had a second bathroom. Barbara's father had worked for the telephone
company before he died, installing jacks and insulated lines in
neighborhoods like our own. Barbara's mother held a clerical position in a small business office downtown. And Barbara's sib-
lings — sister a nurse, older brother an alcoholic transit worker,
younger brother a part-time computer programmer, ex-Marine
enlistee, his hand heavily into the drug trade — each plied blue-
collar trades, as did all her uncles and cousins. My family on my
mother's side was a stacked deck of professionals — doctors, den-
tists, a lawyer, one insurance mogul. My father was the Irish out-
cast, the junior executive who had married into this unforgiving
Mafia. It was her status-seeking and my father's hard-knocks bitterness and drive that propelled me into college. Barbara's parents
had adopted a laissez-faire attitude toward Barbara's education.
They kept letting out line, feeding her directionless, evening-and-
weekend-oriented drift. When she finished high school all she had
was the buoyancy of youth supporting her, and me.

"Can I tell you something?" Hammer said, offering a piece of
over-lunch wisdom many years later. "It wouldn't be love if you
didn't try to make the other person over."

"Why don't you try going to college?" I said to Barbara. It was
my first Christmas break and I was home with long hair and the
black stubble of a new beard. Some brand of jock bohemianism
dictated my taste in clothing, thought, and speech in those days,
and my parents instantly regretted their decision to foist the ben-
efits of higher education upon me. I came to the Sunday dinner
table in faded Lee jeans, an unpressed flannel shirt, and Li'l Abner
work boots. My brother, Bennie, had been sent up to our room
to rouse me — for the third time — at one P.M. With my eyelids
pleasantly bloated by hangover weariness, my hair still rooted, in
those now weightless years, to my scalp and uncombed as a bird's
nest, I descended the stairs.

"You're going to sit at the table like that?"

My mother, seated at one end of the table, was looking at me as if she were the Virgin Mary and Christ had just told her he'd spent the night in a whorehouse. My father was in his usher's outfit: white shirt, sober tie fastened to a buttonhole by his USMC tie clip, beige cardigan. Beside me, Bennie, a recent porker, victim of some glandular havoc, the onset of puberty turning his once underfed frame into a sixty-five-inch knockwurst, was jacketed like a sausage in a honey-colored turtleneck, his polished face moony as a beach ball and soft as an uncooked biscuit. I was content, a woozy holiday cheer slumbering in my bones. No part of me wanted a didactic confrontation with my mother. And, after nearly eighteen years, I had mastered the art of deflection, learning that the absurd and glancing reply was the most effective stutter step when faced with the grim defense of my mother's conforming passion. I turned to Bennie and said, "Yeah. Put something decent on, would you?"

As Bennie stared at me in dumb amazement, I reached for the bowl of mashed potatoes, a toe-in-the-door ploy, instinct telling me that with a forkful of dinner in my mouth I could claim squatting rights and the entire discussion would be dropped. I set the clockwork of manners in motion — "Could you pass the gravy?" "Would you like some carrots?" — then directed the conversation with a free-ranging, undergraduate vigor. Mao, Norman Mailer, and pantyhose commercials all made brief, unscheduled appearances in my Cliff Notes dissection of the American Zeitgeist, my entire freshman Weltanschauung crammed into one long, run-on sentence, which culminated with the not outrageous idea that Nixon should be shot. A shocked speechlessness gripped my immediate family for a moment, some mute horror and mortification. It was as if I had mooned the republic on national TV and they had to face the world and own up to the fact that, yes, we were related by blood.

"He's gone three months and he's Abbie Hoffman," my father said. A bewildered sense of defeat seemed to overtake him. The first in his bloodline to attend college and the kid turns out to be a mail-order revolutionary. "Let me ask you something," he said. "Don't they teach accounting courses at this school?" He meant it, knew I knew he meant it, but I ignored him anyway. "Go ahead," he said, pulling apart two biscuits that had cooked together, then tossing one back into the basket with disgust. "Be an idiot."

I will, I thought, not giving any weight to his first signs of resentment.

"Just go take some classes," I said to Barbara. "See if you like it."

"I didn't like high school. Why should I like college?"

"There's a greater license to fuck up. Look at it like a gigantic kindergarten. Instead of milk and cookies, everybody has beer and pretzels. I do, and I still pulled a three point oh."

Barbara was not genetically drawn to reading the way I was. Some anxious need for completion and succor drove me to read before falling asleep, regardless of sobriety. I dropped off every night with an open book in my hands, my lower lip drooping, I assume, like a flounder's. She wasn't built for discipline, something that had become second nature to me after years of batting practice, wind sprints, and pop fly drills. I set up a private course of instruction, but we bogged down after her initial contact with Hesse and Vonnegut.

"You've got to stick with it," I said. "It's called practice."

"All right. I'll practice."

"Wait a minute. I want you to do it because you want to do it."

"Fine. I don't want to do it."

"What are you, nuts? You have to."

I fell in love with Barbara the instant I saw her. Knee socks, plaid skirt, the hips of a boy. Seen through my own watery reflection in a storefront's window. Two years later, my image changing with the gravity of years, I began sculpting Barbara with a more deliberate thumb, the sharpening of my own identity working on hers like a trowel. I wasn't all that aware of what was happening to myself during those mind-quickening days. Gravitating toward what naturally suited my temperament, I grew like a gawky adolescent, my intellectual legs bird thin and four feet long, my squat chest boxy as an old suitcase. I had no proportion. What I could pass on to Barbara was soft and untested, the plumb line of my thinking as wobbly as an egg noodle.

"Look. It really can't hurt," I said. "Go at night for one semester, then we'll see."

Barbara registered for two courses at a local community college — Introduction to Literature, and Beginning Philosophy (my choices) — and did extremely well in them, on paper. She received an A-minus and a B, respectively. But when summer returned, so did Barbara's natural inclination to drift. I picked up nine credits in summer school, while she spent her afternoons on the beach, toasting her skin until it turned the color of a walnut.

"I don't think I'm going back," she said over a sunset beer in late August. We were sitting on the beach, the sand cool as clean sheets beneath our bare feet.

"Why not?"

"By the time I get out of work every day, I'm tired."

"So quit your job."

"Who's going to pay my car insurance?"

"Sell your car."

"What if I want money to go dancing?"

"Why go dancing?"

When I returned from college the following Christmas, I looked at the houses in the neighborhood closely for the first time in my life. They were larger, less submissive somehow, in my parents' part of the neighborhood. Driving down to Barbara's, I noticed that there were fewer trees, the houses were smaller and shoved together like warehouse cartons, and over their roofs you could see, in the near distance, the smokestacks of the machine parts factory.

Anxious to sign with the pros, I picked up my degree — American Literature with a grab bag of minors — in three years, then sold myself to Mr. Percy. Barbara married me and we rented a small house in the midwestern town where I was stationed to play. I hit .432, then lost a close friend. Even then, before I jumped to the majors and we moved back to the Northeast, I began to make a mark for myself on the tablet of the game, wrote the first faint lines that would bear my name in the book of myths. As for Barbara: her undelineated future was wedded to the history of my accomplishments, unless she chose to begin to make her own. And as that did not appear likely in the waning days of our youth, we started out with an unbalanced and precarious foundation, upon which we would build, like unskilled apprentices, the untrue skeleton of our house.

Twelve

"DID I WAKE YOU?"

It was — who else? — Hammer. I opened my eyes and looked around the room for a clock. Three numerals and a colon glowed in the control panel column of the TV. The constant beam of electronic reassurance. It was 6:47.

"No. I always get up to watch the farm report." I pushed myself into a sitting position, the light around me suddenly pulsing with a spectrum-wide array of colors, bright as little chips of sun-struck stained glass, the colors mingling like the tinkling of wind chimes. The room exuded a frat house squalor, all empty beer cans, strewn clothes, and the smell of yeast.

"You don't sound well."

"I'm hung over."

"Why do you do this to yourself?"

"I figure it's an objective correlative to the world. Keeps me in touch. What's up?"

"I'm just checking in. A little day-after-the-press-conference touching of bases."

"What are you, my nanny?"

"I just wanted to make sure you were all right. Nothing unusual to report? No death threats or bomb scares?"

"What aren't you telling me?"

"No complimentary bottles of champagne with hair-trigger C-4 explosive corks?"

"I'm universally hated, right?"

"Let's say I've received some expressions of ire from peer-group representatives."

"My teammates want to kill me?"

"I wouldn't be so specific. Let's just say it's a leaguewide feeling of rage."

"Wonderful."

"Can I tell you something? I didn't think the word 'wrath' applied in corporate settings."

"Is it going to blow over?"

"In terms of public animosity, no question. Out there you're in an either/or type of —"

"Not so early with theory, please."

"— situation, they either love you, or they hate you, regardless of specific content. Public opinion is one huge coin toss. Don't worry about it."

"Then who am I supposed to worry about?"

"I don't want to name names. I don't like the McCarthyesque emanations that throws off. All I can say is don't hesitate to bail out on high inside fastballs."

"Terrific."

"Don't worry. This is probably overzealous caution on my part, but I can't help it. I think I have a deep maternal streak. I get this mother hen image every time I think of myself nurturing a nestful of fledgling ballplayers."

"I'm hanging up now."

"Can I say one thing?"

"No. You're insane."

"Bodyguards. Just for a while. Think about it. My treat."

I emptied my bladder, showered, slipped on a pair of loose jeans and a polo shirt — nothing limb-constricting — and rubber-soled shoes, for purchase. A good outfit to throw a punch in. The dark glasses were an obvious final addition. I wore them to keep me anonymous, immune to the grim visage of the sun. And also because you're not supposed to hit a guy wearing glasses.

If I had what might be called a friend on the team it was Greg Arthur. He was from Louisiana and we had begun a wary, laconic friendship the summer I was brought up from the minors. Greg had been the starting second baseman at the beginning of that season, and had played well until June. Then his glove began to be on the wrong side of the ball — always.

"Guy plays like he's got his dick up his ass."

"Guy is a motherfucking bonehead, is what he is. I'm getting tired of losing."

I was unlacing my cleats after another loss, early in the course of my tenure, while Mel Thorn and Oscar Rife were discussing Greg's recent caliber of play.

"I wish he'd get his shit together."

"I wish he'd get a terminal disease is what I wish he'd get."

Greg's style of play up until that slump had been freewheeling, electrifying, and natural. He enjoyed stretching out, left arm extended twenty-four inches beyond the bill of his cap, in order to make diving catches behind the bag at second, landing sometimes, after his brief stint of self-levitation, as far out as the clipped fringe of outfield grass. He made the easy plays look technically complex, fielding lackadaisical grounders that dribbled halfheartedly off a bat as if handling them required all the expertise he could muster. When your fielding percentage is .999 and you execute difficult or nearly impossible plays with such sleight-of-hand dexterity that fans believe you'd be able to field two balls hit ten feet to either side of you simultaneously, then throw out successive runners at first, self-serving histrionics don't nettle. Pull a few boners and they want to burn your house down.

Greg was overlooked in the All-Star balloting. Whim and stupidity almost always govern such lottery-style events. But some players — some men — cannot handle being excluded, passed over. Insecure to the bone, they feel that many of those singled out for glory are inferior, overrated. Quite often, they're right. But rather than taking it indifferently, just getting on with their game and letting time put the yardstick to their contribution, some guys get nuts.

Greg began leaping all over the place. He'd dive for balls that the shortstop, Dickie Tibbetts, had only to move a few waltz steps to his left to pick up like a piece of litter. Rick Muller, the interim center fielder, a whiny, unnecessarily boring presence on the team who lived with his high school trophies and baseball memorabilia, often found himself in shallow center field, waiting under a feathery, slow-dropping pop fly, only to have his toes stepped on by Greg, who was backpedaling like a clown on a unicycle, his mitt appearing in Muller's face and blotting out the sun.

"That's not fair. I play center field," Rick once protested.

"We only let you stand around here to round out the side, dickbrain," Greg said, turning and pegging the ball in to the first baseman, Two-Tone ("Paid like a white man, fuck like a black one") Concepción. At six five and two-forty, Two-Tone seemed more like an embankment, some river-chewed face of rock, than your basic human being, and he had a disposition to match. You had to climb over the initial, low-level rudeness and rudimentary arrogance in order to reach the peaks of indifference and fuck-youism that he shared with only his closest friends.

As the All-Star break approached, coinciding with my arrival, Greg began making force-outs at first himself. Rather than tossing the ball to Two-Tone, who was standing, archerlike, glove hand forward, one foot back on the bag, awaiting the conventional, side-retiring, underhand lob from the gliding second baseman, Greg ran the ball to first himself, making the mistake — while we were playing on national television — of not taking Two-Tone's advice, which was: "Cut it the fuck out." Greg's thrashing went nationwide, the one-sided bruising delaying the beer commercial by fifteen seconds. When Greg knocked out a fan's tooth by lunging over the first-base railing to snag a pop fly foul, chipping in for a contract on his life was seriously discussed by an unforgiving contingent on the club.

"Jesus shit almighty!" Cap screamed at him from the dugout. "You'll be sticking your mitt up snatches next!"

I was assigned to be Greg's roommate, temporarily, as Ted Monday, his former roomie, had checked out before things got out-of-hand gruesome. Distrustful at first, Greg and I worked out a tacit agreement to speak freely between ourselves about the team, the game, the press; about our longings and fears; about the never-saw-it-coming injury that might knock us out of the game forever.

Greg began playing a fairly steady, respectable second base a few weeks after I arrived. The game was not much fun for him, or for me, playing as I was in the shadow of a dead man. Ted Monday's ghost seemed to haunt that verdant pasture. In what was considered by some to be a ghoulish, self-serving, and ostentatious display of piety, he had been buried in left field before the start of a Sunday afternoon doubleheader. The fans in attendance had been supplied with black armbands to wear during the ceremony, and a backhoe was brought in to dig a swimming pool-sized hole in the ground so that Monday could be interred with his brand-new Chrysler Le Baron, a last-minute gift from Mr. Percy, bestowed after Ted's seventh consecutive All-Star selection was announced. The bonus vehicle, lashed with a huge funeral ribbon made out of sailcloth dyed black, a pine-scented air deodorizer hanging from the untouched rearview mirror, was towed in from the bullpen. Greg, Two-Tone, and the rest of us, caps to breast, formed a grim gauntlet as the bereaved immediate family trailed the pennant-shrouded casket, wept, and got the first and only ride in the new backseat. There were times, that first summer, when, as I sprinted back to the warning track, my cleats digging into the still soft, still settling earth beneath the meticulously sutured sod that capped Ted Monday's grave, I felt I was about to fall into the earth, through the matter-packed and gravity-bound shell of the world into the zone of the dead. Caught between the vacuum of history and the unwritten void of the future, ballplayers tend to press, to go flat out in pursuit of ground-breaking numbers. Then ten years later, we find ourselves stuck at the bottom of a deep hole, a pile of recorded dust sitting on the edge of the precipice above us, waiting for word that the time has come to cover us over. We get a little nuts, a little edgy. We don't take kindly to slumps.

"Shove over."

Greg was seated on a guacamole-colored love seat in the motel lobby, the entire room furnished with a dental office flair, all vinyl, plastic plants, and a carpet that looked like someone had splashed paint through a kaleidoscope and had the pattern woven into nylon pile. As I sat down beside him, he held up the edges of the sports section like a Welcome Home banner. My face — my faces — were center-page newsprint ghosts, the headline reading, "Will the REAL Mike Williams Please Stand Up?" I put my left arm along the back of the couch, and leaned in to read the fine print of my egregious public debacle.

"They make me sound like Nixon, for Christ's sake."

"You sound like a jerk is what you sound like."

"It was scripted."

"Which part?"

"Both."

The article suggested that I had "negotiated" my contract with Mr. Percy on the basis that I would serve as a union scab, a pawn in an owner-backed public relations charade designed to turn the public against the players. My agent, listed as the "elusive Mr. Alvin Hammer," then scheduled the press conference when he foresaw player reproachment turning into public animosity and endorsement-negating image tarnishing. "Williams," the article continued, "responding to a question, said he felt players were entitled to a larger piece of the baseball pie, but signed his contract because it had been implied that if he didn't, he would be blackballed by league owners." Owners from both leagues, the article said, were accusing me of defaming Mr. Percy and slandering the rest of them by concocting a paranoid, self-indulgent scenario of collusion.

"Percy told me if I didn't sign the contract I wouldn't find a job in the Appalachian League."

"You still fucked up," Greg said.

"How do you figure that?"

"You should've held out for more."

"Wait a minute. Last year all of you were pissed off because I was the second highest-paid player on the team. Which is it supposed to be?"

"If you had held out you could've gotten three times what you're getting."

"Never."

"Twice. Then it would have been easier for the rest of us to get raises."

"Great. So now everybody hates me because I signed and make more money than they do, and they also hate me because I didn't hold out for even more. Right?"

"Right."

"Terrific."

A front-line edginess and dread infects ballplayers, our slim histories subject to the shakes when confronted by any sudden apparition of eternity. Every un-understandably dropped fly ball, every lapse of error-preventing concentration, is a little death. Mental collapse, some new tic in your hitting or throwing motion, the whittling of your talent by the years, Lou Gehrig's disease. There's a prairie-scouring vortex of doubt pirouetting out there on the horizon, waiting to suck each and every ballplayer into it. A brief hitless streak, a line of negative criticism in the paper, the manager's guarded, cloaked tones and slippery glances when he tells you that you need a day's rest. Keeping the ball down, making contact, moving the runner from first to third. These tasks are painstaking and attention-demanding enough: we didn't need the burden of money thrust upon us, as well.

I sat there beside Greg, too disgusted to look at the paper any longer. I was a ballplayer. I was built for speed and power. It went against the grain of my being to be involved in the Machiavellian clockwork of legal suits, contract negotiations, and press conferences.

"What are you going to do?"

Good question. The sort that hounds men in hopeless situations, some no-win limbo where the misdirected and the hapless always seem to dwell. I could remain silent for the rest of the season, if there was to be one, referring all questions to my agent-attorney. Or else be converted on TV and vow to spread the word of the Lord. I could whine and stamp my feet, make an infantile spectacle of myself, and wait for the news-starved public to come and stick a bottle in my mouth. I could spit at anyone who came near me. Any or all of the above. But none of these possibilities seemed soul freeing. What I wanted was the grace of undistracted play, the redemptive magic of fresh beginnings. Pristine baselines, spotless ball, gleaming bat.

"Paging Mike Williams. Would Mike Williams please come to the registration desk at the front of the lobby."

"What do you suppose that could be?" Greg asked.

"I don't know. Percy's an advocate of capital punishment. Maybe a public execution."

"You rate yourself pretty highly."

I walked across the lobby and was directed to a phone at the front desk by a blazer-and-tied clerk who looked as soulless as an insurance policy.

"Hello."

"My water broke."

"Get to the hospital. I'm coming."

I was out of the motel and screaming north, howling through space at ten miles a minute, less than an hour later. With the spirit-sapping tedium of the lockout left behind, and my child ahead of me, a headlong lust was restored in me, an embrace of time I hadn't anticipated, the heedless plunge into the future mollifying, if only for a moment, the tick-tock insatiability of the clock.

She was beautiful. Spiked hair and a skinned nose, ears the size of butterfly wings. A pensive, leave-me-alone pleating bunching her brow in a pique of virgin anger: in the world three hours and already she's pissed off, her rough sleep won by a sapling will already as hard as an acorn. When she unclenched her monkey hands, I noticed that her nails needed clipping.

"Can I have her?"

"She's asleep," the nurse said.

"She's been asleep for nine months. What's five minutes wake time?"

"I've told you, you should really come back during visiting hours."

"If you don't give me my daughter in five seconds, I'm going to set fire to your uniform. Okay? This is a sacred moment here. Don't piss me off."

I had been prepared for beaming, cigar-bequeathing pride, perhaps even a sense of redemption and infallibility. What I hadn't expected, though, was the way the event transformed me into a creature of instinctive distrust and territorial privilege, a thoughtless, den-protecting beast. In my daughter's world-shunning scowl I saw the twin of my own anger. Cave dwellers by nature, we were both unhappy with our contracts with the world. She wanted sleep, I wanted the peace of the lair. If my tolerance for red tape and authoritarian machinations had been minimal in the past, it seemed to have evaporated completely during the previous forty-eight hours. Between the lockout and the assorted press conferences I had lost all patience for things organized and institutional. I wanted a lion's life, a daily cycle of regal sunning and heavy-lidded dozing. I wanted my cub tucked in along my smooth flank as I groomed it with a tongue as rough as an emery board. The wife would bring home antelope or zebra for supper. Anyone gives me any shit, I tear their head off. Instead, I got the zoo — batter's box and a patch of fake veld. We all get it. I looked through the glass that separated me from my daughter and saw her ready-and-waiting cage: a yard-long mattress with tiny bars creeping up the sides of the crib. On her wrist was a plastic identification bracelet. Above the crib was my last name and Barbara's Social Security number. No wonder we come out screaming.

"Look," I said. "I'm sorry. That's not directed at you." She was a huge, round-shouldered woman with hips the size of an on-deck circle. She wore Buddy Holly glasses, black Poindexter-type frames usually favored by scrawny, buck-toothed kids and Cold War Rotarians. It took me a moment to see past her uniform and realize she wasn't here to be abused. If my uniform transformed me into a god, hers reduced her, at times, to a servant. She didn't need some out-of-work ballplayer giving her lip. "I apologize," I said. "I've had a bad week."

She reached into a hip pocket, removed a set of keys, then went over to the mint-green nursery room door. The sound of the key biting into the tumbler was amplified by a speaker suspended over the semicircular nurses' desk. The slumber room was miked in order to monitor whimpers and phlegm-snapping coughs. My daughter's head lolled like an apple floating on water as the nurse lifted her from the crib, the stern mask of fought-for sleep tightening at the first signs of movement and disturbance. By the time the nurse hoisted her a foot above the mattress she had hacked three times, finally finding the right pitch and boring into a long, slow cat-wail, the unconsonanted gift of the speechless and the perturbed. Other babies — pod-shaped things in blankets, the unclad frozen in body-builder poses, tiny hands clawing the sheets as if they had fallen asleep in midcrawl — began waking up. The nurse looked at me through the glass as the crying swelled with an undirected rage, a blind, I-don't-like-this-anymore pissing and moaning. She mouthed the words "You see. I told you so." I shrugged and turned up the palms of my hands. She left the room, shushing the squirming menagerie as she cradled my daughter, the entire nursery now filled with infant bodies wriggling like worms.

"You couldn't wait, could you?" she said.

But my eyes were on my daughter, my hands opening like petals to take her. Her face, distorted by rage, looked like a Janus mask. Unconcerned with the nurse, I made a polite apology, the automatic pilot of manners keeping me on course in the navigable world, while I drifted down into the circular, merry-go-round loop of love. I took her in my arms and turned away from the nurse; all sight and sound faded beside the hypnotic presence of my daughter. There was something magical about her. That she existed was extraordinary to me. I wasn't afraid of dropping her, wasn't made nervous by the fact that rocking her in my arms produced only a more pointed and persistent wailing. None of these tactile, in-the-world, first-time-father fears made me anxious. Instead, a vast sadness swept through me, some low-pressure system of the spirit. The feeling of never-before pleasure, a virgin sense of wonder associated with first-time delights — lovemaking, driving, hitting a single — was replaced by the abyss of mortality. As I held my daughter, jogging her lightly in my arms, I felt that I had failed her, had lied by bringing her into a world in which I would die and no longer be able to protect her. One in which she would die as well, helpless and apologizing perhaps to her own child, but inescapably powerless. And in the quick of my dishonest soul, I felt ashamed. It was as if I had made a promise I could not keep. Always uncomfortable with my connection to the great chain of being, I was able, now that I had contributed to it, to see the thing for the fiction that it was. Box scores, career totals, who was better than who. All brute facts and conjecture, supposition being the hollow conversation that supports day-to-day existence. And I had brought her into this place, a world held together by bloodlines traceable to ghosts and the long-ago forgotten. She rolled her head and squirmed in my arms as she howled, and the one time she opened her eyes and glanced at me, I looked back at her and said, as honestly as I could, "Sorry." Then her wailing swelled to horror-movie decibels. She closed her eyes again, the mere light of the world an insult. And I thought: "Absolutely. Wail."

Barbara began crying the moment she opened her eyes and saw me. It was as if my presence gave her license to collapse, to drop the pose of stoic reserve and wallow in the cyclone havoc of her emotions. Or perhaps it was some pathetic aspect in me which uncorked the tear ducts of the women I loved. If my daughter had been crying for herself, then Barbara was crying for all of us, for the end and beginning of things, an across-the-board sense of grief with which I had no trouble identifying. I took her hand, put it to my lips, and let myself go in a fit of weeping as I squatted beside her high bed. When the downside of our emotions had spent itself, I looked up at Barbara and we both began laughing, a shuddering, postorgasm sort of laughter, stunned, exhausted.

"We're a mess," I said, sniffling. I wiped the tip of my nose along the cloth cuff of my winter jacket. Barbara nodded. Reaching up, I dabbed at the tears leaking down into the sunken canals beneath her eyes and stroked them away, the color of those pockets bruised with the effects of sleeplessness and exhaustion. Her hair was sweat dampened and matted to her forehead and temples, and I brushed it back with the tips of my fingers. "How do you feel?" I said.

"Awful." Barbara's voice cracked, half the word all air and no sting, hollow as a reed. "When did you get here?"

"A little while ago."

"Did you see her yet?"

"Uh-huh. You were asleep. I came by here first. They gave you some pretty strong knockout drops. You were out like a light an hour ago." I could see any wafting anxiety disappear from her eyes, as she squeezed my hand.

The nurse brought our daughter in shortly after visiting hours ended. I hadn't telephoned my family with the news. I knew that once I did, they would descend. In topcoats and hats, breathless with the cold, they would arrive bearing gifts wrapped in brightly colored papers. I would be embraced and congratulated, Barbara sympathized with, the baby oohed and aahed over with the requisite nod to tradition and mimicked delight. It was an act of confirmation, an affirmation of our good standing, security, and moral health. Quasi-sacred, the event bequeathed the random chance for a gathering upon everyone. The older women would enjoy the regeneration of their industry, as schedules for baby-sitting, cooking, and the knitting of sweaters and booties were discussed. The men might look around at the equipment — the heat lamps and the intravenous tubes, the charts and screens and graphs — and feel a renewed sense of pride in their association with the nearly death-defying security of technology. As the nurse laid our daughter on Barbara's chest and pulled down one side of the hospital smock so Barbara could breast-feed the child, I felt that the oncoming communal goodwill was an intrusion, a dis-location, something out of synch with the intimacy of the event. A cave with a glowing fire, the skins of hunted beasts heaped under and around us as I huddled with Barbara over the infant, a rank, unbathed glory conjuring a comforting, animal heat between us — that's what I wanted.

I sat on the edge of the bed when the nurse left, finally alone with Barbara and our child. Barbara was sitting up, pillows stuffed behind her back. Her breasts were swollen, the nipples dark as milk chocolate. When our daughter took one between the lips of her toothless, old lady's mouth, the line between man and beast dissolved for me. Awed, content simply to watch, made happy by my dumb and private wonder.

Thirteen

WHEN I WALKED into the house later that evening, the telephone was ringing. I dropped my bag in the hallway, nudged the kitchen light switch with the flank of my index finger, and lifted the receiver from its cradle.

"Hello."

"I don't remember giving you permission to leave camp."

I had momentarily feared that it was going to be someone from the hospital calling, some public relations employee roused at home and charged with the duty of relaying the mystifying, never-happened-before events of the tragedy to me, the husband-father. "I assure you she had impeccable references when she came to us," the voice would say. The next day the nurse's abused childhood and warped past would be revealed in the yellow press. A photograph of the nurse standing at the center of a coven — black dunce cap on her head, eyes dead as nickels — would appear at the top of the feature story. "Just twenty-four hours after his controversial press conference, tragedy struck Mike Williams, baseball's brilliant Rookie of the Year." Tragedy had come to be exploited, in those commodity-crazed years, as the antipodal pole of celebrity, the twin of wealth. Both were capable of stirring up feelings of restlessness and passivity in the soul of the republic. On the one hand the masses were fed the stuff of envy. Then the wheel would spin and tales of horror and grief would soothe

the slumbering millions, forcing them to retreat into platitudes and their own tenuous sense of security. Reports of fortunes and early death tick-tocked back and forth in the media, the pendulum of our lottery-fevered longings wagging like the tongue of a grandfather clock. Celebrated, highly paid, emulated by millions, young, I felt the undercurrent of resentment working its subtle and perhaps unconscious voodoo on my life.

"You there, Williams?" It was not a member of the hospital staff telephoning to inform me of some life-shattering news, though. It was Cap Carver. And judging by the late hour and the sound of whiskey in his voice, I imagined that he was calling to taunt me and threaten to see that my mutinous flight from camp ended my career, the call initiated, perhaps, by Mr. Percy himself, who might have been listening in.

"I'm here," I said, though I had been silent for several moments in order to put Cap's call into perspective. What I decided was that I really didn't want to talk to him.

"Do you remember me saying to you that you could leave camp? I don't."

"My wife just had a baby."

"Yeah? Who's the father?"

"Camp's closed, Cap."

"There are camps open in the minors, Williams." Cap's voice had the lilt of condescension dancing in it, a got-you-by-the-shorthairs style of inflection honed to perfection by senators and men in the upper echelons of the military hierarchy. Cap had never cracked the superstar ranks in the course of his playing career. He had come up in 1952 at the age of twenty-four. Scrawny, weasel-faced, ears the size of ballpark pretzels, he played a tenacious second base and choked up halfway on the bat in order to scratch out 140 singles a year. Known for his drinking and gnarled animosity, he once had been suspended for spiking an opposing player in the abdomen during a double play, his cleats traveling what seemed to be a good six inches out of their way, as the legend goes, in order to stab a player who had outpointed him in the All-Star balloting. Devoted to the horses, he had led an isolated life once he left the locker room. Never married, he lived with his mother, a chain-smoker who had overmatched three husbands — one of them a prizefighter — and made a living as a handicapper for the ponies. When Cap signed to a long-term contract his gift to her was a local saloon. Cap's devotion to the team and the town won him a minor league coaching job within the organization after his final season as a player. Mr. Percy seemed to have a special relationship with Cap. More than just a henchman, Cap was unmotivated by greed or egocentric doubt; his loyalty went beyond ideology and the need for a father figure's unflagging approval. Selfless as a Doberman, his limbic system possibly stunted by the shock of early sorrow or his childhood nicotine addiction, Cap seemed to have a working dog's on/off switch at the helm of his cerebral cortex. When Mr. Percy said, "Sic 'em," Cap Carver went for the throat. It seemed as if instinct drew him into baiting, confrontational relationships with his best ballplayers. A good barometer of how well you were playing was the degree of contempt you elicited from Cap. A lifetime .240 hitter, he scorned you if you didn't play better than he had, despised you if you did. And if you threatened his position of favor in Mr. Percy's realm of feudal patronage, he went after you — and always on a personal level — with the unleashed viciousness of a pit bull. "I don't think you heard what I said," he continued. "There are minor league camps open at all levels in the South and Midwest, Williams. Dickhead, North Carolina. Bumfuck, Iowa."

"I heard what you said."

"You already got yourself a hundred-dollar fine. It goes up a hundred more a day each day you stay away."

"I think you should talk to my agent."

"Fuck your agent, Williams. I'm talking to you."

"Look, deal with the Players Association. When I go back on salary, then you can tell me when to show up and where I'm hitting in the lineup. In the meantime, watch how you talk to me, and leave me alone."

After I had slammed down the phone and released the receiver, I noticed that my hand was shaking. Though I was never one for confrontations, some intangible metal in my being had nevertheless been tempered by the steady fire of my first year in the majors. The heat of playing under the nation's eye, compounded by the convective influence of the media, the double-jointed contortions of the new salary structures, and the dual resentment of my teammates and the management, was distorting me in a disturbing, almost inverted way. I was changing so as not to have to change.

It seemed to me that Cap understood this, made it the toehold of his mockery. Which, I knew, would persist throughout the season. Cap had a history of never letting up on a player once he decided to harass him. He humiliated players in front of their teammates and didn't hesitate to criticize a player's attitude or performance in the press. A number of players in that situation asked to be traded. But Cap, with Mr. Percy's blessings, had the final say concerning a player's fate. Even Lee Wheeler, the club's general manager, was forced to barter with Cap Carver before initiating a trade. With the reserve clause in effect, Cap's power over a player's career was essentially limitless. Disfavored players found themselves inexplicably demoted to the minors, or else riding the bench while less capable players assumed their place in the lineup. An outfielder named Wes Ryan had been benched by Cap even though he was hitting .325. Cap attributed his decision to Ryan's mediocre fielding and general inclination toward under-achievement. Ryan was second string for three straight seasons, starting a total of sixteen ball games. He retired at twenty-six when his contract expired, and sat out a full year. A lifetime .300 hitter, he announced his desire to play the following winter and was immediately signed by another club. Mr. Percy claimed that he still owned Ryan, as he had offered him a new contract — with a 50 percent cut in salary — which Ryan had rejected. Initially, the management of the other clubs scoffed at the idea. But Mr. Percy's lawyers were able to persuade the other side's brigade of litigators that the deal could be successfully stalled in the courts, and that the signing club might even be liable for court costs and damages. Mr. Percy met personally with the contending owner, Bob Dockey, a pathologically shy recluse who had inherited a string of auto plants as an eight-year-old and purchased the team for his own twelfth birthday present. Unmarried, alcoholic in his boyish middle age, Dockey was uncomfortable with confrontations and legal harangues. Mr. Percy invited him to a members-only resort in the Bahamas, calling in all the other owners at his own tax-deductible expense as well. When Dockey returned to the Northeast two days later, Wes Ryan's contract offer was rescinded. It was obvious to the press and most of the fans that Mr. Percy had convinced Dockey that Ryan's ploy had been to circumvent the reserve clause, and allowing him to sign with another club without contesting the action would threaten the entire monopolistic foundation of baseball. Wes Ryan was thrown back into Mr. Percy's jurisdiction. Asked to assess his general plans for Ryan's return, Cap said that a year in Double A ball would be the first step, then maybe a move up to Triple A the second year. "I don't expect to see Wes Ryan playing in this stadium for at least two to three years," Cap said. When a reporter mentioned that might mean Ryan was returning to the majors at thirty, Cap replied, "Well, if a player wants to go sit on his butt for a year, this is what he can expect." Wes Ryan returned to his father's North Carolina tobacco farm and stayed there. Freddie Fields, a third baseman who had been a friend of Ryan's and had suffered equally at the hands of Cap Carver, went after the wiry little misanthrope with a thirty-two-ounce bat shortly after the season began. He had smashed and battered a whirlpool unit, the water cooler, both refrigerators, and most of the shelving on which the team stored its chewing tobacco and bubble gum before stadium security arrived, calmed Freddie Fields down, and escorted Cap Carver from the office in which he had locked himself. Not one player had tried to stop Freddie. Carver's single quote to the press was, "He just swatted his way out of baseball."

I looked around at the kitchen appliances, the newspapers and the dishes, the framed prints hanging on the walls. I bore a paradoxical resentment toward them now. For even while they were the makings of our nest, the comforting, familiar, sheltering elements to which we retreated from the outside world, still they were necessities — cold and indifferent to us — which neverthe-less dictated the regimen of our material lives. Every new purchase was another loss of freedom. And as I stood there I wondered how long before Cap Carver would be able to say of me, "He just swatted his way out of the game."

Fourteen

IN THE MORNING, before I left for the hospital, I tried to reach Hammer at his office. The phone rang eight times before Angela, Hammer's secretary, answered it. When she picked up, I could hear a morning talk show squawking in the background, and laced with that the sound of her baby crying. Hammer's office was the top-floor apartment of one of his investment properties. The three floors below had been sold as cooperative apartments. Victim — as well as beneficiary — of a legal conundrum of his own making, Hammer the tenant was forced to join the other members of the coop when a leak in the hall skylight caused water damage to the stairwell and sue himself, Hammer the owner.

"Can I tell you something?" he said to me at the time. "I came out better than if there had never been a leak. You know what that tells me? I have to love insurance."

I believe what attracted me to Hammer was his basic insincerity. He exuded some sort of marshmallow-soft aura of intimacy, came on as if he were a feather bed of trust, a plump, cushy beanbag of a friend and father-confessor to whom one could turn after plunging headfirst through the gauntlet of celebrity. I didn't buy it for a second. He was so congenitally specious, such a hammish representative of trust, that I let him sign me as a client. For him, truth did not possess any sort of absolute value. It wasn't a fixed and inviolable constant, like the speed of light. Instead, he saw it as simply one more particle existing amid an infinite number of particles which, when closely observed, changed intrinsically. Truth was some quantum-sized subcategory of phenomena to Hammer, governed solely by the subjective force field of interpretation. "Which, of course, we discount," he admitted to me the one time I called him on a flagrant lie. This was early on in the course of our relationship. He made apologies, and picked up the tab for lunch. In his book, all was forgotten and forgiven. It was this attitude of amiable condescension toward the entire matter of truth that won me over to him. He was such a liar that I knew I would always be able to construct my own vision of the truth out of the tangle of his fabrications.

Hammer had sought me out during my senior year in college. I was icing down my left hand, which had been clipped by a pitch during a warm-up game, when a pro scout named Howie Hawk approached me.

"Got a minute, kid?" he said, already talking the shorthand of a road-weary salesman. There was the dead cylinder look of boredom in his stare and a bottle of Pepto-Bismol nestled in the right pocket of his tartan plaid blazer. He wore yellow double-knit pants and a pullover sweater the color of orange soda. The laced black shoes pulled the whole outfit together nicely.

"What's up?" I said, leaving my bruised hand in the pail of ice, squeezing the metallic-green handles of a forearm developer with the other. That was when a third voice interrupted, one I had never heard before.

"I'm sorry, but Mr. Williams cannot, or finds it in his best interest not — at this juncture — to enter into any preliminary contractual discussions, arbitration, conversations, or anecdotes relating to his play, both past and future —"

"Who are you?" Hawk said.

"Hi, how ya doing? Alvin Hammer. Player representative. Counsel at law."

"You represent this kid?"

"I'm speaking on his behalf now, yes."

"But do you represent him?" Hawk said, putting a combative topspin on the word "represent."

"I think that my talking to you represents my representing him. If you'll notice, he's seated *behind* me."

"That's because you stepped in front of me," I said. There was a growing third-party quality attaching itself to my existence, and I didn't care for it. Hammer turned and faced me.

"No, I didn't," he said. "That's merely your perspective. What's your name? Mike? Mike. You're taking — and I can't fault you for it — a totally subjective perspective here and holding it up as truth. I didn't step in front of you. I stepped in front of him," Hammer said, pointing a finger now at Howie Hawk.

"You're still standing in front of me."

"Can I tell you something?" he said. "One day you'll thank me for it."

Howie Hawk did not discuss the possibility of my future with the team he represented that day, and, although I was selected in the first round of the college draft that spring, Howie Hawk's club passed me over for a southpaw right fielder named John Laun.

"The name has no charisma," Hammer said to me, as we monitored the selection process. "On the basis of his surname alone, I can call that a bad pick. Where's the cash register ring to it? Where's the fan-endearing handle? The name has no grit, no purchase. Mike Williams, Ted Williams, you see? Sandy Koufax. You see what I mean? There's cinder in that name. Bill Mazeroski. You get the steel-mill, wooded-mountainsides connotations in that name? Let me tell you something. That name is Pittsburgh. Abba Dabba Jim Tobin. Foghorn Myatt. Sig Jakucki. I grew up with those names. Summer afternoons. The maple-colored radio sitting on a crocheted, eggshell-white doily in the living room. The curtains snapping like sailcloth. Out back, sheets are drying on the clothesline. The house smells of lemon wax and Lestoil. A hooked rug sits on a section of parquet floor like a magic carpet. I lie on it and stare at the ceiling, factory-autographed Joe DiMaggio glove on my left hand, right hand slapping the ball into its pocket. One knee is bent, the other hooked over it. I have never been seriously sick or injured. My body has never been bruised by alcohol, caffeine, or tobacco. Women have yet to make sport with my genitals. I have no conception of social disease, and only great-uncles from distant parts of the borough die. A crowd of sixteen thousand murmurs in the background at a Tuesday afternoon game. On the mound it's Ellis Kinder against Tommy Byrne. There are gaps of silence in the running commentary. It's almost as if there was a time when the world existed before hype. Before the constant buzz of statistics and information. Phil 'Scooter' Rizzuto and Tommy Henrich draw walks. Rizzuto and Henrich. You know these names. They're from the neighborhood. All those first-generation immigrant images well up in the mind. You can see ships gliding into New York harbor, men wearing caps and ill-fitting woolen suits standing in the bow beside women whose heads are wrapped in kerchiefs, their eyes fixed on the gray and black spires of the cathedral-like city. Do you get the sense of fraternity and hope in those names? The sense of melting-pot enterprise and promise? I'm sorry, but John Laun is about as emotionally enthralling as a dial tone. I don't know. Maybe that's what we've become. Anyway, bad pick. Not to let your ego be bruised by it."

"He has a great arm and he stole a hundred and seven bases this year," I said.

"Statistics don't make the player. From a totally profit-oriented stance, if I was his owner, I'd have to force him to change his name."

A catcher from Arizona State went next, then a Chicano pitcher who played in San Bernardino. It was still early in the first round and the teams with the poorer records continued to make the selections. The scouting report on me — another step in the incessant sifting process that begins for each of us the moment we let go of our mother's hand and march in alphabetical order across the threshold of our grammar school building and into its dim, sterile hallways — was favorable, and there were supposedly several teams interested in drafting me. But Hammer had made overtures, as he put it, to one team in particular. Their scout, Kurt Buttle, a former third baseman, rated me highly, and he was on a rare streak in scouting circles. Five of his last six "can't miss" draft selections actually made it to the majors. The average is generally more like one out of thirty-six. Slipping into the majors is equivalent to a full-grown man's snaking through the eye of a sewing needle: a little bit of magic is required. Careers can take off in the minors like combat jets, then lose a wing two miles above a cornfield and pirouette to the ground nose first at nine hundred miles an hour. Or else they idle for a while, have their nuts and bolts tinkered with by mechanics and structural engineers, then wind up rusting in some cavernous hangar, microscopic flaws in the engine and hairline cracks running through the fuselage. That Kurt "The Kid" Buttle was convinced I was the real thing meant there was a possibility the gods were on my side. And Hammer had intimated to him that in contract negotiations he and I would be flexible.

"They've already got Ted Monday," I had said to Hammer, several weeks before the draft. "He's made the All-Star team five years running. Why don't you just sell me into slavery?"

"I hear the sense of insecurity in your voice, and I sympathize."

"It's not a sense. It's on-the-money insecurity."

"This is understandable, given your lower-middle-class upbringing. Can I ask you something? How was your relationship with your father?"

"My father's not a left fielder."

"I'm not saying anything negative. I'm just saying examine the relationship. Maybe we can slip a clause into the contract where you get analyzed at the club's expense."

"I don't want to be analyzed. I want to play in the majors."

"This is beyond a doubt the end and foremost goal of your professional career game plan. But just stop and ask yourself one question. How old is Ted Monday?"

"I don't know. Early thirties."

"A babe in the woods. He's thirty-two. Have you seen X rays of him?"

"Yeah. They print them on the back of baseball cards now. Would you just please say what you're going to say if you're going to say it?"

"Sciatica. He has a disk in his lower back that's worn thin as a potato chip."

"How do you know?"

"I see his chiropractor."

"I don't believe it."

"It's true. I've made appointments. I've undergone spinal manipulation."

"You just happen to see the same chiropractor he does. By chance."

Hammer chuckled. "Not by chance."

"You spied on a man through his chiropractor?"

"What's this Watergate-style backlash against picking up a little information? I went in, he fine-tuned a few vertebrae, we chatted. It was a chat. A series of chats."

"And you found out . . ."

"And I found out that Ted Monday has about two years before he starts moving like the Tin Man. By which time, of course, you will have proven your phenomenal capabilities in the minors, and the parent club will be only too happy to have you step into the role of young, full-time outfielder."

"Have you spoken to Buttle about this?"

"You mean, have I 'leaked' any of this information to him?" I glared at Hammer. "We discussed vertebrae, yes. But it was in your best interest."

I was made unhappy by this revelation. My dream of perfection had been built around an inviolable talent and a universal acceptance of it. Both, I felt, were necessary. If one voice questioned my abilities or quibbled about the importance of my presence in the game, the dream would be revealed to be nothing more than petty egomania. But if I could become a hero of huge and selfless proportions, then the dream would be able to feed, and feed off of, a chorus of communal hosannas. In my dream (which I never put down on paper, by the way; in fact, I hardly ever thought about it) I learned the genius of immortality, which is that everyone shares, everyone counts. At twenty, I was deaf and blind to the fragmented exigencies of the republic. Perhaps it is a quality latent in all ballplayers: eternal hope. Nevertheless, I felt that the dream had been tainted by Hammer's machinations, by the corporate impieties of deal making and computer-generated player profiles. I was in the realm of men who reduced dreams to the bottom line of profit-and-loss sheets, and Hammer read in my eyes the disappointment that I felt when I realized this.

"Come on," he said. "You have to grow up a little bit." I didn't give him any indication that I concurred. "You're getting what you want," he said. "You should be happy."

I was selected a third of the way into the first round, Mr. Percy tabbing me on the generally astute — and this time chiropractically abetted — advice of Kurt Buttle. On the day Hammer and I were supposed to sit down and discuss the initial terms of my contract with the club, though, no one had any idea where Hammer was.

"Angela, did he say he'd be back?"

"No."

Angela was at the kitchen table in Hammer's office, spoon-feeding mashed turkey to her ten-month-old. The baby, Sammy, sat in a high chair, his limbs twitching, straining to reach seemingly ineffable objects that floated by, invisibly, in the air. His mouth hung open in dumb distraction one moment, closed and chomped away the next. There was a miniature television set on the table. Battery operated, it had a five-inch screen and could be carried in a briefcase. Another of Hammer's technological playthings, the tiny screen riveted Sam's attention the moment Angela snapped it to life.

"Sammy, stop playing and eat."

"Angela —"

"What? Sammy, eat your food."

"Angela, is there any possibility that he left a number where he could be reached?"

"I don't know."

"Well, could you check?" I could see the exasperation of the clerical and the underpaid lift her shoulders and then set them down like two sacks of groceries.

"Angela, please."

I could see her weakening. Not out of any sense of obligation, but possibly from a feeling of pity combined with a desire for me to shut up and go away.

"Ange . . ."

"Oh, all right. You feed Sammy." A red-alert status of politeness went out to every neuron in my body the moment she stood up and slapped the business end of Sammy's dinner utensil into my palm. "Don't give him too much at once, or he'll throw up."

"Ange, I'm —" and she was out of the room. I looked at Sammy. He was a dark-haired baby, burly as a bear cub. And not happy. Shameless, he grunted, begging me to feed him, despite the fact that he found me strange and quite possibly loathsome. "Don't you have any pride?" I said to him. My words only provoked more of the same twitching, chair-bound frug, so I shoveled up a stingy portion of food. But before I could get the first spoonful to his lips, Angela was back.

"I can't find anything," she said. "Here, I'll do that." She took the spoon from my hand.

"You were gone only ten seconds. Where could you have looked?' She sat down and changed television channels. "Angela —"

"This is my favorite show. No talking."

"Fine. I'll look myself."

"Good."

Angela's desk was a muddle of unsigned contracts, deposition copies, clipped savings coupons for canned foods and detergents, Chinese restaurant take-out menus, and back issues of *Cosmopolitan*. When I found her calendar I flipped to the day's date and discovered that nothing was listed under "appointments."

"Angela," I said, restraining my voice just enough to keep any sort of impatient edge out of it. "What's Hammer's home number?"

"Look on the Rolodex."

"Great," I whispered to myself. I thumbed through the file and found Hammer's card. Half a dozen numbers were crossed out. Others were followed by parenthetically enclosed qualifiers: home, boat, club. Club? What club? The home number had a suburban area code and had been changed six times. Hammer's boat was in Florida. I didn't even want to think about calling there and having him answer. But, as I was to find out, Hammer never answered a phone himself. I dialed.

"Downtown Athletic Club."

"Is there an Alvin Hammer there?" I said, thinking: Hammer? Exercise? The man was a walking coronary, a monument to cellulite and caloric excess. I heard the guy who had answered say to someone who was obviously in the background, "Hey, Harry. You seen Hammer around?" Harry's reply came through the receiver with the hollow, disembodied feel of a transmission from some orbiting space capsule, all muffle and shadow. "No," the guy who had answered said. "We ain't seen him."

"Well, do you think you could —" I heard the knocking of the receiver at the other end, as it stumbled into its cradle. Then dead air. The power and indifference of telephones began to grate on me. I cursed while I dialed Hammer's home number.

"Hello." The voice was young, somewhere in the six-to-nine range, I guessed. And frail. It had to belong to a four-foot-eight boy with the arms and legs of an extraterrestrial, all fig-shaped torso and limbs as narrow and unmuscled as soggy french fries.

"Hi. Is your father home?"

There is a brief period of silent option-weighing, a sounding of the depths of his befuddlement. "Uh. . . ."

But before I can say, "Listen, kid," a voice approaches from the background. He mumbles in reply to it. Then there is a staticky rustle of the receiver changing hands.

"Who's this?" A female voice. The tics of teenage coyness and pointless vim animating it. Not Hammer's wife, as I had hoped, but a step up on the information food chain nonetheless. Desperate, I'd talk to anyone even remotely connected to Hammer by a common roof.

"Mike Williams. Listen, is your father home? We're supposed to negotiate my contract in about fifteen minutes."

"He's not here," she said, a practiced confidence in the way she handled my call. Also the singsong lilt of a pampered adolescent.

"Well, do you know where he is?"

"I have absolutely no idea."

"Did he leave a number where he could be reached?"

"Try his office."

"I'm at his office."

"Then I can't help you."

"Is your mother around?"

"No."

"When will she be back?"

"I have no idea."

There was an almost arrogant glee coloring her rebuffs and denials. It was as if she had studied copies of her father's depositions, the tactics of evasion and abjurement addling the unchiseled foundations of her ethics.

"Thanks," I said. "You've been a tremendous help." I hung up hoping that she would marry into permanent penury. I scanned the office, looking for any clue as to Hammer's whereabouts. Cardboard boxes and transfiles the size of treasure chests were stacked against the wall, the corners of the lower ones crunched like the hood of a car after a head-on with a light pole. The records were marked, some of them dating back to 1963. Two bicycles — one racer, the other a kid's trail bike, thick tires and custom-painted racing stripe — leaned against one corner of the embankment of files. Beside them, the tips of its rigid tail spanning eighteen inches of carpet and supporting the body with the seemingly precarious strength of an arching, cast iron, modern sculpture, stood a seven-foot wooden marlin, its dorsal fin as ribbed, papery thin, and crisp as a Chinese fan. Its mouth was open, teeth as sharp and beveled as the ragged tongue of a handsaw. Next to the marlin was an unplugged jukebox. If I put together the clues that were in front of me, Hammer was either at a flea market or in an insane asylum.

I made my way to his office, feeling empowered, by his negligence and unavailability when my career was on the line, to ransack the place. Angela was engrossed in her soap opera, Sammy's fat left cheek nestled into his left shoulder as if he were nuzzling the cleft of a Stradivarius, eyelids drawn like a pair of bedroom shades after dark, as I passed the kitchen and moved down the hallway. The small bathroom was as cluttered as the reception room. Bottles of after-shave, vitamins, prescription drugs, and over-the-counter pain relievers were jammed onto the ledge of the sink. A suit jacket hung from the shower curtain rod, angling in the slight breeze let in by the grimy airshaft window.

I moved further down the hall and opened the door to the one room I had never been in. I half expected to find something gothic and macabre — the disinterred and mummified corpse of Buddy Holly, dressed in a powder-blue suit; or a twelve-fifty Harley, gleaming like a chrome god, its front tire aimed at a wall-sized black-and-white blowup of a fishnet-clad Marilyn Monroe. Instead of a pop icon graveyard, though, there was only mundane clutter. The glass top of a coffee table, more boxes, an uncartoned air conditioner. Dejected, I closed the door and crossed the hall into his office.

He had done a little redecorating since I had last been in it. The kidney-shaped oak desk sat in front of his cases of law books as it always had. Black, four-drawer-high file cabinets stood in the corners of the room like palace guards. The TV had not been removed from its niche in the long, wood-paneled wall opposite the desk. It continued to stare out at the room like a dead prophet. But in front of the window that looked onto a brick wall streaked with the white drippings of rooftop pigeons sat an exercise bike. I wondered what sudden craze for health and fitness had overtaken Hammer. Had he been set on a righteous, low-fat path by his rabbi or cardiologist? Hammer, the devoted fan of all-you-can-eat salad bars. He relished them, he told me, for their fusion of the organic and the synthetic, for their shameless abundance.

He had taken Barbara and me to dinner the day I signed a contract with him. A bunker-style building, squat as a pillbox, on the commercial highway near home. It hunkered on a plot of ground surrounded by a gravel parking lot. We arrived in Hammer's white Eldorado, a car conspicuous for its cheesy grandeur. The hostess seated us in a large, semicircular booth that hugged a round, oak-stained table. We ordered three steaks — Barbara an eight-ounce portion, Hammer ordering the sixteen-ounce size for himself and for me. "You have to eat more," he said, then led us off to the salad bar.

Barbara and I followed him across the carpeted dining room to the buffet. Middle-aged couples and teenage kids out on dates maneuvered around the island, selecting greens and dressings and condiments, the older people with the care of home buyers, the friction of experience tempering the haste of their choices, the kids heaping items one on top of another with the abandon of sweepstakes winners. Hammer picked up a plate and made his way around the bar. It was the size of a lifeboat and lit up like an altar. There was something daunting and tawdry about it, like a recreational vehicle. Hammer built the foundation of his salad around the basics: shreds of iceberg lettuce, slices of cucumber, halves of cherry tomatoes. Then made the obvious move toward accenting items — the heart stoppers and artery hardeners. Using a tablespoon, he speckled his salad with croutons and bacon bits, loading up on the latter as if they were a seasoning, like salt. The unexpected fillip was the laying on of chickpeas, cheddar cheese bites, and a pickled three-bean salad, then topping the entire plate off with a cross-cultural combination of Roquefort dressing, Thousand Island, and a dollop of barbecue sauce.

"Did you see that salad?" Barbara said, walking back to the table with me.

"Maybe we'd better not judge the man who controls my life too hastily," I whispered.

"Are you sure he's a real agent?"

"That's what it says on his card."

"I think he's nuts."

"So do I."

We rejoined Hammer and our steaks arrived. Hammer drowned his in A.1., slathered sour cream onto his baked potato, then, before he began eating, he took the tip of his wide, striped tie and tucked it inside his shirt, feeding the material in between two buttons just below his sternum. Barbara and I glanced at each other as Hammer finished and looked up at us. "Otherwise I get gravy all over it," he said.

I sliced away the fat on my steak and ate gingerly, requesting another pitcher of beer from the waitress. Hammer, mouth grinding the last morsels of a bite of steak to crumbs, said, "Barbara, why doesn't he eat more? Look at him. He weighs one-sixty."

"A solid one-sixty," I said.

"So, a solid one-sixty. The point is you should be one seventy-five, one-eighty."

"I'd never get around the bases."

"Don't worry about the bases. Worry about hitting the ball out of the park once in a while."

"My game is my game."

"Did you play professionally?" Barbara asked Hammer, reserving any inquisitorial glances.

"No. With this body?" He laughed. "Barbara, come on."

"How did you get into representing players?" She continued cutting her steak.

"It was a decision I made. Can I tell you something?" He put a chubby hand on Barbara's arm. She held her utensils still and looked up at him. "The legal profession is very boring."

"So that's why you represent players?"

"I'll tell you. I'm a fan. I'm a fan of the game. Any suggestions I make to Mike," Hammer said, deftly acknowledging the thrust of Barbara's remark, "are purely as a fond and caring amateur. I throw them out as food for thought. I make no claims to authority. But I'll tell you something else. At one seventy-five he'd be worth twenty-five percent more on the open market."

"He's not a piece of beef."

"Barb," I said, "it's all right."

"No, that's fine," Hammer said to me. "I like that. I find that admirable. Kids starting out, sticking up for each other. It's touching. It's not easy to find things to be moved by in the world. Hold on to that. Barbara," Hammer said, leaning toward her, "I'm going to tell you something I never told anyone else." Packed into his camel-colored corduroy suit jacket and white shirt, he looked like a stuffed teddy bear. I knew he was lying through his teeth, but I couldn't help smiling. He was so grossly intimate and completely caught up in the fiction of the moment that he didn't believe he was lying. He kept Barbara waiting a moment for his revelation, then said, "Most of the time, I'm really full of shit." Smiling, turning back to his steak, Hammer said, "So don't be afraid to call me on anything." He lifted a forkful of baked potato gleaming with streams of melted butter and sour cream to his mouth. "Can I tell you one last thing?" he said, this time with the natural declivity of humility in his voice. "If God hadn't given me this body, I would have been a ballplayer. That's how bad I wanted it." Hammer paused for a moment. "Well, you don't always get what you want," he said, then put the tip of the fork into his mouth. And, for once, I believed him.

So what was I to make of the exercise bike in his office? Hammer basked in his chubbiness. His arms were fat, his neck was fat. His fingers were as pudgy as cocktail franks. Portliness was Hammer's natural condition. To upset that at this point in his life would be a shock to his system, both physically and psychologically. Was this a reaction to some dire health warning? A new trend Hammer was onto? Was he in love? How would Hammer, after forty-odd years of corpulence, adjust to a sleek, healthy body?

The Elvis poster I had less trouble accepting. Leaning against the wall behind one of the two armchairs provided for clients stood a huge lithograph of the King. Forty-eight inches high and at least thirty-six across, it was an enormous headshot. In its grim, sanctimonious style, it bordered on the totalitarian. When I checked more closely I found a tag on the back that read: Shelley's Posters and Framing, Kings Plaza Shopping Center. Mall art. I didn't think that even Hammer would stoop so low. It rekindled my fury. I remembered what I was doing and went over to his desk. Opening legal-size folders I found copies of *Sports Illustrated*. I didn't recognize any of the names of the players on the tabs of file folders in his drawers. Then I realized that they were divorce cases. I wondered if Hammer handled any pros besides myself. My father had warned me about checking Hammer's credentials before signing with him, and lamented the fact that Bernie Papy had died before inking me with his club. But I never checked Hammer's credentials. Instead, I let him charm me.

When I opened the center drawer of Hammer's desk, I found baseball cards. Thousands of them, lying there like the pieces of a puzzle. I brushed through them, thinking I might find some professional, agent-attorneylike clues to Hammer's whereabouts — or at this point his sanity. But it was a two-inch-deep baseball card slush pile. I grew furious, until I saw a 1951 Mickey Mantle. Rookie season. A twenty-year-old phenom, blond crew cut and teeth as white as lime, out of Spavinaw, Oklahoma, a place no one had ever heard of. (If you're from a place, you don't count.) Collector's item, less for its monetary value than for its totemic stature. I considered stealing it, but felt that if I did the card would be tainted. I put it back and closed the drawer, vowing to come back and pinch it if Hammer ever really pissed me off again. I searched his other drawers and found notes, old files, socks, ties, and uncashed checks for huge sums. I began to get the feeling that I had not signed with the man, but with his estate. I checked my watch. Our meeting with Mr. Percy was in ten minutes. Traffic going across town would be moving at a caterpillar's pace at this time of the morning. I decided I would take my chances on my own. I had read Joyce's *Ulysses* in college. A legal document couldn't be any longer or more complex. Wing it.

"Angela, I'm leaving." She looked up at me, didn't say a word — from the blankness of her gaze I believed she had forgotten who I was — then turned her eyes back to the television set. In the high chair, Sammy was sound asleep, head rolled to one side, his Winnie the Pooh bib stained the color of a pumpkin. "Right. Great. Well, if the elusive one surfaces, tell him I'm headed for Mr. Percy's office." No answer. I left the office and bounded down the stairs.

When I turned onto the avenue at the corner of the street, I saw Hammer through an antique store's window. He was talking with a man wearing an olive-green pin-striped suit.

"What are you doing?"

Hammer stopped babbling and looked at me. "I'm glad you're here," he said. "I need your opinion." No hello, no surprised reaction, no guilt.

"I don't have time to give you my opinion," I said. "We have to be at Mr. Percy's in seven minutes."

"Relax. It's only negotiations. Come over here. I want you to see this."

Hammer walked me to the back of the cavernous store —

brick walls, cement floor, dim as a cathedral — in order to discuss barber poles. "I've bought into an investment group that's doing sports bars. The barber pole. Eighteen-nineties. Abner Doubleday look. What do you think?"

Two years later, I didn't think, I knew. Hammer was certifiably insane. And, as I had allowed myself to become his exclusive property, I imagined that the same could be said of me. Not a good thing to realize one day after becoming a father. Impatient to leave for the hospital, I was about to hang up when Angela picked up the telephone on the tenth ring. Her answering a call at nine o'clock in the morning was, in itself, miraculous, a just reward for my ludicrous hope. I didn't expect to be able to talk with Hammer himself. I was certain he was skulking about the Caribbean in his sloop, entertaining the wealthy and the divorced, talking investments with men who wore cream-colored suits, black silk shirts, and patent leather loafers. But I at least wanted to find out if he had left a number, or said when he'd be check-ing in.

"No."

"He didn't say anything?"

"No."

I could tell I had annoyed Angela. I was interrupting her mid-morning talk show. She would be missing out on a moderator-led discussion on the problem of transvestite airline pilots — should they be allowed to fly in drag? — or a heated debate over the question of whether massage parlors should accept MasterCard.

"Well, if you hear from him, please ask him to call me, please. Beg him if you have to. Will you do that for me? Please?"

She hung up. Even kowtowing failed to move her. My agent was at large and my one link to him loathed me. At least, she did to the extent that her indifference allowed her to give me a second thought. Despised by my teammates, annoyance to on-duty nurses, new prey for Cap Carver's chamber of professional hor-rors, I began to wonder if I invited sadism and shows of otherwise buried contempt. I put down the receiver, grabbed a jacket, and walked out of the apartment. On our doorstep was a copy of the morning paper. I picked it up, opened to the sports page, and saw my name in the headline. "Mike Williams should speak softly and carry a bigger stick." I was even a whipping boy for hung over and embittered sportswriters. I got into the car and left for the hospital, moving deliberately through the static February gloom.

Fifteen

"THAT IS NOT a happy face."

I was leaning over my daughter, talking to her, as a nurse, one I hadn't seen before, wiped her small, taut belly with a tuft of alcohol-dipped cotton. Where her navel would be after ten days was a gleaming scab the size of a raspberry. She had stained her diaper and covered her thighs and buttocks with a snotty, cherry-colored vaginal discharge that mixed with her first bowel movement, a runny porridge the color of pea soup laced with ballpark mustard. I could see on her face a look of for-this-you-dragged-me-into-the-world irritation. But that small and all-consuming ire, combined with her innocent helplessness, had the effect of wiping out every lick of my own brooding and self-concern. Rather than complicating my life, her presence made it burdenless.

I turned to Barbara and said, "This is a quality baby," then, once the nurse had finished changing her, lifted her and laid her on Barbara's chest.

"Ah! Careful."

"What?"

"I'm sore."

I caught the full weight of our daughter before she settled onto Barbara's breasts, and lifted her away. "Sorry."

Barbara put one hand to her breast and massaged it softly. A few drops of milk leaked from her nipple and stained the white smock she was wearing.

"Where should I put her?"

"Here, next to my arm." She pushed herself upright, wincing, in order to be able to lean over our daughter. Together, we marveled at the almost impossibly small fingers and toes, the uncoached grumpiness and thrashing, the bags under the eyes.

"How can she be tired? She's been asleep for five thousand hours." In spite of this, she yawned like a grandmother watching a bad prime-time movie, then sighed, her small body rising and settling with a weariness I didn't associate with infancy. I put my nose to hers, looked directly into her eyes until they crossed, then said, "This is not good, this laziness. Do you hear me? This is not a good thing." An instant later, she burst into tears. A mewling, low-pitched whine crested into a blaring, I-want-my-mommy wail. Barbara said, "Aw," and stroked our daughter's damp scalp. I stood up and said, "What'd I do?"

Barbara was saying, "Shh, come on. Shh." I watched as she calmed the child as if by an act of magic. "I think it's your tone," she whispered.

"What's wrong with my tone?"

"You sound too . . . intimidating."

"I'm supposed to sound intimidating. I'm the father, the pillar of strength, the figure of inexorable moral authority. Right, baby?" She simply whimpered this time, her sobs not opening up their strides. Just a little low-level blubbering, eyelids squeezed tight, her lips as crimped as the fluted edge of a pie crust. "We need a name for her," I said. "I feel like she has this generic canned food quality, something we picked out of the baby patch like a head of cabbage."

Barbara and I had discussed names, both male and female. We spent nine months psyching ourselves up for one gender or the other. At first, Barbara wanted a girl for the same reason I wanted a boy: mirror image, protégé, chip off the old block, jr. A miniature reproduction of ourselves that we could mold from step one, thereby leading our lives over again the way we thought we wanted them lived. Barbara would teach her daughter a fierce, implacable, and heedless independence. I would teach my son to hit sliders. The idea of recapturing our lost youth and remolding it through our progeny was enticing and, I suppose, telling. The impulse pointed to some basic sadness in our constitutions, a shakiness and flaw. I began to see the idea of a little Mike, Jr., as ghoulish and appalling, a thought winging well beyond the gyre of narcissism, out into the disorienting ether of the grotesque. Baseball pajamas, a mitt for his third birthday. Little League tryouts, my well-remembered ghost haunting him in his first unsuccessful at bat. The inevitable comparisons, the daunting specter of my stats. My looming record in the game. Vaguely insecure throughout his early years, Mike, Jr., a .140 hitter, would become a drug-addicted neo-Nazi by the age of fifteen. I was siring a doomed life, a rebellious, inarticulate kid who would turn hostile and self-destructive because he had seen my disappointment as I stood behind the backstop and watched him miss pitch after pitch. All my worst traits would be passed down to the boy, my one redeeming talent withheld by some spiteful gene. I began to dread the thought of having a son.

But all my anxiety evaporated the instant my daughter appeared. It was replaced by a deepening sense of freedom that seemed to spring from the clarity of newborn responsibilities. The hue of the future brightened, and the cycle of passing time seemed liberating, celebratory, and deeply necessary.

"What should we call her?" I said, watching Barbara play with her hand. "I'm thinking Sandy, after Koufax."

"No," Barbara said, drawing out the lowing of the vowel in response to the silliness of my suggestion.

"Well, what? If we go with Regina, we could call her Reggie for short. There's Babe. Babe is good. Melissa. Then we could go with Mel. Mel Ott, Mel Allen, Mel Stottlemyre. You get a lot of range with Mel. It's a kind of a discount-store-type name. What do you think?"

"We're not naming her after a baseball player."

"I already promised the game. Besides, we're getting off light. If we were ancient Egyptians, we'd have to immolate her in center field, then dance naked for three days."

"I don't care."

"What's wrong with Mel or Reggie?"

"I'm not naming my daughter after a right fielder."

"Well, I'm not naming her after a saint. Saints are out."

"I want to call her Elizabeth," Barbara said firmly.

"That's a saint."

"That's too bad."

"Name one good reason for calling her Elizabeth," I said.

"It was my mother's favorite name."

I paused, caught in an argumentative balk. I had already started the motion of my comeback, cocksure for no reason at all that I would be able to shoot down Barbara's reply as easily as I shagged fly balls during off-day practice sessions. Instead, there was nothing I could say. If for me our daughter filled, in some way, the void left by O'Kane's death, then she also, I saw for the first time, healed the deep, unclosed wound left in Barbara by the swift taking of her mother. There had been no period of preparatory grieving for either of us, no time to say last things, make final promises and bedside confessions. Perhaps there was some unconscious or karmic correlation between the alacrity with which death worked and the suddenness and undiscussed speed of our daughter's conception. Perhaps all entreaties are not ignored. Or possibly you just have to make your own answers. I had no argument for Barbara, only the sympathy of a ready and reverent sense of agreement. "I like it," I said, nodding slightly as I looked at Barbara. "Elizabeth."

"Am I interrupting?"

I do not pray, I play baseball. I do not kneel and finger rosary beads, I run down fly balls and chase outside pitches that have no right being hit. I am a baseball player. I put my faith in effort and desire, and make the world as I go.

So I didn't expect to hear Hammer's voice in the hospital doorway. I had done nothing to earn his near-miraculous appearance. Instead, I had imagined that I would either have to wait eternally for him to rematerialize and untangle the cat's cradle of animosity and threats which my career had suddenly become, or else hire a Sherpa guide and seek him out like some holy, eastern mystery found only on the peaks of snow-tipped mountains. To have him simply show up was beyond the realm of miracle. It was ludicrous.

"I'm hallucinating, right? You're not really standing there."

Hammer chuckled, and stepped into the room. He was carrying two dozen roses, his briefcase, and an overloaded shopping bag. There was a plastic bat handle sticking out of it, as well as the flat top of a gift-wrapped box. In his overstuffed parka he was bear-sized, his broad, padded body nearly filling the doorway. Flaps jutted out from both sides of his neck like the sprung collars of a tuxedo shirt. The hood of his jacket was thrown back, revealing a patterned wool lining, and on top of his head was a furry, black cap. The coat was unzipped to the waist, and a bulky sweater the color of eggnog billowed out from between its flanks. He wore pleated, chocolate-brown corduroy pants. They looked as soft as angel cake and he had stuffed the cuffs of them into the tops of his ankle-high hiking boots. Shielding his eyes was a pair of mirrored, state-trooper sunglasses. He looked like a crazed fusion of Admiral Byrd and a Hollywood director, and, for a moment, I did think I was hallucinating.

"What are you doing here?"

"This is a blessed event," he said, glancing at Barbara and smiling. "What do you mean, what am I doing here?" He approached the opposite side of the bed, set his briefcase and the shopping bag down on the visitor's armchair, then extended one arm and offered Barbara the roses. "Hi. How ya doing? You proud to be a mommy?" Barbara smiled as Hammer leaned over and kissed her lightly on the forehead. She took the flowers and began to blush, the first color coming into her face since I had been back home.

"Thanks."

"I paid for those with after-tax dollars, so you know I'm sincere." Hammer laughed at his own joke, then put out one hand and wiggled his chubby index finger under Elizabeth's chin. She tucked her chin in against her neck and stuck her tongue out, her eyes crossing and rolling up beyond the almond-curved ellipses of her eyelids. Croaking sounds escaped from her throat in brief, broken fragments; then her arms twitched and flailed wildly, tiny feet pedaling the air.

"You're giving my baby convulsions," I said.

Hammer snorted and laughed. "I'm not giving her convulsions. She's laughing," he said. "I am right in calling her a she, correct?" Barbara and I nodded. "I thought so. You know why? She goes for me. All women do. I drive them wild."

As Hammer winked at Barbara, I tried to imagine him being intimate. I pictured sex being a secondary concern to him, some activity not on a par with shopping for electronics products and ordering Thai food in a chic new restaurant. The art of seduction might appeal to him, but the act itself would have to be anticlimactic. Or perhaps I was imagining only one side of him. He may have been a satyr, a connoisseur of erotic potions, oils, and gadgetry, his bedroom a purple-and-black temple presided over by a bronze statue of Priapus and a collection of pornographic movies. Who knew? I just couldn't see him spending time engaged in an enterprise that required so little wheeling and dealing. It wouldn't appeal to the con man in him.

As Hammer was taking the gifts out of his shopping bag — a solid gold spoon from Tiffany's being the last and most special — my parents arrived with my brother, Bennie. Dressed in topcoats and caps and scarves, they had a meek and persevering quality about them which filled me, all at once and unexpectedly, with great sadness. I felt as if I were outside the room, looking in from another dimension, some Dickensian character taken on a nighttime journey through the sites of his irrevocable past. They had all tragically aged somehow, while I remained inert, free-floating and disembodied. Even though I had left for spring training only three days before, the hue of death — a blackish-brown tint found in the corners of worn and somber daguerreotypes — had darkened the outlines of each of them. They stood out against the background of flat, milky-green walls, anonymous light switches, metal doors, and mute wall sockets. Perhaps it was the sterility of the hospital that focused their frailty in my mind's eye. Or the new addendums to their identities: grandfather, grandmother, uncle. Each of them had been nudged another step further from their beginnings. No one likes to make room for someone else coming into the game, and I thought I felt an unspoken resentment radiating from my father in particular. He was being forced to relinquish another handhold on his vanquished youth, and, knowing him, he wasn't going to give it up easily.

They shuffled into the room and around the bed. My mother was the only one who moved with any sense of authority. She went straight to Elizabeth, the power source. I noticed Hammer lurking merrily in the corner and I began introductions, which then found their own momentum.

"Hi. Alvin Hammer," Hammer said to my father, extending a hand.

They had not met before, Hammer's appearance in my life sudden and taking place away from home. Signing with him had been my first notable act of independence, or heedless idiocy, depending on how generous an assessment I was in the mood to make. My father viewed the relationship dimly. I suspected there was more than one reason for this. True, he thought Hammer was feckless and unprofessional. He blamed my tax problems and the pressure to perform immediately at superstar levels on Hammer's insatiable and impatient need for endorsement opportunities.

"All he sees is the bucks, and a quick way to make a name for himself," my father said, shortly after I had been left in the lurch by Hammer to sign, unassisted, with Mr. Percy. "His best interests are his own interests, not yours."

I didn't disagree. To my mind, Hammer was indefensible, practically a joke. That the man was a successful attorney and a rising sports agent cast a shadow of ludicrousness over both professions. But I won't deny that I succumbed to the sway of Hammer's charm, the breathy and seductive voice of money. As a middle-class boy, I was not long on identity, or a sense of personal worth. At my worst, when I saw a scrap of wealth or upper-class credentials dangling before me, I snapped at it like a starved, stray mutt. I was not immune to the shallow nobility offered by money. In our materialistic age, nouveau riche wealth is the only grail in town. Still, I was not completely taken in by Hammer and the sirens of celebrity. If I wanted greatness — which I did — I wanted it for more intangible and abstruse reasons. I played with faith and an undiminished sense of hope, was playing — without realizing it — toward a fuller, possibly complete understanding of the genius of immortality, that improbable, yet nevertheless powerful, fiction. So I hadn't yielded to Hammer and his seductive promises in toto. But, at the same time, I was moving more deeply into realizing my own vision. And I knew that this subtle cleaving, this shift beyond the sphere of parental influence, chafed at my father's sense of pride.

Hammer was effusive, laying on the I've-heard-a-lot-about-yous and the pleased-to-meets with the polished, indifferent air of a presidential candidate. It was an automatic friendliness, projected as mechanically as an insurance company's false aura of beneficence. No thought went into Hammer's goodwill, no effort. It was one of the reasons I found him lovable. He cheated at everything.

As Hammer worked his way through my family, greeting each of them heartily, I watched my father. He had taken Hammer's hand warily, and his greeting had been perfunctory, iced with a smooth malice.

"Yeah, hi. How are you?" he said, shaking Hammer's hand unenthusiastically. He released it quickly, freeing it to go on its way. But his eyes stayed with Hammer, sizing him up slyly. In a glance I could see that my father disapproved. Hammer's presence, his appearance, seemed to confirm for my father all his doubts, reservations, and prejudices about Hammer's flimflamming, my cocky independence, and, unconsciously, his own sense of inadequacy. My father had been a loyal Democrat throughout my childhood, voting for Kennedy in 1960, Johnson in 1964. But by the time I was in high school, there had been a seismic shift in his political temperament. He voted for Nixon in 1968 and spoke at the dinner table of Hubert Humphrey as if he were some sort of social disease, something debilitating and shameful. I suggested that Jimi Hendrix be elected president, and my father snapped back at me with a vicious racist remark. Traveling to work every day, he rode an elevated train through a ghetto that had once been the segregated, immigrant neighborhood where my mother had grown up in comfortable, middle-class style. Now it had deteriorated into a wasteland of hopelessness and poverty, and the summer Nixon made his successful bid for the White House, it had burned to placate an inarticulate and frustrated rage. The high school team I was then playing on won the divisional championship and, in order to reach the city finals, had to play a ghetto-based team, on their turf. There was talk of canceling the game because of the riots, or moving the site to a neutral ball field in a less troubled area of the city. But the home team protested, their request was sustained, and the game was scheduled to be played on their field. Normally, our team rode to away games in the school van. One of the coaches drove, and the players without rides from their parents filled the bench seats in back. On that morning, though, we rode out to the field like a funeral procession. Car following car, each driven by a grim-faced father too anxious to speak to his own son. My father even rounded up a few friends to come along. As I rode in the backseat, I felt ashamed for us all. When we stepped out of the car, my father held me back, his hand squeezing my arm more firmly than I think he knew. "If anything starts," he said, "get your goddamn ass over to me — fast. Understood?" He was speaking from fear and anger, even resentment. Something had to be to blame for the loss of control he felt. At the moment, I was the nearest target.

I didn't understand until later that it was Nixon's promise to restore law and order that appealed to my father. Just as he felt intimidated and cornered that day on the ghetto field, he also felt this loss of freedom and control over his life in a number of peripheral and almost intangible ways. He became more rigid in his support of the war in Vietnam, as if his nostalgia for patriotism kept his sense of material inadequacy at bay.

By the time he met Hammer, my father was filled with a distrust born of his own frustration. He held Hammer in contempt, simply for what he assumed Hammer represented. What I did not realize, and what my father did not, most likely, see either, was that what Hammer represented most literally was me.

I walked toward them, and as I approached I could begin to make out the mumbled, fragmented sounds of conversation. Hammer was talking theory — endorsement deals and salary arbitration possibilities — and my father acknowledged Hammer's cheerful, profit-scamming suggestions with a minimal number of curt grunts. His eyes were fixed on patches of tile or spots on the walls — anywhere but on Hammer's.

"Hi. We were just talking about you," Hammer said.

"Yeah? What were you talking about? My undeniable television charisma?" I was answering Hammer, but looking at my father. At least until his undisguised displeasure forced me to look away from him, and at Hammer.

"That didn't go as well as we hoped," Hammer said, seeming to cover my embarrassment.

"That's an understatement. Listen, we have to talk."

"Of course!" Hammer said, as if my request was a grand idea, something he looked forward to with delight.

"I mean it. I want out."

"I already have feelers circulating."

"What do you mean, you want *out?*" my father said, mocking my wish.

"I mean, I want to be traded."

"You haven't even been with them a full year yet. Get your picture on a magazine cover, think the goddamn world revolves around you."

I was dumbfounded by his scorn. The suddenness of it carried the shock of betrayal. "What's that got to do with anything?" I said, a slight, shrill whininess creeping into my voice.

"Of course, we're going to proceed slowly," Hammer said, neither to my father nor to me directly, but to the shame of our public disagreement. A slowly intensifying force field, as resonant as a piano chord, was resolving itself out of my father's disdain and my own bewilderment, and I was embarrassed for Hammer. My father's anger seemed to be drawing on deeply private sources for its energy, and I sensed — but did not understand — that my career was not the cause of his reproving coldness, but the magnet to which all his latent, free-flying bitterness was drawn.

"What have they done for me?" I said to him. "I don't owe them anything."

"Who do you think pays your salary?"

"They drafted me. I was one of the top players picked in the first round. I'm supposed to thank them for being talented? They were lucky to get me." I couldn't believe the words coming from my mouth. Kept in check throughout my success-laden youth, the deep but, to me, distasteful desire to proclaim my specialness had finally slipped free. After Cap Carver's threats, Mr. Percy's deceitful and self-serving machinations, the petty vituperations of the press, and now my father's condescending ire, my poise and sense of restraint evaporated, and I was, instantly, heedless, arrogant, and self-protective.

"You think you're something, don't you?" my father said. For some reason — spite, bitterness — he was shameless in front of Hammer. Mr. Percy, then Cap, and now my father: each of them felt he could talk to me as if I were a child, none of them measuring the limits of their reproofs, as if they each resented me deeply, perhaps even despised me. In Cap Carver's case, this was totally understandable. As for Mr. Percy, he was a ham, a manipulator, and had played off my gullibility with the ease of a Shakespearean villain outwitting some dutiful and earnest go-between. But the shift in my father's attitude was more insidious, deeper, and more reverberating because it echoed through the ruins of love.

"What I think of myself has nothing to do with wanting to be traded," I said. "They've screwed me since day one, and it's only going to get worse." I turned to Hammer, who was making an effort to be as inconspicuous as possible. "Cap Carver called me at home last night."

"I wasn't aware of this," Hammer said, looking at me now, full of concern. "He was the one who told me you had come back home."

My mother joined the circle, slipping in between Hammer and myself. "Why are you raising your voice?" she said to me. "The baby's trying to sleep."

"I'm not raising my voice."

"What did Carver say?" Hammer asked.

"That I'd be playing in the minors for the rest of my career if he felt like it."

"He actually said that?"

"What are you talking about?" my mother said. "Who's Carver?"

"His coach," my father said, attaching an aura of unassailable authority to the title.

"Manager," I said.

"I want you to know that he's not allowed to speak to you that way," Hammer said.

"The man has a team to run," my father said, addressing Hammer for the first time.

"Yes, well, but —"

"The man is a petty psychopath," I said.

"What did he say?" my mother said.

Bennie drifted to the fringe of the circle, behind my father. I could see that he was puzzled, as well as concerned, by the tone of the conversation. It seemed to have taken on a chafing, argumentative edge.

"The main thing is for Mike to be playing where he feels happy," Hammer said. "If he's going to be productive, he has to feel appreciated."

"Oh, bullshit," my father said. The bluntness of his remark stunned us. There was a subtle measuring of worlds going on, and even Bennie, hovering at the edge of the circle, seemed aware of the charged force that my father's words carried.

Hammer, adjusting the tilt of his gilt-framed glasses, tried to defuse the remark with a patient, conciliatory approach. "Actually, no," he said, "they have found that —"

My father cut him off. "It's a job." There was a dense, compacted bitterness in his words. He used them like jabs — terse, to the point, punishing. "He gets paid to do a job. That's it. I don't get asked if I'm happy. It's a job."

"And if you don't like it," I said, "you find another one."

"You're not quitting?" my mother said.

"No, he's not quitting," Hammer said, immediately reassuring not only her, it seemed, but himself as well.

"What would you do if you quit?" she asked me. "You have a family to support."

"I could teach American literature for three thousand dollars a year. That's why I went to college, remember? To have something to fall back on." I was looking directly at my father as I spoke.

"I don't think that would be wise at this juncture," Hammer said.

"Who told you to take those idiotic courses, anyway?" my father asked.

"I think we're getting off the subject here," Hammer suggested.

My mother turned to him. "You're not going to let him ruin his career, are you?" Even though she didn't understand what a squeeze play was, or a hit and run, or the infield fly rule, my career was of supreme importance to her. I appeared on magazine covers, in newspapers, on television. I was somebody. I had escaped the shame of anonymous obscurity in the land of the noted and the famous. The fact that Cap Carver hated me and the public and players despised me in a collective, almost abstract way was beside the point.

"I won't let him ruin his career," Hammer said, putting a hand on my mother's wrist. "Trust me."

I could see by the way my mother was looking at him that she did. He had the charm vacuum on high, and she was sucked up into it as easily as a ball of dust. Hammer was a successful attorney, a player representative; he wore brand-name clothing from head to toe. My mother was willing to trust him on the basis of net worth alone.

"Yeah, the two of you have been doing a great job so far," my father said, his voice tinged with an undercurrent of acrimony that eerily matched Cap Carver's.

"I'll admit there are a few things I'm not happy with," Hammer said.

"Dad," I said.

My father cut us both off. He pointed a finger at me. "You were nobody when they signed you, and you're nobody now," he said. He stared at me for a moment, then lowered his arm and pushed past me to see Barbara and the baby.

Hammer, Bennie, and my mother were silent. Barbara was as speechless as I was. Only Elizabeth had the courage to speak. Her cries filled the room for as long as it took us to say our good-byes, and my family and Hammer to leave.

Sixteen

TWO WEEKS after Elizabeth was born, the owners yielded on the issue of free agency. Not completely, but enough to prompt the players' union to agree to negotiate, and Bowie Kuhn, the commissioner, ordered spring training to begin. I had not spoken to my father since I had seen him at the hospital, and refused each time my mother called and asked me to.

"He's very hurt."

"He's not hurt. He's just not in charge of my life anymore."

"He wants you to call him."

"Then let him call and ask me to."

"Would it hurt for you to pick up a phone?"

"Yes."

"Then just do it anyway."

"No."

The day I left for spring training, Bennie drove me to the airport. He checked his side mirror and darted into the left lane, where we rode six inches from the tailgate of a family-sized wagon, Bennie's pedestrian insecurities overcompensated for by his behind-the-wheel Will to Power.

"You get points for arriving in one piece," I said. Bennie smiled, and eased up on the accelerator. The drop in speed tugged me forward. When the traffic thinned and we sped up again, I turned and looked out the window. I felt what must be an astronaut's melancholy, a sense of gravity-thwarting thrust and the leaving of a familiar world behind.

"You think I'm wrong?" I said. It was the first time I had asked Bennie what he thought. "Not calling him. Am I wrong?"

Bennie watched the road, then tilted his head slightly to one side, testing the weight of his reply. "I don't know."

"It took you that long to come up with 'I don't know'?"

He shrugged. "If it's going to bother you, call."

"Should it bother me?"

"That's up to you."

"Would it bother you?"

"What difference would it make? You're not me."

"Nice eye, Williams."

It was Cap Carver's voice. He was standing behind the backstop as I took batting practice the following morning. We had not spoken since the night he called me at home. At the team meeting, he seemed to look straight through me. Drunk the night he called, he may have forgotten the incident, I thought. Lost any memory of it in one of his periodic blackouts.

Winston Page, a Cold War pitching ace who came down to spring training each year, wound up and threw me a lazy curve. I jumped out ahead of the pitch and ripped it foul down the third-base line. Overextended, I lost my footing and had to hop, pivoting on my left foot, to keep from falling. When I glanced over my shoulder, Cap was staring at me with a look of contemptuous displeasure, as if he were bored by the fact that he hated me.

"Good footwork, Williams. You're really hitting with power."

I hit poorly during the exhibition season, my mind literally a thousand miles away. The first game broadcast back home I went oh for four, and committed an error. In a cloud-nine fugue, I didn't see the ball until the shouting of the fans in the leftfield seats called my attention to it, sailing over my head. When I reached the dugout at the end of the inning, Cap was standing beside the bottom step. One foot was raised, propped on the railing, his arms crossed. He hunched over and stared out at the field with a pointedness powerful enough to make me feel my presence had been eradicated. I walked past him without uttering a word, my initial eagerness to apologize overtaken by a vindictive and self-rationalizing anger. I strode sulkily down the dugout, flung my glove at the shelf above my teammates' heads, then dropped myself bruisingly onto the bench. Lunch Molloy, seated in his usual corner spot, lineup card in hand, leaned forward, eyed me, and said, "That's nice, but you're up."

Greg Arthur slapped my butt with his mitt. "Get a hit."

"Yeah, right."

I took the dugout steps in two leaps, then reached down to pick up my bat. My eyes met Cap's. It was not an innocent, ingenuous glance. I was hoping that he had merely been distracted when I clomped down into the dugout, that his silence was impersonal, without scorn. I was hoping that he would respond now with a look of sober encouragement, even just the small blessing of a nod.

His stare went through me like an X ray. Icy to a point that seemed to pass beyond hostility, it weakened me like a flu. As I straightened up, bathed in the corrosive glare of his seemingly all-knowing contempt, I felt as if I had been dropped to the bottom of some huge, transparent bell jar, my internal atmosphere contracting to where I thought I would implode on the spot. I walked toward the plate, my legs moving with an underwater deliberateness. The crowd, in spite of its tidal murmurings, blurred into a six-story-tall wave of circus colors. I felt as if I were a film character shot in deep focus, some unmoored being seen at the far end of a tunnel of dense, almost syrupy, four-color space. I fouled off the first pitch — a slider with about as much heat as a cup of lukewarm water — into the mitt of Bernie Offut, the opposing catcher, and was called out before I had a chance to get it through my head that I was up.

"The late, great Mike Williams," Offut said, coming up out of his crouch. "Have no fear, he'll be gone in a year."

Two hours later, the south Florida sun cool as a dinner plate and glowing like a navel orange, I was Visa-carding beers and bourbons at the first oceanside bar I could find, the fingernails of my right hand tapping out an unconscious Morse code signal that could only have been deciphered as "Help!" when Two-Tone and Oscar walked in and found me.

"Hey, slow down, man," Two-Tone said. He gave me a puzzled, reproving look. "You drink like you're carrying the entire white man's burden yourself."

Oscar, wearing a scoop-neck mesh sweater the color of a manila envelope, beige double-knit pants, and matching patent leather loafers, stirred his gin and tonic, then tossed the swizzle stick onto the bar. "You think you're going to come out of this slump, start getting on base?" he asked.

It was the first apparently sympathetic voice I had heard since arriving at camp, aside from Greg's. My salary, and the press conference debacles, still seemed to bring out the piranha in most of my teammates.

"God, I hope so," I said.

"I hope so, too. Because I go free agent this year, and I need some numbers in my RBI column."

"That's cold, man," Two-Tone said.

"What? This is business. Williams knows that." They stopped talking over my head and Oscar leaned down and looked at me. "Am I telling you anything you don't know?"

"No." I ran my finger around the inside of my bourbon glass.

"See. He knows Carver'll have his ass in Poughkeepsie long before I get on it about anything." Oscar looked at me again. "You know this, right?"

"Right." I didn't look at him.

"See. The boy ain't stupid."

"I ain't saying he's stupid. Maybe he just don't need to hear this shit right now."

"Aw, man. I ain't hurting him. The dude's playing so bad he's beyond criticism."

The next day, hung over to the point of near-blindness but feeling giddy from a sense that I had somehow survived a night of monumental abuse — who knows, maybe I was still loaded — I went three for four and banged in the winning run. The RBI was meaningless in spring training. Still, I felt it put up a buffer between Cap and myself. After the game, Oscar stopped by my locker while I was dressing.

"Our talk helped," he said.

"Looks like it." Our talk had nothing to do with anything, I thought to myself.

"That's good," he said, nodding. "One thing, though. If you get on base too much once the show gets under way, that could be bad. They're going to start pitching around me, giving Concepción all the meat."

"Are you saying you want me to go back to slumping?"

Oscar's eyes widened. He put his thick, pinkish palms up, as if I had him at gunpoint. "No, no. No."

"Because if that's going to help you —"

"No. The thing I'm saying is — forget me — the thing I'm saying: You can hurt the team by helping too much. You see what I'm saying?"

"So what do you want me to do?"

"I can't tell you that." His next words were tinged with a solemnity he usually reserved for quoting the Bible, or assessing his own talents for the sporting press. "Remember. A real ballplayer just knows. You see what I'm talking about?"

"Yes." I had no idea what he was saying.

"Good. Hang loose."

Ten minutes later, Oscar had a private meeting with Cap Carver in which he declared me erratic, selfish, and a detriment to the ballclub. He suggested I be sent down or traded.

"Who the hell told you that?" I was seated on the team bus beside Pete Hendley, a beat writer who traveled with the club. We were heading to Sarasota for a split squad game, Oscar staying behind with Cap and some of the others for the home game. Hendley was a few years older than me. He had worked for a radical underground paper in San Francisco, then a gossip sheet, and finally with a daily owned by the parent company of a communications empire based in our city.

"Carver."

"When?"

"Last night at the bar. When else?"

"And you believe it?"

"I'm running it."

"You mean it was on the record?"

"He said print it. It runs this afternoon."

I threw myself back against the seat. "Fuck. Why would Rife do that?" I didn't need to ask why Cap had revealed the conversation.

"Oscar's a Pandora's box of insecurity. Tell him he's great and he'll say, 'Damn right.' Ten minutes later he'll be asking if you really think so. He can't have you coming up hitting four hundred and holding press conferences."

Hendley told me that Oscar was the subject of an opening-day cover story and interview in *Sports Illustrated*. In the article, Oscar mentioned my press conference appearance with Mr. Percy. Hendley flipped through a kid's homework-sized assignment pad and stopped on a page covered with chicken scratch, coffee stains, and doodles. "Know what he said about that?" he asked me. I shook my head. " 'It's going to be kind of hard to hit, if he doesn't let go of the old man's hand.' "

"He said that?"

Hendley nodded, then flipped ahead several pages. "Listen to this. 'Williams may be smoke, but I'm fire. With him, the club smolders. With me, it burns.' You're his new competition. Or whipping boy. Depends on how you deal with it."

"Two days ago he told me he needed me to get on base."

"Then he turns around and tells Cap to trade you. That's Oscar."

"What did he go to Carver for? He hates him."

"The lesser of two evils," Hendley said. "At the moment, you're the bigger threat. Want to comment?"

Two-Tone had driven to Sarasota by car. He was on the field warming up when I approached him. "Hey, I have to talk to you."

"Don't ask me, man."

"You don't even know what I'm going to say."

"You got that scared, rabbit-shit look in your eyes, so I know it can't be good."

I told him what Hendley said.

"So why are you telling me?" He continued throwing, loosening his arm.

"You're his friend."

"Don't be hooking me up with that vanilla bean. You see me sucking up to Carver and Percy?"

"No."

"No is right. Learn from it." He paused and looked at me, holding the ball in one hand. "You still don't know where you're at, do you?"

"No," I said. "Where am I?"

"Alone, sucker. Alone."

That afternoon, I collected four hits under the generously indifferent eye of Lunch Molloy. My mind was on hold, nothing but a narcotic, self-propitiating emotional Muzak ringing in my ears. Alone. I reacted to the shock with a kind of autistic alertness. My reflexes were intact. Put the ball anywhere in my vicinity and I attacked it, lashing out at rising, inside fastballs that charged like bloodthirsty Dobermans, diving in the outfield for sinking Texas leaguers I was insane to even try for. Your basic, everyday psychopath — insecure as an overweight schoolboy, homicidal as a college linebacker. I had a contract to play baseball. Thank God for sublimation.

But two months into the season Dickie Tibbetts broke his wrist and Cap pushed Greg Arthur to short and moved me to the infield to play second base. My protests were ignored, my average plummeted. By the All-Star break I had committed seventeen errors and — with the unfamiliarity of the new position affecting my entire game — was hitting .231. The press grew increasingly acerbic and disparaging. Hammer's attempts to have me traded were met by management with derision and scorn. Fans, even my teammates to a certain extent, began to forget about me.

For years I had been a streak hitter on a roll, my rookie and minor league seasons prodigal, wild with innocence. My game collapsed the moment the world ceased to feed it adulation and unrestrained affection. I hit below .300 — well below .300 — for the first time in my life. By season's end, when Hammer saw that the brightness of my future and chances for a successful career were fading, and my tenure with Mr. Percy was unalterable, his became a distant and seldom-heard voice, like my father's. Barbara, caught between the new and nearly ceaseless demands of Elizabeth, and a surfacing and inarticulate restlessness of her own, had little time and even less energy to devote to the wounds and confusions of my career. I found myself hitting infrequently and with no sense of magic, questioning the worth of my efforts, alone with the specter of my own shortcomings.

BOOK II

How they are provided for upon the earth. . . .
How all times mischoose the objects of their adulation and reward,
And how the same inexorable price must still be paid for the same
    great purchase.

— *Walt Whitman*
"Beginners"

Seventeen

THE PLAGUE of dispiriting failure beleaguered me for two full seasons. Having made the leap to demigod, I was now disdained for falling back into the race of mortals. Fans began razzing me from the sidelines, telling me where to play, and how to hit. At one point I was even sent down to the minors, a swift lesson in humility. It was a nakedly spiteful move by Cap, coming just as I was beginning to get my rhythm back after its two-year absence. Also a payback, I felt, for my successful salary arbitration even though my stats were only slightly better than passable. But millions were being paid to lifetime losing pitchers and washed-up utility infielders, and by late in the seventies the average league salary had leaped into the six-figure category. When I began hitting well again, the onslaught of attention began once more, an all-is-forgiven attitude characterizing reports of my rebirth. Even Mr. Percy came forward and praised my efforts at second base as selfless, overlooking the fact that I had protested the move every day of each season until I was returned to left field. Along with the raise came more resentment — a petty authoritarianism from management, boos from a steady and resilient contingent of unhappy fans.

Even now I cannot fully account for my turnaround. It's strange: the things that bring you peace are always simple and mystifying. I was still signed to Hammer, but he was elusive,

relegating me to the back burner, as the possibility of multimil-
lion-dollar contracts was still too far in the future to get excited
about. And I'm fairly certain that I can't attribute the resurgence
to Barbara. After four years of marriage, we were simply trying
to hold ourselves together, and, distant as I'm sure I seemed, Barbara's own affection appeared to be more focused on her accounting classes and appointments at the tanning salon than on me. In
a way, though, I expected no less. As my career bottomed out
down in the minors, I turned not so much to women but to sex.
I was away from home, not wanting to uproot Barbara and
Elizabeth from the Northeast, or do anything to suggest that I
considered my demotion permanent. But it wasn't the distance
that spurred my infidelities. It was a hope (a deranged hope, I
agree) that by reconnecting with something primal, something in
which I could lose myself — even if that something was dark —
I could return whole. And I suspected that Barbara, through some
divine power of selflessness, understood this, and let me explore
what I needed to. The downside of this, of course, was that she
could not surrender her own needs, and to compensate for the
license she granted me, there was a reciprocal diminishment of
affection. I also thought there was more to it than my womaniz-
ing, something evolutionary, a simple growing apart. Barbara began to go her own way.

As for my father, he and I had barely spoken to each other in
years. My only solace, then, was hitting, and it had been a long
way back. But finally I just put aside everything that was wrong
and crushing and foolish in the world and myself and began to
hit again for the sake of hitting, for the rigor and beauty it
brought to bear on everything shoddy around it. At first I was
wary, handling my recaptured grace as gingerly as a beakerful of
hydrochloric acid. Drop it, I thought, and the floor beneath my
feet disintegrates into a cloud of steam. Nevertheless, I hit. I hit
when I was so hung over I could barely see; hit when Elizabeth
was home in bed with a 104-degree fever and Barbara was threatening me with divorce. I hit as the economy reeled and the fans
turned to the game for an impossible affirmation of a long-gone
past. The wall that had existed between myself and the game dis-

solved. Only this time, instead of being connected by the magic of youth, I had a feel for the tension of mastery.

In 1979 I hit .341 and was paid $185,000 for doing it. That winter, as the presidential primaries were beginning — inflation peaking at 14 percent, the value of the dollar deflating like a pin-pricked balloon — I took my contract to arbitration and, with near-MVP stats, walked away with a $500,000-per-year raise, the going free-agency rate for a player of my caliber. Mr. Percy vowed not to pay it, threatened to sell me for a handful of batboys, then relented and called me the best hitter since Ted Williams. His new promise, he announced, was to make me the highest-paid player in the game. Someday.

A year later, 1980, I had yet to hear him reiterate that promise. The team, though, had been picked — and ordered — to win the World Series. Money had worked its superficial voodoo on the roster, and that spring the best-hitting lineup in baseball belonged to Mr. Percy. So we were expected to win, and, in truth, we were hungry. Beyond hungry. We felt bullied, adored, despised, and confused. It had been a dispiriting half-decade, the late seventies, a time of plummeting hopes and floundering resolutions. Yet, despite our new salaries — or possibly because of them — we, as ballplayers, were idolized. The brief chill that had tempered our relations with the public gave way to the awe of six- and seven-figure salaries, and million-dollar endorsement deals. Attendance boomed, the statistics leapfrogging as quickly as real estate prices and inflation figures, as if we had been charged with the duty of releasing the republic from its torpor and setting it right again, even if for no more than a few instantly replayed moments a night.

In return for his market-enforced generosity, Mr. Percy, long insidiously aloof from the day-to-day mechanics of the game, demanded a championship, and, to remind us of his expectations, he visited the clubhouse that summer with the regularity and bluster of a thunderstorm. Unannounced, he would descend on us, a bevy of swirling, ushering aides stirring up a small whirlwind around him as his wheelchair crashed through the swinging steel doors of the bunker, the acrid smells of old sweat, tobacco, and heady disinfectant overpowered when he was swept into the room amid a cloud of after-shave, new leather, and the faint effluvium of rot and halitosis that seemed to escape from him like an invisible gas. Mr. Percy once even expressed an uncharacteristic displeasure with Cap Carver's managerial ability, and Cap responded, in stoic fashion, by going on a three-week bender.

We began the season brilliantly. Through May we were nearly untouchable, reeling off a record twelve straight wins, winning forty of our first fifty games. We led the league in runs, hits, walks, and steals. But the average age of our pitching staff was thirty-three. Johnny Clemmons, a sinkerball pitcher, was nearing forty and hadn't pitched a complete game since Nixon was pardoned. Prayer Pearson, at thirty-six, had been reconstructed by prosthetic surgery, a bionic elbow replacing cartilage and bone in his pitching arm. Ron Donaldson, a former Cy Young contender, had joined Alcoholics Anonymous for the third time and pudged out on sweets to circus fat man proportions. The fade began as the temperature rose into the eighties. By the dog days of summer, with our combined earned run average hovering around a mark that could only be considered good for a low-interest loan, we slipped into a footrace for first, Cap Carver's benders deepening as Mr. Percy's wrath swelled, and the humidity grew so thick you could almost carve your initials on it as it hovered in the virtually unbreathable air.

But we were still scoring, and Otis Armstrong, our center fielder, was the key to our offense, as well as our sense of decency as a team. A year younger than me, he had hit twenty-six home runs and stolen thirty-six bases as a rookie. He was compared to Willie Mays and Hank Aaron. His speed and solid, left-handed bat were supposed to generate pennant-winning numbers, and the burden of run production was set down in front of him in black and white every morning. He was praised to the press by the front office, then told in private by the club's general manager, Lee Wheeler — an old-timer who had worked for Branch Rickey — exactly what the club expected of him. Haircuts. Jackets and ties on the road. Fines for lateness, unexcused absences, subversive behavior, and bad attitudes. Then he was handed a computer printout, and there they were — his projected numbers. Live up to them, or perish.

Otis was our leadoff man, though he could hit for power as well. His main job was to get on base, steal, and come home on anything hit through the infield. In spite of his youth, he delivered, shedding whatever naïveté and innocence he had had in the minors, ascending to the plane of near-superstar within months of coming up to the big time. The leap from prospect to product is often instantaneous, though, and it can be disorienting. The forward momentum of personality explodes, flying off in a million directions, as it succumbs to the pull of celebrity and seemingly limitless wealth. Yet, in spite of this, Otis performed. While the rest of us were playing badly, he was making things happen on the field, and Cap was uncharacteristically generous with his praise, shielding Otis from the press — even from Mr. Percy. Then someone — a disenchanted and embittered sportswriter, some activist with a political agenda, Mr. Percy himself — decided that Otis's role was too cuddly. The situation reeked of near-harmony, and harmony didn't sell tickets and newspapers, or cow City Hall and borough commissioners. A black writer in one of the liberal weeklies called Otis an Uncle Tom and accused Cap of making him the team's "boy."

It was the end of the decade. The city was bankrupt and mismanaged, its bridges and immigrant-laid tunnels and elevated train tracks crumbling, its manufacturing base in flight, taking off for Sunbelt industrial parks, tract houses, tax breaks, and the fluorescent beneficence of malls. Fifteen hundred people a year were murdered within its riverbound limits; junk was peddled openly in downtown parks; and the illiteracy rate was reaching daunting and irreversible proportions. Saigon was an unspeakable memory, auto plants were closing up shop, and Elvis was dead — a bloated, drug-addled behemoth who shot out television picture tubes and got twisted on codeine, stuffing himself with deep-fried peanut butter and banana sandwiches as he wallowed through his fading days. We were oil-starved, inflation-battered, and depressed. A contagious sense of floundering, of being at sea, had infected the will of the republic, optimism and our sense of divine right vanishing along with the borders of South Vietnam and single-digit unemployment figures. With this sense of diminished promise and deracinated national identity came a craving for the superficial and the gilded. If Moscow paraded surface-to-air missiles through Red Square, we overpaid celebrities. So why not add a little racial melodrama to the ongoing soap opera? Crank up the grist mill of speculation and prejudice, link the breadbasket panacea of wealth to the shame of our deepest and most persistent sin, and sell some tickets.

Amazingly, Otis managed to stay above it, at least on the field, and usually by being reserved — which doesn't always translate well through the press. His on-base percentage going into the final month of the season, just as our pitching began to fail us, was .425. He had scored over one hundred runs, stolen seventy bases. He was even closing in on thirty homers. MVP stats, without question. Stumpy from the waist down, lean as an Olympic swimmer on top, Otis ran like a cheetah. Forty-two-inch chest, thirty-inch waist, one percent body fat. A million-dollar-a-year machine, which, nevertheless, had its limits. Legging out an infield hit as we tried to keep pace with the division leaders, Otis touched the first-base bag, then screamed — an instinctive, involuntary howl, selfless, unmoneyed, oblivious to sympathy. His right knee was pulled up waist high as he hopped three pogo steps down the line before momentum overtook his balance and he tumbled onto the grass, his fall silencing the thousands of late season apostles. The moment Otis's leg hitched and caught, Cap Carver yanked his hand out of his back pocket, kicked Ollie Sutkiss's catcher's mask, and swore like a madman, cursing the bad luck that plagued him and, it seemed, fed off his own meanness. An instant later, the dugout phone rang. Lunch Molloy uncradled the receiver without getting up from his spot in the corner. Keeping his left hand tucked into his windbreaker pocket — his arm pressed against his side to keep out the first of fall chill that had descended on the city — he extended the instrument to Cap without even checking to see who was calling. On the field, Otis lay on his side, clutching his leg, the intimacy of his pain beaming out to the millions, while our trainer, Cliff Thompson, raced out to first base. The rest of us sat still. Injuries spooked us, as if there were a dark magic in them, some ability to leap like electrons from the orbit of one body to another.

"Mm-hmm." It was all Cap uttered into the telephone's mouthpiece. While he paced at the end of the dugout, I leaned forward. I could see the windows of Mr. Percy's suite above the upper deck. His thin, ministerial figure — the white shirt, the black tie, the jacket with the padded shoulders — was visible from the waist up. An aide stood to one side of his high-backed leather chair, waiting to take the receiver whenever Mr. Percy was finished shouting into it. "Right," Cap said.

I sat back and looked at him. He handed the receiver to Lunch, a look of grim and dejected disgust lending his face an almost thoughtful cast. He gazed out beyond the dugout railing and watched Otis being lifted from the ground. As Cliff Thompson supported him, Otis hopped along beside him on one stiff leg, the other bent at the knee and held up like a flamingo's. The fans — in a dutiful and grudging show of appreciation (Otis, since the racial flap in the papers, was perceived as moody *and* black) — slowly rose to their feet and applauded. Cap glared at him as he hobbled down the steps.

"What the fuck is wrong with you now?"

"He may have a ruptured hamstring," Cliff said.

"I didn't ask you. I asked the prima donna."

Greg Arthur, sitting beside me, hung his head and shook it. "I don't believe he's going to start this shit again," he whispered.

Otis seemed stunned by Cap's malevolence. It had, until that moment, been reserved for the rest of us. Cap was also particularly restrained with the black players. He addressed Two-Tone only when necessary, and then with an attitude of professional solemnity. He was reported to have called Oscar Rife lazy and spoiled, then claimed he had been misquoted. But there was a lack of control about him now, something unhinged.

"You're a candy ass, Armstrong. You're in pain because that fourth grader's brain of yours can't make it *past* the pain."

No one in the dugout made a move to stop Cap as he stalked Otis down into the maw of the clubhouse tunnel. A state of catatonia seemed to have come over us, some unwillingness to respond to the world we found ourselves in.

"You're a disgrace," Cap yelled after Otis. "And you'd better think twice about playing for this team again."

We lost eight of our remaining twelve games, the division title, and the favor of the fans. In a funk, I hit .250 over the final fortnight and failed to be the first player since Ted Williams to hit .400, my average fading to a season-ending .386, four points shy of George Brett's title-winning stat.

I spent the off-season bickering with lawyers, talking to other agents, then listening to Hammer's reinvigorated predictions, his assertions of undying fealty and innate wisdom. And when I returned in the spring of '81, I was being paid 20 percent less than the season before — still almost $600,000, but nevertheless an insulting although totally legal salary cut while my contract lingered in option-year limbo. All I wanted was good numbers and low visibility.

At the beginning of the final year of my contract with him, Mr. Percy was still impossibly alive. But then, little else had changed. Czech television was broadcasting mock devastations of cities and countryside every evening as a coercive warning to Polish Solidarity members; Alexander Haig was sending "advisers" to Salvador; and assassins and baseball players were still making the headlines. Mehmet Ali Agca, a Turkish terrorist, tried to assassinate Pope John Paul II before a thronging mass of the faithful in St. Peter's Square; John Hinckley, Jr., crotchety, lovelorn, an obscure figure in the land of the pampered and the famous, took a shot at the Gipper in order to impress a teenage actress; Mark David Chapman, another drifter in the four-color maelstrom of the republic, had murdered John Lennon moments after telling him that he was his biggest fan; and I was asking for $2 million a year. Bang! Pistol shot, clean single. Terror and entertainment. The American yin-yang. The stuff to cow and appease the millions.

The day I showed up at spring training — two days late and coming off the best season in my career, as well as a winter of extended and bitter contract negotiations — I expected the assault of adulation and spiteful opprobrium to begin at once. A fine, owed by me and amounting to $5,000, had been reported in the paper I read that morning on the plane. Outside my hotel room when I arrived were two teenage girls wearing Keds, cutoffs that seemed to have been painted on, and uniform shirts bearing my number.

I had begun sleeping with different women, sometimes girls, on the road. Though never with girls this young. The first one had been a starry-eyed college junior. She came out to the park early, in time for batting practice, and stood at the railing, her hands clinging to it as if she expected someone to come along and try to drag her away. Each time I looked in her direction, she was staring at me, or actually trying to stare into me, to pour every ounce of her being into mine — as if that were possible. And her expression, a sort of bottomless vacuity in her eyes, told me one thing: that I could take her and do with her whatever I wanted, which was, of course, what she expected I wanted. She had to completely eradicate herself, allow herself to be my object, an extension of my consciousness, as if that surrender would give her an identity, a bizarre sense of satisfaction. After the game, I walked along the railing and, without even looking up at her said, "Meet me by the gate." When I strolled out of the clubhouse, she was there, dressed in a cheerleader's uniform, hands clasped around a rolled program held to her breast. She looked like some demented version of a bride. When we got back to my room she fingered the odd items I had laying on my dresser as if they were totems. And when we fell into bed, she offered herself up to me as if she expected to be anointed, to be penetrated by the primal force of the universe. And the image of her that resonates in my mind is of her lost face, a wild mane of hair spread out around it, hovering above the almost hypnotically vibrant black-and-red lettering of her uniform top, which she had left on. It was the incongruity between that pulsating, neon-bright surface — the uniform turning her into an icon, something permanent and deathless — and the paleness of her face, signifying the unfathomable, perhaps desperately empty being inside the uniform, that haunted me, and, in a way, made me feel that I had touched something dark, something empty, the obverse of innocence perhaps. And yet it energized me. I began to hit again. When I did, the world came back to me. Not in abstract terms, but concretely. I returned to the majors, returned to my home with Barbara and Elizabeth. Praise was squandered on me without end. My name began appearing once more on the covers of newspapers and magazines. I had made the trip down and back, and now everyone wanted to welcome me upon my return, take part in my resurrection, as if in some way it was what they had all along wished for and, somehow, even arranged. There were days, as the fans leapt to their feet watching me rocket a fastball out of the park, when I wanted to surrender myself to them, to bound over the stands and fall into their arms and be passed among them over their heads.

Then there were times when I felt nothing but disgust and revulsion for myself, and the allure of celebrity, my susceptibility especially keen that morning I arrived for spring training and found two girls, barely in their teens, waiting outside my room. It may have been the lingering jet lag, or the soreness in my limbs scraping through the fading layers of my hangover, but when I looked at the dark-haired one, her face as flawlessly innocent as Barbara's had been the first time I saw her, a sense of longing plunged through me, and my heart became an iron weight. For a moment, it was difficult to remember where, or even who, I was.

"Can we help carry your bag, Mike?" the dark one asked.

I looked at her for a moment and, because I truly wanted to know, felt myself on the verge of asking her, "Who do you think I am? What do you think I'm going to do for you?" But it was not her place to answer these questions, or to be thoughtlessly confused and hurt by them. So finally I just said, "No. Thanks, though. It's all right."

"We could hold your bat." The one who said this giggled.

"I think you'd be better off boning up for your SATs."

"How about your balls?"

I smiled as I closed the door to my room. "Bye." When I threw the bolt, I heard them in the hallway, laughing like the schoolgirls they were. I stood there a moment, then unpacked, showered, and left for the stadium.

In the clubhouse, one of the batboys, a 130-pound kid — twenty-five-inch waist, arms as undeveloped as hot dogs, a chest as flat and unmuscled as a cereal box — was standing, shirtless, a towel draped around his neck, in front of a group of sportswriters gathered around my locker. They laughed whenever the kid finished speaking. As I approached, I could hear what they were saying.

"You think you deserve all that money, Mike?" one of them asked the boy.

"Hey, when you hit three eighty-six and have the biggest dick in baseball to boot, see if you're happy with the minimum wage."

The writers laughed again and the boy beamed like a Little League MVP. Until he saw my face. A few of the writers turned, lowered their eyes, and began to move away from my locker, several of them meekly, a few others lingering, staring at me as if to say that, in some way, they owned me, and wanted me to know it. One or two even said hello. Another asked me if I would give him an hour for an interview.

"Talk to me about it another time," I said, my eyes holding the boy where he stood. As I walked toward him, my teammates taunted me, adding to the weight of the boy's humiliation.

"Thrash him, Mike."

"Whip that boy's ass, dude."

"Make him balance your checkbook for you."

The boy had pulled the towel from around his neck and was holding it in his hands. I stopped in front of the chair separating us. He looked at me directly, as if that were the only way he could redeem himself. "Sorry, Mike," he said.

I made him look at me for another moment, then said, "Don't worry about it." I said it lightly, holding back the heft of the words, and with their weight any clear reading of them. It was only day one. One-eighty to go. Six years had taught me two things: you came back as someone else every spring; and save a little for the end. It was a long season. If I didn't know who I was yet, or what they would turn me into over the relentless nights and headline days of the coming year, why should anyone else? I dropped my bag onto the chair and looked away from the boy. The moment my eyes released him, he stole away as if he had been given a telepathic hit-and-run signal. When I looked up, I saw an envelope with the club's insignia embossed in the upper left-hand corner tacked to the crossbar of the locker's top shelf. My name was printed on it in Mr. Percy's spidery script.

"The kid's got you down pretty good," Otis Armstrong said. He was seated beside me at his locker, taping his leg.

"Yeah, not bad," I said, taking the letter. No chance it could be good news. If they like you, they call. I dropped it into my gym bag, then took out a brown plastic bottle with a prescription label taped to it. Otis had a Coke sitting beside him on the floor. I slipped one of the green amphetamines into my mouth, then picked up the can and washed the pill down with some of the sweet, flat liquid. Otis looked up at me.

"Man, are you doing that shit to your body already? It's only spring."

"Yeah, well, you know. Avoid the Christmas rush." I looked down at Otis. His hands were still wrapping an Ace bandage around a thigh as squat and thick as a fire hydrant. "How's the leg?"

He shrugged. "We'll see."

I changed into my uniform, Otis suiting up beside me, then reached into my bag and opened the envelope that had been left on my locker. Inside, on a piece of pale blue rag paper, were the words, "Mike, come and see me. Let's talk." And his baronial signature, E.P.P., in a filigree worthy of Age of Enlightenment script. I exhaled, and Otis, reaching for his mitt, looked over at me.

"Looks like they're planning on getting an early start on you this year."

"Then they'd better change their plans. I'm not in the mood."

I went out onto the field, loosened up, did wind sprints until the southern heat and humidity opened my pores like a hot bath and the speed kicked in. When it was my turn for batting practice, I drove pitch after pitch over the outfield fence, the drug making the ball seem as if it were winging in from the mound in slow motion, nothing around me moving as fast as I wanted it to. An infernal tirelessness began to drive me, my limbs propelled by a synergistic force that was part drug and only part me. I repeated to myself with every swing, "Machine, machine, machine." When I was convinced I was one, I turned. Up in his rooftop bunker, behind the tinted walls of his suite, Mr. Percy was staring down at me through a pair of binoculars, which were held up to his eyes by a stock-still aide. Knowing he could read my lips, I raised one arm, pointed toward the main offices, and said, "Now."

Eighteen

"YOU LOOK GOOD, Mike."

"It's the steroids."

"Come in and sit down. Sit."

The office had been redecorated, enlarged and depersonalized like the rest of the spring training complex. With attendance booming, Mr. Percy announced his decision to update our antiquated facilities. The old park had been a shaky rink of flaking, forest-green bleachers bordered by three-foot-high fences and a mud parking lot. Capacity: thirty-two hundred, max. Press box the size of a lavatory stall, loudspeaker system made out of baling wire and used soup cans. Waist-high clapboard separated the stands from the field. When I first came up we played for white-haired couples and dozing retirees. Die-hard fathers my age, or slightly older, capped sons and daughters in their arms, speckled the crowd, their enthusiasm as fresh as roadside flowers. Once, I even had a foul ball tossed back to me. Someone hit a loping, opposite-field line drive that hopped over the fence into the stands before I could run it down.

"You lose this?" The ball, bright white except for one mint-green smudge where the grass had brushed it, was held up by a thin man in a cream-colored short-sleeved shirt, his arms and face toasted the color of an almond. He snapped his wrist and flipped the ball over the fence. Beside him was an elderly woman, broad as a barrel in her chintz dress, who patted his other arm and smiled, nodding, like it was nice to meet me. The last time I went to the wall after an eyebrow-high bullet heading foul, somebody ripped the glove off my hand and bolted. I stood there like my pants had fallen down, while the rest of the fans hooted with pleasure.

Our new complex, twenty miles up the road from the old site, had seven-foot-high chain-link fences surrounding the field, a rooftop press box, and nine thousand plastic seats designed by a Japanese bus manufacturer who guaranteed them to be rust-, scratch-, and graffiti-repellent. Minimum-wage security guards protected the entrances, forbidding any unauthorized individual access, a cheap militia rounded up from the ranks of the pensioned and the bullying. Parking was orchestrated by short-tempered men wearing reflective orange vests over blue uniforms. Batting practice was held in secret, the two-story-tall outfield fences draped with sea-green plastic tarps lashed to the uprights. Broadcast rights had been sold to a cable sports network, blacking out all other coverage, including the local station back home. The media department operated out of a pair of trailers behind the clubhouse entrance, the area cordoned off by police horses and more chain-link fence. Thin strips of metal, as flimsy as venetian blinds, were woven into the fence, giving the place the look of a Federal Witness Protection compound. Naturally, the slats matched the color of the piping on our uniforms.

Erected on old swampland, the stadium had been donated to the team by a real estate consortium based in the Bahamas. A motel for the players had been included as part of the package, and Mr. Percy received royalties on all rented rooms at the public hotels and rides at the theme park that had been constructed along with the complex. Condominiums with twenty-four-hour-a-day golf courses, an on-the-premises shopping mall, and the first oceanside emergency room were available. Prices started in the low six-figure range, ballooning to the half-million mark for a three-bedroom-and-Jacuzzi model with on-line stock market capacity, and free lifetime passes to the roller coaster. For a price, Mr. Percy allowed the builders to name streets after team players, living and dead. A mortuary had been named after my predecessor, Ted Monday. It offered the first drive-through viewing facilities in the area. Videotaping of wakes and interments were also available, as were headstones in the shape of home plate.

I sat down in a chrome-and-leather chair opposite Mr. Percy. Behind him, through the plate glass, I could see the arched metal girders and poured concrete roof. Beyond that, a Ferris wheel surrounded by new construction sites, a few coconut palms, and an expanse of land-filled swamp.

"Well, what do you think of the new place?"

As he was wheeled toward me, his spine bowed, pitching his upper body forward, his arms hung from his pinched frame like pincers. He looked like a huge insect, something that fed on strange, milky fluids. A subtle change seemed to have overtaken his features during the off-season. Perhaps it was some new medication, or the lowering of his tax rate. He seemed more decrepit, his skin hanging from the bones of his face like a wrinkled shirt, yet, at the same time, more charged and animated. There was still no color in his eyes, but they seemed somehow more beneficent and insidious. Radiant, and black as onyx. And they matched his suit. He appeared to have invested in a new one of those, as well. The fabric was richer than his old ones, less synthetic. Dandruff speckled the shoulders of the jacket like a fine spray of salt, and a regimental pin was tacked to his right lapel, which had been tapered to a traditional width, the rococo fashions of the seventies left behind as we swung into a new decade. His tie was pure silk and appeared not to be clipped on like a schoolboy's. I could smell his fetid breath as he came close to me.

"It's nice," I said. "All you're missing is the machine-gun turrets."

He laughed, which was always a sign that he wanted something from me, also, that threats and tantrums were lurking just behind the fugitive show of civility and ostentatious goodwill. I was struck by an odd sense of having lived the same moment before. I had a memory of it, one that was connected to the idea of the moment (is this possible?) but not its physicality — that all seemed different. The angle of the light, the fanning out of the room around me, the absence of Cap's chain-smoking pacing, of Lunch dozing in the corner chair. Even the mute sense of my own heft. I was twenty pounds thicker than I had been my rookie year, muscle that translated into dollar signs and decimal points. Yet I had the feeling that the moment was being repeated, or had in some way occurred and was now being distilled and deepened, leaving only Mr. Percy and myself face to face with each other, all the rest sucked into a void.

"Always the kidder," he said, angling his chair closer to my own until we were sitting arm to arm, his face no farther from mine than the width of a generous strike zone. With half a wave of his hand he dismissed his aide; an instant later it seemed as if the two of us had been alone together in the room for centuries. The smoked tint of the wall-to-wall glass window gave the sweep of sky surrounding us a flat, opaque cast, a colorlessness that was either devoid of meaning or pulsing with it. The central air-conditioning vent blew cool, hushed, damp air into the room. And, as the rankness of Mr. Percy's breath mixed with it, I had the sense of being entombed.

"How are you, my boy? Happy?"

"With a twenty percent salary cut?"

Mr. Percy brushed my protest away. "Pennies."

"One hundred and forty-three thousand dollars' worth," I said. In spite of the sum, Mr. Percy remained unimpressed.

"I've lost more being on hold to my broker."

"I didn't think you owned stocks. Just industries."

"Ah, wit. The balm of the overeducated and the middle class."

"Upper middle class."

"Hair splitting! If you work for someone else and need medical insurance, you're middle class."

"You don't have health insurance?"

"Boy, I have hospitals."

There was something tantalizing in Mr. Percy's bluster. In a curious way, it was endearing, or at least seductive. To be allowed near the source of such immense wealth, to be treated to the appearance of being taken into his confidence, was also loathsome, somehow obscene. Perhaps because there was something depraved about the limitlessness and scope of his influence. He counseled heads of state, underwrote covert military operations, funded campaigns, bought elections, employed and laid off hundreds of thousands. He dictated the fates of major corporations, and directed the progress of several ostensibly sovereign nations. He owned the patent on the cure for cancer, but wouldn't release it for spite; he had purchased a country when an exiled tyrant who had befriended him required asylum. Who he was depended on how freely you were willing to let your imagination run with rumor, or the tenuously substantiated facts circulated by a king-making press — a large portion of which he himself owned. Reclusive, bound to a wheelchair since childhood, he had inherited a chain of steel mills when he was nineteen, then collaborated on the genesis of fiber optics technology in a private laboratory located on an island off the coast of Nova Scotia. He expanded his financial empire into communications, purchasing the team as part of a packaged buyout of a major media conglomerate. He became notable for his eccentricity, first by introducing, and then trashing, the first and only tie-dyed uniforms. His parsimony when it came to player salaries was well publicized, and his attempt to have the reserve clause guaranteed in perpetuity by Congress was heralded as an act of impudent Americana. Celibate by circumstance, he never married. Without an existing heir, he was reported to have designated Cap Carver the beneficiary of a sizable portion of his legacy, including full ownership of the team and all its minor league affiliates. This was repeatedly denied by Cap and his attorneys, and scoffed at by Mr. Percy, though documents concerning his efforts to legally adopt Cap were said to exist on microfilm in a locked, underground vault. He had become notorious, larger than the game itself in a way, when, in 1977, a female reporter sued him for denying her access to the clubhouse. She claimed that the action was sexually discriminatory — women were allowed in the locker rooms that year and ever since — and thereby illegal under the equal protection and due process clauses of the Fourteenth Amendment. In a fearless move that forever endeared him to misogynists, and caused a temporary decline in female attendance, Mr. Percy countersued, saying to her in a publicly recorded conversation, "Go ahead, girlie. I've bought off more judges than you have pubic hairs." When he lost in circuit court, he responded by purchasing the publishing company that owned the magazine she worked for. Attorneys advised him that firing her would lead to another round of lawsuits. So, not to be stymied, he raised the magazine's cover price to thirty-five dollars. It went down the tubes in three months. Shortly afterward, he was voted "The Most Despicable Man in America." To some, Mr. Percy's contempt was so absolute that it inspired a nihilistic sort of faith. There was something grand in his unbridled scorn. If you were a tad insecure or needy for a moment, his spell could have the overwhelming pull of a black hole.

"So, did you get me up here to tell me how much you're worth?"

"I wouldn't insult you by being so boring."

"No, you'd rather do it by trimming my paycheck."

"I assure you I had nothing to do with it."

"Right."

"The computer spits out paychecks. If you're unsigned during your option year, it deducts twenty percent automatically."

"Technology with a human face. Nothing like the pastoral life of baseball."

"Why do you always have to reduce it to money?" he asked, feigning genuine anger. Or perhaps he was genuinely angry, which I couldn't accept.

"You want to be friends?" I asked him.

"That would be nice."

"I'm no longer 'nice.' Five years ago, I was 'nice.' "

"Don't pity yourself. It's beneath you."

"I don't. Let's just say I have a low threshold for flattery. I don't need you, or anyone else, telling me how bright, great, and wonderful I am. Okay?"

He pointed a finger at me. "If you're unhappy, you have only yourself to blame. You're who you are because you wanted it. You used us as much as we used you." He lowered the finger. "I'm just disappointed to see that someone as bright as you hasn't realized that we can use each other on another level. What the hell are you stopping for?"

I didn't know. He'd lost me once we left the rhythm of baseline-to-baseline insult and retort behind. The truth was, I'd taken him for senile. The call to his office, the annual coddling and reproof. It had become a rite of spring, something dependable, like the change of seasons. I believed he indulged in it merely out of habit, a gruff pageant that restored his self-confidence, the event followed by an immediate loss of memory and a brief nap. I imagined he spent most of his time with his knees tucked under an afghan as he drowsed in the subtropical sunshine like a fading hibiscus. When I looked more closely, I could see that he was anything but withering, though. There was a splendid firmness in his wrath. And his disappointment in me seemed to promise the unraveling of secrets, life-altering glimpses into the clockwork of my own being.

"You don't know, do you?" he said. "You think we've come as far as we can. Now you're speechless because you know I'm right, and you realize we haven't." He sat upright in his wheelchair, leaning his weight on the arm nearest me. We were silent, and I felt my mind going blank under the resolve of his scrutiny. "Of course you're no longer nice," he said. "Do you think I would have let you stay that way?" As if certain that he would not be rebuffed, he reached out and laid one hand on one of my own, then patted it firmly. He seemed to be reassuring me that it was all right for me to silently acknowledge the depths of my debt to him. "What did I say to you nearly six years ago when I signed you to your first contract?" he said.

" 'I've suffered financial reversals. Forty-four five.' "

Mr. Percy burst into a fit of laughter, tickled, it seemed, both by the acuity and pettiness of my grudge, and by the memory of his own resplendent cheapness. "I knew you'd slip that in somehow. You think I screwed you? Sure, fine, all right. But be objective for a moment. You've made out handsomely. You were a rookie on a roll, and you stepped into a quarter-million-dollar contract. Big money for those days."

I hesitated, then grunted in assent, conceding the historical accuracy of the remark, nothing else.

"The only reason you were unsatisfied was because that walking quagmire you've got for an agent filled your head with gibberish about instant pots of gold. That's the trouble with all of them. They think in terms of fourth-grade addition, and not one of them has the foresight of the six P.M. weatherman. You want the biggest numbers? Put the number you want on a piece of paper, and I'll sign it."

"I'm gone at the end of the year," I said, immediately regretting it. There was something shallow and aggressive in the remark's finality, a gloating, payback type of spite. I felt it was cheap, and lacked class. There was also a clarity to the decision that made me doubt its validity. Or perhaps this was simply Mr. Percy's insidious ability to make all decisions that ran counter to his own wishes seem ill conceived and intrinsically wrong.

"If that's what you want, so be it," he said. "I won't stand in your way."

"You can't."

"Don't be so sure." He was leaning forward, mixing the allure of whispered revelation with bare-toothed threat. Then he sat back again. "Nevertheless, I'll help with the transition if you like. I can bid you up, then let one of the other lunkheads in the league feel he's stealing you away from me." He leaned in again, his hand settling back on my own. "But where will you go, Mike?" He said this to me like I was five. "Atlanta?" Pause. "Cleveland?" Pause. "Minnesota? What will you do in Minnesota? Go into iron mining in the off-season? Start a dairy farm? I'll be frank with you. The idyllic life sucks. It's leaky roofs, bad weather, and mud tracked across the kitchen floor. Dealing with it is inherited stupidity. Believe me, it's not for you. Especially — I'll be honest, I've heard it — when your marriage has the life expectancy of a hundred-watt bulb."

"How would you know?"

"I know." He took my question the wrong way. As a challenge not to his authority in the area of intimacy, but to the veracity of his charge. "Lou Gehrig you're not," he added, raising his eyebrows.

"You compared me to him when you signed me for a song."

"You were an innocent. I used innocent symbols. It was part of your education."

"Which included screwing me in dollars and cents."

"The five hundred was didactic, I'll admit that. But it's time you saw that money isn't the stumbling block between us. Answer something. Not for my sake — I know the answer — but for yourself. When have I ever denied you the money you've deserved? Think about it."

I didn't have to. My image bank was flashing highlights of the scenario like a card sharp dealing blackjack. My financial situation, his intercession. Forcing me to take a loan I didn't want — or did I? — when I needed money for a house and the IRS as a rookie. Six years later, he was still fishing for a thank-you. Perhaps something even deeper — devotion.

"You've always gotten it," he continued. "Haven't you?" He wanted an admission. Or perhaps he wanted me to dispute his claim, tell him I hadn't asked for the money. That way he'd know he owned me completely.

"Okay. I've gotten the money," I said. "So what?" I was certain that the sound of resignation, of an accepted bitterness, was evident in my voice. Letting him have the victory was mechanical, the pleasure I granted him by acquiescing as meaningless to me as praise shouted down from the stands. Every inch of my personal life which Mr. Percy, the fans, or the press insisted on taking, either by condemnation or flattery, I willingly gave up. Implosion: the cleanest form of suicide. No spattered brains, no corpse as chilled as a refrigerated side of beef to bag and cart down to the morgue. Very corporate, actually. I had a wife and child, put on a uniform, went to work, and created a mountain of paper wealth. I could self-destruct and yet be extremely productive at the plate at the same time. I seemed engaged in a headlong retreat from the world. Who knows, maybe it was a lingering inclination from my Cold War childhood, some generationwide desire to make ourselves small in the face of seemingly inevitable global annihilation. Freedom through contraction. Shrinkage was all. At any rate, the only thing I was willing to hold on to was my hitting. Singles, doubles, home runs; they were the only part of my life that wasn't compromised.

"All right. Fine," Mr. Percy said. "You've decided that you want it to mean nothing to you."

"It doesn't mean anything to me."

"Come on. I know you. You speculate on the way your toast is buttered. You're rankled over the salary cut."

"I can live with it."

"Would you sign a new contract if I put one in front of you right now?"

"No chance."

"It would make you the highest-paid player in the game."

I paused. Mr. Percy's eyes were mischievously bright. I began to smile at him as I fought back a smirk. "How much is it going to cost me?"

"Save the naive cynicism for your intellectual friends."

"You expect me to trust you?"

"God, no. I just expect you to see that we can use each other more productively. There's money out there to be made."

"Good. Then you can start helping me make it by paying me my full salary."

"Why should I?"

"Because it would be the right thing to do."

"What's right is that I shouldn't pay you a penny more than I absolutely have to in order to keep you."

"It's also right that I shouldn't make a cent less than I'm absolutely able to."

"Agreed."

"But you'll screw me just because the rules are in your favor."

"Absolutely. Just as you're going to do the minute your contract's up."

"Aren't you worried that my productivity will flag if I'm not happy?"

"I wouldn't care if you were the most miserable son of a bitch on earth. Do you honestly think I believe you're going to let your statistics fall off with a free-agency opportunity coming up?"

"It was a cheap argument. I didn't think you'd buy it."

"I don't. Which is why I think we should settle our differences now."

"Why?"

"Because at the moment I'm dealing from a position of strength. I'm always more amenable that way." He said this with a sternness that puzzled me. I had been ready to stand up and leave. The likelihood of going around in circles seemed inevitable. But Mr. Percy's sudden move away from a coy friendliness caught my interest. There was the possibility that I would be able to watch him operate on a new, perhaps more elegant level of deceit. I'll confess to being perversely fascinated by the man. There was a tidal pull to his loathsomeness, a regularity that was hands-down hypnotic, if not daunting. He could be supportive, prom-ising you the world — and able to give you most of it — if he wanted to be. I stayed because I wanted to know where I stood, at the moment, in his conception of things.

"So, is this a new tack? You're going to be honest with me."

"I've never been anything but honest with you. You've just always managed to turn my words around in order to keep your-self mired in abject confusion. That's why I keep telling you the money is beside the point."

"You've never lied to me?"

"Of course I've lied to you. But you were supposed to see through that. Do you think you're going to play baseball for the rest of your life?"

"What does that have to do with anything?"

"Ah. I have your attention. Finally." He said it like a school-master, condescending yet genteel, as if displeased by the ersatz form of intelligence he was forced to educate. He leaned forward, his eyes bearing down on mine. "How would you like to run a network?" he said.

"Excuse me?"

"Television. A network. How would you like to be president of one?"

Right now I was about to say, I'm all sweaty, my self-protective patter operating on automatic pilot. But I caught myself. I could hear Mr. Percy's vilifying bluster, his impatient disappointment with me thumping inside my head like shutters banging against the side of a house during a summer storm. I felt aware of being beyond glibness. It struck me as retrograde, used up, good only for self-deprecating evasions and pat, subject-closing retorts. For keeping myself locked up and in the dark.

I shifted position in the chair, slouching now and crossing both my arms and legs in a sort of fetal crouch. Involuntarily, my right foot, dangling six inches above the plush carpeting, began to twitch, pumping the air as if spastically working an invisible bass drum pedal. Its ticking measured the pulse of my thoughts.

"Why?" I said.

"Why?" He looked at me. He was, or seemed to be, incredulous, as if he were consciously misunderstanding my question. "How about money? Power? An endless supply of eighteen-year-old beauties? Son, let me tell you something. The script doesn't change."

"I meant, what is it going to get you?"

He looked up at the ceiling as if he had to think about it. Then said, "Oh . . . the network."

"That has the ring of truth to it."

"The pursuit of power usually does."

As the two of us sat there, I noticed that, despite the amphetamines, I felt inordinately calm. There was a reassuring end point to Mr. Percy's quest: the balm of nihilistic, predatory despair. His rapaciousness precluded any sense of doubt, and without that the final quivering of moral tension vanished. Experiencing this was cleansing, free of cant and hypocrisy. Aesthetically, it was pleasing as well. A nice straight line — clear, spare, and elegant. But morally I was numb to it. Having reduced myself to a hitting and fielding machine, shutting down my emotions in order to drift in a cocoon of economically protected solipsism and celebrity-fueled catatonia, I was the wrong guy to ask. In terms of conscience, I was inert.

"Think of it," Mr. Percy said. I felt as if I were being told a bedtime story by Richard III. "Tremendous wealth. Limitless cultural and political influence. And, if that's not enough, a steady supply of the world's finest pussy." He put one hand on my arm. "I didn't offend you by saying pussy, did I?"

I frowned at him for a moment. "I think I've heard it before."

"I thought so. You chase enough of it." He said this with a tinge of judgment and, I thought, even envy.

"Are you spying on me now?"

"I read it in the *Sporting Times*."

"That was a hatchet job."

"You mean not a word of it was true?"

"They were trying to make me look like a satyr." I paused. "Don't you own a piece of that rag?"

"I'm a loyal subscriber," he said. "Have been for years." His sincerity bordered on the Nixonian. A moment later, he burst into a grin. "I lied. I set the whole thing up."

I yanked my arm free of his placating grip and bounded out of my seat. "Jesus Christ!"

"Calm down." He seemed legitimately afraid.

"I have a fucking wife."

"Well, if that's who you were fucking, you wouldn't have this problem."

I spun on the balls of my feet and lunged at him, grabbing the arms of his wheelchair and swinging him toward me until we were face to face. "If I lose my daughter over this, I'll kill you. You hear me?"

"You don't have to —"

I shoved his chair backward, slamming it into the wall behind him. A potted palm shivered from the vibration, and the old man's head snapped back as if he'd been jolted by ten thousand volts. The crown of his skull smacked the wall, his eyeballs crossed and rolled back up into his head.

"I said did you hear me?"

"Yes." He spit the word back in my face, refusing to acknowledge for an instant that he was at a disadvantage. I glared at him, then released the iron rungs of the chair and stood up.

"Who the hell do you think you are?" I said to him, feeling, for the first time since we'd been cast together, like his equal.

He stared at me with what seemed to be a sense of profound desolation, which was outdone by an even more acute self-knowledge, and said, "I'm the only friend you've got."

"Right." My cap had fallen out of my back pocket. I scooped it up off the floor, then turned and headed for the door.

"Look at yourself," he shouted, his voice, for some reason, sounding to me exactly like my father's. He caught up to me as I neared the door, and blocked my path. "Who do you have besides me?" he shouted. "You've been swindled and abandoned by your agent. You have no friends, no faith, no family. You loathe the game as much as I do. And now you're losing your wife. So you idealize your daughter because you think that redeems you."

"Get out of the way."

"Kick me out of the way. Go ahead. Hit me. I won't sue. I'll just release a press statement. 'Frustrated golden boy strikes crippled owner.' No team would offer you the minimum wage come November."

"Move." I gripped one arm of the chair and spun him aside. His hand darted for my wrist and clamped itself around it.

"You're nothing without the money," he said.

"Let go."

"You have no center, there's nothing you believe in. Look at yourself, for God's sake. You're twenty-seven and you're falling apart from booze and drugs." I looked down at him. "Don't think I don't know about it," he said.

I pulled my arm away and moved toward the door.

"Do you really think any judge in the world is going to let you anywhere near your daughter?" He paused and waited for me not to turn the doorknob, which I did not. "Ah, guilt," he said. "Sometimes I'm nostalgic for it. Sit down, Mike."

"No."

"No? Fine. Stand there like a fool. Or else get out. You'll have to forgive me if I'm testy, but I don't like being manhandled in my own office." He turned away and guided himself back toward his desk. I hesitated, unable to look at him, unable to leave. "Go on. What are you waiting for?" His tone slipped an octave, glowering now with an unrestrained contempt. "I only made you the highest-paid rookie in the game when you came up."

"In that market, I was a bargain."

"A bargain's what you pay yesterday's prices for. You got top dollar when I signed you. So go on, leave. You don't owe me a thing. Just ask yourself who kept a roof over your head."

"I would have survived."

"You would have folded up like a cot and died. You're only able to stand on your own two feet now because of me. Who do you think kept you in the majors? Carver? He wanted to put you on waivers when you couldn't hit a softball in a bar league contest. He sent you down to the minors and then wanted to get rid of you. Yes," he said, nodding as he looked at me. "Now you remember. Who do you think ordered you brought back up?"

"I came back, didn't I?"

"Absolutely. You know why? Because I had faith in you. I gave you the chance. You've got the rest of the world licked, face it. You've won the batting crown, you're making over a half-million a year. The only one you're fighting is me. So if I want to help, why don't you let me?"

All the momentum of my anger was spent. Mr. Percy seemed worn out as well, somehow beyond malice, and without the will to sustain his relentless energy for deceit. He turned away from me, squaring his wheelchair with the wide plane of his office window. As I watched him sitting there — the hunched and bony shoulders, the frail hands gripping the handles of the armrests, the bald crown of his skull shining like a dance floor — I thought I saw in him the small boy who was, perhaps, once daunted by the world. I stood behind him, and the silent sweep of the room held us within the stasis of our mutually defeated truce. Mr. Percy was looking out at the field. Below us, on the nearly iridescent arc of outfield grass, players in gleaming white uniforms were running wind sprints, their throwaway grace thrilling even from this height.

"Do you know what it's like never to have walked?" he said. "A simple thing like that." He paused for a moment, watching several of the men he owned dash across right field, racing one another like schoolboys. "They say every infant has the instinct for it." He looked down at my teammates a bit longer. I saw Oscar and Otis jog onto the field, Otis flipping the lenses of his shades down as he trotted out beyond first base. "They're children, Mike. They need someone to lead them. Do you think that any one of them comprehends the possibilities we're being offered by cable television, satellite dishes, global markets? The limitless potential for profit is merely the icing on the cake. There's a higher moral imperative at stake. Civilizing the world." He spun his chair around and faced me again. "Civilizing the world, Mike. This game," he said, opening his arms in a river-parting gesture to indicate and embrace the glories of the club's imperial past. The polished brass and gold plaques hanging on the walls, gleaming like chalices. The championship pennants as garish as the colors of a pirate ship. The framed and yellowing publicity photographs of former stars, including the first black player to join the organization, several years after the lifting of the color ban. A bronze bust honoring him was kept locked in a case with other assorted team memorabilia and a boastful array of civic awards. "This game is America. Freedom. Individual effort. Democratic mobility and racial harmony. It's all there. With the game, we can bring America to the world."

As I listened, I didn't question Mr. Percy's madness. That he was cynical and misanthropic failed to amaze me. He was simpler and more naive than I ever imagined. A deep streak of sentimentalism ran through him, a patriotic plumb line that balanced him like the centerboard of a sailboat. The will to power is the sound of one hand clapping. Face it, even the best of tyrants needs a teddy bear, a little nationalistic ballast to smooth out the trip through the void. "For God and Country" has been the security blanket for who knows how many despots. Why not Mr. P.? In a perverse way, this instinctive drive for symmetry was, I suppose, actually a sign of health. But I still didn't go for it. When he appealed to me on a level of pure malevolence and greed, he had a chance. But buy into his Norman Rockwell version of apartheid? No way, José.

"You don't actually expect me to buy that bullshit, do you?" I said.

The expression of benign enlightenment that glazed Mr. Percy's features was suddenly curdled by scorn. "You wouldn't, would you?"

"Bring America to the world? Give me a break."

"Yes, bring America to the world. Have you got any brighter ideas?"

I was silent. Up until that moment I believed that his public shows of patriotism and soapbox jingoism had been carefully contrived charades designed to boost gate receipts and mass media revenues. The fervor was pure advertising, no more sincere than a life insurance ad. True, there had been rumors of political ambition on his part in the past. A Richard Nixon–Edmond Percy ticket had even been referred to by several hawkish and nostalgic sportswriters. But promoting a man confined to a wheelchair as one of the leading symbols of America was not what the Republican party had in mind. Mr. Percy's political role was reduced to backroom lobbying and a slew of illegal campaign contributions, one of which he was indicted for, sentenced, and then pardoned — by Nixon himself. Still, I never credited these ventures with being any more than flirtations with tangents of his outsized and apparently shameless craving for power. I couldn't imagine him, after all, placing himself in a position where he was answerable to anyone, i.e., public office. (Though, on second thought, maybe a pathological, Nixon-style presidency did appeal to him.) Shortly after his failed political bid, he purchased the team, talked the city into refurbishing the stadium, then promised to restore pride to a once great baseball dynasty. His civic boosterism was considered eccentric — he wanted fifty blue stars painted on the ball so it would match the colors of the flag — but, for the most part, harmless. This gave him a good deal of range in terms of manipulating his public image. He seemed conservative and refreshingly radical at the same time. The city was entranced. Headlines came his way with the regularity of junk mail. Attendance tripled, revenues from TV and radio increased, and the team became a hot ticket. All he needed to put him over the top was a winner. During the time I had known him I could never bring myself to accept the idea that he even remotely considered taking himself seriously. As I stood there, though, I realized that he had never considered anything else.

"No," he said, responding to my silence. "I didn't think you would have. That's what's sickening. All this pampered cynicism. Tell me something, what gives you the right to reject what's made you what you are?"

I thought about this for a moment. What was I? Headed for divorce. Hooked on amphetamines. Addicted to a high style of living, and paid half a million dollars a year for being a mass market product. A walking, talking Ken doll. "Listen —" I started to say.

"Listen, nothing. Let me tell you something. You're the pathetic one."

"Look," I said, "if you want to help me with a judge in case it comes down to a custody hearing about my daughter, fine. Name your price, and I'll consider it. Outside of that, skip the lecture bullshit. You're not my father."

As stunned as I was by my callousness, Mr. Percy seemed even more shaken. "This is what you've turned into?" he said.

"Don't start moralizing."

"I wouldn't know where to begin. Does anything affect you? Or are you completely dead inside?"

I moved away from him, toward the window, following some inarticulate urge to stare at a vast, almost barren expanse. Below, my teammates were lined up in rows, boot camp style, working their way through calisthenics. At one time I had been able to see order in the rigors and laws of the game. It seemed to me now no more than a sprawling, inherited inertia, institutionalized entropy. "You're right," I said, finally. I turned and looked at him. "Sorry."

"Right about what?"

"It's impolite of me to feel superior to you." Manners were all I had the stamina for. Mr. Percy grinned. "Don't gloat," I said.

"Who's gloating? Did I taunt you with a mock headline? 'Golden Boy Succumbs to State of Corrupt Despair. Goes 0 for 4'?" I looked away from him. "No," he continued. "Why not? Because I don't take advantage of someone when he's down. I help him. The way I still want to help you." I turned and beseeched him, with my expression, to cut the shit. "Okay, and help myself in the process."

"That's better."

"You didn't buy that manifest destiny horseshit for a minute, did you?"

"No."

"I had you going, though," he said, enjoying himself.

I nodded. "I was ready to be disappointed."

He laughed, one hand pounding the arm of his wheelchair. "I thought that pure greed had scared you off." He began coughing, long, hoarse, phlegm-cracking eruptions that left him breathless. "What a pair," he said. "Huh?" All our caginess and distrust of each other had been exhausted, and I was aware of, but only dimly bothered by, our new, somehow welcome intimacy. I felt as if I had arrived at a place I had been moving toward for a long time. "You know," he said, "you're more of a son to me than you can imagine." Then he let the suggestion drift away without making anything more of it. "It's so good to corrupt someone with a brain," he continued. "You don't know how tedious it can be otherwise."

"Now I'm corrupt?"

"Don't discredit yourself by denying it. You've come so far." I turned my head for just an instant to look at him. "What did I call you when you first came up?" he asked me.

"It slips my mind."

"An idealist. You've just come full circle, that's all. Stick with me and everything will be fine." He put his hands to the wheels of his chair and pushed himself around the side of his desk, speaking as he rolled toward me. "Now this divorce business, and your daughter. If it comes to anything, let me know and we'll fix it. I guarantee you that you'll come out of it all right. But if you can hold things together till the end of the season, it would be better for all of us."

"Why? What's my marriage have to do with anything?"

"Revenues. Team image. Endorsement contracts. I'm not saying it's imperative. Do what you have to to keep your mind on the game. That's what's important. But a divorce could tarnish your image a bit. Nothing catastrophic, you understand, but it could be detrimental around contract time. Particularly if what comes out is a little sordid."

"I haven't done anything sordid."

He held up his hand to stop me. "I'm not passing judgment. Fuck hamsters, for all I care. But, Mike, see, this is the thing." He paused and breathed deeply, almost as if reconsidering his decision to tell me what he was about to. Then he plunged in. "We're in the richest per capita television market in the world. Not only that, our local viewing population reaches upwards of forty million, and it stands to increase by nearly half over the next ten years. Do some simple calculations. Take a four percent share — just four percent — of forty million, which is our current market share for all television games. What do you get?" He slipped a pocket calculator from the accessories sleeve attached to the arm of his wheelchair and punched in the numbers. "One million six hundred thousand," he said. "Now, say the sum total that all your advertisers put together are willing to spend per viewer per broadcast adds up to forty cents a head." He multiplied the preceding number by the new one, saying, "Trust me on these figures. They're accurate. Okay. What's that give you?" He looked at the slim gray bar at the top of the instrument. "Six hundred forty thousand. Fine. Six hundred forty thousand in advertising revenues per game to the network. Now, they keep half, and we get half." He mumbled as he pecked at the tiny keyboard. "Divide by two that's —" He paused and squinted at the figure. "Right. Three hundred twenty thousand. Lost a zero there for a moment. Okay, so: you multiply that three hundred twenty thousand per game by one hundred and sixty-two games." He did. "Fifty-one million eight hundred forty thousand." He looked up at me. "Fifty-two million a year for the TV rights alone. Just the exclusive local cable rights. I'm not even talking about the league share we get from the big boys. I mean just cable."

I was silent. The sum was staggering, but in a self-defeating way. I tried to comprehend the magnitude of it, make the number as literal and daunting as it should have been, but I couldn't. It was as if the century — with its obsessive and mind-numbing rush toward quantification — obviated the possibility of awe. I was able to react to the relative and abstract impressiveness of Mr. Percy's figure with no more than a cerebral sense of excitement.

"Wow," I said.

"Wow? I offer you plans for establishing a global communications empire and you say wow."

"It's not a ninth-inning grand slam in the Series."

"Child's play. This is real power."

"Yeah, but where's the hero?" He was unmoved by my argument. "Okay," I said. "It's a lot of money."

"Damn right it's a lot of money. And it's only the tip of the iceberg. The network's got a ten-year offer for five hundred and twenty million on the table right now. It begins effective January one, 1982, end of this season. You know what I think?" He paused. "I think if we win the pennant, we can squeeze them for another two hundred million. You bring me a championship, I'll share it with you."

"Fifty-fifty?"

He snickered. "This is how it works. Watch." The pennant, Mr. Percy calculated, would bring our audience share up to 6 percent of the market. "More if there's a good race in September." He could hold off on signing the contract until the season was over, then go in with a figure showing a 50 percent share increase and negotiate a higher selling price for the broadcast rights. "Even if I get only one and a half percent," he said, "that's still one hundred and fifty million over the five hundred twenty." He sat forward in his chair. "And do you know what the beauty part is?" He arched his eyebrows. "They'd be financing their own takeover."

Mr. Percy unraveled the scenario for me. He already owned

10 percent of the network's stock. With additional revenues from the sale of the broadcast rights he would be able to buy up more shares, eventually purchasing the network outright. In other words, by increasing its own earnings and profits, the network was selling itself down the river.

I wondered why I wasn't appalled by the overarching specter of his greed. The truth is that it struck me as a paltry and recyclable thing, as much a part of our time as the aluminum can. Greed had created a monstrous void, and I had been playing at the center of it for six years. Left field, batter's box. Newsprint photos, magazine covers. Ten-second close-ups on the Monday Night Game of the Week.

"The point is," Mr. Percy said, "the market's limitless. In ten years, we'll bring it to the whole world."

My attention wandered out through the window again. Blank sky. Empty, cathedral-like sweep of stadium. Teammates moving about like automatons. When I looked back at Mr. Percy, his eyes latched onto mine with their bottomless stare and he said, "I'll give you twenty-five million for ten years, then a network presidency when you hang up your cleats. Just hit four hundred and bring me a championship."

I continued to look at him, nothing registering inside me. I turned away and stared at the broad spine of the outfield, the immense reaches of sky above it. Mr. Percy wheeled himself up beside me. Hands crossed in his lap, he gazed out at the diamond, raising his chin slightly. "It is impressive, isn't it?" he said. I didn't answer. And, as if by instinct, he said, "The important thing is that I have someone to share it with now."

When I glanced down at him, he didn't look back.

Nineteen

I MADE no immediate plans to lead the team to a pennant, in spite of Mr. Percy's lucrative offer. My first concern was hitting, my own numbers and statistics. Mr. Percy announced at the beginning of the season that, as we had folded and finished second the preceding year, every one of us was expendable, including, for the first time in his tenure, Cap Carver. Unloved, his status as a hatchet man diminished by the booming growth of free agency, Cap, a lifetime losing manager, seemed to realize that he was fifty-five, ulcer-ridden, alcoholic, and replaceable. His natural reaction was slow suicide — nonstop drinking, pills to mask its effects, and an implacable plunge into rancorous despair. When an unemployed manager who had won a pennant two years earlier appeared in Mr. Percy's suite one evening at game time, Cap berated Lunch Molloy for no reason, went out, got tanked, and attacked a pool salesman in a roadside bar. Perhaps motivated by an unspeakable sense of pity, we pulled together and won six straight, and the incident, in the light of our first-place standing, was ignored by Mr. Percy. But by mid-May, with Cap changing the lineup daily and for no apparent reason, and Mr. Percy belittling us in the press for floundering in second place, we began to play with a sense of disgust. The money, the greed, the insatiable appetite of the fans — they became larger than the game, the field ceasing to be a sanctuary and becoming, instead, a place to dwell on our bitterness and frustrations. Cap's sole obsession became a championship. Chasing it seemed to be the only thing keeping him alive. And the further we slipped from dominating our division, the more he drank, pulling us down into blackness and despair along with him.

He had gotten drunk more quickly than usual during a night game we were losing pathetically. We knew he kept a flask in his windbreaker pocket. He would disappear into the dugout bathroom three or four times a night, then emerge with an expression of wide-angle obliviousness on his face, a what-did-I-miss look of inquisitiveness and concern. In time, we simply ignored him. But that was what Cap couldn't stand. He required Mr. Percy's unwavering approval; he needed our unflagging attention. It could come in the form of love or hate or fear, but it had to come. And, almost in spite of himself, he always managed to produce a player who was devoted to him. Usually it was the poorest kid on the team, a ghetto-born rookie with a quick bat and a bad attitude. Someone out to prove himself, and too naive to understand that no one cared. But with the average salary hovering at $185,000 a season, disciples were hard to find. The only one of us who still seemed to elicit Cap's approval was Otis. Cap had done the miraculous and apologized to Otis after the incident in the dugout the previous fall, and Otis seemed to accept it. Six weeks into the new season, he was the only one of us playing with any sort of enthusiasm, let alone enough faith to believe that what we did mattered.

Otis was at the plate, leading off the inning, when Cap stepped out of the bathroom. At first Cap seemed not to know where he was. Then he looked up and my eyes met his as he scanned the faces lining the dugout wall. A sure sign that he was wasted — eye contact. Unafraid to look at us, numb to the contempt we had for him. The crack of Otis's bat meeting the ball snared his attention, and Cap's head snapped to the right like a startled cat's, his eyes following the scudding, jackrabbit charge of the ball over the clipped surface of outfield grass. From the bench I could see Otis's arms and legs hammering the air and ground like pistons, his cleats making the leap from distinguishable objects to high-speed blur as he rounded the bag at first and kicked into overdrive going to second. Cap seemed awed by the purity and rough grace of Otis's flight. There was something untainted and regenerative about it, an unmediated desire, elemental as love, that seemed capable of purging all the commercialized rancor from our souls.

"That's fucking baserunning," he said, turning to glare at us. "If half a dozen of you were as fucking hungry, we wouldn't be pissing around in second place."

Oscar Rife stood, pulling on his batting gloves, and said, "If you love him so much, why don't you fuck him?"

Cap, weaving as he moved down through the dugout, squinted at Oscar. "What did you say?" His tongue was thick as a sausage from the booze. "What did you say to me?" It was as if Cap had heard the words but couldn't believe them.

"I said, why don't you fuck him." Oscar stood in the center of the dugout as Cap reeled toward him. Brought up on the streets of a Depression-crippled ghetto, Cap liked to settle matters with his knuckles. For Cap, at five eight and one-forty, with the pectoral muscles of a chicken and the pencil-thin arms and distended belly of a full-time boozer, taking on a half-gassed pool salesman in a tacky, overly air-conditioned bar may have passed for nostalgic machismo. But going mano a mano with Oscar Rife when he was slumping, being sued for divorce, and trying to shake a coke habit was hands down suicidal.

"I'll show you who I'll fuck, you cocksucking coon."

We were playing on national television, filling airtime between the jism of commercials for cars, jockey shorts, cologne, and catastrophic health insurance. So even though I was seated only five feet from the actual event, my memory of it is inverted to some extent, complicated, and at the same time simplified by the ubiquitous, unrelenting presence of videotaped replay. Before any of us could grab Cap — not to save him, but to avert an all-out disgrace while we were being beamed coast to coast — he scooped up a handful of dirt from along the dugout's lip and, following through as if he were swatting the air in front of him, flung it at Oscar's face. Oscar put his hands over his eyes to shield them.

But from two hundred feet and three decks away, it appeared to the eye of the camera that Cap had dismissed Oscar's challenge and Oscar had waved him on, begging Cap to come and get him. Which, an instant later, Cap did.

Moving with a speed and dexterity none of us suspected was any longer possible of him — those shortstop's reflexes still quick after forty years of wear and self-inflicted abuse — he grabbed a warm-up jacket that was hanging on a peg over Johnny Clemmons's head and, brandishing it with matadorial panache, spun it around Oscar's skull. Blind, Oscar stumbled in midcharge. Cap kneed him in the groin, then drove an elbow into his kidneys as Oscar pitched headfirst past him. On screen it appeared as if Oscar had rushed Cap, who, in self-defense, clutched helplessly at the nearest object and tossed it into Oscar's path. When Oscar fell to the dugout floor, Cap began kicking him. Three of us — Cecil Ffolkes, Ollie Sutkiss, and myself — grabbed Cap and wrestled him away, his small, wiry body trying to jerk itself free of our grip with an almost rabid ferocity. A moment later, the fans seated across the stadium who had a clear view of the event rose and began cheering. Others began hooting when the home team's scoreboard monitor cut to cover the tail end of the brawl, the sight bringing the rest of the crowd to its feet. Above us, baseline ticket holders, the half-tanked and innately riotous, began beating on the dugout's aluminum roof, filling the trench with a warped, metallic pandemonium until Mel Thorn bolted up the steps onto the field and challenged the entire loge section to a fight, ending his dubious and impromptu stint as the club's PR man by grabbing his crotch and giving the whole west side of the stadium the jerk-off sign.

"On goddamned, fucking national television!" Mr. Percy burst into the clubhouse moments after the game ended. "You're a fucking disgrace. All of you! When you signed your contracts it was an agreement to produce. And if any one of you doesn't, I'll sue you for misrepresentation. And if you screw up together — collusion! Rife!"

Oscar was pacing at the far end of the clubhouse, swearing to himself, it seemed, and eyeing Cap, who was separated from him by several players as well as a contingent of Mr. Percy's private security force — ex–city cops and semiretired soldiers of fortune.

"What?"

"You've got yourself a ten-day suspension and a ten-thousand-dollar fine."

"Fuck you. Try collecting it. And I'm telling you, trade me — now! I don't have to take this from some white motherfucking juicehead."

"This is baseball, not the NBA. You'll play wherever I tell you to play."

"Bullshit!"

"I said ten days. And do some community work, visit a ghetto while you're moping around. Make yourself useful."

Sitting beside me was Otis, bent forward, his broad back flaring from the waist as he unlaced his cleats.

"You'd better listen or you might wind up with a red star next to your yearbook picture," I whispered.

"Why don't you just shut up, okay?" He didn't look up at me.

"Okay. Relax."

He stopped tugging at his laces, stared at the floor, and shook his head.

"Thorn!" Mr. Percy growled. "You want to tell a city it can whack off, you can pick up the tab for the Kleenex. Ten thousand and ten days."

"You can kiss your fucking pennant good-bye," Thorn said. "Your run production's going to be dick."

"Fifteen thousand. And if you tell me what I can kiss again, you'll be cleaning toilets in Pizza Hut for a living."

"What about him?" Oscar shouted from the back of the bunker, charging forward now to point at Cap. "What about that lowlife scum? " Cap was skulking behind the pack of Mr. Percy's aides, a cigarette clamped between his right index and middle fingers like a syringe. "You going to fine his ass before I break it?"

"You worry about breaking three hundred. I'll worry about my manager."

"You're not going to do anything to him?" Two-Tone said, cutting in.

Mr. Percy turned, looked at him, and said, "Carver's fired."

A feeling that a veneer of reality had been superimposed on the life in the room swept through me and, I was certain, all the others, the trapdoor type of vertigo that generally follows news of assassinations or the death of a parent: all placid surface and nothing but floorless abyss beneath your feet.

Yanking the cigarette butt from between his lips and flinging it past the ear of one of Mr. Percy's blue-suited aides, Cap bulled his way through the guards. "What?" he shouted, leaning down near Mr. Percy's face.

"I said you're fired. Lunch Molloy is the new manager."

"I don't want to be manager," Lunch said, slumped in his corner seat.

"You'll manage if I tell you to, or you'll get a job selling shoes."

Lunch took a moment, then said, "Men's or women's?" with an off-the-wall earnestness that made it hard to read the remark as either dry wit or witless musing.

"He couldn't manage to get mustard on a hot dog," Cap shouted.

"And you can't manage to keep your lips off the nipple of a scotch bottle long enough to discipline these overpaid five-year-olds."

"That doesn't affect my judgment."

"You mean it's always pathetic. Come on," Mr. Percy said, waving over an assistant, "get me out of here."

As the aide took hold of the wheelchair's handles, pivoting the carriage on its heels, Cap reached out and grabbed one arm and spun Mr. Percy back toward him. "You withered old crank. You're pissing away a championship."

"I'll piss away whatever I want. Now get your hands off me, or I'll have you arrested."

He yanked his arm free of Cap's grip and signaled to the aide to wheel him out of the room. Face flushed, the veins in his neck as thick and taut as bass strings, Cap walked in step with the chair, leaning over Mr. Percy and spitting epithets at him with the heedlessness of the truly possessed, a decade's worth of frustration and entombed rage suddenly given over to hysterical articulation. Ten steps later, a foot from the clubhouse doors, Cap darted in front of the chair, dropped to his knees, and began weeping. The roomwide sense of astonishment seemed to yield to a disconcerting feeling of shame, Cap's naked display of blind and helpless need embarrassing everyone but Mr. Percy.

"He's sick," Oscar muttered, "the man is certifiable," amazement cutting through his bitterness.

Oaths were sworn, promises made. Drinking, gambling, griping to the press — all would cease. "Just let me stay. I'll lie down and die for you," Cap said, his palms cupped over Mr. Percy's knees, "if that's what you want."

"Then do it." He shoved Cap aside and rolled out of the room, bodyguards and assistants following on his heels.

Kneeling, head hung, arms draped in resignation, Cap stared at the clubhouse floor and wept. The rest of us remained still and silent, leaving him untouched. Finally, Prayer Pearson, our reconstructed knuckleballer and founder of his own independent mail-order ministry, walked over and said, "Are you all right?"

"Of course he's all right," Oscar shouted. "He's still got his booze and liver pills."

Raising his head, Cap seemed to growl, a deep, instinctive reverberation starting an inch above his scrotum and shaking his frame all the way to the tips of his fingers. He sprang to his feet, grabbed a bat from the rack beside Lunch Molloy's shoulder, and rushed at Oscar, who froze. As Cap charged, thirty-four-ounce bat over his head and no obstacles in sight, his cleats skittered over the rock-hard face of the tile. Two-Tone, leaning back against his locker, deftly shoved the upright chair his foot was resting on forward, into Cap's path. The seat flipped, cartwheeled, and caught between Cap's feet in midstride. The head of the bat hit the floor first, a dull, semihollow ringing filling the room. Cap landed on his chest, his left knee, pulled along by the torque of his body, smacking the tile with one brief clap — *thwack!* — like a single firecracker exploding. When Cap let out his first low-pitched, seemingly involuntary moan, the silence in the room was nudged into the background. The sigh had a pissed-off edge to it, as if Cap would kill somebody if he only had the strength to move.

"Cap, you all right?" Prayer Pearson asked again, moving closer.

Cap, seeming to want to bend his left knee, didn't answer. With his left hand he reached down and touched his pant leg, squeezing the joint gingerly, releasing it an instant later as if he'd received a shock. Blood began to blot through the material, a cherry-colored stain nibbling at the white cotton.

"Why doesn't someone get Cliff?" Lunch said, pushing himself out of his armchair.

"Nice fucking move," Mel Thorn said to Two-Tone, who immediately stood up and kicked aside the chair he'd been sitting in.

"You got a problem?"

"Yeah. Your fucking existence."

Otis grabbed Two-Tone by the arm before he could make a move toward Thorn. "Get your hand off me."

"Come on. Relax," Otis said.

"I'm supposed to take advice from a white man's pet?"

"Why don't you all just bag that noise for now, okay?" Lunch said. He eased down beside Cap, every muscle in the ex–third baseman's body as stiff as beef jerky. If Cap or Mr. Percy had told any one of us to back off and settle down, it would have had a compressing, explosive effect. But Lunch's distracted, off-the-cuff style of authority was palliating. He lacked a sense of malice, and seemed to have no capacity to hold a grudge, particularly one built on petty complaints, and heated, later regretted remarks. Two-Tone untensed a moment later, as Otis, visibly stung by his words, released his arm.

Otis stared at the floor, aware perhaps that Two-Tone was looking at him. But if he was, he refused or simply could not bring himself to acknowledge him. When Two-Tone looked away, his eyes met Mel Thorn's. Hands on his hips, undershirt hanging over his trouser belt, grass-smudged white socks making his feet stubby as mittens, Thorn looked like a pissed-off homeowner roused from his recliner to see what idiot was fucking with his front lawn. The homicidal edge he had at times — particularly if he'd been doing too many greens, either to get up for a game, or to level out the coke-induced hangover from the night before — had yielded to an expression of barely patient expectation, an I'm-waiting attitude usually reserved for stern fathers demanding an apology from an oldest son.

"What do you want?" Two-Tone said.

Thorn stared back at him for several moments. Then, with a look of disgust cinching his features, said, "Fuck it," and turned away.

Lunch ministered to Cap while Ollie Sutkiss ran to the trainer's room to find Cliff Thompson. I turned to Otis, who was leaning forward, one elbow perched on each thigh. His fingers were wrapped around one another, his head down. Several of the others sitting around us — Greg Arthur, Ron Donaldson, Aureliano Santana — stood up and went over to where Cap was lying. Two-Tone tore his shirt open, midnight blue buttons flying off and skipping across the tile floor. He stripped off his T-shirt, threw it into the bottom of his locker, then walked to the buffet table at the other end of the room and looked down at it. A moment later he swept half the dishes from one corner of the table onto the floor with a single swift pass of his hand. He stomped out of the room, bulling his way past Ollie Sutkiss and Cliff Thompson, who were hurrying back in through the doorway.

"Look," I said to Otis, "blow it off. It was a stupid comment."

"Do me a favor," he said, not looking at me. "When you don't know what you're talking about, don't say anything." He said this with an air of almost magnanimous patience, as if he pitied me for being so dumb. There was an undercurrent of entreaty running through it, too: Just leave me alone, was what I heard.

"If you change your mind, I'm here," I said, then stood up and let Otis be by himself.

Red Summers, the clubhouse manager, came into the room, a pack of sportswriters clammering in the tunnel behind him. "They want in," he said to Lunch. "Their thirty minutes are up."

"No press in the clubhouse."

"What do you want me to tell them?"

"I'll tell you what to fucking tell them," Mel Thorn said, moving toward the doors. I caught him by the arm.

"Mel, you pissed off a whole city. Lighten up."

"Tell them no press in the clubhouse," Lunch said, looking at Red with an is-that-so-hard-to-understand expression on his face.

"They're not going to like it."

"So they don't like it."

Red shrugged. "Okay," he said, and turned toward the doors.

Cliff Thompson rolled Cap onto his back. There was a bright red bruise on Cap's right cheekbone, a no-question shiner in the morning. Lying down, the thin shade of skin covering his facial bones pulled tight by gravity, Cap looked almost young. The smooth lines of his youth burrowed through the etched map of his face everywhere but under his eyes, where the bags were the size of pigeon eggs. He put one hand to his forehead and lay there as Cliff snipped a hole in the blood-soaked fabric covering his knee. The tile was cracked where he had landed, a circle the size of a half dollar smashed into hundreds of tiny chips.

"Get me an Ace bandage and call an ambulance," Cliff said. "He has a compound fracture."

One of the batboys ran to the trainer's room for the bandage while Prayer Pearson went into Cap's office and dialed the stadium's medical unit. Cliff tore open the leg of Cap's pants. Covered with blood, a thin shell of bone the size of a thumbnail jutted through the flap of broken skin. A viscous, cranberry-colored glaze surrounded the opening, and blood ran down the outside of his leg. When the batboy returned, Cliff took the bandage, wrapped a length of it twice around Cap's leg just above the knee, cinched it tight, and tied it off.

"Ambulance is on its way," Pearson said, emerging from Cap's office.

Oscar Rife joined the circle, lurking just behind Ron Donaldson and myself, and peering over our shoulders to look at Cap.

"His leg looks like it's shot," Greg said.

Cap lay there, not acknowledging the remark, or, for that matter, even our presence.

"You want to lay off the amateur diagnosis, Arthur?" Lunch said. He kept one hand on Cap's shoulder and gently massaged it.

"You think he got what he deserved?" Oscar whispered to me, tugging at my arm to lead me away from the group.

"I don't think it works that way, Oscar."

"Why did he always have to be starting with me?"

"You started with him."

"Because he was riding me."

"How do you figure that?"

"With all that Otis shit."

"He gives everybody that Otis shit. Don't flatter yourself."

"No, man. He was saying it to me. The man wants to see me go down."

"The man wants to see us all dead. It's a kind of perverse love."

"He embarrassed me on national TV."

"We're all a disgrace. You'll blend in."

"You think I offended Percy the way I talked to him?"

"He doesn't know most of us are alive. Forget it. Just worry about your game."

"I am worried about it. You think it's true?"

"What?"

"That I'm through. I'm thirty-two. I ain't getting any younger."

"Oscar, you're in a slump. It happens. You'll come out of it."

He nodded. He'd gotten what he wanted, what he needed to hear at that moment. This was Oscar. Arrogant as a rooster, insecure as an orphan. His personality fed straight through to his hitting. Forty homers a year, two hundred strikeouts. He chased bad pitches like he'd chased Cap in the dugout, rashly and head-first. And when he finished his motion he was usually in the same position — twisted up and face down on the ground. The fans loved him when he was on top, despised him the moment he fucked up. Surrounded by hangers-on and dubious off-the-field business associates, Oscar either came and went in a whirlwind, or moped in front of his locker wearing nothing but a jockstrap, asking batboys if the fans really loved him. For some, he was hard to take. Others just plain hated him. Now he was silent for a moment, his head bobbing almost imperceptibly as he tallied his gains, trying to determine if he'd gotten everything he'd wanted. That ten minutes later he would be pressing another sympathetic or naive listener for the same boost of reassurance, and by the next day — oblivious to everything that existed beyond the horse-blindered periphery of his ego — would have totally forgotten our conversation and walk past me without a word, I found somehow endearing.

"You really think I started with him?" he asked one more time.

"I don't think you tell the manager to fuck his center fielder."

"I only meant it figuratively." He seemed genuinely surprised to find out he'd been misunderstood.

"I don't think you get points for that, Oscar."

"But he still overreacted, right?"

"I think you could call wrapping a windbreaker around your head overreacting. Sure."

"Okay." He looked at me, waiting for confirmation, nodding, now that he had a handle on the situation.

"Okay," I said, then shrugged.

"Thanks."

"Anytime."

An ambulance arrived and took Cap away. Ten minutes later, Oscar went into the hospitality room and told the press that Cap had "overreacted" to a suggestion he made on how to play Otis, and Cap attacked him because he was deranged from drinking.

"Come here and look at this," Greg said to me. He was sitting in the lounge, watching the news with Mel Thorn, Dickie Tibbetts, and Aureliano Santana, when I stepped out of the shower.

"What's up?"

"Check this out."

I looked at the screen. Oscar, his back to a wall of photos from the club's past, was surrounded by a circle of beat writers who were jotting down every word he said.

"The thing is," he was saying as I edged into the room, "I am the situation. The way I go, the team goes."

"Then I wish he'd go get fucked," Santana said. "I need some pussy."

"Try dating somebody besides your sister," Tibbetts came back at him.

"Shut up so we can hear him make an ass of himself," Greg said.

"All you have to do is dress beside him every day, if that's all you want." Mel Thorn's eyes were riveted to the set as if he were waiting for Oscar to say one word about him so he could run out into the hall and thrash him — for the second time that night — on national television. "This guy makes me sick," he said.

A reporter asked Oscar why he had attacked Cap.

"I didn't attack him. I made a suggestion, and it was misconstrued. And — because I believe the man has a drinking problem and is deranged — he threw dirt in my eyes."

"Aw, the big bad man threw dirt in his eyes," Tibbetts said.

"But —" A guy from the local TV station tried to cut in.

"Don't you understand," Oscar continued. When he rolled, he rolled. "I am the situation. I have a one hundred and fifty IQ. White men can't deal with that because they like to see the black man down. I'm smart, I'm successful, and I'm this big black stud. So the man says, 'How are we going to keep this . . .' " — the next word was snipped out of the seven-second live delay loop — " '. . . in line?' Well, I'll tell you something. People see me and you know what? I intimidate them."

"Yeah," Thorn said. "You intimidated Carver into slapping the shit out of you."

The transmission cut to a clip of the fight. On screen it indeed appeared as if Cap had dismissed Oscar's remark, that Oscar had egged him on, and that Cap had grabbed a windbreaker in self-defense. Cap's kidney punch seemed to be an effort to keep Oscar from falling, and once Oscar was on the dugout floor, the camera lost sight of him. The newscaster stated that Oscar had been experiencing severe marital and emotional problems, as well as slumping at the plate.

Then transmission jumped to a scene outside Mr. Percy's office. Lee Wheeler stepped into the hallway and stood at a make-shift podium. "I have just gotten off the telephone with Edmond Percy, and he has asked me to read the following statement. 'Due to a variety of intimate and complex reasons, which are not connected with the incident this evening, we have unconditionally released Tom Carver from his contract as manager of this team. Charles Molloy will serve as interim manager. As we are close to completing negotiations with an extremely qualified candidate, we expect to announce the name of a new manager within a few days. Mr. Percy wishes to express to the city, the two leagues, and the rest of the country his sincere apologies for tonight's outburst. Thank you.' "

Lee turned and walked back into the office, refusing to answer questions. In the studio, the broadcaster said that a poll in progress was already showing that 90 percent of those surveyed supported Cap, and felt he should be reinstated.

"Reinstated in a rubber room," Tibbetts said.

"They don't have to play for the son of a bitch," Thorn said.

"What did they do, poll three people?"

"Yeah. His mother, his bookie, and his druggist."

"What do you think?" Greg asked me.

As I shrugged, Oscar appeared in the lounge doorway and looked over us as if we were members of his flock. "I think I cleared the air," he said. "And I just want you all to know that I love you, and forgive you."

None of us, not even Mel Thorn, said a word.

By the time I woke the next morning and picked up the paper outside my hotel room door, Cap had been rehired. A picture of Mr. Percy, wrapped in a black trench coat and white scarf, his hand reaching up to clasp the outstretched palm of prone, white-sheeted Cap Carver as he was being wheeled into surgery, was blown up to full-page proportions on the back of the local low-rent daily. "We just couldn't let the best manager in baseball go without a second thought," Mr. Percy was quoted as saying. I ordered coffee, pulled open the curtains — the grimy inner-city light filtered in as if through a dirty glass — and sat down in one of the room's armchairs, guessing that no one in his right mind would take the job.

Mr. Percy admitted that some people in his organization had been precipitous in announcing the decision — in spite of the fact that he had ordered it himself. Heads would roll to preclude any such hasty tendencies in the future, he swore. An expiatory statement by Cap was released. In it, he admitted that he had been suffering from a rare disease (unnamed), emotional exhaustion, and a crisis of faith. He vowed, with God's help, to recover quickly, and guide the team to a division title and the pennant. For beating up Oscar Rife, or shattering his own kneecap — we couldn't decide which — he was given a new contract and a raise. In addition, Cap was presented with a two-week lease on a timeshare condominium in the tropics, the certificate accepted for him by proxy while he was undergoing surgery.

Ten days later, our home stadium packed with die-hard fans — the inner-city and suburban regulars who couldn't afford beachside vacation homes and mountain retreats — Cap appeared, moving under his own power, to a standing ovation. He was introduced as an honorary member of the Old Timers squad that was playing a warm-up contest before the start of our Memorial Day weekend series. Sixty thousand plus greeted him as if he were a military hero. Hobbling slowly toward the first-base line, his leg encased ankle to midthigh in a plaster cast, a gleaming black cane — a permanent addition, we were told — spiking the sod beside his feet every few inches, he limped onto the field, buoyed by the cheers of the forgiving masses. Cap had an underdog quality in the public's eye, was a throwback to a rugged and manly baseball past, an era of postwar prosperity, zero inflation, and low player salaries. In him, the fans found a focus for their resentment, a channel through which they could express their distaste for our new wealth, media-generated celebrity, and princely distance. The blatant polarization sweeping the rest of the republic — cutting taxes for the rich, slashing social service budgets — found its mirror, it seemed, in the relation of fans to the game. The game was getting rich; most of them were not. So when the public was presented with an opportunity to vent its displeasure, it seized the moment with an instinctive swiftness.

An ugly, and previously buried, enmity toward Oscar Rife surfaced in the hometown crowd. Fans called for his banishment. The feeling of discontent grew when Two-Tone's involvement in Cap's accident and subsequent crippling was revealed in the press — leaked, some of us felt, by Mr. Percy himself. Oscar was struck by a bottle flung at him from the rightfield bleachers as he went back for a long fly ball. During our home stand, Two-Tone was booed each time he appeared at the plate.

Lunch was nominally in charge while Cap was recovering. Before the start of the Sunday doubleheader, he walked up to Two-Tone in the dugout. "You want to sit a couple out?" he asked, tapping the lineup card against the palm of one hand.

"What for?"

"You know. Mental health, the good of the team, protection of life and limb."

"You think I can't handle it?"

"I think it's getting ugly. Let it blow over."

Standing up, Two-Tone said, "Any of those fucking peons in the stands got a problem, you tell him to bring it to me. You hear?"

"Just checking."

Three innings into the game, Two-Tone went to the source, leaning over the first-base railing and dragging a heckler onto the field by his necktie. It took several seconds for a pack of security guards to pry the man out of Two-Tone's headlock. In the dugout we could hear him shouting, "You like your tongue on the inside of your head?" He was wrestled away from the man and ejected from the game. The next day, he was fined by Mr. Percy, reprimanded by the commissioner, and sent a dry cleaning bill for the man's pants. Our anger got the better of our talent, and we went into a ten-game tailspin, losing miserably each time. We were sinking toward third when we returned home for a two-week stand.

Hitless in my last six games, I came to the plate with two on in the bottom of the ninth when we were down by a pair of runs. On the mound, relieving, was Lynn Pike, victim of my minor league biting frenzy, his arm obviously healed these many years later by his hefty salary and his jump to a new league. I hadn't faced him in the majors before and, as if he wanted to pick up where we left off, he came in with a screamer that disappeared into thin air ten feet in front of the plate, then rematerialized six inches from my left temple a nanosecond later. Dirt was in my nostrils before I had time to see the ground. I stood and brushed off, took my stick from the batboy, stepped back into the box, cocked, and, letting go of the handle momentarily with one hand, gave him the finger. I yelled at him as he started his windup, "Come on, fucko," the words carrying, I'm sure, up to the press deck and upper loge seats, then stepped into a knee-high slider and bulleted the ball in a screaming, diagonal arc over the left center fence. Before I started for first, I knew that the ball was gone and I stood there, watching it, then flipped my bat toward the pitcher's mound and took off down the line, pointing at Lynn Pike and shouting, half out of my head, "You like that, chump? Huh?" Rounding third, the crowd on its feet, I punched the air over my head, crossed home plate with both arms raised, then strutted in front of our dugout, inciting the fans, at one point kicking over a Gatorade cooler and screaming like some berserk tied to the prow of a Viking ship, before flinging my helmet into the stands, leaping onto the dugout roof, and pounding hands with front-row fans who swarmed me like some long-gone king.

Things have a way of turning around fast. We won our next eight games, the last one on a ninth-inning double by Mel Thorn, and moved into a tie for first place. At the end of that game, the last of our home stand that stretch, the crowd of fifty-five thousand plus burst onto the field after the final out. It was a sky-scraper-high fly ball. At its peak, I lost sight of the ball as it climbed above the band of light that crowned the stadium, into the envelope of darkness and low-flying smog. When you can't see the ball, it's best just to follow your feet. I drifted to my right and back a few steps, and when the ball materialized I was standing directly under it. The hush lifted from the stands like the sound of a thousand pigeons flapping their wings as my glove went up into the air. When it came down with the ball and I looked back at the field, a motley stampede was already in progress. I thought for a moment that a bomb had gone off in the stands. Fans were charging over the first- and third-base railings like protesters fleeing the sweep of a riot-quelling army's bullets. Oscar was sprinting in from right field, dodging fans who swarmed around him as he reached the infield dirt. Thousands of rolls of toilet paper were hurled out over the field and the mezzanine boxes from the highest tiers of the upper deck, the white wingless birds unfurling like banners, like bales of ticker tape heaved by profit-crazed traders out through the windows of hundred-story-high monoliths. Clumps of sod were yanked out of the ground, the fist-sized caps of earth tearing away from their roots as easily as rotted teeth. Stunned for a moment by the sight of fans rushing toward me with a spirit of Comanche abandon, I didn't hear Otis screaming at me from center field. The cacophony of war whoops and banshee shrieks had begun to slice through the jet-engine roar of the crowd, the frenzy breaking into fragments, specific howls and rampaging cries. When my feet started to move, I saw Otis running in toward second base. He was waving to me, his right arm reaching behind his shoulder, then coming forward as if he were swimming, his mouth open, his face haunted by determination mixed with a look of battlefield panic. A moment later he was sucked into a maelstrom of faded jeans, windbreakers, caps, and shirts that were as bold, bright, and iconic as flags. I broke into a gallop. The infield was a crush of bodies. Beer cans and cardboard containers, tossed into the air from the high rows of seats, cartwheeled as they floated down into the crowd. A helicopter, gleaming with the hard, dark polish of an insect, descended from the sky and touched down behind the press box roof. Through the wide windows of the executive suite, I could see an aide gripping the handles of Mr. Percy's wheelchair. Fireworks began exploding, streaks of party-light colors whizzing across the screen of space just above the field like electrified lances. The sound of my own footsteps pounding the outfield grass was swallowed by the cresting pandemonium of the pack of fans racing toward me from the sidelines. They charged with open, outstretched hands, the frenzy of the overlooked and forgotten all tumbling into the arena with riotous delirium. Blue-coated policemen brandishing nightsticks began billowing out of the dugout trenches as the leading wave of the crowd surrounded me. I darted between their first thin ranks as hands clawed at my jersey. A rainshower of beer tossed from a cup unfolded like a fan and wet my face and hair. As the packing in of bodies thickened, hundreds of fans beelining for me with a coagular fury, I bounced off shoulders as heavy as tackling dummies, by accident knocking a woman down onto the field. As I tried to reach for her, a wave of bodies moving with the slow force of a barge shoved me past her. A stray hand rapped me on the side of the face. The cap was snatched from my head. Someone ripped my glove off my left hand. I could see a line of blue bulling its way through the bedlam and I struggled toward it, driving my way past bodies, using other shoulders and arms for purchase. Voices came at me like blows. Declarations of love and encouragement, offers to come to dinner or get laid. Prick, hero, faggot. The epithets were hurled at me with a mix of malice and adulation, the Babel-like madness zeroing in on the alternately resented and deified spectacle of my celebrity. By the time I reached the gauntlet formed by two rows of city police, the shirt had been ripped from my back. I broke loose of the last clinging hand and sprinted for the dugout. Lunch Molloy was on the top step, waving me on like a retreating general, screaming, "Come on!" A beer can catapulted over the line of policemen and smashed into my right temple. On the ground the thick black shoes of the guards dug for leverage against the swelling thrusts of the crowd. I was ten feet from the lip of the dugout when a young couple appeared, almost magically, on its roof. A small boy holding a pair of crutches dangled between them. His toes pointed down, his legs limp as noodles. He was wearing a home team cap and a uniform shirt with my number on it. I braked two feet from the dugout steps. "Please sign an autograph for him," the woman said. To my left, a new stream of fans began rushing into the far end of the dugout. Others were barreling down along the roof of it. I turned back, saw the boy's eyes — blank, bewildered, pitiful as a poster child's — hesitated for a moment, then began to reach up to him as the pounding on the dugout grew louder. Then Lunch Molloy's hand tugged at my arm. "Forget it. Let's go!" he shouted, his strong hand pulling me down the dugout steps. As I reached up and grabbed the roof to catch my balance, the father of the boy above me began bellowing. "Overpaid scum! You should be crippled!" With Lunch at my heels, I plowed my way through the dim canal of the clubhouse tunnel, the pandemonium fading behind me like the ebbing of a clamorous dream. But the resonance of the public's bipolar passions, its love-hate affair with the players of the game, stayed with me. If I warily accepted the public's love, I also remained mindful of its hair-trigger loathing. If we love our heroes, we also love to see them vanquished. As I said, things turn around fast.

Yet, we continued to win. Two-Tone was back in the lineup, taunting fans and driving in runs. Otis was stealing bases and saying nothing. Oscar was pontificating to the press like an urban guerrilla leader. And I was hitting over .350 again and had taken to painting large, black streaks of greasepaint across my face before games like some Sioux brave. As long as we kept coming out on top, the turnstiles clicking away like tickertape machines, no one raised a hand to stop us.

During this stretch, a package arrived Express Mail from Hammer. There was a note enclosed.

"Mike, Please give the attached a read-through. Baseball flicks are always solid box office packages, and, with the current state of your marketability I have to tell you that I've had some interest in your life. Not to be presumptuous or anything, but I've had a screenwriter acquaintance develop a synopsis. Of course, I would sell nothing without your approval, but I have to add that we're in a primo position to capitalize on your flavor-of-the-month appeal. I think we can get six figures for the option alone. So give this some serious thought. If you need me, you know where I can be reached. Best, Alvin."

The suggestion that he was reachable inclined me to toss the envelope away immediately. But I was curious, in a morbid sort of way, to see what my life looked like on paper, via Hollywood.

The team is a bunch of misfits, their losing ways a source of amusement to the fans and the press. They suffer through a winless April, then a sub-mediocre May. Dissension erupts in the locker room, the kettle-drum roll of frustration climaxing with a cymbalic clash. (Translation: there's a brawl.) Disgust subsequently settles over the team like a fog. The stage is set for my arrival. The appearance of my figure on the field, a bit tattered, weary, an innocent in the city, is accompanied by the somber, stoic melody of the hero's theme, which is played on the sound track by a single French horn.

In June, we begin winning more than we lose. At first, the fans do not take notice. The sportswriters are amused. They find our newly won confidence clichéd, our optimistic pronouncements at the All-Star break positively Falstaffian. By August no one is laughing. The press is suddenly comparing our lineup to Murderers' Row. They say our pitching has finally put it all together, "it" remaining undefined. My own hitting streaks, dizzying and intoxicating to follow, to speculate upon, to imagine never ending, function as the equivalent of Shakespearean soliloquies in the pinstripe drama that is unfolding. I seem to exude, like some divine young prince, an aura of magic. (In the movie I am blond, beyond blond, my face a polygon of lines and angles, looking more geometric than human but nonetheless appearing, in a pose seemingly motivated by a state of mind I can only describe as one of stern vacuity, on the cover of *Gentleman's Quarterly*. The ad for men's briefs that I do is a scandal. The women of the country are polled, and dejected housewives and eighty-year-old virgins name me the "Sexiest Man in America." Compared to me, Robert Redford looks almost Latin.) Anyway, I'm Shane in the middle of a pennant race. And, as the last rays of the relentless August sun beat down upon us, we find ourselves only two games out of first place.

Then, tragedy strikes.

Unable, because of his male pride, to confide in any of his teammates, Mook Montana, the team's brawny, dumb-as-an-ox first baseman, suffers laconically and alcoholically through a personal crisis brought on by an "unmanly incident" that he was party to with a TV weatherman shortly after Mook's wife, Con-

nie, the women's free-style mud-wrestling champion, left him for
a Chicano shortstop from the Mexican League. In an alcoholic
stupor, Mook steps off the team's chartered 747. At the time,
Cleveland is still six miles below the jumbo jet. Mook's death,
however, fails to galvanize the team, instead casting a glum funk
over it. We lose three straight and fall two back in the standings.
By early September we're five back and the champs, locked into
first place, are looking "tougher, and meaner, and more ornery
than ever," while we, definitely the more modern of the rivals,
seem to be wallowing in guilt and self-pity. Finally, Fez, our ancient right fielder and captain, calls a team meeting. His body, like
that of an old warrior, is bruised and aching; his knees are taped
and braced, his lower back is supported by a corset made of can-
vas and piano wire; his wrists, both bionic replacements made of
ball bearings and waiters' corkscrews, rotate with minds of their
own; his thinking, meanwhile, is impaired by the third in a series
of concussions he has suffered from running repeatedly into the
outfield wall. Fez stands before us wearing his specially designed
eyeglasses, so thick they look like a pair of framed ice cubes, and
begins, solemnly and forgetfully (sadly, he keeps losing his train
of thought and says the greatest hitter in the game was Babe
Cobb), to invoke the names of great baseball legends, their never-
say-die style of play, the money they took under the table. We are
moved by the nobility and greed of their heroic efforts. At stake,
Fez tells us, are the hopes of little fellas all over the country —
orphans, sick kids, little geezers born with two heads and six
arms, kids in Catholic school. We have to win for them, Fez says,
his speech culminating in a spasm of inane and childish squealing.
We all jump up and cheer, then charge out onto the field to win
"this thing" (the championship) for Mook, his stupidity and basic
mean-spiritedness atoned for in death.

We begin to once again play tough, smart, heads-up ball, a lot
of high-fives and ass-slapping punctuating our collective effort,
and by the last week of the season we are breathing down the
champions' necks. The division title comes down to a three-game
series in their ballpark, and during the titanic battle for first the
city watches in a state of volatile expectancy and fear. The Friday

night game goes fifteen innings, causing a panic as word goes out around the city that late-night delis have run out of beer. I knock in the winning run long after the "Tonight Show" has put all the civilians to bed and, with only two games to play, we are in a tie for first place. After the game I am interviewed. When asked what I think of the champs, I say, "They ain't so tough." This earns me a fastball up and in around my left eyebrow during my first trip to the plate the next day. I fling my bat aside and charge the mound. Both benches empty onto the field. We are one swarming, tripping, biting, punching beehive of bodies until the umps stop the row and the game is resumed after a commercial break. I stand in the batter's box, allowing my bat to rest on my right shoulder as I stare down my opponent. The catcher razzes me, but I remain unperturbed, determined looking but somehow also omniscient, incapable of failure. I leave the bat on my shoulder and take two called strikes without even attempting to lash the ball down the third-base line. I am, then, where I, pagan egomaniac, want to be. I lift the club from my shoulder, burrow my cleat tips, pestlelike, into the dirt, then stand not quite deathly still, glaring through my opponent into a clichéd and heroic vision of the future. The pitch comes. It has a good bit of snap and movement, arcing troutlike for a moment, shoulder high, then breaking sharply down and away in a whiplike motion, arriving at the plate doing about, oh, let's see, eighty-four miles an hour, a millimeter above my shoelaces. By this time I am halfway through the torque-driven thrust of my swing. I follow every inch of the ball's flight, then golf-stroke it up from down around my shoetops and drive it over the centerfield scoreboard. Majestically, I round the bases, all the while exchanging unprintable epithets with my opponents. A pall falls over the defeated city. We go on to win the division crown — the nation's sportswriters concurring that the outcome was decided by that all-telling swing — and the pennant, then take the Series in a melodramatic, seven-game cliffhanger. After the last game, while the rest of the team is popping champagne bottles and changing into ill-fitting street clothes, I slip off into the night, a true loner. But the world has been restored — for a vast and simple portion of the republic — to order. Good is once again triumphant. And the hero's spirit, eternal and sublime, continues to hover over us in a repose of Olympian vigilance, ever watchful and at the ready, as compassionate and self-sacrificing as Prometheus.

Well, this ain't that life.

Eternal verities. Ptolemaic symmetry and moral order. Corn gods. Ritual love and death. Pennants.

You expect a lot of us. After all, it's only nine not-so-bright, half hung over jocks trying to hit and catch a lump of horsehide-bound cotton yarn. I know. The almost perfect balance between offense and defense, the delicate equilibrium of skill and chance. Beauty. Rootedness. The exaltation of the individual, the search for the perfect community. The basic, do-it-yourself American dream kit.

Granted, stepping off the Mayflower onto the unblemished coast of a 3.5-million-square-mile ballpark must have filled the first Pilgrim's already overwrought soul with a mania bordering on the truly possessed. Edenic lushness. Paradise regained. The New World. Heady stuff, no question. But manifest destiny? America as the embodiment of prophetic universal design?

Okay. I'll accept that the terror inspired by standing on the edge of this vast, pristine abyss fuels our love of stadiums. Open spaces. Pastoral setting. Then, too, there's the civilizing aspect. Batter up. One man against nine. The individual testing his will against the repressive forces of society. Bases loaded, two out, the count is three and two. The stands are full, the bleacher section is chanting like revolutionaries — strike, strike, strike. Nothing ecumenical here. Bury the bastard at the plate and confirm us in our righteous and self-elected destiny.

We must have had grave misgivings about what we were doing here in the first place, we must have stopped to question the possible insanity of the quest. Something had to underwrite it, either God, or profit. Secular process becomes sacred teleology, and vice versa. Uncivilized nothingness? Beatific grandeur? Kick the moral rhetoric into overdrive.

The genius of America is that it is constantly advancing. Okay,

I'll bite the Emersonian apple. If the literal grass and roots and trees frontier is gone, hasn't it been replaced by the frontier of before-tax dollars, corporate profits, global markets? Even three-, four-, five-million-dollar-a-year ballplayers? Aren't we, the players, fulfilling America's destiny by holding out for as much cashola as possible?

Face it, no one likes to see a major league All-Star despairing by himself in an air-conditioned hotel room. It's a rejection of the national dream. A symbolic gesture on a par with losing faith in God. Cotton Mather would disapprove, big time. So if money is the only thing keeping our heads above water, why deny us? Why lay all the pseudomystical Americana on our back? It sells tickets, fine. But it's illusion. Think of the game as one big movie. Unlike three other nineteenth-century industries (steel, whaling, auto [shy by three short years]), baseball has gone from the pastoral to the profitable. The extremely profitable. It's entertainment — what America brings to the world.

So. Mystical underpinnings? Eternal truths? Sorry. No dice. It's like evolution — accept it.

On the other hand: Is it possible to buy this spiel and still be a ballplayer? Is it possible to believe this and call yourself an American?

One never knows, do one?

Twenty

SPRING RARELY ARRIVES in northern cities before late May. Until then, rebirth is a false promise, every tentative offer of warmth revoked with mocking swiftness by tulip-killing frosts and relentless, stinging, late April rains. It is a kind of death to be in a strange city, staring down from the window of a twelfth-story hotel room and waiting with a diminishing sense of hope for the lashing showers and inexorable grayness to pass. There is an anonymous uniformity to these inner-city landscapes, something utilitarian and failed in their celebrations of bleak opulence and hulking corporate grace. Taxicabs washed bright and slick as banana skins by the rain dart past the gliding limousines on their way to state luncheons and government scandal investigations. On the sidewalks, men and women course in long, unbroken streams, moving under their umbrellas or folded newspapers in opposite directions with a sense of huddled purpose. Jets circle the horizon, drifting above the city like desexed Valkyries. Bank buildings and life insurance towers loom over the streets, signature logos beaming the names of parent companies and multinational conglomerates out over the metropolis from their mile-high rooftops. Hospitals nest among rows of cooperative apartment complexes and sweeping, block-long shopping centers, only their names — Mercy, Redemption — distinguishing them from the rest of the sandstone-and-glass shelters. There is a river. There is always a river, or harbor, or decaying railyard languishing in the distance, a fossil of the city's Industrial Age nadir, some low-lying plane clinging to the fringe of haphazard urban sprawl. Polluted or rotting, they are sequestered behind the dump sites and the power plants, miles from the downtown financial-service district and information-processing centers. Out near the horizon's vanishing point is the stadium. Ringed by interstates and connecting beltways, it seems like some distant planet — awe-inspiring, insensate, pulsing with promise, as if it were capable of unveiling a life-blessing mystery, some key to the workings of the universe. In early spring, only the arcing, beneficent sweep of outfield grass defeats a loneliness that cuts to the bone, placating, for a moment, the sense that we have somehow gone astray, and are now forsaken.

"What are you looking at?"

"Rain. Midwestern rain."

"Fuck." Otis closed his eyes and allowed his head to drop back onto the pillow. Thirty seconds later, he was snoring again.

While Cap Carver was recovering from surgery, Lee Wheeler made some personnel changes on the team. We were loaded with left-handed hitting, but weak on backup defensive players and pitchers who could go the distance once the midsummer heat kicked in. Lee swapped three Triple A prospects for a nineteen-year-old fireballer named Odell Harriman, brought over Al Friendly, a steady long reliever, in exchange for two third-string outfielders and an undisclosed sum of cash, then picked up Tom Beattie, one of the game's most highly regarded starting pitchers, after an arbitrator declared him a free agent. Beattie's owner had failed to invest the $300,000 per year in thirty-year bonds that Beattie's contract stipulated and therefore was in breach of contract, leaving Beattie free to sign with the team of his choice. Mr. Percy interceded, agreeing to pay Beattie $6 million for five years' service. The news was greeted by everyone connected to the game with a feeling of puzzled exasperation. As players, we were getting conflicting signals. With one hand, the owners were turning their pockets inside out to show us they were empty. With the other, they were signing seven-figure contracts. They seemed to take a perverse pleasure in this, announcing every can-you-top-this salary increase with self-congratulatory pride.

The year that Ronald Reagan took control of the White House and declared that a renewed sense of moral and financial vigor would soon overtake the republic, full-time player salaries jumped by 30 percent. Three of us on the club — Otis, Oscar, and me — were earning over half a million per season, and two others — Two-Tone, and the newly acquired Tom Beattie — were signed on for over a million apiece. As for the players' union, the owners were out to destroy it. They seemed to feel there was something evil and tainted about our ability to mount an organized rejection of their wishes and commands. But one on one, they couldn't pay us enough, praise our abilities more, or, in Mr. Percy's case, use every opportunity to belittle and humiliate us in public.

"Mike, why don't you come up and see me after tonight's game?" Lee Wheeler had stopped me as I was walking onto the field to loosen my arm. There was some stiffness in my shoulder. An area the size of a quarter ached, ringed by a halo of prickly heat. It was as if a small sun had been inserted under my skin, a chunk of battlefield flak or smoldering meteorite. The ache seemed to be burrowing into my joint like a tick, spiky claws crimping around the stringy comb of muscle on the front part of my shoulder. Normally, I would have dismissed it. Sat in a whirlpool, popped a handful of extra-strength pain relievers, and washed the pain — or my consciousness of the pain — away with no more thought than I gave to falling asleep. But there was an insistent pitch to this injury.

The night before, I had missed home by six feet on a long throw from left field. It wasn't a mental error. My arm simply didn't behave the way I commanded it to. That had never happened to me before. There had been errors in judgment, distractions, misseeings. The play opens up before you, if you're playing right field, as if it's set out on a table. But left is the funhouse corner, full of shrinking angles and the vertiginous, tunneling pull of home. All the stabilizing and orienting perpendiculars of center and right vanish on plays at the plate. Coming up with a back-handed grab down the line the preceding evening — one of those spooky urban twilights when a vaporous blue light hovers over the crown of the stadium, obscuring the night sky behind a veil of swirling inner-city emissions — I braked, came down on my heels to decelerate once I had the ball, then turned. My body instinctively lined itself up with the plate. Or, if it wasn't instinct, it was a state of having been drilled beyond any distinction between instinct and conscious thought. My left leg was forward, stepping into the throw, right side back and rearing, even while the wordless computations of distance, angle, speed, and force were being determined someplace — not in the muscles of my arm, and not quite in my mind, but some guardian angel composite of memory, touch, faith, instinct, rote, sight, luck, and the voice of the ball — which floated just behind me. When I pulled up one foot beyond the leftfield line and saw Freddie Teuful's cleats picking at the clay of the third-base line as he dug for home, the ball was already rising from behind my right thigh and burrowing its red threads into the callused fingertips of my right hand. Ollie Sutkiss, our catcher, stepped into my sight lines down near the vanishing point of home plate. Nailing Teuful demanded a peg as sharp as a paper cut.

Straight lines — with the exception of uniform pinstripes and foul lines — are an illusion in baseball, once the ball is put into play. Television, that great flattener, reduces the movement of tosses and hits to unruffled flights, smooth as violin strings, when actually the flight of the ball is warped, bowed, at times even zigzagged. The ball tails or slices, sputtering if it's scuffed; if not, it just scoops across the vast screen of space like a hot spoon along the surface of a pint of ice cream. But never straight. I could, with a healthy arm, bring the ball within half an inch of Freddie Teuful's ear, painting his peripheral vision with a streak of vaporous whitewash, zipping the missile past him close enough to divide his attention between home plate and the fact that he'd almost just become a vegetable for life. It's an edge as thin as a split hair, but an edge nonetheless. Make a great throw one time and it's magic. Do it day in and day out and incrementally it opens a chasm between levels of performance bordering on the infinite.

When I came up throwing from three hundred feet down the third-base line, there was only my body and the ball. No corn god trips or seven-figure contracts, just a stripped-bare intuitive strike fired to catch the runner going from third to home, all the mechanics of weight shifting, arm cocking, back bowing, reduced to a single, instinctive response. And with all the intangibles, prep time, and mind games processed and forgotten, my shoulder seized like an overheated piston and I missed home plate by six feet.

"Open your goddamn eyes, Williams!" a voice in the stands admonished me. I turned and walked back toward deep left field, the man's distinctive tone of superiority, dissatisfaction, envy, outer borough grieving, and tabloid-fed disgust ringing in my ears like a dulling, almost buffering white noise. Swirling around me in the air were jeers, instructions, and cries of "Nice fucking throw, Williams," anonymous, good-natured, envious, and spiteful exhortations drifting down from the tiers of stands like confetti tossed from skyscraper windows. Normally, I would have ignored the heckling. It was a quotidian event, the inalienable right of bleacher bums and outfield disciples. Part of the juice for them in their trips to the park was the opportunity to force me to acknowledge their existence. I was like some piece of modern sculpture, abstract as a Rorschach blot, the sum of whatever any given fan chose to make of me. Accepting the projections of their fantasies — both benign and psychotic — was as easy for me as discarding them. Inside the foul lines I became porous. The whirling fanfare surrounding the game blew through me at times as if I were a celluloid phantom, some ethereal figure haunting the outfield, my ghostly outline barely discernible against the royal-blue backdrop of the outfield wall.

A throbbing halo of pain circled the front of my right shoulder, a spiking sensation at the center of it careening through the alleys of my deltoid muscles like a bottle rocket. But I let my arms hang along my sides, not windmilling my right arm to loosen the joint or work out a knot in it. The problem was apparently more than that. Something in it, or something in me reacting to it — age, anxiety, a sudden epiphany revealing the swiftness of the body's decay — told me this was a pain with deep roots, that there were ramifications connected to it: contingencies that would require consultations with dour physicians in white lab coats bearing clip-boards and test results, visits to downtown medical facilities equipped with state-of-the-art scanning devices, probes that could be passed over my body like magic wands. And, if it sidelined me long enough, the loss of freedom.

I was up for free agency at the end of the season, provided I logged 109 days of major league service to qualify. It was late May and the first two months had netted me 52 of them. But there was a strike looming over the issue of player compensation, which the owners insisted become a staple part of the Basic Agree-ment. A strike could erase the remainder of the season, or, at a minimum, a substantial part of it. There was the possibility I would lose credit for playing time. If I was injured and my service time was on the borderline, I wouldn't put it past Mr. Percy or Cap Carver to send me down to the minors for "rehabilitation." One day short of a full six years and Mr. Percy would own me for another season. So I dropped my head and stared at the ground, as if reflecting on the mental error I'd made. At least, the mental error I wanted everyone watching to believe I'd made.

As usual, Mr. Percy was in attendance, observing the game from his celestial suite hundreds of feet above home plate. In his private box adjacent to the press level was Lee Wheeler, our gen-eral manager. With him was Don Stone, one of the club's vice presidents, in charge of operations, and the only ranking member of management with a hands-on knowledge of the game. A former first baseman, Stone was a shrewd judge of talent. He had engi-neered the pursuit and signing of me, Otis, and Mel Thorn, as well as being the architect of trades that brought the club Two-Tone and Oscar. I knew that if anyone could detect the retarded motion in my arm and pin it to an injury, it would be Stone. Mr. Percy understood my soul, or lack of one. Lee Wheeler knew the bottom-line me, what I cost and earned the club, *Homo econimus*

Williams, that creature made up of stats, ratios, averages, and integers, a deathless being whose numbers would exist long after he was gone. But Stone fathomed my body. He had read into the lean, unremarkable twenty-year-old physique a potential for combined speed and power which would take three to five years to develop. So I stopped. Stopped in the middle of left field, looked up at the rising tiers of fans seated in the deep outfield seats, and, with their voices raining down around me, some with reckless sincerity, some fevered by mockery and spite, spread my hands, shrugged, and yelled, "What?"

In the clubhouse, the inevitable nosegay of microphones appeared inches from my face minutes after the game as I sat in front of my locker.

"I was saying, 'Hey, I made a mental error. Lighten up.' " As I looked at the mob of reporters I felt them pause, some sort of instinctive caesura generated by the lack of a closing line. "I was having fun," I said.

The beat reporters jotted the phrase down, jerked upright, issued a collective thanks, and were gone as swiftly as a handclap, video and audio technicians trailing them like dust. The following day I appeared, Job-like, on the back page of three dailies, the gist of the caption under each photo being, "Why me?" Five hours later, Lee Wheeler said he wanted to see me in his office.

"I missed one throw to the plate, Lee. We have to have a discussion about it?"

"Just stop up to the office. It'll take five minutes."

Later, as I passed him in the clubhouse between batting practice and game time, Don Stone nodded to me. It wasn't a formal hello. There was something more complex going on in the gesture, something eerily omniscient and judgmental. During BP, I had sensed I was holding my bat an inch lower than usual while I waited on a pitch, the crabbed pain in my shoulder clenching like pincers. With Stone watching from behind the backstop, I left my hands where they felt comfortable, worrying that perhaps they *were* in their natural position, that I wasn't unconsciously compensating for the ache in my shoulder by dropping them, but simply thought I was. Trying to hide this confusion, I felt guilty, clumsy, and distracted. So I told myself to just swing away, then proceeded to hit six balls into the dirt.

"Swing's a little short there," Stone said as I came around the cage.

I looked at him while I pulled my batting gloves off. "Yeah, well, I'm saving the whole thing for the game." Then I tossed him a smile and walked toward the dugout holding myself unusually erect.

Stone's cool rebuff in the clubhouse, though, told me he wasn't buying my line. I went one for four in a tight game, using the shortness of my swing to advantage by just meeting the ball on one pitch and slapping it to the opposite field for a single.

"Going to the opposite field the way you used to," Lee Wheeler said as I took a seat in his office.

"I just hit 'em where they throw 'em, Lee." As I spoke, Stone walked in. He closed the door with an unhurried equanimity, slid into the armchair beside mine, and nodded at me, saying my name solemnly, as if he were about to tell me I had cancer.

"Well, I'm going to turn that business over to Don," Lee said. "There are a few things he wants to go over with you. Don."

Stone, staring at me the entire time, simply opened his mouth and said, "Is there anything bothering your right shoulder?"

The specific nature of the question startled me, though I showed no surprise."No," I said. "Why?"

"You missed the plate by six feet last night."

"My computer malfunctioned." I tapped the side of my head. "Gave me the wrong coordinates. I've already explained this to Lee."

"He told me."

"Mike, we're not trying to back you into a corner," Lee said.

That was a weird remark, I thought, but I simply said, "I don't feel backed into a corner."

"Good."

"Maybe you're compensating for something you don't even realize is there," Stone said.

"We just don't want you getting hurt," Lee said. "We can't

afford it. You guys may go on strike in two weeks and we're a game and a half out of first. Who knows what's going to happen to the rest of the season? But I can tell you one thing. There's no better place to be than in first if the shit hits the fan. Right now you're carrying the team offensively. Attendance is up. You're an attraction, no two ways about it. I'm being honest with you. The two of us are going to have to sit down sometime in the not-too-distant future and discuss money. I'm aware of that. But I'm telling you if you don't let us help, then you're hurting both of us. So listen to what Don has to say, and keep an open mind."

"I always do," I said, in spite of the fact that I distrusted every word he said. In the long view, this may have been immature. On the other hand, if this century has done nothing else, it legitimized paranoia.

"I'm not worried about you missing the plate," Stone said. "What bothers me is that there was a hitch in your throwing motion."

"Were you aware of this?" Lee asked.

"No."

"Nothing felt off, or unusual?"

I shook my head.

"He may not even have been aware of it," Stone said. "This is what I mean by compensating." He turned back to Lee. "Let's show him the tape."

Lee leaned forward, picked up a remote control box as sleek and black as a Luger, and handed it to Stone. Behind me a television set came on, its screen bristling with static as it was bombarded by a flurry of electrons. "You can swivel around," Lee said to me, his index finger twirling above his desk top as if he were controlling the strings of a marionette.

The TV beamed with a mute, garish authority in the corner of the room, the figures on the screen swirling like elementary particles once the ball was put in play. As Stone fast-forwarded, players sped through motions like silent movie comedians. We were the size of toy soldiers, flat as baseball cards, as close to weightlessness as motes of light. The game was no more than information on the tube, soulless as a ticker tape report. Stone slowed the action when, with Freddie Teuful at third, Clayton Firestone laid a rope down the leftfield line. I had seen the seams of the ball spinning like the blades of a cake mixer set at "frantic," and broke for the line even as the ball bowed toward short, knowing that no matter how the ball seemed to be hooking toward left center, it would be true to its arc and swerve back toward the leftfield foul line. I stumbled on my second step, grunting as I recovered. Then my breath came in erratic bursts and reedy, rabbit-punch clutches as the air was jogged out of my ribcage while I accelerated, each breath more deeply lost in the cresting roar of the crowd, until I was gliding. My steps became lighter, the grass streaming by beneath me smelling as clean and sharp as chives. The ball tailed toward me and I fine-tuned the angle of my approach, the pitch of the crowd's voice dovetailing with the ball's wingless, space-capsule descent and my own deceleration. It was as if all of us — the ball, the crowd, other players, and me — were nosing toward an embrace of the inevitable with a time-slowing sweetness. Everything began shutting down around me as the ball comet-tailed the last few feet toward earth. The sour perfume of the cut grass, the conch shell roar of the crowd, the passing of time, and the tracks I left behind me in left field — all of it vanished the farther I went into the rabbit hole after the ball. I was coming at it on a forty-five-degree angle, which meant I would have to pick up the ball on a short hop, stabbing down at it with my glove and stopping in the ball's path as well, just to insure that if I missed it on the hop it would hit me rather than skip past my legs and carom off the wall into left field, which would rematerialize if the ball slithered out there, just to make me look bad. Balls will do this sometimes. Some of them are spiteful and devil possessed. Some can seem to be in two places at the same time, like the tip of a sprung diving board. You don't know which is the ball and which is the ball's after-image. Others can change direction like a bumblebee, or zigzag like a lightning bolt, so that when you lunge for them a voice over your shoulder says, "Psst! Looking for me?" And when you crank your head around, the ball is sitting in the shadows of the leftfield corner, and you feel like the dick of the universe on national TV. But this wasn't that kind of ball.

As it dropped, the spinning of its seams slowed and their rotation became as easy to read as a model of the earth in orbit at a high school science fair. The spin was going to make the ball leap toward me after it bounced. Although my eye had been on the ball, I knew Teuful was hovering near third. I could feel his presence tingling down the left side of my body like a mild electrical charge, as if the two of us were held together by magnetic force. I braked in order not to overrun the ball and fracture the line of approach I had been developing from the first step I took eighty feet away in left field. I grabbed it waist high, keeping my center of gravity floating around my hips to get some zip into my throw. Clayton Firestone was taking a wide turn around first when I looked up. Keeping him from going to second was academic. But I followed my body. It was the only way I knew how to play. If I thought too hard about what I was doing, I lost the edge, started swinging early, or else misjudged the flight of the ball and watched it blow by me into some pull hitter's left center power alley. Yielding to the purity of the ball's intention, rather than attempting to dominate it — to pull an outside pitch, say — was, for me, key. Going with the flow, an embrace of what is. So when I found myself in a position to grab the ball on a short hop, downshift, and make a throw to the plate, I followed my body's lead and did it.

But all you saw on TV was me backhanding the ball and whipping it toward home.

"There. You see that?" Stone rewound the tape and replayed my catch and peg. "There's a hitch in your motion, halfway through."

"You mean on the upswing?" Lee asked.

"Right there," Stone said.

"Slow it down."

And they watched as the tape ran at one-quarter speed.

I stopped. My left shoulder was forward, pointed toward the plate. As my stride opened, my left foot came off the ground and

I leaned backward. My right hand floated higher, and when it was even with my shoulder, it seemed to lock.

"There," Stone said. "You're not getting the full extension of your right arm."

"It seems like you're pulling your arm in closer to your body," Lee added. "Not really letting it rip."

"This is TV, Lee. I'm flat as a pressed shirt. You can't tell if I'm doing something out of whack from this."

Lee, arms folded, looked over at Stone. "You think he could be right? The camera's playing tricks?"

"We weren't looking through a camera last night."

"Don, you were two hundred feet away," I said.

Stone continued to stare past me at the television. He reran my throwing action in slow motion while I looked to Lee, hoping for a companion in dissent. Oddly, the ache in my shoulder seemed to have relented, chased away perhaps by the hot postgame shower I had taken. This recovery of my sense of well-being only made me less patient with Stone's scrutiny. "Okay," he said. "Then tell me why you kept your elbow below your chin on the delivery." He raised his eyebrows a millimeter, and inclined his head toward the screen.

It was true. My motion was constricted and awkward, the line of windup and follow-through cinched and irregular. Finishing the throw, I brought my forearm down like the blade of a guillotine, then snapped my wrist, hoping to put a little sting into the ball. It never climbed more than a dozen feet above the field, tailed weakly toward the pitcher's side of home plate, and arrived behind, rather than in front of, Freddie Teuful. Ollie Sutkiss picked it up six feet in front of the batter's box, after two feeble hops. Teuful scored, tying the game, and Clayton Firestone, the go-ahead run, was standing on second when I turned and began walking back into left.

"I was making an adjustment."

"So you sabotaged your natural throwing motion and missed the plate by half a dozen feet?"

"I've told you. It was a mental error. I knew the throw was off the mark the second it left my hand."

Between the unexplained remission of pain in my shoulder and the hundredth telling of the story, I was beginning to believe this myself. Maybe I was finally putting the pain into perspective. Arriving with a sudden and unexpected sharpness, it had loomed, its appearance magnifying the tentative, promissory quality of existence. I had played a flawless season in left field the year before, the team was picked to be this season's champions, and I hadn't thought of George since I last hit .250, in my slump-ridden sophomore year. But the thunderbolt of pain, and the loss of movement that besieged my shoulder, had brought him back with brooding authority. I had been playing without any sense of death, or even failure, and had managed, somehow, to deny the existence of each of them. I felt invulnerable, as if I were living in a zone where death couldn't touch me. Then one bad toss and the sense of doubt it unleashed sucked every molecule of confidence out of me, my sense of invulnerability imploding as if it had been dropped into a vacuum.

"It was a mental error?" Stone said.

"Yes," I answered, though, in truth, I could not believe it. Some part of me wanted to admit to Stone what was wrong, to share the knowledge, or suspicion, of my decay with him, as if that would somehow deter its progress. But I didn't trust him. Ambitious, intelligent — he had picked up law and business degrees after finishing his minor league career — he also seemed to be without an identity, or a center. He was a hybrid, spawned by the mating of a solid, Ivy League education and a dogged minor league history. Never having ascended to the majors — despite a tenacity which, some said, bordered at times on the pathological — seemed to have left a hole in him. Media room and front-office talk around the league tagged him as a "genius," the type of executive who could take an organization, restructure it, and turn it into a dynasty. As our attendance climbed, I thought I detected him slipping a bit toward pretentiousness. He refused to have his judgment questioned. If he said you were doing something wrong, you'd better agree you were doing something wrong. So there was no way I would confess my problems to him. His word could cost me a fortune, as well as my freedom.

"Well, if it was a mental error," he said, "why has your top hand dropped below your shoulder when you're waiting on a pitch?" Stone nodded, as I looked at him in silence. "When you're swinging well, your right pinky is dead even with your right shoulder. It means you have the bat up, for quickness."

"Where's my finger now?"

"In your armpit."

"If my bat's dragging, maybe I need a day off."

Stone shook his head. "I want you to hit for me tomorrow before game time," he said. "Down in the cages."

I sat there, not answering him, knowing there was no choice.

"You're a very expensive piece of equipment, Mike," Lee said, leaning forward now, his hands clasped in front of him like a financial adviser addressing the issue of a billion-dollar tax shelter. Then his reverence shifted, edging toward the fatherly. "We only want to look out for your best interest. For everyone's best interest."

Several moments passed while they studied me. Then I said, "Can I go now?" Lee nodded, and I felt like a schoolboy.

As I stood up to leave, Lee's eyes followed me. "We're going all out for the pennant this year, financially and every other which way," he said. "We don't want it jeopardized."

I looked at the two of them for a moment, in their suits and polished shoes, then turned and opened the office door. "Tomorrow," Stone's voice said behind me. "Three o'clock. In the cages."

Twenty-One

AN ACHE as dull and solid as the head of a lug wrench, and a blotting, late morning heat, carried me up out of sleep. Even before I moved, I could feel that my right shoulder was locked as tight as a rusted nut and bolt. With my eyes closed, I tried to move my arm, sliding it across the mattress. A white-hot pain roped from my shoulder to the tip of my index finger. When I pulled my arm close to my right flank again, the merry-go-round of stained-glass colors stopped spinning inside my head, bleached to transparency by the leaking away of the pain. A brimming light, golden as corn, replaced the carnival colors, and the heat of the day seemed to melt my eyelids like pats of butter. "Fuck."

"Who are you talking to?"

The voice — earnest, inquisitive, soft as the cooing of a pigeon — surprised me, appearing, it seemed, out of nowhere, like an angel's. Elizabeth was standing a foot from the side of the bed when I opened my eyes. Clad in an oversized white T-shirt gathered at the waist by a leather, western-style belt studded with turquoise medallions, thirty-five-dollar designer blue jeans, and brand-new, snow-white running shoes — compliments of one of the companies I endorsed — she looked like a mail-order catalog's model, some not quite substantial being. She had Barbara's complexion, cupid-white cheeks, round as oranges, tinged with a pinkness bright as a sunburn. There was a sweetness about her —

thick, lush hair the color of caramel, hazel eyes deep and large as marbles — that I found, on occasion, almost eerie. Only advertising was capable of spawning such an unblemished being. I had to wonder if after-school cartoons had performed some insidious invasion-of-the-body-snatchers soul swap on Barbara and me, taking our real daughter and leaving in her place a brand-name-crazed demon who had an insatiable appetite for nationally promoted clothing, games, movies, toys, and fast food.

"When did you come in?"

"Mommy told me to stay here till you woke up."

I knew without checking that Barbara was not in bed. Slipping into bed at night with the stealth of a cat burglar, then waking solo, was becoming an increasingly frequent and disturbing pattern in my life. Our life.

"Where is Mommy?"

"She went out."

"That's pretty open-ended." I pushed myself back on the bed with my left arm and leaned against the pillows. "Didn't you get anything more specific?" She shook her head, then waited on my next word, a look of rapt attention and dutifulness on her face. "Well, did Mommy say when she'd be back?"

She shook her head with a grim, witness-stand solemnity, her failure infusing her with a sense of gravity. "She left a note."

"What's it say?"

"I didn't read it."

"That's good. Because if you had, and it wasn't addressed to you, you could've gone to jail. Did you know that?" Nod. "Good. Give me a kiss."

I sat forward, my left hand taking hold of hers as we touched lips. From the waist up I felt bisected, as if half my body was atrophied, or crippled.

"You love me?"

"Yes."

"Good. Down two. Man on first, two out, bottom of the ninth. Hit and run, or steal?"

She thought for a moment. "Pray," she said, remembering the line I'd fed her.

"Good. Let me up. I have to go to the bathroom."

I kicked the sheet off and pivoted on my butt. With my right hand in my lap and feeling dead as a fish store flounder, I cocked my head and rolled it clockwise. The muscles beside my right shoulder blade were knotted, their tightness pinging like an injection of Freon when I swept my chin across my sternum. I arched my back and let the crown of my head fall backward, loosening my lower back muscles. I could already feel the heaviness in my legs, a fatigue that left them as dead as sides of beef. All I wanted was coffee and an hour in the Jacuzzi. When I stood, a knot of pain bulleted through my shoulder. "Shit."

"Who are you talking to now?"

"A part of my body."

"Which part?" She was following me across the carpet toward the bathroom, not thrown for an instant by the idea that mind and body are split.

"The part that doesn't hurt is talking to itself about the part that does hurt."

"What hurts?"

"Name it."

"Your head?"

"No, that's the part that gets me into trouble."

"Your feet?"

"What happened to everything in between?" I stopped and looked at her. "Can I ask you something? Should you be following me when I'm walking around in my underwear?" She nodded. "It's okay?"

"Yes."

"You're not going to come back to me in twenty years and tell me that it mangled you sexually and psychologically, are you?"

"No."

"Okay, then. Just remember one thing. You listening?"

"Yes."

"Don't compare the men in your life to me. You'll only be disappointed with them. Want to do me a favor?"

"Yes."

"Go get Mommy's note."

I stepped into the bathroom, emptied my bladder, then went to the pine-framed medicine cabinet for pain relievers. A burst of cloyingly sweet air from inside it whistled through my nostrils and made me momentarily light-headed and nauseous. A potpourri of cinnamon sticks, vanilla bean, petals of dried flowers, and tissue-thin shavings of fruit rinds nested in a handmade basket in one corner. The mixture gave off a perfume that smelled like Ripple Red cut with room deodorizer. Barbara brought home a steady supply of it from specialty stores in the city, its odor one more thing that cut us off from the rooms in which we had each grown up.

"I don't know. Barbara seems to have changed," I said, waving my discontent away with one hand. "It's like we're cut off from our old life." I was unburdening myself to, of all people, Hammer, who, in spite of his complete lack of sincerity, had become my sole confidant. Once my salary had jumped to $715,000 per year, Barbara and I built a new house on six acres of primo north-shore real estate. We were over our heads in a sea of money, and I was lost in my own day-to-day celebrity. We seemed to have misplaced our faith in who we were — if we ever knew — and, in order to protect ourselves, we each refused to acknowledge the fact that we didn't know what we were doing.

"It's definitely a late capitalist thing," Hammer said from, of all places, behind his desk. I wasn't sure what had happened to him — maybe it was turning forty-five, or a drop in his testosterone level — but once Reagan took up residence in the White House, Hammer began to act with a sense of at least fiscal responsibility. His lingering, late sixties and seventies tics and fetishes — sideburns, flare-leg pants, Birkenstocks worn with sky-blue knit socks; the pro bono work he did for political activist groups, the occasional joint we'd share; his sense of irony — receded. In their place he adopted a demeanor that was, at least superficially, straitlaced and unashamedly corporate. Though his eating habits hadn't improved.

"Barbara and me splitting up is tied to economic theory now?"

"Absolutely. Inflation, two-income households. The pill, Japanese expansionism. No question. There's a restless need for self-creation brought on by a volatility in market forces. The childhood sweetheart number is touching — I state this without reservation — but only as product, revisionist nostalgia. On a practical level, it's an Edsel."

I dragged on my cigarette — new habit, something picked up between innings (though we were ordered to smoke in the clubhouse tunnel so we would be hidden from the eyes of television cameras, and sentimental fans hooked on notions of an idyllic pastime played by untainted demigods). Meanwhile, Hammer broke up a Twix bar and sprinkled it over his diet fruit salad. He was eating off a teal-green cafeteria tray, die-molded into compartments, which had a distinctly penal aura about it. Sitting beside the fruit bowl was a diet Cherry Coke, a bag of puffed cheese balls, and a cinnamon-raisin bagel with garlic-dill cream cheese.

"Are you sure you wouldn't like any of this?"

"Positive." I sipped some coffee, then waited for the caffeine to slash away the edges of my hangover.

"That's all you're going to have?"

"I'm in training."

Hammer shook his head. "I can only approve on a film noir level. The coffee, the cigarette. The look of rumpled, unshowered despair. Very French. If you had fifty percent more hair, I think I could promise film roles. But outside of a certain celluloid resonance, I have to frown on your habits. You're poisoning vital organs, not to mention risking possible endorsement-opportunity suicide. Hit three-fifty again and I can vouch for delivery of a binding and lucrative contract with a razor blade company. Again, with the communications boom, we come full circle to your marital woes. As markets open up and the potential for profit increases, there's a fracturing of self-image resulting from the proliferation of new and more readily acceptable role models. Americana, as a concept — the white picket fence, the sloping lawns, the chintz-covered couches — sells. As a packaging concept, it's a gold mine. Greeting cards, gift wrap, linen lines. It's the grist of all television commercial brainstorming sessions. Without it, we couldn't sell an English muffin. Why? Because nostalgia is the only culture we have."

Hammer, in his blue, pin-striped suit, a shirt as white as a cotton ball, rep tie, and fire-engine-red suspenders, pushed the tray aside. "Let me ask you something. You and Barbara, how are your eating habits? Do you have conventional dinners? Repasts from the meat, potatoes, and vegetable genre?"

"Who eats together?"

Hammer nodded knowingly. "Definitely a symptom in the last stages," he said. "But perfectly natural. We need to maintain a sense of fluidity, the feeling of being at one with a product, which that type of dining denies us. Do you own a microwave?"

"No."

"I think we should make it part of your free-agent package. I'm hoping that with microwave ovens we'll get away from the idea of food as economic and social symbol, and begin to see it in its purer form as entertainment. Nacho cheese–flavored popcorn; diet, cholesterol-free, high-protein pizzas; frozen egg rolls cooked in cardboard crisping sleeves. Sort of a remote-control, cable TV–style, restless-sampling approach brought to the concept of meals. Knoshing as a pluralistic substitute for canon items such as roast beef and mashed potatoes. I'll be honest with you. I can't eat that type of food anymore. The social and religious implications of it are too overwhelming. Though I love Thanksgiving. The whole Stouffer's-Hallmark-Pillsbury commercial quality of it. History as advertising. The packaged effluvia and aromas. The E-Z Lite Yule Log at Xmas. That sense of having purchased your way into the national collective unconscious. Purchasing. Can I tell you something? Every time I use my Visa card . . . ? I forget I'm going to die."

Hammer took a pad from his desk drawer and laid out the details of my upcoming free-agent package. I hadn't mentioned Mr. Percy's offer, wanting to see what Hammer would come up with on his own. His plan called for a $2 million-a-year raise and a four-year contract. There were clauses in it for straight income of $750,000 per season. Twelve checks, two a month April through September, for $63,000 apiece. The rest was to come in the form of deferred income: annuities, long-term bonds, a college fund for Elizabeth, who had yet to enter kindergarten, and a below-market-rate mortgage for our new house. "I've also taken the liberty of discussing your portfolio with a financial-planning acquaintance," Hammer said. "We think it's time for you to start moving out of money market accounts and short-term instruments into something more forward looking."

"Like what?"

"High-interest bonds."

"Never heard of them."

"That's why you want them. High risk, high yield. Stay ahead of the pack. Also, I've accepted a position for you on the board of directors of a very well intentioned charitable foundation. My marketing acquaintances tell me it's a one hundred percent bona fide excellent move — even though I myself knew this in advance. Nevertheless, all people with the proper university degree concur with the strategy."

"What kind of foundation?"

"It's an ineffective, heart's-in-the-right-place kind of venture, with a high and favorable media profile, and connections to other celebrities whose names it wouldn't hurt to have yours sandwiched in among on thousand-dollar-a-plate, gold-leaf-embossed dinner menus. You make a few appearances, read off a cue card, take some publicity shots, and exit. In the meantime, twenty-four city kids get to go to a baseball camp in the country for six weeks. It's sincere without being condescending."

I was accustomed to Hammer's scheming, had come, in fact, to expect it of him. But there was something unsavory about this new posture, his blind, or perhaps just smug, acceptance of celebrity-led noblesse oblige. Not for its cynicism, but for its moral hollowness. Over the long, occasionally storm-tossed career voyage I made, almost by default, with Hammer, this was the one time I actually disliked him.

"I don't care about being 'sincere without being condescending.' The whole thing's a scam to make a few overpaid entertainers feel guiltless."

"It's a good cause."

"It's self-congratulations."

"You play left field. Since when are you so cynical?"

"Now you sound like Percy."

"Can I tell you something? He's not the worst person to have on your side."

"Why do I need someone on my side? Who am I against?"

"The downwardly mobile, the disempowered. It's a shrinking world. Resources are scarce, goods expensive. You're a bit too dark-complexioned to make a serious bid for federal office, so I think a behind-the-scenes position in an executive capacity is more in line with a realistic assessment of your future. In the meantime, charity work is looked upon very favorably by major corporations who dole out millions in sports celebrity endorsement deals. Let's face it, financially you're at a critical point in your career. One more season with Hall of Fame–sized numbers and you make the leap into economic hyperspace. From a strictly marketing point of view, on the endorsement angle you need all the help you can get. Frankly, you don't have the boy-next-door quality. And you're obviously not in the ebony god class — which, by the way, is a very easy TV sell because of the pagan undertones. The tube just eats that up. So the charity thing is one more item on the plus side of your balance sheet. It's a competitive world. You take whatever you legally or illegally can. The only penalty is finishing out of the winner's circle."

Hammer paused, dropped my contract proposal on his desk, and slumped back in his leather chair. "I can tell by your moody silence that you're disgruntled." He let one arm fall onto his desk top in a pose of mock defeat. "What can I say? Once you move into a substantially higher income bracket, you lose old ways. The affection for a childhood sweetheart fades." He looked away for a moment before looking back at me and continuing. "This situation with Barbara," he said. "I understand the impetus, the inevitability of it. It's natural selection. The institution is obsolete, like the reserve clause. Nonetheless, this news saddens me on an emotional level I rarely have need to call on. Friend to friend, is there anything I can do?"

"Yeah. Tell me how you and Rachel have managed to stay together for fifteen years."

"We're divorced."

"What?"

"Eight years."

"You live together."

"Cooperation. Social hierarchy. Organization of the hive. It's man's oldest instinct. Community. We have offspring. There are hunting and gathering tasks that we share in equally. We enjoy the same nighttime television programs. We're cave dwellers. It's the best of all possible worlds." He paused. "I think separation is a despairing necessity. No one can maintain the level of self-lessness necessary to make a marriage work. There are simply too many other outlets that accept and return our affections indiscriminately — cars, computers, mail-order catalogs, home entertainment centers. Where else can I find the selfless devotion of a Mr. Coffee? We're too accustomed to the relentless concern and subservience of technology. Marriage is a perishable item, like fresh fruit. All certificates condoning any said unions should bear a stamp on them that reads: Better if used before this date. What can I tell you? The institution has a brief shelf life? Can I offer one suggestion? Divorce and remarry each other. It could be a good career move, and it might even save the relationship."

Hammer turned and looked out the window. "You know, I used to think youth ended at twenty-five," he said. "Now I realize it ends when you start earning six figures annually." He looked at me again. I saw that there was a seriousness — actually something more like sadness — in his expression. All the satisfaction usually evident when he expounded his off-the-wall theories of existence was replaced by a sense of gravity, almost defeat. "You don't have friends at your income level. You have acquaintances, colleagues, teammates, peers. You talk money with them, sports, dining out, movies, weather. Superficiality is the key, the operative mode. And you want to know something? One evening, in another recycled city, while you're sitting at some TV sitcom–style chain hotel bar — one of those places with plastic beer tap handles, cheesy butcher block tables, the bright green mantra of Astroturf on the wall-sized television screen in the corner — you'll reveal to one of these acquaintances — in a fit of nostalgia, in a sweeping gesture of self-pity directed at lost emotion and spiritual burnout after one too many nights on the road — you'll reveal, over your fifth watery cocktail, your most intimate and painful secret. Know why? Because like you, it will have become superficial, too." Hammer paused for a moment and regarded me silently. "People don't get older," he said. "They evaporate." He sat in his chair for another moment, then stood up. "So I understand your insecurity," coming around his desk now, "the deterministic lack of self-esteem. But I'm going to say just one thing. Don't go public with it. It gets old fast."

I closed the medicine cabinet and reached for my toothbrush. Barbara kept them in an antique white mug, hand decorated with a blue heart. The cup sat on whipped-cream-white marble. Porcelain tile, in matching white, lay on the floor and up the walls. The vanity held two large porcelain sinks, each adorned with nickel-plated hot and cold water handles, their faucets fat as garden snakes. Two bars of handmade, heart-shaped soap, each red as a valentine, huddled side by side at the bottom of a shallow blue-and-white spongeware bowl. Grapevine wreaths hung from antique peg racks affixed to the walls. Beside them, salmon-pink towels, soft as cotton candy, sat on stripped pine shelves. Sunshine came barreling in through the row of French windows open over the golf-course-smooth lawn leading down to the woods behind the house. How was it possible my arm had no lateral movement, that there was a pain as though someone had just driven an ice pick into my shoulder? It was embarrassing to be mortal and given to decay — maybe even to conscience — in the face of such pristine opulence. Maybe that was the game plan, success as the appropriation of obliviousness. Everything from the rage for health and physical perfection to perfectly decorated homes the true and universal American longing. Consumerism as the fulfillment of manifest destiny.

The mirror failed to reveal any discernible bruise or deformity that might explain the pain. I'd hoped to see some discoloration, or evidence of a contusion, so that I could get an ETA on healing. Shadowy, insidious, under-the-skin nadirs of pain spooked me. They were the cancers and degenerative viral diseases, illnesses that showed their faces only to radiation, and dyes which, when ingested, turned your organs to inky shapes, dark as midnight.

I walked back through the bedroom to the exercise room. There was a sterile, almost vacuum-chamber hush that enveloped the place. White, ice-cream-smooth walls; a bank of glass-cleaner-clear picture windows overlooking the stream at the end of the property; mirrored folding doors closed over the closets where we stored our athletic clothes. Panels of fluorescent bulbs, hidden behind sheets of translucent fiberglass, exhaled a long, steady curtain of light. AC slithered into the room through narrow rectangular grates, the damp tongues of air curling invisibly into the corners. A Nautilus machine sat in the center of the room like a piece of industrial sculpture, or some refurbished thirteenth-century instrument of torture. Opposite it was a small alcove with a sink, an under-the-counter refrigerator, and an automatic drip coffeemaker. Rows of vitamins stood beside it on the countertop.

The coffee was bracing, although, after sitting for several hours on the warming plate, bitter as aspirin. I added several teaspoons of nondairy creamer to it and the off-white powder melted into a boggy, swamplike puddle. The act of stirring the coffee, then raising the cup to my lips was awkward but manageable. The pain had shrunk my perspective, every movement sucked in by the question, If I do this, will that hurt? All I generally asked of my body was not to make me think about it, so I felt betrayed. I decided to treat it with Tylenol and the moist heat of the Jacuzzi until I could get my hands on some heavy-duty narcotics and a shot of muscle-numbing cortisone. If there was a point to technology, after all, it wasn't to pinpoint the beginnings of the universe, or introduce us to God; it was to make life painless. Take away pain and you lost the need for God anyway.

I carried the coffee back into the bathroom and turned on the Jacuzzi, then flipped on the television set at the foot of the tub. As I tested the water, Elizabeth appeared in the doorway. She was clasping the note from Barbara like a visitant, some innocent extraterrestrial bearing news from the leader of another, hopefully benevolent, planet.

"I brought you the letter from Mom."

I unfolded the rabbit-shaped notepad paper. Printed across the bottom of it in bold red letters were the words "Hop To It."

"What are you doing?"

"I'm going to sit in the Jacuzzi for a few minutes."

"Can I, too?"

"Sure. Go put your bathing suit on."

"Okay." She turned and bolted from the room, as though if she were gone too long, the offer, or the room itself, might vanish.

"Had to leave for summer registration," the note read. "Didn't want to wake you. Elizabeth needs to eat lunch and be at play group by one o'clock. See you later. B." No salutation, no closing intimacies or patented avowals of affection. Even the romantic Morse code she used to scribble on the most incidental of notes — love, followed by an ampersand and a string of X's — was missing. Or withheld. Was the reason for the demise of our marriage cultural, historical? There was a reassuring allure in the idea of blaming social forces. It saved me the trouble of admitting I was often incredibly distant and self-concerned. But I couldn't speak for Barbara. All I knew was that there was a charged atmosphere between us. I would have liked to believe that it wasn't Barbara and me arguing, but some force-field poltergeists, aural projections of our least compromising, most infantile impulses and rock-bottom wants. But I couldn't do that either. By falling in love at sixteen, each of us still unformed, as open as furrows, as resilient as we were naive, we were fused in a way that no longer seemed possible to me, the purity of youth eclipsed by the looming presence of the world. It was this same presence — I'm not blaming it; it merely brought out what was latent in each of us — that split us like an atom. High school sweethearts marry. Boy becomes baseball hero. Get real. You can only stretch Americana so far.

"You always expect me to be right there for you," she'd said. "Miss Perfect. You're not the only one who feels alone, you know."

"You're telling me you feel abandoned?"

"Emotionally, you're not here."

"How much more here can I get?"

"Forget it. Just forget it."

Sometimes I had the feeling that Barbara had married a fake. Despite all my accomplishments — the batting titles, the scholarships and contracts, the on-camera glory and in-print praise — I always felt they had the wrong guy. I was an imposter, some escaped paranoiac imitating a promising All-American. Perhaps Barbara hadn't noticed because she was rebounding from her parents' deaths. Maybe I had simply been the nearest thing to grab hold of to at least slow her look-ma-no-hands tumble from security into Chicken Little chaos.

Our sexual life took on an unbridled urgency after her mother's funeral, and our separations — perhaps part of some vast pattern — when I left for college after summer and holiday vacations were intolerable. They were filled with post-phone-call depressions, and middle-of-the-night panics.

"Are you coming back?" It was Barbara, her voice coming at me through the midwinter night's blackness like a bright, dream-lit phantom.

"What?"

"You're not, are you?"

It took me a moment to realize I was holding the receiver in one hand, that I was in the Raskolnikovian garret room I had rented at the beginning of the semester from a man clad head to foot in double knit, five hundred miles away from her. I sat up and looked around the room, the bed covers falling from my shoulders. The window curtains, wrinkled and thin as paper towels, sawed back and forth, their ends fluttering in the draft like the skirts of a ghost. There was an arctic clarity infusing the room, a beyond-the-grave placidity and chill that bordered on the timeless. Even Barbara's voice was elemental and spooky, stripped of all pretense, and unashamedly infantile. It seemed to be coming to me from the deepest griefs of memory, like the voice of a child speaking across the vast, Ferris-wheeling gyre of the universe.

"Barb?"

"I don't want you to leave me," she said. Then I lost her to tears.

The conversation made no sense for several minutes. "I'm not going anywhere," I said. I felt as if I were trying to talk someone down off the ledge of a building. "Come on. I'm here." I spoke in measured, reassuring tones, never above the whispered pitch of a lullaby. I felt a swelling helplessness, which was only deepened by the distance between us. "Come on," I said. "It's all right." I hoped to calm her with the authority of my confidence. Her weeping subsided, slightly.

She sniveled, gathering herself. "Can you come home?"

"Now?"

"Uh-huh."

"It's" — I reached for my bedside clock — "three in the morning."

"So?" There was a croaky, almost willful childishness in her tone.

"I'm five hundred miles away."

Barbara burst into tears again, though this onslaught seemed to possess an almost reckless quality, signaling perhaps an inconsolable, even elemental despair. Something permanent and life afflicting. She slipped beyond my ability to comfort her. Clipped, sputtering noises punctuated her gasping for breath, and a renewed sense of surrender overwhelmed her. I imagined her disappearing, sucked down into a great, swirling blackness.

"I'm coming."

Twelve hours later, after driving through a petulant slush storm, fat, gumdrop-sized beads of watery snow pelting the windshield of my Nova, I arrived at Barbara's office, a tiny, ill-lighted room in the basement of the hospital. I suppose we both looked like zombies, midwinter pallor and crescents dark as plums under our sleep-starved eyes the only color either of us had. The instant she saw me, she leaped out of her chair, and, giving in to an almost ecstatic sadness, flew to me, tears streaking her face. Now, our love used up, her notes shared with me no more than a few rigid, listlike thoughts, and merely the initial of her name.

Elizabeth came back into the room after I disposed of the note, put on swim trunks, and lowered myself into the tub. She was wearing a one-piece swimsuit designed as boldly as a toothpaste tube — all bright, look-at-me colors, and lettering like cannon shots. "GIRL" was spelled out across the front of it, as if the concept were a challenge, some role to be asserted and defended. There was something confrontational creeping into her style of dress, an almost territorial aspect that worried me. Also a uniformity bordering on the totalitarian. Mail-order catalogs arrived at the house daily, selling everything from $300,000 necklaces to soldier-of-fortune flak jackets. Packages descended on our doorstep, the local UPS driver leaving box after box on the front porch like foundlings. If Barbara's clothing had evolved into a decidedly upscale blend of bohemianism and revisionist, aristocratic Americana — pleated linen pants worn with plastic, jelly-colored sandals; to-die-for cashmere sweaters draped over prison-quality work shirts and paint-spattered jeans — Elizabeth's had degenerated into a cloying version of assembly-line cute. Armies of kids — racially mixed according to some marketing strategist's blueprint — were lined up in catalogs like members of some hedonist youth brigade. There were cross-eyed nerds, and gawky though confident-looking adolescents; Oriental hipsters with slicked-down hair, and black kids with Ivy League, tortoise-shell glasses; white kids from the heartland and Indian kids from innercity ghettoes were dressed in $400 leather jackets and $60 ski sweaters. Back-to-school notebooks bound in kid leather cost $45. Every item bore a logo, some identifying mark that seemed to have a hypnotic effect on her. I wasn't sure she even knew why she wanted the things she wanted, but she pursued them with fiendish intensity nonetheless. It was as if she were wired to self-destruct if she didn't.

"We have to cut back on the amount of television she watches," Barbara said, after we had put Elizabeth to bed early one evening. Homemade hamburgers had evoked in her a response that can only be described as psychotic.

"There's no paper on them."

"What?"

"There's no paper on them!" she had said, her voice shifting gears from high-pitched trepidation to horror-movie frenzy. When Barbara admitted a moment later that the burgers were not, indeed, certifiable, Ronald McDonald–approved burgers, the shrieking commenced.

"Maybe she's not programmed to ingest nonsynthetic food-stuffs."

"I'm telling you, she needs to watch less television."

"She needs an exorcism is what she needs."

Draped over one shoulder, covering her bathing suit strap, was a Smurfs beach towel the size of a magic carpet. On her feet were banana-peel-yellow flip-flops with treaded, black rubber bottoms. Die-molded sand sharks were attached to their straps. A bracelet adorned with miniature charms — fruit, hearts, tropical birds, their surfaces painted with glossy, lacquered colors — wreathed one ankle. Shielding her eyes from the bathroom light were Beat poet sunglasses — sleek, pitch-colored frames, lenses black as espresso. She put her towel on one of the antique benches and climbed up to the level of the tub.

"Why are you wearing sunglasses?"

"You said to put my bathing suit on."

"You can't wear your bathing suit without shades?" She shook her head. "Fine. Get in the tub."

The water, sizzling around me, bubbles surfacing and snapping like thousands of milk-soaked Rice Krispies, seemed to be loosening my shoulder. I was submerged to my chin, my head peeping out above the surface. The sharp edge of the ache had been dulled, either by the pain relievers, the heat and motion of the water, or a combination of the two. All the other minor cramping and soreness was evaporating, rising out of my body. Every morning when I performed this ritual, the years seemed to drop off me like old skin. But no matter how deeply I slipped into a groove of looseness, the buoyant, walking-on-air sense of lightness and vigor that I had in my youth never came any closer to me than a memory. I was driven now less by vitality than by the engine of a slowly eroding will.

The telephone rang as my eye was following headlines on a television news update. Stock prices, printed in thumb-sized electronic lettering, scudded across the bottom of the screen. Above them photographs of a controversial new bomber were flashed, interspersed with congressional committee reports on its viability, cost, and instant obsolesence. With my body numb and weightless beneath the water, I felt like some futuristic, science fiction being, a floating brain connected by tie lines to information-spewing devices. My torso and limbs had been traded in for a sexless, pain-free, data-driven immortality, an emotionally nil existence in which I was simply aware of information winging bloodlessly into being, then vanishing without echo or shadow instants later.

Elizabeth answered the phone on the third ring as I watched the final news hook before the commercial. "Strike looms as baseball talks stall. Next." Half submerged in water, shades wrapped around her temples, she looked like some hip mermaid, a fantastic fish-child I had befriended while scuba diving. Turning and extending the receiver to me, she said, "It's Grandma."

I took the handset from her, then cradled it between my ear and shoulder. My mother was crying. I knew then my father was either ill or dead, and when she told me he had had a heart attack, my silence broke with a chest-clearing exhalation of breath which she mistook for a bereavement that went beyond words, instead of a forgiving grief I wanted to reject. "I know," she said, "I know." But she didn't. And there was no way she could without my telling her. Which I did not.

Twenty-Two

MY PARENTS had suddenly become old. I wasn't certain when it happened, or if the process had been gradual, the way one can't tell if a spouse is aging, gaining weight, or losing hair. There's a patience to decay, and a stealth to it, an invisible yet fluid clockwork that denies measurement on a quotidian scale.

The last time I had seen them — and it had been several months — my parents were conspicuously middle-aged. With my brother and me grown and out on our own, and the mortgage on their house paid off, there was an abrupt turnabout in their level of disposable income. Some kind of middle-class joie de vivre infected them, and there was a rash of purchases. Mostly durable objects: car, dishwasher, twenty-four-inch color TV, his-and-her recliners. There was also an oblique yet nonetheless distinct upgrading of their sense of self-worth, particularly in my father. His insecurity, masked over the years by hardheadedness, defensive parochialism, and — as his youth fell away from him, taking with it the illusion of second chances and new lives — an almost fearful intractability, was slowly replaced by arrogance, as if the new money made him somehow indestructible, and above reproach. Our relationship, never a paragon of father-son affection to begin with, had cooled over the years, iced down by our respective stubbornnesses, which seemed to grow in proportion to our individual net worth, as if what we earned inured us to the other's criticism.

Before the money, all my father had was the authority of size, his looming figure dwarfing me as a boy. And all I had was hitting.

My father was in the stands the first time I stepped into a batter's box. A pockmarked infield surrounded by grass bleached as yellow as the faces of daisies by a lack of water and the heat of the sun. The mound a flat dirt disk, irregular around the edges and primitive-looking as a Druid altar. On it a second grader. One year my senior, he appeared to me daunting, terrifying, and at the same time confused, as if he was stepping into a role he only dimly understood.

As I walked to the plate, Mr. Damm, one of the local fathers who acted as a coach, encouraged me from third base with handclaps and dispassionate, matter-of-fact cries of, "Let's go, Mike. Get a hit." I saw the boy on the mound look over to the small bank of stands behind the first-base line, not as if for instruction, but for validation and approval. In the bleachers, luminous in a white T-shirt and cap, was a large man wearing sunglasses. In the brightness his head seemed to disappear around their black frames until there were just two black holes, as if his eye sockets had been eviscerated. "Strike this little shit out, Deke. Strike him out."

I noticed my own father sitting on the edge of the bottom row. Alone, he was leaning forward with his hands clasped when he heard the other man's voice, and looked up at him. Not to challenge him — the man was oblivious to the stares of those around him anyway — but simply, it appeared, to take stock of him. My father seemed to grow angry with himself. He crossed his arms over his chest as if he felt the need to assert himself yet felt unempowered.

He wasn't an athlete, and my accomplishments were always something of a mystery to him. For some reason — impatience, insecurity, an inability to express, or even fathom, an affection for the process of the game, for living itself — he never reconciled himself to the incremental manner in which a career, like a life, is made. He responded only to the home run blows and the somersaulting catches in deep left field, the grist of instant replay slots and thirty-second sports news highlights. Putting the ball in play, advancing a runner, keeping a grounder from getting through the infield — this pecking approach he found tedious. Big innings, runaway games he could turn off in the seventh inning, ten-game division leads on Labor Day — a having-it-over-with state of existence is what he aspired to in all things.

"Well, that's done and out of the way," he said, the day I signed Mr. Percy's first contract offer.

"What is?"

"The contract."

"I got screwed on my contract."

"Be happy you got anything at all," he said, then turned on the television set. We were in my parents' living room just after dinner.

"I am happy. That's why I signed." He ignored this, pausing for a few moments before speaking again.

"I've been looking around and I think certificates of deposit are the best place to dump the money."

"Who said I want to 'dump the money'?"

"What did you plan on doing with it?"

"Barbara and I want to buy a house."

He lowered the TV's remote control box and looked at me. "What do you know about buying houses? What do you know about mortgages? What do you know about anything besides swinging a club like an ape?" He turned away from me again and said, "Nobody's going to give you a thing."

"They already have," I said. But when I said it, I didn't realize that my contract represented for him the end of his attempt to orchestrate my life and therefore live through me, an effort that began with my first at bat.

"Come on. Hit this bum," he had yelled suddenly from the base of the bleachers. "Let's go, let's go!" his uncharacteristic demeanor drawing from me what I'm sure was a look of noncomprehension and confusion. "Let's go, Mike, let's go. Hit, hit!"

And I did. The first pitch. Adjusting to a twenty-odd-ounce bat, which felt as if it were half my body weight, I took the pitch inside out, rapping the ball down the first-base line to a stunned, weak-armed kid in right who made a torpid throw, Mr. Damm waving to me from third to come on, come on, then yelling slide, slide, which I also did, about a foot from the bag, more or less just falling on it and jamming one knee into my Adam's apple. When I came up through a cloud of dust to sporadic applause from our team's parents, and way-to-goes and ass-slaps from Mr. Damm, I saw on my young father's face — his arms crossed, lips as expressionless and even as a knife's edge, head nodding almost imperceptibly in stern approval — a look that seemed to say he felt momentarily impregnable, and somehow avenged. Unlike the state I found him in at the hospital.

My mother was in the waiting room when I found her. After a quick glance around the room, I'd asked for her at the desk. A nurse looked up and pointed her out to me. When I turned, I saw my mother walking toward me from a spot I'd just glanced at. I hadn't recognized her. The stiffness in her gait was new to me, and there was something strange and unfamiliar about her appearance, a ghostliness or pallor, some lack of definition that was disturbing, and momentarily unnameable. As I bent to kiss her, I became aware of the fact that her skin, until recently fairly smooth, was deeply, and perhaps more startling, irrevocably lined. I hadn't recognized her because she was an old woman instead of my mother. Her hair was gray and thinning. It shone dully, like freshly polished pewter. The rectangular frames of her glasses dwarfed the upper part of her face, as if she had shrunk, or subtly withered behind them. When we sat down, she took hold of my hand. I let it stay there, although I felt she wanted me to feel helpless. That through some perverse optimism she expected this to bring me close to my father again. I was sure she wanted some sort of television Movie of the Week version of grieving — the kids rallying around, the comforting nurse, the gifted and sympathetic young intern subbing for the silver-haired heart specialist who was away on an extended golf vacation.

"Barbara couldn't come?" she said, when she stopped crying. It was an oblique but unsubtle dig, and I let go of her hand.

"Barbara wasn't home when you called."

"Who's watching Elizabeth?"

"I dropped her off at play group."

"She'll be safe there?"

"No. She'll be taken hostage by terrorists and sold into slavery in the Middle East," I said, unfairly directing my anger with the situation at her.

We were silent for several moments, my mother's hands clasped around the brassy gold buckle of her purse as if it were a lifeline. I tensed without wanting to, and a knot of pain began to swell in my shoulder.

"I think your father would like to see you," she said.

I was leaning forward, head in hands, and I closed my eyes. I simply closed my eyes.

"You can go in now." A nurse was standing in front of my mother and me when I opened them. Hands pressed against her white skirt, she seemed as solicitous as a stewardess. When she turned her eyes to me — deep brown circles as large and dark as chocolate kisses — I realized I had seen that stare thousands of times outside clubhouse entranceways. But here it was stranger, as if celebrity had a way in our culture of taking precedence over death.

"Do you want to go in first?" my mother asked.

"No, you go in."

"You are going in, aren't you?"

"Yes, I'll go in. Just go."

My mother walked toward the wide, swinging doors of the ICU, one hand tugging her blouse down around her hips, her pocketbook dangling from her other hand like a child's lunch box. Oblivious of me, she seemed small and intimidated by the world. The nurse left and I sat by myself and smoked half a cigarette, wondering if I was blind to my own shortcomings due to pride. Or maybe not pride. Maybe I had been reduced to a machine. I hit off machines, trained with them, was examined and rehabilitated by them. What if I had become a machine? Was I supposed to be capable of pity and compassion? Or was this merely nostalgia for some fabled and illusory past, an atavism motivated by fear of death?

Minutes later, my mother came out through the ICU doors, a tissue crumpled in one hand. She was walking with her head down, as if there were shame attached to the situation. The unyielding sterility of the room only intensified her look of helplessness. Molded plastic chairs and machine-cut Formica counters, Sheetrock walls and a rigid grid of linoleum tile. There was a denial of pain here, an emphasis on the efficient and the anonymous, as if this were a virtue, some blind modern grace.

"How is he?"

My mother shook her head. "Not good. He asked to see you."

I didn't believe her. I had no trouble imagining her spoon-feeding my father suggestions for a reconciliation, even while his vital signs were faltering, plunging off the charts into nothingness. But I could not picture my father's dying breath being expended on a request for my presence. "Please don't argue," she said. "In a minute they're going to tell you that you can't go in." I began to move away from her, but she reached out and laid a hand on my arm. "Say you're sorry to him," she said. "He wants you to."

I felt separated from her at that moment by some abyss of understanding, as if we had come from two different planets. She seemed to have stopped somewhere in time, her capacity for rearranging the disordered, random elements of the world into new perceptions atrophying. I thought at first that this was a willful rejection of change, an extreme form of insecurity. But as I looked at her I realized that her understanding of the situation between my father and me was fixed inextricably in the past. What I was seeing was my mother dwindling, receding — not just physically, but retreating from me in time. I turned and walked away, leaving her behind as if she were a figure in a dream.

The room beyond the doors was filled with beds. Men and women were lying in them, their arms attached to monitors, intravenous feeding devices, and waste retention tubes. With their eyes closed and heads fallen to one side, they looked wasted, crucified, dead to everything but some faint hallucination of the world around them. As I made my way, a team of physicians and nurses responding to an alarm raced by me clutching charts, hand-held instruments, vials, and syringes. I felt as if I were in the chamber of some vast machine, beds aligned on either side of the corridor like pistons, technicians repairing and replacing faltering parts.

Beyond a partially closed screen my father lay propped up against the back of his bed. With skin the dead, grayish white of putty, a deep, plum-colored rut beneath each eye, and his hair spread out wildly around his skull, he looked like an end-of-the-world Beckett character, a picture of immobility and nearly spectral luminescence. Covering his nose and mouth was a clear plastic mask, held in place by a rubber harness strapped around the crown of his head. A canister of oxygen, grim as a torpedo, stood beside his bed like an angel of death. Flesh-tinted electrodes clung to his arms and chest, measuring the electrical projection of his heartbeat. IV bottles fed a steady stream of sugar and antiarrhythmic agents into his blood. It was as if he were some high-tech science project, a twentieth-century Frankenstein kept alive by a network of stimulants, monitors, and pumps. I felt as if I were standing in front of an icon, something imposing and silent. I considered that he was conscious and aware of my presence but in an act of supreme disdain was ignoring me by feigning sleep. Filled with an overwhelming sense of waste, disillusionment, and loss, I removed the tips of my fingers from the foot of the bed and, with the rhythm of his heart beating as indifferently as a blip on a radar screen, turned to go.

Then I noticed his hands. Clenched into fists the size of soft-balls, they lay at his sides as if pinned there by invisible restraints. I stepped closer and, as if it were an amulet or sacred stone, took hold of the one nearest me. There was a leathery grit to the skin, like the hide of a baseball. It felt like Mr. Percy's hand — parched, skeletal, bloodless. As I looked down, my father seemed to go through some fast-forward, horror-movie metamorphosis, his flesh revealing a death mask that was the shape of Mr. Percy's skull. My father's fingers began to wrap themselves around mine and he drew me closer, exactly as Mr. Percy had drawn me to himself countless times to whisper commands, secret pacts, and temptations. With his chest rising and falling, he opened his lips, his breath fogging the surface of the plastic mask until — more hypnotized than dutiful — I lifted it and brought my ear to his mouth. The lids of his eyes rose as if he were coming back from the dead, his pupils glazed and lifeless as marbles. Then I heard the susurrous outlines of his voice, the nearly breathless, misshapen words he spoke, the last syllable trailing off with a faint, hoarse, stertorous whisper. "You're nothing. . . ." Then he let go of my hand as if he had passed on some eternal curse. Released, he closed his eyes, and withdrew into a peace indistinguishable from death.

Have you ever held a baseball? It's like touching a mantra. There's a completeness and inscrutability in the way it settles into the cradle of your fingers. The true marvel is its perfect fit in any hand of any size beyond an infant's. Give a baseball to an infant, though, and you'll see it rub the ball like some magic object or talisman that possesses gift-granting powers, then pop a section of the ball between its lips and suck as if it had hold of its mother's breast.

Circle: completion, perfection, never-endingness. The wheel. The roundness of the globe, the New World. The bending of light. The cyclical expansion and contraction of the universe.

Know what the sweetness and peace you feel emanating from a baseball when you hold it is? The universe. Not just a representation of it, but your basic Kantian thing-in-itself. Self-contained, complete, whole. Circles are the noumenal outlines of the infinite. Fuck with them, you get A-bombs.

Bat, ball. Male, female. Coupling, creation, oneness. The impulse is toward union, reintegration. A melding into something singular and indivisible.

Home. Om.

The Sanskrit word for energy centers distributed throughout the human body is *chakra*. In paintings, these are represented by circles with red centers. There are nine *chakras* in the body. Nine *chakras*, nine fielders.

Question: Where does the stitching on a ball begin, where does it end?

Second question: Red stitches? *Sattva,* the binding force in the universe, the one which pulls us toward wholeness and cohesion, is represented by white. *Rajas,* the tendency toward circular movement — the spin on a fastball, the rotation of the universe, the creative force behind all things — is represented by red.

To digress for a moment: Balls are also called "seeds."

Did we derail somewhere along the time line? Get sucked into this obviously fallacious patriarchal "image and likeness" deal without realizing its implications? Submission, judgment, punishment. Maybe our representational deity needs a serious overhaul.

Father figure. Phallus. Fallout.

Beauty. (Beg)innings. Baseballs.

Circles. Case closed.

Twenty-Three

THEY WERE WAITING at the end of the tunnel. Lee Wheeler, Don Stone, Cap Carver, and, in his wheelchair, Mr. Percy. We were in the bowels of the stadium, a labyrinth of girders, pipes, cement, and cinderblock passageways buried beneath the lower mezzanine seats and street-level concession stands. Water-stained sheets of corrugated fiberglass lined portions of the tunnel. They had fallen away in spots, exposing a shallow valley of rubble, discarded beverage cups, and sewer mains like some post-holocaust city of the future.

Don Stone, arms folded, feet planted half a bat's length apart, was staring in my direction when I turned into the corridor. It may have been the light — bare fluorescent strips suspended from thirty-foot-high girders by rusted chains and corroded metal cages — but Stone's face was pallid, and his glasses — polished, gold-framed windows that had a militaristic rigidity and intransigence about them — reflected the light directly back at me, turning his eyes into gleaming silver dots. He looked like some futuristic android law enforcer.

Behind him, Cap Carver, leaning on his cane, stood looking off to one side. He was smoking a cigarette and flicking the ashes into the pit below the walkway. His leg was sheathed in a flexible, wire-mesh cast, thick ribs of stainless steel stitched into a casing of black nylon. The brace was strapped to his limb just below the

severed end of his uniform pant leg by Velcro-coated tongues. He
looked up when he heard the clopping of my cleats on the wooden
walkway, then flipped his cigarette butt into the rubble and pivoted on his cane.

Lee Wheeler came forward. "You're a few minutes late, Mike."
"I know."

As I approached them, I tightened the wristbands of my batting
gloves and ignored Lee's mild rebuke. I checked to see if Stone
noticed that I was carrying my bat under my left arm rather than
my right, but he was staring up at the riveted metal arches over-
head in disgust.

"So, he's a few minutes late," Mr. Percy said, nudging Lee to
one side. He came toward me in his wheelchair. Its belts and gears
hissed, driven by the machine's electric motor. This was one of
the few times I had seen Mr. Percy without a blanket draped over
his knees. The legs of his suit pants were hiked above his shins.
Just above the ridges of his thin, midnight-black socks were two
shafts the color of mercury, each as smooth as the barrel of a bat,
and gleaming like polished chrome. No flesh, just dead metal
limbs running down into a pair of well-shined black shoes, the
tips of which pointed toward one another, making him seem,
from the waist down, as lifeless as a marionette. "How are you,
boy?"

I stopped several feet in front of him. "I'm fine," I said.

"You hear that?" he brayed to the others. "Boy says he's fine."
Wheeler and Stone nodded with grudging obedience. Meanwhile,
Cap leaned over his cane and spit on the floor. Mr. Percy turned
back to me. "You're fine," he said.

"That's right."

"You look sullen, though." His voice rose an octave. "Are you
sure you're fine?"

I began to wonder if he knew about my father — he owned
the hospital my father was in — and if this grilling and mock
concern was simply a sick joke. While I was in the hospital it had
seemed that he was there, hovering like a spirit, prompting my
father's contempt with a malicious, almost diabolical sense of mis-
chief. "I'm positive," I said.

"You're not upset about anything, are you?"

"No."

"This slump hasn't got you down?"

"It's a slump."

"Good, good. Keep your mind in the game."

"It ain't his mind we're worried about," Cap said, his tone walking a line between glib disdain and let's-get-on-with-it boredom.

"The peanut gallery's not interested in your mind," Mr. Percy said.

"I heard." Cap shot me an I'll-take-care-of-you-later look.

"Think the problem's just mechanics?"

"I think we're dealing with more than just mechanics here," Stone said. He stepped closer to Mr. Percy, as if this enhanced his authority.

"We just want to find out," Lee added.

"As a precaution?" Mr. Percy asked, with an air of curiosity.

"Yes."

Mr. Percy winked at me. "I pay them to take precautions so I don't have to. You don't think this could be the distraction of free agency?" he added, turning his head to address the brain trust behind him. "Lot of money out there," he said, his face coming around to meet mine again, his expression inscrutable.

"He's a pro," Stone said. "Nothing but hitting and fielding should be on his mind from March until October."

"Nothing is," Cap said. "Including hitting and fielding."

"Mike and his agent know where to find us," Lee said. "And Mike knows my door's always open."

"Well, maybe we should ask Mike if he wants to sit down and talk," Mr. Percy said. "Do you want to sit down and talk, Mike?"

"I'd be happier doing it when all the facts are in," Lee added cautiously. "I think free-agent discussions are premature at this point."

"You don't foresee him becoming one?"

"Absolutely. It's just that I think it would be wiser not to have uncertainty clouding the process. It's not my place to advise him, but it could be in his best interest to play out the rest of the season, then worry about a contract."

"That could be very good advice," Mr. Percy said to me. "How many days do you need this season to qualify as a free agent?"

"I don't know."

"One-oh-nine," Lee said.

"He can't count above three," Cap said. "Walks confuse him."

"Well, you're only halfway there," Mr. Percy said.

"And they're threatening to strike," Stone added. "No play, no pay."

"And no credit for time in the majors," Lee said. "A strike could negate your free-agency status."

"Not to mention anger and disappoint a lot of devoted fans," Stone said.

"So if Mike were to go on the disabled list . . . ?" Mr. Percy threw the possibility up for consideration.

"If we were convinced there was anything seriously wrong that required rehab time in the minors . . . ," Lee said, then shrugged his shoulders.

"No credit for minor league time," Stone said.

"No credit for minor league time," Mr. Percy echoed, with a faint, feigned hint of remorse. "So, I guess it would be in your best interest not to have your teammates strike," he said. Then waited for me to answer.

"Could cost you a year and a lot of money if you don't have the days to qualify as a free agent," he reminded me.

"I know what it'll cost."

"Do you?" he said, staring at me. "Since when are you the laconic hero?"

"I'd just like to get this over with."

"We all would. This isn't pleasant. Do you believe we really want to see that you're hurt?" I didn't know what I believed at that moment, so I kept my eyes on the ground. "Without you," he said, "we're nothing." I raised my eyes at this unexpected reversal of my father's words. Mr. Percy was staring at me with, for once, an intensity that bordered on conviction, even envy. His lifeless legs, thin as bamboo shoots, propped on iron pedals, and his atrophied figure nearly as immobile as my deathbed-bound father's sent a sadness that outweighed my anger coursing through me. I sensed that what he saw when he looked at me was the embodiment of some phantom he was fighting — time, mortality, powerlessness. "You're the game, boy," he said. "You need to play it."

"But there's one catch."

"You can't play it without me," he said, nodding slowly. "Good," he added, growling the word as he studied me. "You catch on quick. Carver," he shouted.

"What?"

"We have a pitcher?"

"If his arm isn't dead yet from waiting."

"I didn't ask you for a scouting report."

"He's ready."

"I thought I was hitting off a machine."

"What's the difference?" Mr. Percy said.

"You can't move the ball off the corners of the plate with a machine," Stone said.

I released the bat from the crook of my arm and started toward the mouth of the cage. "I think you miss the point, Don." The frame of Mr. Percy's wheelchair creaked as he pivoted on the walk behind me. Stone looked over my shoulder toward the old man, confused.

"What the boy means," Mr. Percy said, "is they each do what I tell them to."

I pulled the green, diamond-shaped netting to one side, and slipped inside the batting cage. The platform, eighty feet long by twenty feet wide, sat on carbon-steel stilts like a landlocked oil rig. Thousand-pound sheets of grid metal were bolted to the frame, then covered with Astroturf carpet. In the subway-station light of the cage, all glare and shadow, the fake grass glowed with a filmy, almost extraterrestrial iridescence.

There were three cages. Two were equipped with pitching machines, olive-green arms with hands like garden spades. Run by pulleys, they scooped balls up off a tee and hurled them toward a makeshift batter's box at eighty-five miles per hour. The other cage was for live-arm batting practice. There, flesh-and-blood pitchers fired split-finger fastballs, which dove like gulls ten feet in front of the plate, or full-tilt sliders, which hummed in toward the box with enough spin to make the seams of the ball bleed into a single red dot the size of a thumbprint. Half a foot from the box, the ball would sidestep the plate and drop half a dozen inches faster than you can unzip your fly.

Cap limped down the tunnel to the dugout telephone and called the pitcher in from the bullpen. His cane could be heard thumping against the planks of the walkway as he made his way back.

Mr. Percy wheeled himself down the short ramp onto the runway that connected the cages. Lee Wheeler followed, with Don Stone, looking chastened and sulky after misjudging the breadth of Mr. Percy's scorn, trailing behind.

I turned my back to them and began stretching, corkscrewing my upper body in each direction, holding the bat waist high in front of me. When I went to my right and my shoulder opened up away from my body, there was a sensation that felt like threads snapping. Moving faster consolidated the effect, bunching it into a tight clutch that popped. The pain rang down my arm and across my back in long, sweeping waves. I bent forward from the waist and dropped my arms toward the floor, bouncing lightly to loosen my hamstrings. When I stood upright again and took a couple of cuts with the bat, I found I couldn't extend my right arm.

"A little stiffness in the shoulder there, Mike?" Mr. Percy, his wizened hand cupped over the starter switch of his wheelchair, was staring at me with an expression of mock puzzlement.

"Just a cramp. This place is like a dungeon."

"You wouldn't cramp if you stretched a little more, and drank a little less," Stone said.

"Right. And if I say my prayers every night, my soul will go to heaven."

"All I do is explain why you're in the shape you're in."

"Sorry. Thought I detected a tone of moral superiority." I punctuated my remarks with half swings of the bat.

"Why don't we get on with this?" Lee said. "Where's Cap?"

Cap yelled from the tunnel, "I'm coming, for Christ's sake."

"Why?" Mr. Percy reached up and patted Lee's arm. "Mike's letting us in on the state of his soul. I think we owe it to him to listen."

Cap limped in through the doorway and made his way down the ramp. "Pitcher's on his way."

"Mike's just been wondering if he has a soul," Mr. Percy said to him.

"If he does, it's for sale like everyone else's."

Mr. Percy made a lowing, gutteral sound, pensive, brooding. "Sounds bleak, Mike. Are you having a crisis of faith? Do you think that could be the cause of the slump?"

Stone, who had the sense of humor of a computer terminal, rolled his head back in frustration.

"I think I'd like not hearing that cramps are the result of moral dissipation."

"It's a retreat toward conservatism," Mr. Percy said. "Happens with age. Or to nations and baseball teams in decline."

"Look, if Mike is tight, let him warm up against one of the machines," Lee suggested.

It would be the best way to test the range my shoulder had. I waited a moment, then Mr. Percy said, "Don't let me stop you. Go ahead."

I ducked through the flap in the netting and walked past them into the adjacent cage. Someone had left a footstool on home plate. I moved it to one corner, then putted the few loose balls lying near the batter's box up toward the other end of the cage. A thick, black electrical cable ran down one of the corner seams of the cage. At the end of it was a dull silver box with black on/ off buttons as fat as checkers. I hit the starter, then backpedaled into the box. The motor that drove the machine's pulleys clicked on and the cage filled with an accelerating hum. When the belt speed peaked, the noise thinned to a soft whine, a familiar white noise that triggered my concentration. I touched the outside of the plate with the head of my bat and eased into a loose stance. My weight was back lightly on my hind foot, my arms were relaxed, my hands even with my right shoulder. The metal arm started a slow cartwheel and swept down to scoop a ball up out of the chute. Then it crept upward in an arc, like a roller coaster climbing a steep hill. At a position of five minutes before the hour the arm whipped forward and the ball sailed the length of the cage, tailing down on a smooth line as it approached the plate. I waited. There was a grace, an apparently effortless freedom in the ball's flight that transfixed me, a loveliness I simply liked to watch. I held my position and let the ball wing past me into the net. Then the arm came forward again and released a second pitch. As it swooped in toward the plate, I opened my stance, stepping up to meet it, allowing my hips to carry my hands and arms forward. All I wanted to do was put the barrel of the bat on the ball. I had no intention of driving it. I let my left arm guide the bat and took my right hand off its handle as the knob rolled past my belt buckle. The front half of my torso went with the rotation of my hips and thighs, my left shoulder opening as it followed the sweep of the bat, my right arm closing over my chest. My shoulder felt tender, but looser. I hit the next pitch harder, stepping into it with more quickness. By the fourth pitch I was uncocking my wrists sharply as snapping a twig; I began to sting the ball. Everyone was silent, down to business.

As I rapped pitch after pitch into the dim corners of the cage, my rhythm etched its way into a thoughtless, reflexive groove with the machine. My awareness of the others faded. I broke out in a light sweat, beads of perspiration no larger than the tips of sewing needles springing out of my pores. The pain in my shoulder either receded or was numbed by the soothing repetition of thrusting forward, then pulling back. I wasn't conscious of compensating for any tightness or lack of movement. The bat was firing through the strike zone, my hands driving it into the first half of its arc, then giving up their momentum to the forward motion of the stick. My rhythm became as mechanical as the machine's. Set, tense, fire, reset. Wait, react. Maybe this was what I had been looking for, a binary existence, some on/off mode of being in which I was oblivious to my father's words, Mr. Percy's money, and, in a larger sense, death. The peace of a machine. Maybe this was what the game gave me — dehumanization rather than transcendence. Perhaps I was a technological pagan, homages to corn gods, divine animals, and tree spirits replaced in my world by a worship of the man-made, the mechanical, and the comfort-bringing. The frenzied dances of witch doctors and shamans had yielded to the sober readings of charts, X rays, and electronically produced graphs. In place of fire festivals, we had the playoffs. As a machine, I rendered my father's judgment of me meaningless. Maybe everything isn't permitted, as Ivan Karamazov suggested, but is simply denied meaning, is mechanical. And perhaps the reason my father was bitter was because he had failed to reduce himself to the state of a machine, and so he passed on his sense of nothingness to me like some primitive transference of evil, or the purging of a demon.

As if running on the same current as the machine, I waited for the next pitch. Its arm sprang forward, clanging like bells at a railroad crossing, and delivered nothing. When the arm came up empty a second time, I relaxed my grip on the bat, came out of my trance, and crossed the cage to the turn-off switch. The whine of the machine faded around me.

"Not bad, Mike," Lee said. "Any stiffness?"

"I didn't notice." I actually hadn't.

"Maybe you would have if you'd made contact with two hands," Stone said.

I came out of the cage onto the ramp with the others. "I wasn't following through?"

"You looked like you were trying to fling the bat halfway across the infield," Cap said. A tall, choirboy-faced kid stood behind him, as wide in the shoulders as a refrigerator. A second kid, stumpier, red-haired, and corseted in catcher's gear, waited beside him, his mask resting on his hip. I didn't recognize either of them.

"Your left arm was flying away from your body because your right hand was leaving the bat handle before it even got over the plate," Stone said.

"Maybe he's invented a new swing," Mr. Percy said, his voice a spry mixture of bemusement and sarcasm.

"Yeah, one without power or control," Cap added.

Mr. Percy looked at me like a guilty puppy. "You probably should have one of them," he said meekly, seemingly sad to have to disappoint me. I didn't trust him when he was solicitous. This was the flip side of his ruthlessness, the joy he took in deceit. I felt more secure when he was berating aides, firing coaches, and castigating his top brass. "Which do you think he should have, Cap? Power or control?" Mr. Percy looked at me as if he were speaking in a code I should have understood.

"He's batting third in our lineup," Stone said. "If he's not our strongest hitter, he has no business being there."

"With a strike possible, being in first when it starts is the best place to be," Lee added. "We can't afford to make ourselves vulnerable at this point."

They spoke as if I weren't there, Lee and Stone trying to persuade Mr. Percy that I was the part of the machine that wasn't functioning, Cap dreaming of some ideal machine from his past. Only Mr. Percy paid me any attention. His hands, arthritically gnarled into claws, lay between the thin shafts of his prosthetic thighs. A thin, almost rueful smile flattened his pale lips, as if his power over me saddened as much as pleased him.

"Are you making the team vulnerable, Mike?" he asked. "Hm? Maybe just a little bit?" His eyes lost their blackness as they warmed to his mockery. "Come on. You can tell me. You can tell Mr. Percy."

The others around us seemed to recede in space. It was only Mr. Percy and me. Through some infernal process of the game — traveling, negotiating contracts, being reduced to baseball card size then blown up to billboard poster proportions, diminished and refined by drills into a machine, then deified by a god-hungry audience — I had become lost. And this being lost was what my father meant when he said I was nothing. I was this small thing, this boy tethered by fear to the death-driven phantoms of the male world. And because I was this small lost thing, all I did have was

Mr. Percy. And the sadness in his smile was there because he knew it.

I climbed into the cage with the two unnamed boys and, with Stone, Cap, and Lee Wheeler conferring mumurously behind me, swung at pitches that moved further and further toward the outer edge of the strike zone, until the pain in my shoulder increased to a point where will no longer had any sway. My muscles and ligaments locked, and Lee finally said, "Okay, Mike. That's it."

I lowered my bat and stood in the box for a moment, the kid behind me moving away in silence. I tore back the Velcro bands of my batting gloves, stripped them off, and dropped my helmet onto the fake turf. When I turned to find my way out of the cage, Mr. Percy was not gone, as I expected. Instead he had wheeled himself close to the edge of the cage and, leaning forward in his chair, was holding the diamond-shaped netting to one side so that I could step out.

"Wheeler," he said, looking at me with an unreadable expression, "make sure this boy has every ounce of medical attention he needs."

"We'll get him to the doc first thing in the morning."

"Whatever it takes," Mr. Percy said, ignoring Lee, and smiling at me as if he'd won. "He's still our boy," he said. "We're not going to desert him now."

Twenty-Four

LEE WHEELER scheduled an appointment for me with the team physician, and Cap removed my name from the clubhouse lineup board. Cecil Ffolkes, who had lost his starting position to Otis, took my place, and the team's PR man, Harvey Beckenbridge, announced that I was being placed on the fifteen-day disabled list, pending examination. As I stripped off my sweat-soaked clothes, there seemed to be a hush in the clubhouse. My teammates dressed with grim haste, then wordlessly slipped past my locker. To be out of their way I went into the trainer's room, people stepping aside as they sailed past me, their eyes directed at the floor.

Otis was on one of the tables, naked except for a white towel draped across his rump as Cliff Thompson massaged the back of his left leg. My shoulder was numb, a fevered deadness echoing through it. I moved along the white countertop, past glass jars filled with cotton swabs, bandages, pills, and gauze. When I reached the acetaminophen tablets, I plucked four out of the jar, then went to the water cooler and took them.

Oscar Rife, a copy of the *Wall Street Journal* spread across his lap, was sitting up reading when I turned and headed for the open table beside Otis. Chunk Stallings, one of the rubdown men, a burly, ex–minor league left fielder with a ruddy complexion and a hairless skull smooth enough to fry an egg on, was seated on a stool in front of Oscar, taping his ankles. Thick as a bull from the hips up, Oscar had tarsal bones brittle as dry toast. Stress fractures and sprains plagued him throughout his career, limiting his range in right field. Before every game he had to have each ankle braced by a tourniquet of Ace bandages.

In response to his public fistfight with Cap Carver and the subsequent humiliation Mr. Percy had subjected him to, Oscar was excelling on the field. Leading the league in jacks with fourteen, he was second in RBIs at thirty-six, and fifth in average — a remarkable stat for him — at .315. He was up for contract renegotiation, so perhaps he thought the best way to sting Mr. Percy was through his pocketbook. But I felt it had more to do with preserving some untouchable center of grace within himself. Of us all, Oscar seemed most comfortable with our role as hero-machine, reconciled to the split in a way most of us were not. Some felt this was because he was more talented than the rest of us, others because he was a heartless, self-indulgent egomaniac. Both arguments had their good points. He looked up from his paper when I climbed onto the table between him and Otis. He studied my eyes closely for a moment, as if upset over my condition in a way I hadn't expected of him. He actually seemed sympathetic. Then he said, "Do you own IBM?"

"What?"

"Reagan's forcing tax cuts through Congress to stimulate business. IBM's at sixty and a quarter. Would you bet on that, or T-bonds at thirteen-three?"

Otis opened his eyes. "He's on the DL, man. He don't care about your financial empire."

"Maybe he hasn't heard," I said. "Tell me you haven't heard, Oscar, and restore my faith in a small portion of mankind."

"I heard. At least I don't go around treating you like some leper."

"You don't have to be asking him about no stocks and shit though, man."

"I'm asking him because I respect his opinion."

"Would you take my advice?" I asked him.

"No."

"Then why are you bothering everybody?" Otis said. "We know you can talk. Don't say nothing, but you can talk."

"I'm just polling the dude. Seeing where the white man's putting his money."

"You think I have the inside track?"

"Only in matters of privilege."

"Oh man, don't be pulling that whiny-ass shit where my ears can hear you." Otis dropped his cigarette into an ashtray.

"It ain't whining if it's fact." Oscar turned to me. "Not to take anything away from you, but you're overrated because you're white. They expect me and that Milquetoast nigger over there to do what we do. Everybody'd be happy with you if you mowed the lawn right."

"How can he be overrated," Otis said, "if he's leading the league in hitting?"

"That's a white man's feat."

Mel Thorn rolled over on the rubdown table behind Oscar. "Yeah, leading the league in strikeouts every year is a real credit to your race, Rife."

"He thinks the bat's his dick," Otis said. "Always waving it around, but it hardly ever touches anything except his own hands."

"Listen, homeboy, don't you come crying to me come contract time when they offer you half what he gets."

"Don't worry. Getting your advice isn't high on my list."

Oscar slid off his table and stepped into his shower clogs, not taking his eyes off Otis. I wasn't sure what drove Oscar, but the story was — and Oscar supported it, adding variations depending on his mood — that Oscar's father was white. Reputedly the owner of a minor league club — in either the Carolina or the Texas League, the tale varied — the man was among the first to begin recruiting and developing black ballplayers for the majors. Attendance in the Negro League was faltering in the late forties, its decline precipitated by the breaking of the color barrier and the advent of television. On one of his scouting trips, the man supposedly met, seduced — some, including, at times, Oscar himself, would say raped — and abandoned the younger sister of one of his Birmingham, Alabama, prospects. The boy, unsigned at the time of Oscar's birth, committed suicide, believing, according to the note he left — a barely literate dispatch filled with misspellings and inverted consonants, scrawled in a childlike hand — that his sister had given herself to the man in exchange for a contract for him. Oscar claimed to have the letter, admitting once in a national interview that he reread it before a big series, or whenever he found himself in a slump. Orphaned at two — his mother was killed suspiciously in an automobile accident on an unlit secondary road — he was taken in by his mother's cousin, and moved north in the midfifties. There he came under the wing of Jake D'Amato, manager of his inner-city baseball league team. D'Amato trained him, and supposedly even arranged a scholarship for Oscar to one of the city's leading private schools, noted for its peerless athletic program. D'Amato died of cancer before Oscar was drafted, but one of the clauses in Oscar's contract called for the club to donate a low four-figure sum to the American Cancer Society every time Oscar hit a game-winning home run. As with every other legend connected with Oscar, the story was mythic, self-propagating, and apocryphal. Though no one questioned Oscar's racial mix. The truth of it — perhaps the only truth about Oscar, aside from his record in the game — lay in his skin. It had the silky veneer of coffee flush with fresh cream.

"Don't listen to me," he said to Otis. "You're nothing but a white man's puppet, anyway."

"And you ain't gonna be happy till Mr. Percy adopts you," Otis shot back at him. "So get out of my face."

Oscar collected his paper and calculator, then started to leave. He stopped directly in front of Otis and pointed at him with a finger thick as a ballpark frank. "Contract time, you watch. This boy gets a piece of the action. We get chump change."

"Any time I get over a million a year, it ain't chump change."

"That's because you're a chump. Too stupid to see the big picture."

"I see the big picture."

"Yeah. What is it?"

"It's you annoying me all the time. Now go on and get your finger out of my face before I bite it off."

"Dumb-ass nigger," Oscar said, then turned. After he'd moved a step, he turned back. He pointed at me with the same finger he'd pointed at Otis. "Yo, this was no disrespect to you. You got talent, get what you can." He paused for a moment, then lowered his arm. "And I hope that shoulder heals quick," he said, then was out of the room before the echo of his voice faded in my ears.

Mel Thorn rose from his rubdown table and followed him. "Get well quick," he said, passing my table. "Right. The only thing he's concerned about is all those pitches over the plate he's not going to see with you out of the lineup."

"Maybe so."

"No maybes about it. Your shoulder just cost him ten dingers for the year."

"He'll live," Otis said.

"That's the fucking problem." Thorn, taped at the ankles, knees, and wrists, walked out of the room.

"The brotherhood of baseball," Otis said. He sat up and extended his leg. Cliff Thompson unwound a snaky length of flesh-colored bandage and began wrapping it around Otis's thigh.

"What do you need, Mike?" he said to me, bent over his work.

"Stone said to get some ice on this." I pointed to my right shoulder.

"Tony, get an ice pack on Mike's shoulder," he shouted. "Hang on, he's coming."

"No rush. I ain't going anywhere."

As Cliff Thompson worked, Otis watched, judging the tightness and position of the bandage. In profile, with his arms behind him for support, Otis looked like a piece of sculpted black marble, the representation of ideal human form rescued from classical antiquity, or else one of those models in street poster ads for designer underwear. He and Cliff exchanged mumbled, single-syllable queries and answers on the fit of the bandage.

Tony, a short, iguana-faced man clad in double-knit pants rolled up at the ankles, appeared with a roll of bandage and a hot-water bag chocked with ice. I raised my elbow and held it away from my side so that he could strap on the ice pack. As Otis and I sat there, our bodies being worked on like machines, I wondered if my father had surrendered his body so readily, or if, closer to death, there was a greater reticence, a sense of invasion and insult.

"You're set." Tony slapped my leg. The ice pack was strapped to my shoulder by yards of Ace bandage, one long loop running under my arm, across my chest, then across my back to the shoulder again.

Cliff hooked the tongue of Otis's bandage to its topmost layer with a metal fastener, then collected his scissors and liniment. "How does that feel?"

Otis tested the support, squeezing his thigh and feeling for tenderness. "Good. Thanks." He slid off the table and we walked out of the room together. "Don't let that shit with Oscar screw with your head," he said as we approached our lockers.

"What do you think he meant, I was going to get a piece of the action?" I decided it wasn't beyond Mr. Percy to have made Oscar the same offer, then to pit the two of us against each other. Maximize our performances, put on a show for the millions, then retract both offers on technicalities in the end.

"What do you think he meant?" Otis kicked a pair of cleats out of the way and sat down in the chair in front of his locker. I reached into my own stall for a shirt to take the chill off my back.

"I think he figures he's getting screwed for being black," I said. "Is he?"

I looked at Otis as he unrolled a pair of socks. I was silent for a moment, the question taking me by surprise. "No."

"There's your answer. You're gonna have enough problems getting your concentration back when your shoulder heals. The last thing you need is to be worrying about some head case. Fuck him." Otis tugged a jockstrap up over his long underwear, and slipped a cup inside it.

"It doesn't bother you, that white man's pet business?"

Pants on, Otis slipped one foot at a time into his cleats. He removed his uniform shirt from a hanger before he turned and looked at me. "That boy's got some jones about Percy loving him. He needs it, I don't. Far as I'm concerned, everything he does is twisted from the git-go. He don't know who the fuck he is. How's he going to tell me who I am?"

I hesitated, watching Otis tuck in his shirttails, then said, "What if I am getting a better deal — because I'm white?"

Otis looked at me, and squatted slightly to adjust the fit of the uniform on his legs. "Well, I'm not here to speculate. Is you, or ain't you?"

I shrugged, tilting my head to one side in a gesture of uncertainty. "There's talk." A moment later, I was stunned to find that I'd revealed to Otis what I had not even told Barbara.

"Well, they don't give away nothing for nothing. Ain't a new thing under the sun. Feel bad about it if you want, but don't think it's something special."

"They're offering me more than just money."

"They would be."

"You don't resent that?"

"I don't want it. Why would I resent it?"

"No blacks in management?"

"A couple of showcase niggers in suits ain't gonna change the day-to-day bullshit. They offer you a chance to do something about that, take it."

"I don't think that's the shot."

"No, I don't think so, either."

Otis took his batting gloves from the locker's top shelf and tucked them into his back pocket.

"They may have offered Oscar the same deal," I said. "What do you think?"

Otis grabbed his mitt, a large black claw with his name stamped on it in bold, gold-leaf letters. He pushed its fingertips down over his own as he looked at me. "I think they're going to go with the color of their choice. Whatever gets them the biggest bang for their buck."

"That's it?"

"That's it."

The last of our teammates darted past us on their way to practice. Across the clubhouse, one of the locker room boys was straightening the pile of shoes on the floor of Oscar's locker, stacking them beside mounds of unopened fan mail. I thought it strange that Oscar and I, apparently so different, were Mr. Percy's favorite wards, the attention he paid us bordering at times on obsession. On the top shelf of Oscar's stall, beside the bottles of deodorant, cologne, after-shave, and baby powder, was an eight-by-ten reproduction of a bearded deity, sunlight ringing the crown of the figure's thick mane of hair. Propped up beside the icon was a photograph, framed in gold filigree, of Oscar leaning over the wheelchair-bound Mr. Percy, a smile as wide as a candy bar parting his lips as he hugged the shoulders of his stern-faced owner.

It may have been the cap on his head — beak up, the pool-table-green lining of it showing — but all the youth in Otis's face seemed heightened when I looked back at him. In spite of the six-figure salary, the inside-the-diamond heroics, the godlike grace, he was still a boy. "Where's your father?" I asked.

"Dead, I hope."

"Really?"

"I haven't seen him for fifteen years. Kind of lost my affection for him. Why? Where's yours?"

"In the hospital. Heart attack. Today."

Otis nodded, studying me silently. "You like him?"

"He hasn't really made that an option."

Otis shrugged, then began unwrapping a chunk of gum. "Then bag it. No percentage in getting all teary-eyed just because he's dying. A prick's a prick."

Cap Carver's voice, stern as a commandment, cracked over our heads like a bullwhip. "Armstrong, get your ass out on the field. You," I turned, "start praying I don't chain your ass to some Triple A bench for the rest of the year."

"Get my drift," Otis said softly, his eyebrows arching in Cap's direction as he went past me.

When the clubhouse was empty I tried to reach Barbara. I let the phone at home ring a dozen times, then redialed and listened to the shrill, unanswered summons again before giving up.

As I suited up the emptiness of the room and the spurious cheer piped into it by the clubhouse speakers struck me as a subtle rebuke. A local DJ gave an upbeat spin to reports of rush-hour traffic jams, tales of celebrity addictions and infidelities, and leaks of fiscal irresponsibility by the city fathers.

During the game I sat on the bench, beside Otis when he was there, alone when he was not. I felt spooked, as if I'd died and come back to see how the world would look without me, whenever Cecil Ffolkes took my place in the batter's box or trotted out to left field. Six innings into the game, the dugout phone rang. Lunch Molloy answered it, listened for several moments, then hung up. He rose and walked down the length of the dugout, then told me, as if telling a third-stringer he was being cut, that I had a telephone call. Before even taking it, I knew that my father was dead.

Twenty-Five

BARBARA WAS straightening throw pillows on the corners of the couch when I found her in the living room. She ignored me, continuing to recenter the spongeware planter filled with paperwhites, realigning the edges of the dhurrie rug with the corners of the Shaker coffee table. It may have been the room, the breadth of it, or its spare opulence — a dried flower wreath hanging over the fireplace, red-and-black antique checkerboards softening the light of linen-shaded ginger jar lamps, white-framed windows and glass doors opening onto a redbrick patio lighted by scented torches — but in that room, so different from the rooms of our childhood, a sense of fugue, of unreality magnified by my father's death, intensified for me until it seemed that Barbara and I had somehow slipped out of time. When she turned, her features, in all their resolute familiarity, passed over into strangeness. At twenty-seven, she had lost all her girlishness. If I had filled out the way Stone had predicted, Barbara had moved toward a more chiseled version of her younger self. Her waist-length hair was a memory now, distant as high school friends, the joints we used to pass back and forth in our old Nova, and four-figure bank balances. She wore her hair clipped just below the ears like an Elizabethan prince's, heightening the angularity of her features, the roundness and softness of them rendered by the heat of time down to a point of lean authority. She worked out daily, either in our private gym or downtown at aerobics classes held in dance studios tucked away above gourmet take-out emporiums and boutiques selling designer combat gear. At first I suspected that Barbara's fitness regime, accompanied by her return to college to pursue a degree in business, was a response to my orgasmic pay hikes. She may have become insecure as the middle-class roles we had been raised to emulate faded into the past, as outdated now as our parents' first, hulking, Cold War appliances and rabbit-eared television sets.

"You've changed," she said one morning, looking across a restaurant table at me. Even then, a short time ago, there was a sense of surprise in her voice, a hint of delight.

"What are you talking about?"

"You. You're reading the *Wall Street Journal* and talking about interest rates."

"What am I supposed to read, *Sports Illustrated?*"

We were in an upscale charcuterie in the city's gallery district, a tony eatery catering to blue-suited money managers, flavor-of the-month painters, and penniless university students reading Verlaine and charging their breakfasts to daddy's American Express card. Around us sat smartly dressed middle-aged women who seemed to have tortured themselves into fragile states of attractiveness. With Elizabeth in nursery school, Barbara and I often ate breakfast out. Over the course of the season, we had the chance to have dinner together, at most, six times. Lunches together never seemed to materialize. By noon I would instinctively begin to get my head into the game, watching videotapes from my last at bats against the pitcher we were facing that night, running through the stats and tendencies I'd noted and logged into my computer files on opponents. Barbara, trying to accelerate her graduation date, ran to class five afternoons a week during summer sessions, the two of us exchanging kisses and the seat at the computer terminal as she came in at three and I left for the ballpark. By the time I returned on home stand nights, Elizabeth was in bed, asleep, and Barbara was dozing on the living room couch, her chest buried beneath an economics textbook the size of a headstone. Summer mornings, though, before thunderstorm-swift

changes in mood, peevish sulking, and workmanlike displays of
affection began to tear at the once unquestioned ardor that bound
us together, Barbara would wake me with coffee that smelled of
hickory and cinnamon, the sweetness in its aroma like a promise
of grace. On Barbara's skin, in her hair, the musk of something
beyond sex or the fragrance of youth, an apple-sweet scent that
Elizabeth smothered me with mornings when I ached and lay in
bed until she came to me. A perfume of innocence that stopped
time. A taste of the sweetness of being. Then, stealing into
Elizabeth's room, tiptoeing through the thin husk of her breathing
without waking her, I would carry her down through the silence
of the house. Outside, the green silence of the woods and the silver
dampness under the bare soles of my feet were indistinguishable
from one another, as if the world was caught in the midst of some
magical state of repose. Even the soft voice of the car's engine
folded into it, the quiet inside the car like a cocoon as Barbara
swung us out of the drive into the deserted streets, rolling past
closed bakeries, greengrocers' shops, and Hopperesque filling stations, onto the empty causeway bounded by salt lands, and sea-
green shacks perched above the tide on spindly stilts. Marsh
weeds the color of wheat reflected the sun's rays as we came onto
the beach, fusing them into a long, solid band, smooth as polished
brass. Elizabeth would begin to stir as I carried her over the sand,
waking for a moment to salt air and a lulling, wave-governed
music as I set her down on the blanket. The three of us would lie
with our arms entwined, huddled together in deep surrender to
the rhythms of the world, until we woke to gull cries and the heat
of the sun. Returning home I felt rejuvenated, as if the wordless
pleasures of the morning replenished something elemental in each
of us. Elizabeth would sit on my lap, covered with salt spray, the
taste clinging to my lips whenever I brushed them against the
wild, knotted strands of her hair. Reaching into the basket beside
me while Barbara drove, I would dig out grapes or berries and
slip them between Barbara's lips, letting her take them from my
fingertips as if they were kisses. By evening, though, this sense of
contentment was gone, defeated by the frenzied clamor of the
money-obsessed world. I was not deluding myself; money made

those mornings possible. Money and night baseball. So I didn't feel bitterness when they ended, merely a deeper sense of loss, a sadness that attaches itself to all things human, and a sense that perfection is humanly possible (there are perfect games, there were those mornings), but that in the long run it is the exception, and, above all, is immediately relinquished to the past.

"Why have I changed? Because I don't talk ball scores anymore?"

Barbara leaned back to allow a white-shirted waiter room to set down her omelette. "You're just different."

"It's called disillusionment. That's the price of being able to pay for this breakfast."

A few steps away there was an antique side table lined with silver coffeepots, chrome buckets stuffed with cracked ice and splits of champagne, marble trays topped with to-die-for pastries, and a wide-mouthed vase spiked with two-foot-long gladiolus. The waiter, maintaining a respectful silence, refilled our cups with fresh coffee, then moved on to another table. When he was out of earshot, Barbara said, "Don't talk down to me in front of other people." The look of amusement was gone from her face. "Or just ever," she added.

"How was I talking down to you?"

"By telling me what you think I'm trying to say. By making out that you're the all-suffering wage slave and I'm some bubble-brained housewife."

"If it wasn't funny, I'm sorry."

"I'd prefer not to talk about it."

"I'm not asking you to talk about anything. I'm asking you to accept an apology."

"Fine. Accepted."

We achieved a tentative peace an hour later over the purchase of a three-thousand-dollar room divider, a cast-iron triptych sand-blasted down to a pastel-soft terra-cotta finish. Each of the panels was embellished with carvings of Apache symbols for fertility, long life, and contentment.

When we arrived home, rather than falling into bed — the spontaneity for which we seemed to have lost — we each went

out of our way to express interest in the other's work, as if this
were the ultimate measure of caring.

The night my father died Barbara stood beside the room divider, coolly ignoring me as she fluffed the pillows of the second
couch. It seemed the less intimate we were, the neater the house
became. None of the comfortable sprawl from our first home remained — the disheveled clutter of the living room, Elizabeth's
toys strewn across the floor, records piled beside the turntable in
the haphazard order they had been played, gloves, balls, caps, and
bats tossed into the corner. From the moment I signed my first
contract with Mr. Percy, our lives had been a continuous process
of accumulation and ordering. Money, investments, runs batted
in and scored, as if these things held at bay the faltering of the
love that somehow — through age, experience, the alignment of
the planets — had lost confidence in itself. We had reached a point
where, just beyond the last breath of every word, I felt the possibility of an exploded future, one absolutely cut off from our
past. I didn't see order in the careful arrangement of the room,
only the outlines of our estrangement.

"Are you going to tell me what's wrong?" I said, finally. "Or
do I have to guess?" I waited, watching the way Barbara's four-
hundred-dollar Italian cardigan fell around her hips as she bent
over the coffee table. Her sleeves were pulled up to midforearm;
a thin gold band hung loosely around one wrist like some delicate
handcuff. I thought there might be some clue to the distance between us in these simple things, or the lean, almost muscular terse-
ness of Barbara's aerobicized body.

There was a patrician grace about her now, something defiant
and self-assured. From time to time we made love in our workout
room. Barbara, breathless, fresh with sweat, would leave on her
leg warmers and sweatbands, occasionally even her Danskin, the
crotch of it pulled aside to accommodate me. At times I wondered
what I wanted — Barbara, or the mystery of those garments, the
way they changed and objectified her. Garter belts and lace-top
stockings, satin chemises and merry widow vests with push-up bra
cups, were back in fashion, along with evangelism, talk of evil
empires, and the promise of prosperity, as if our sexual roles had

to take a leap backward to accommodate our revived imperialist longings. Where we had made love as kids, playing with each other in one long, slow tussle like cubs, it now felt like we were fucking, almost fighting, handling one another roughly, as if in our frustration we were trying to tear out of each other some lost incarnation of youth. As I watched Barbara brush dust from the jacket of a book, just as, in what now seemed to be another lifetime, she had swept dust from a rack of greeting cards while I watched through a store window's glass and my own watery reflection in it, I realized that rather than coming full circle, we had followed the line of our innocence to its endpoint. My dream of completion, once embodied in Barbara's oblivious, ideal presence on the other side of a plate glass window, was now dead — as if our dozen years together had been one long, blind, heedless effort to dissolve that glass, the very thing that separated us and yet, in a way, allowed us to idealize each other, to focus and resolve the strangeness and magic of the other.

When she didn't speak to me after several moments had passed, I said, "Well?"

She bolted upright, a pair of heavy coffee table books in her hands. "Don't think you can bully me just because your father's dead. I'm not in the mood for it."

"All I asked was what's wrong."

"What's always wrong? Right after you call, I get forty-five minutes from your mother about how I need to support you now because of what you're going through. Everything's always reduced to you. How you feel, how you think, what you need. Your father's the one who's dead, but suddenly the situation's about you." There was a hysterical propulsion behind her words, as if my father's death had uncapped all her frustration — with me, with her own struggle to move out from behind my shadow, with her parents dying on her before she was ready or able to assume responsibility for her own life. I don't believe we came apart for anything specific — not a particular infidelity, or a final, irrevocable argument — but gradually, by a process of accretion, the way my father died, his heart attack building for years as the muscle degenerated day by day, then suddenly — pop! — all at once, it's over.

"Listen, this is not about me," I said.

"What *isn't* about you?"

"Look, do me a favor," I said, becoming as unhinged by my own frustration as Barbara was, "drop the pop psychology horseshit and tell me what your fucking problem is."

Barbara started to shout something, to snap back at me. But no words came out of her mouth, and she began shaking, as if she were about to burst, to fly apart like a piece of shattered glass. A moment later, she flung the books to the floor, and they clapped like rifle shots. She was looking down at them so she wouldn't have to look at me, and she started to swivel her head slowly, the ends of her hair slapping lightly against her face. I said her name with an edge of fear, as if I didn't expect to find Barbara inside the face I was asking to look up at me. "Barb?"

She backed away, taking several small steps as she pulled her arms against her sides, and began to curl in on herself. I put my palms under her elbows and her hands shot open like paper fans, as if at my touch she would explode into flames. She was crying, and when she spoke she said, "Please," her voice small, as if only half of it had escaped from her body.

We stood there, Barbara's hands up to keep me from touching her, mine raised to let her know I wouldn't. The books, cracked open along their spines like bodies broken on piles of rock at the base of a cliff, lay splattered at our feet.

"Why's Mom crying?" Elizabeth, in a knee-length T-shirt bearing my number, appeared on the staircase. Her tone of voice went beyond simple curiosity; there was an edge of accusation in it, however tentative and unfinished. When I tried to answer I noticed that my heart was racing, my breathing deep and rapid. My hands were still extended toward Barbara and I held them there, afraid of moving too quickly out of the hysterical clarity of the moment. It took me several seconds to come back inside myself, to leave the force field of panic, and wounded, remorse-filled love. Reentering the non-hysterical world, I found it eerily lifeless, and my feeling of being adrift receded only as the pain in my shoulder restored a sense of weightedness to my thoughts.

"Mom's crying because I said something I shouldn't have said."

"Why?"

"Because I'm feeling sorry for myself." This threw Elizabeth, and she was silent, as if her confusion suddenly reminded her of her exhaustion. "We'll talk about it later," I said. "Okay?" She nodded and I lowered my hands. When I turned, I saw that Barbara was down on one knee, collecting the books. I squatted beside her. "I can do this if you want to put Elizabeth back to bed."

"I'd like to be alone right now." Her voice rose slightly, a controlled, aggrieved plea. She didn't look at me.

Knowing I had hurt her in another unexpected, irrevocable way, that over the course of time I had driven her as far from me as possible, I put my hand on hers, as if by acknowledging this I could tell her one last time I loved her. Barbara let my hand rest on hers. Then, without looking up, nodded, accepting the gesture only because we were beyond redemption. I kept my hand on hers for another moment, then took it away and left her.

Elizabeth was standing, sleep-stunned and slack-jawed, halfway up the staircase. She watched me approach with a sort of dumb sense of trust. I lifted her, surprised not by the pain in my shoulder, but by the degree of weakness in it. Light as Elizabeth was, I felt that my right hand was merely stabilizing her weight in my arms, and this weakness was more disconcerting than the pain. It seemed to evidence some deeper state of degeneration and decay. I shifted all of Elizabeth's weight to my left side and, as I began climbing the stairs, pressed my free hand softly against her back. Her head dropped to my shoulder, carrying with it the dewy redolence of her body, its simple perfume, clean as young fruit. Beside the tortured aura of my own flesh — a haphazard mixture of liniment, soap, tobacco, and the first musky waves of sweat beginning to go stale, the odors all seemingly bound into a single, quavering chord by my anxiety — Elizabeth's scent seemed like some memory of first love, of life being a great hurtling forward into time, as if you became larger the deeper you went into it:

that was its thrill. It was the aroma of innocence coming off her, and for several moments while I carried her through the darkness it tempered and slowed my sense — beginning with the pain in my shoulder, then my father's death and the gulf between Barbara and me — of becoming smaller in time, of the momentum at the center of my being having changed, the thrust of my youth succumbing to time's gravitational pull so that now, at the peak of my ascent, I was turning in space, in slower and slower revolutions until I was almost still. As I laid Elizabeth on her bed, my head swam with an awareness of all things breaking down, decaying, softening in time like the flesh of broken, fallen trees, all living things arcing like achingly high fly balls, their grace bound up in their unquestioning acceptance of descent, the momentary sadness of completion, though all things tended toward it, the universe animated by the process of its own decay, all of us fueling it with our infinite though seemingly discrete deterioration — dwindling, unmoored, adrift, receding from one another, losing energy like unheated molecules. My sense of this free-fall into eventual dust was momentarily arrested by the perfume of Elizabeth's innocence, her newness and sap. I traced one of her eyebrows with the tip of my finger, hooking the hair that had fallen over her face like an untrussed sheaf of wheat behind her ear, lightly stroking the same smooth brow until she sighed, and passed into a deeper cave of sleep.

In the hall, light was blotting across the pine floor in front of our closed bedroom door. For an instant, it seemed as if I could see Barbara moving silently through our bedroom, the walls and door turning sheer as stockings. I left her in the peace the moment demanded and went downstairs, picking up a pack of cigarettes on my way to the car. Outside, I stopped on the terrace, lighted one, then walked down the long slope of lawn, my legs resisting the increasing momentum of my descent, reining it in as I fell away from the veil of light emanating from the house. Hammer's voice was in my head, soft, and for him unenergetic, rising like a bubble through water to the surface of the present from a gloomy, wind-lashed afternoon in a bar where, over the clinking ice in his glass, I listened. His voice, weakened by a visit to his physician's office, a morning of probings and grave, tentative inquiries, ticked off the descending stages of his life: "Alvin Hammer, Al Hammer, Al's hammers, Alzheimer's. We diminish, evaporate, break down. Little black holes show up on X rays of our bodies and we're sucked into them, vanished. Gone."

When I returned from my mother's house, our bedroom door was open and Barbara was lying on the bed in a white tank top, a sheet pulled to her waist. I removed my clothes and slipped into bed beside her. The sheets were clean, a brusque, cool gentleness about them, something of crisp, flawless spring afternoons when the sky is an incomparable and endless blue, an intimation that every trespass may be forgiven and redeemed. With Barbara lying on one side, her hands pressed palm to palm as if she were praying, all the girlishness she had lost over time came back into her features and I saw in the gray dawn light the girl I loved. The one who was timid and helpless, haunted by the death of her parents; the girl who was supportive and clearheaded, and much stronger than me; the girl I wanted to protect and be protected by; the one who clung to me while we slept, one leg hooked over mine, her hand clutching my breast as if I might be snatched away from her during the night. Maybe love is a kind of magic, an illusion. Maybe it's born whole, and complete, the way it was for me the first time I saw Barbara. Or perhaps love is simply a pair of congruous inadequacies and fears coming together by happenstance and finding that they complement each other. As I looked at Barbara, I felt her falling away from me, receding like an echo. It was as if we had served each other as the second stage of a rocket, the engines of adolescence — with all its high-strung innocence and headlong lust for the future — igniting when we met and thrusting us beyond the pull of childhood, family, town, middle class, and, in my case, anonymity. With the energy of innocence exhausted, we were now disengaging, dropping away from each other like the spent shells of booster units. So was Hammer right? We don't so much age as evaporate? Or rocket off into space, in time becoming weightless, beyond the pull of other bodies? Was it love between Barbara and me, or just that for a time the courses of our trajectories were aligned? Or is that what love is, this drift-ing apart simply how love goes, when it goes? I had become every-thing I had set out to become, so perhaps it wasn't the result that drove Barbara away from me, but my seeming stabilization and completeness. For we were largely each other's creations — isn't that what love is, too? — and now the process of inventing each other was stalling, becoming inert. There had been a gap between us, a necessary gap, a space where nothing existed, and in that space we were free to imagine each other. Maybe it's in the free-dom contained in that space that the loved one exists — un-finished, receptive. Somehow this valence had closed up on us, filled to capacity perhaps by time, identity, the atoms of the adult world. Where we once had imagined each other within that space, we now seemed to exist on opposite sides of it. Barbara had be-come all surface to me. I could no longer find a way in, a window that would lead me to a new reinvention of her. Where I had first spied her through a piece of glass, I now saw only a mirror, and my own solitary reflection in it.

"Are you awake?"

I heard her voice as I lay there, my eyes closed. My body seemed to be separating from my mind, my limbs becoming den-ser, exhaustion lending them a previously unfelt weight, my thoughts rising out of the darkness just above sleep and winging away at slicing, breathless angles. The events of the day — the scene in the hospital, the batting cage, the books crashing to the floor at Barbara's feet — were going off around me like fire-works. Barbara's voice — free of accusation, spite, or anger, col-ored instead with a sort of sadness — opened at the center of my thoughts, stopping the riot of images. I raised my eyelids and stared at the ceiling, and when I was certain I was awake said, "Yes."

Barbara drew a breath. I could feel her studying me, knew her well enough to sense the remorse in her silence, well enough to know that her gaze was taking in something she knew she'd lost, but wasn't quite sure how or why. I turned my head toward her, knowing that we had regained a closeness through having drifted so impossibly and irreversibly far apart. It was a closeness of final hours, last words. I hesitated — I was afraid, actually afraid, to touch her — then reached across myself with my left hand and swept the hair off her brow so I could see her eyes. For as much intelligence as they possessed, there was, as always, a nervousness about them, some ghost of fearfulness and insecurity, as if she felt the world might be yanked out from under her at any moment. I let my fingertips linger over her brow, afraid, as well, that if I removed them, she'd vanish. It may have been the light, the way it cast the room in half-shadow and seemed to stop time, but Barbara appeared to me as a memory, a dream figure who would recede in space when the dream ended and time began to lumber forward again.

"We're about as far apart as we can get," I said. Barbara nodded, and I felt formless, without shape or identity.

"You wanted it," she said.

"To be lost?" She shrugged, then nodded again, acknowledging the helplessness that lay behind this truth. "Why would I want that?"

I waited, only for an instant though, as if Barbara needed the moment not to shape her thought, but to prepare herself to let go of me forever. With all my adrenaline spent, I simply stared at the ceiling, able to listen now, to hear her, because I was as blank as the white slate above me. "So you can hang on to your innocence," she said.

"Is that what I'm doing?"

"You're trying to."

I thought about this for a moment, then said, "Why?"

Then deliberately, as if this were a truth she had held for a long time, she said, "So you don't have to take responsibility for anything."

I inhaled deeply, as if the shock of breath would clear my head. Then time started up again — and what is time but the increasing momentum of the loss of innocence. Aside from that, unless I was missing something — and I hoped I was, it was evident that I could — there was only Mr. Percy's inexorable will, his ubiquitous wealth, and the breadth of his power, the lines of which spun out around him in slowly extending arcs, until the farthest reaches of them disappeared beyond the limits of my vision. I had lost Barbara, lost her by trying to remain the innocent I'd imagined I'd once been. And as I rolled on my side and touched the tips of my fingers to her temple, I still wished that the slow circles they described had the power to rewind time.

Twenty-Six

"HELLO, OLD FRIEND." Dr. Lang, tall, narrow as a foul pole, with a waist half an inch below his pectorals and legs long and thin as stilts, tossed one hand into the air to greet me as I stepped off the elevator at the area marked Diagnostic Imaging Center. Dressed in a navy-blue, gold-buttoned blazer, cuffed, charcoal-gray pants, and a maroon-shaded paisley ascot, he crossed the room; its eggshell-white walls, Roman-style sconces, and round-arched doors that retracted at the touch of a button made the place seem like an odd combination of pagan altar and NASAesque sterility. He had round cheeks, slightly large front teeth, and cream-slickened hair parted on one side as if by a straight razor. He was half a head taller than me, and as his hand applied a gentle, guiding pressure against my back, I felt as if he were some escaped, impossibly even-tempered children's show host. "How are you?" he said, clapping a hand against my healthy shoulder as he fell in step with me.

"Are we limiting the question to physically?"

His smile vanished, the expression on his face turning almost histrionically grave. He invariably tensed at receiving bad news. "Yes, I heard about your father," he said. "You have my deepest sympathy. It's a tragic, tragic thing." With that out of the way, a glow returned to his face as we approached the reception area. "I'm going to step into one of the examining rooms for a moment with Mike," he explained to the woman behind the desk. She seemed designed to fit into the surroundings: thirties, fit, rather bland in the way news anchorpeople are. I suspected that when I looked at her, I wasn't supposed to think or feel anything. "I want to go over the steps of the examination with him."

"I'll let them know that you'll be a few minutes."

"Thank you, dear." Dr. Lang extended a hand and I followed him into a small, bright, windowless room. "Just take your shirt off and have a seat on the table." He removed his blazer, replaced it with a white smock, then scrubbed his hands over a stainless steel sink. I slid up onto the table, the skin on my arms springing to attention in the chilled air. Dr. Lang, smock hanging from his narrow shoulders like an alb, dried his hands with paper toweling, a liturgical deliberateness informing his movements. "I'm going to do a brief general exam, Mike. So just relax and look up at me." He took my head in his hands and stared into my eyes, pulling down their lower lids with the surprisingly soft tips of his thumbs. I looked back at him, but there was nothing behind his eyes — his body had turned into a camera. Then he turned my head and began probing the line of my jaws, depressing the flesh inside the mandible, creeping down along my larynx, finally rooting around in the cavity ringed by my collarbone. "Look up." He came at me with a silver-tubed flashlight, the beam emanating from an eye no larger than a pea. "Open." The light tilted from my eyes to my throat. "Do you still smoke?" he said, snapping off the light and dropping it into the large square pocket of his lab coat.

"Usually."

He placed his hands on my right shoulder and focused his attention on it, as if he could see through my skin. "Drink?"

"Only when necessary." A sharp pain lanced through my shoulder when he pressed.

"When is that?"

"Generally just game days and off days." He left his fingertips on my shoulder, but leaned back to look me in the eye. "It's medicinal," I said. "Keeps me from getting too wired."

"You mean hyper, restless?" I nodded. "Is there any history of manic depression in your family?"

"My guess is yes, but undiagnosed."

"You mean there was never any treatment of it?"

"Nothing clinical."

"Well, what did they do for it?"

"Watched television."

Dr. Lang stared at me for a moment, unable to decide whether or not I was serious. I may have been distancing myself from the dreads that awaited me in the other room, the peering inside me to locate the nadir of my decay, my breaking down, the beginnings of my descent into unbeing. Or denying my father's death, running from it the way Barbara had run from her mother's. There was a lightness in me, a mischievousness I couldn't account for. It was as if I had eluded some punishment or confusion, possessed a plan for escape that I wasn't aware of.

Dr. Lang changed the position of his hands. "Now Mike, I want you to understand —"

"Cut out the smoking and drinking."

He nodded, his lips folding in on themselves to accentuate his earnestness.

"What about amphetamines and major hallucinogenics?"

"I can't approve of those either," he said, totally deadpan, his presidential press conference solemnity creating almost a para-reality, something absurd and literal at the same time. "Two ounces of alcohol per day is medically acceptable. Beyond that, I think we would have to talk about your need to become intoxicated."

I saw that he truly didn't understand. That it would be impossible for me to explain that intoxication kept the boredom and anxiety at bay, helped me contain the elation and despair of streaks and slumps. That it just plain washed away the merciless groundswell of inanity rolling across the nation on T-shirts and bumper stickers proclaiming everything from love for puppies, grandchildren, and Jesus, to life-sucks teenage nihilism and death by heavy metal; in calls for miraculous healings and prayer dollars, and multimillion-dollar-a-year ballplayers signing autographs for the unemployed and the disenfranchised.

"You're a very lucky person, Mike. You should count your blessings."

You mean I should see God's hand in my princely wealth and celebrity? I wanted to say. That I'm the anti-Job? But I didn't.

"This isn't a lecture, Mike."

"I understand that."

"You're a good boy. Now —" The remark stunned me, but he rolled past it. "There's a little tenderness in your shoulder," he said. "Can you raise your arm for me?" I hesitated, then did. "Okay, stop." He kneaded the tendons in my shoulder. "Any pain in there?" He depressed a spot the size of a penny until his thumb began to dig into my skin.

"Yes."

"Sharp or dull?"

"Sharp."

"Here?" He shifted his grip.

"Yes."

He ran the fingers of his hands lightly down the length of my arm, almost as if he were caressing a racehorse, then turned my palm face up, studied it, tugging slightly on each of my fingers as he traced their bat-callused outlines. "Okay, you can put your shirt on." I stood and slipped into my shirt while Dr. Lang re-washed his hands. "There's obviously some sort of tissue damage or irritation," he said, turning to me. "It could be a strain, a slight tear, or simply inflammation."

"I figured it was a pull. I rushed the throw; it was a cool night."

"Well, we may be into something slightly more complicated than that."

I stopped tucking in my shirttails. "How complicated?"

"That's what we're here to find out." Instinctively, I was wary of his evasiveness. It was tinged with finality, and intimations of the irreversible progress of some invisible disease rolling through my system. "Let me just run through the test we're going to do. Why don't you sit for a moment." Dr. Lang indicated a hard plastic chair, then pulled one up beside me. "Now, Mike, the first thing I want to reinforce for you is not to be anxious. The test is extremely simple, and noninvasive."

"I thought we were just going to take some X rays."

Dr. Lang shook his head. "No. X rays pick up only bone. Your problem, whatever it is, lies in the soft tissue. Since it produces little or no shadow, the usefulness of X rays in this case would be negligible." He was speaking slowly, and the racing of my heart seemed to attach itself to the rhythms of his voice, slowing even as my chest expanded. "Now in most cases, we would do an arthrogram," he continued, his careful tone suggesting that he was taking on all the pain and responsibility for the injury. I felt myself losing shape, almost melting, as I transferred my trust to him. And, for the moment, my fear began to drain out of me. "We do them all the time, on pitchers especially, in cases where we expect to find rotator cuff damage. But because of the limited amount of throwing you do as an outfielder, and the natural motion of that throwing, I don't expect that to be the problem. Also, with this other test we save time and avoid the use of needles."

"Needles?"

"Yes. Basically, what we would be doing in an arthrogram is injecting a radiopaque contrast dye into your shoulder, presumably underneath the rotator cuff." My stomach twinged as I imagined a three-inch needle slicing through the thick elastic of my ligaments, a dull, hard bubble of pressure shuddering into my shoulder as the dye was plunged into it. "Then we would allow you to exercise. X rays would follow, and they would tell us if any of the dye leaked out. If it did, then you have a damaged rotator cuff. Do you follow?"

I nodded.

"That's why this is such a lovely, lovely test. It's one hundred percent noninvasive. We don't have to open you up to see what's inside. And there's no encounter with radiation. It's totally patient-friendly."

"What are you going to do, pass a wand over my shoulder?"

Dr. Lang brightened at the mention of this. "Almost. We're going to put you inside a magnet."

"A magnet?"

"Yes."

"Then what?"

"Turn it on." The test was referred to as magnetic resonance imaging, or MRI, the process originating in the 1970s when researchers developed the first two-dimensional image of proton density. "They ran the first brain scan in 1978," Dr. Lang said. "It was successful, even though initially there had been some fear that too strong a magnet might remove memory centers from the brain."

"What?"

He pressed on my leg as I tried to stand. "The danger doesn't exist. We've had years of trouble-free testing, and have one of the most advanced machines in the world," he said, informing me that there were only six in operation in the U.S. "Mr. Percy wanted the best medical equipment available for his players. You see, Mike, you're the first player on the team to undergo the test."

I was silent, and afraid, even though I knew that my fear was irrational. After all, would Mr. Percy spend the $1.8 million that Dr. Lang told me the machine cost simply to yank memory centers out of my brain like rotten teeth? Maybe. But despite making no sense, my fear seemed to grow in direct proportion to its irrationality. Memory pockets? Were they the size of dimes, or the head of a pin? Was there a pocket for each individual memory, or were they gathered by time period and categories — childhood memories, painful memories, good memories, memories of gross humiliation and shame? Was a memory singular and discrete, focusing on one thing? Or was all memory aggregate, linked, so that if I forgot what a steak was, just lost the concept of it, I also lost the memory-concepts of cow, cattle, herds, milk, udders, grass, pasture, barns, hay, cowboys, cowpokes, medium, medium-rare, milk cartons, manure, hamburgers, cheeseburgers, buns, ketchup, pickles, McDonald's, money, towns, cities, states, nations, planets, evolution, creator, deity, being, eternity? When I emerged from the magnet, would I even recognize a bat? Would I know that I had once loved Barbara and lost her? Would I any longer understand that I would one day die?

"There's absolutely nothing to fear, son." Dr. Lang patted my knee as I looked at him. "It's an elegant test, simply splendid. Let me show you how it works." Sketching hastily on his clipboard pad, he drew a cluster of arrows, their spear-shaped tips appearing to rotate in tight circles, the head of each arrow pointing in a different direction. "These are the protons, or nuclei, of hydrogen atoms," he said, telling me they existed in abundance in the human body, spinning at random. "We'll lay you down on a comfortable bed, then slide you into the tunnel of a magnet." Which weighed fifteen tons, the electromagnets encased within its walls supercooled to minus 452°F by liquid helium. The result was a magnetic field thirty thousand times stronger than the earth's. "This is why you have to make certain you surrender your watch, wedding band, belt, keys, any loose change, even credit cards. Everything. You'll hear a light tapping inside the tunnel, like rain falling on the roof of your car. That will be the electromagnetic field building up around you." And when it peaked — at some point where memory pockets in my brain were clinging by their quivering roots to the subsoil of my unconscious — the protons of the hydrogen atoms would spring to attention, lining up beside one another like an infinite row of exclamation points. But their heads would still be wobbling slightly, precessing in almost infinitesimally small revolutions. "At this point, we'll direct a radio signal at your shoulder, energizing the protons and momentarily knocking them out of alignment, like a bowling ball scattering pins." Imagine the pins being able to leap back into place on their own, though. The protons would do this, would spring back to attention once the signal was cut off, this springing back, or realigning, producing its own signal. A computer would track the rate of realignment, then produce an image based on the variation within that rate. "Since hydrogen atoms reflect water content, we can use the image to make distinctions within the tissue, see if it's inflamed, torn, et cetera. All without invasive surgical techniques. And, most splendidly, without the use of radiation. It's a marvelous, marvelous machine." We were silent for a moment. "Well?"

"What are my options?"

Dr. Lang let the metal clip at the top of his board snap down over his pencil. "Long-term health risks. Needles. Inelegance. Uncertainty. Pain."

"No 'Rest and drink plenty of fluids,' huh?"

"I'm afraid not."

After checking that I did not wear dentures, or have any metallic implants lodged within my body, the receptionist took my silver-studded belt, wallet, and car keys. I hesitated for a moment before removing my wedding band.

The viewing station — sterile and spotless as the inside of a spaceship — vibrated with the scent of new plastic and vinyl. Dr. Lang introduced me to the imaging technician, a soft-faced man who seemed almost featureless. A glass door retracted, and I followed Dr. Lang past the computer console into a large, dank, white-walled room, bright as the inside of a refrigerator. The only sound was the faint, steady exhalation of the air-conditioning ducts, and the muffled flapping of Dr. Lang's lab coat as he crossed the carpeted floor to the examination table.

"We're going to want you to lie here, Mike," he said, indicating the padded top of a hard plastic slab. "If you'll just make yourself comfortable, I have to go retrieve a coil."

The table was pigeon's-neck gray, supported by a metal base. Barbell-thick handles ran along its side like the grips of a casket. A thin mattress lay on top of the table, its fabric the color of my uniform's pinstripes. Two pillows, propped at forty-five-degree angles, leaned back toward the mouth of the tunnel. The peak of the tunnel's arch was an inch or two taller than me. Above it was a long black monitor, glowing green numbers floating on its surface like digits on a scoreboard. I lay down and clasped my hands over my waist, feeling eerily corpselike. Dr. Lang reentered the room, carrying a white tube shaped like a trash pail, with an oval opening in the center.

"Comfortable?"

"It's not exactly a white sand beach."

"Well, we'll have you out of here in twenty minutes. Right now I need you to give me your arm so I can slip this over your shoulder." Dr. Lang held up the tube as if it were an impossibly light watermelon. I extended my right arm toward him and he nodded, pleased with my ability to follow simple instructions. "This is a surface coil," he said, sliding it up my arm. The inside of the tube was a brassy, highly polished gold plating, like the inside of a chalice. "It will direct the radio signal to the spot on your shoulder we're interested in. That way we get a clearer picture, more distinction between soft tissue and bone. Hurt?" To accommodate the coil, my shoulder was opened outward, my arm crooked at the elbow, then hanging straight down like a scarecrow's. I nodded. "Hm . . . Oh, well, you're just going to have to hold it there. We need an axial view, and a sagittal, cross section and side to side. There's nothing we can do about it."

"Forget it. You owe me twenty free Percodan."

"All right." Dr. Lang was completing his final inspection of my position, oblivious to my pain or remarks. "You'll be able to hear us talking to you through an intercom inside the tunnel. Just follow any instructions we issue." I nodded, and he patted my chest. Then he reached up to a long panel of buttons beside the tunnel and pressed one of them. The table jerked into motion, then slowly backed into the mouth of the tunnel.

As Dr. Lang's white lab coat swept past the receding opening, the tunnel began to taper and shrink around me. I felt what must be an astronaut's anxiety. Slight fluttering in the pit of the stomach, film of sweat breaking out along the ridge of my forehead, a tingling fatigue deadening my arms and legs. The light inside the tunnel dimmed as the roof glided by, inches above my eyes. I began taking deep breaths, as if having difficulty finding enough air in the tight, shadowed space. I closed my eyes, hoping that the darkness would open around me once I was inside it. In the blackness, with the table still sliding into the tunnel, the sense of its almost calibrated motion slithering through me as if the tongue of a tape measure were being very slowly unspooled, I felt that I was falling, the type of falling that precedes sleep, only this was deeper, bottomless. "Relax, Mike." A voice, as distant as childhood, and oddly reminiscent of my young father's voice on those nights when he would sit on my bedside in the dark and calm me after I'd had a bad dream, filled my head in tones as clear and sonorous as church bells. "Let it go," the voice said. "Let everything go." And, for a moment, I thought I had fallen through layers of being, passed through them as if they were clouds or streams of air currents, falling the way the body of a plane begins to fall, or maybe a soul, slicing down through levels in which being either dissolved or thickened — became denser but somehow less packed. I couldn't tell because I seemed to be lighter, yet all around, diffuse, yet solid as ropes of light and gravity, and permeated by this voice, which seemed to be my father's, saying, "Let it go." When I opened my eyes a red beam, thin and taut as a fishing line, shot from the roof of the tunnel down to a point on my right shoulder. The hammering started, a light tapping at first, like a series of drummers testing the tautness and pitch of their snares, the last few raps fading like distant gunshots. Then a cresting of hammers began all around me, the single raps accelerating, almost instantly engulfing thousands of others until, like the revving of a jet's engine, there was a peaking, the sound spinning around me in a single, high-pitched cacophony as if a million high-speed jackhammers were rapping against every square inch of the tunnel, and then this sense of thrust, like I was falling again, falling forward after an instant's stillness at the peak of a roller-coaster hill when your breath catches and the gravity of flesh kicks in — the way our souls must leave our bodies when we die — and then there's this giddy, screaming sense of release and terror as the pit of your stomach rockets up through your insides like a bubble the size of a basketball and your limbs shudder like roller-coaster tracks as the cars thunder over them. The skin on my face began to tighten, stretching over my skull like a shrinking Halloween mask, and my teeth began to sing in their sockets, quivering at first like tuning forks, then ringing inside my head as if angels on speed were drumming on them. I imagined the skin of my chest splitting open from sternum to navel, my ribs springing open like mousetraps, heart, liver, and entrails exploding out of me like cannon shot and splattering across the roof of the tunnel. Then it was over. They cut the magnet's juice and I fell back inside myself, spent as a gun shell.

"Now that wasn't too bad, was it?" Dr. Lang seemed as

pleased as a secondary school dean complimenting his prize student. He threw his long arm around me as I stood up from the table.

"I thought my chest was going to explode."

"Pure anxiety. Nothing to worry about."

As we entered the viewing station, a grainy, bluish picture of my shoulder was tracing itself onto the face of the monitor. It looked like a map of some seabound peninsula, rounded, well-defined shoreline abutting an ocean of black, TV screen abyss. Inside the line were long canals and waterways wrapped around solid masses of bone or muscle. One was shaped like a Brazil nut, another like a timed-release cold capsule. A third, the largest, had the shape of a human skull. Just above it, floating in a thick, purplish-blue canal, was a small cloud, black as a collapsed star.

"Hm." Dr. Lang made a sound beside me. There wasn't really any emotion invested in it, just bafflement, as if he'd overlooked an opponent's chess move.

"What's wrong?"

He covered his lips with an index and second finger, thumb hooked under his chin, then leaned close to the monitor, the reflection of his face expanding like a funhouse mirror image. He passed his eyes over the picture, horizontally first, then vertically, as if he were a jeweler inspecting a rare gem for flaws. When he stood up straight, he folded his arms, pursed his lips, and seemed to want walking space. "Well, I thought we'd see a small tear, due to the suddenness of the injury's onset."

"We're not seeing that?"

"No."

I hesitated before speaking, as if that might allow the black spot on the monitor a chance to vanish, evaporate. "What are we seeing?"

"This little dark mass right up in here." He outlined the cloud's perimeter with the tip of his gold pen. We leaned in together to look at it, reassure ourselves that it was there. "I expected to see something more precise," he said. "I'm very disappointed."

I had the feeling he wasn't connecting the disturbing, imprecise information on the screen with me, actual living tissue. Instead, he seemed dejected over the limits of his cherished machine. "Could the picture be incorrect?" I asked.

"No. My guess is that we'll see the same mass on the sagittal image." He pressed a button and a new image, a side view of my shoulder, popped onto the screen. "There it is."

In the glass I could see his eyes making slow revolutions around the circumference of the cloud. "That's the one drawback of MRI. It's sensitive but nonspecific. We could be looking at just a little fluid from swelling. Or we could be looking at a tumor."

My heart expanded like a balloon, the beating of it thumping all the way up to the base of my skull.

Dr. Lang backed away from the screen without looking at me. "We'll put you on anti-inflammatories for a few days, then come back and have another look. If the fluid's gone, then we have no problem."

"And if it's not?"

"Then we'll have to explore other possibilities. But we shouldn't get ahead of ourselves. We have to do the only thing we can do."

"What's that?"

"Wait."

Minutes later I had a prescription form, an appointment for another test in five days, and Dr. Lang's hand on my back. When the elevator arrived I stepped into it alone, pressed the lobby button, and turned. As the doors began to close, Dr. Lang, beaming once again like a children's show host, happy to be free of me, of the unspeakable cloud inside my shoulder, raised one arm into the air and shouted, "Farewell, old friend!"

An instant later the elevator plunged downward, like a penny into a well.

Twenty-Seven

"HEY, MOOSECOCK." The voice passed through me in sleep as if I were air. "Hey," a second time in a whisper thin as tissue.

"What?"

I rose into the weight of my body, the lightness of dreams feathering away from me in the dark. George was sitting on the edge of my bed, his white T-shirt luminous as the numbers of a digital clock, or the hovering veil of a ghost. Outlined by shadows black as pitch, he seemed almost insubstantial, his presence no more palpable than fog, and I thought that if I reached out, I could pass my hand through him.

"You awake?" He was still whispering, his voice cracking like an eggshell in his effort to be quiet.

I looked at him for a moment, waiting for an exhibition of some sleep-defeating urgency, or red alert. When he didn't do anything, I said, "No," then dropped my head back onto the pillow, its softness immediately releasing me to the first gravity-shedding stages of sleep.

"Hey." There was something pained in his tone this time — insistent, fearful, embarrassed. His voice reminded me of a young boy's, one who had a shameful admission to make, all sense of play gone out of it. I sat up, his unusual seriousness catching me before I could drift back into sleep.

"What is it?"

"My back is fucking killing me."

"It's probably a cramp." The bed creaked as I curled into a sitting position. It took a moment for my thoughts to reinhabit the heft of my body. I leaned back and exhaled, then looked at George again. He was shaking his head.

"No," he said. "I don't think so."

The darkness seemed to recede as my eyes became accustomed to the dim, cavelike light. Our motel room windows were open, a warm, boggy air ruffling the curtain hems. Each breeze was shot through with the sharply sweet aroma of tobacco. We were on the road, playing night games across the South in humidity-drenched towns like Jackson, Mississippi, and Columbia, South Carolina. Crowds of at most fifteen hundred turned out each evening at the tiny ballparks ringed by rural blackness, the interstellar velvet above us softening the abyss in which we all seemed, some nights, to drift. Evenings the temperature cooled down into the upper seventies, and George and I preferred to sleep without the air conditioning on. That damp, chilled, unnaturally cooled air seemed to lull our muscles into cryogenic sleep, leaving cramps that rang through our bodies like piano chords in the morning. Shirtless, I slept on top of the sheets in my jockey shorts, the back of my neck and head dewy with a light sweat. But as George sat on the edge of my bed, I saw that he was shivering, his arms twitching as spasms zinged through him like bolts of electricity.

"Are you all right?"

He shrugged. Another body tremor rattled him from the pit of his stomach. He pulled his head down between his shoulders like a turtle, and shook it off. With his arms folded across his chest, and one hand tucked under each bicep, he looked like an escape artist, someone straitjacketed and helpless.

"Do you want to go see the doc?" I said, sitting forward in order to make him look at me directly. He shook his head. Then fell forward onto one side of the bed, arms still wrapped tightly around his chest, feet pulled up against his butt. As his head came to rest beside my hip, his back pressed along the length of my thigh. I leaned over him, putting one hand softly on his shoulder to balance myself.

Listening, I heard clenched, fist-sized breaths burst from between his lips every few seconds. An involuntary precision governed the workings of his body, even under siege. We were lithe, smooth-skinned assemblages of fluids, gears, and pumps, machines driven by plugs, hoses, and ropes of muscles, each part oblivious to its own day-by-day degeneration. Fear of death has to exist outside the body, in some place beyond the indifferent decay of limbs, organs, and senses, some quintessence of being in which the body becomes merely a conduit of our yearning to exist. As I curled down over George, his arm warm to my touch, the heat of his body caressed my face. Another shiver raced through him and his bicep tensed under my hand, a soft explosion inside his flesh, which then fell back in on itself. He drew a deep breath, then let it go, as if he had found a temporary peace.

"Do you want me to do anything?"

George shook his head, my eye following the mole just below his temple as it moved back and forth in a slow, short arc.

"You think it's what you ate?" Images of George chewing Slim Jims three at a time, wolfing down beer nuts, and knocking back schooners of beer in the roadside bar we'd walked to after the game flashed through my mind like police blotter photographs. Gas seemed a likely explanation for his pain, though I'd never known George to succumb to despair over the misfirings of his physiology. In fact, he appeared to relish them. Lighting "zorches" in the dugout to the exasperated disgust of our manager, Houston Slaught; farting on cue; belching the "Star Spangled Banner," his cap clasped to his breast in deadpan reverence. Sprains, pulls, hairline fractures: they seemed to excite him, as if their existence complicated and deepened his sense of being alive. He played taped, strapped, aching, and half dead from hangovers. "Perfect health" seemed to include, for him, a consciousness of some debility or crystal-clear sense of pain. He used infirmity as a sounding board, bouncing an irrepressible vigor off it, playing with the downside limits of his body as if the yin-yang of health and decay were a game. So I didn't know what to make of his fetal-coiled figure beside me. I felt helpless, stupid, anxious, and frightened.

"How could it be what I ate?" he said. "The pain's in my fucking back." The idiocy of my groping-in-the-dark hypothesis had roused him from pain-induced lethargy to a state of short-tempered irritation.

"I thought bowels went all the way around," I said. "I thought that was the point of bowels."

"You have a brain the size of my right ball."

"Maybe internally you're a mutant. I saw a picture of this bushman once. The guy's dick was the length of a necktie." George's shoulder began to quiver slightly under my fingertips. "I mean the guy could use the thing as a nine iron. And he had this knot in it. A little loop halfway down about the size of an apricot." The dampness on the back of George's T-shirt rubbed my thigh as his body shook. "Maybe you're in that type of category. Bowels the size of bowling balls, or watermelons, or something."

George inhaled sharply through his teeth, a rigid, hissing sound, narrow as a needle, the small of his back arching away from my leg.

"What?"

"Don't make me laugh." His body slumped. Then, after a moment, began to shiver again.

"I think I should go get a doctor."

"I don't want a doctor!" He waited a moment, letting his petulance pass. "I'm just cold." A fine spray of sweat lay across his forehead. Taking my hand from his arm, I leaned forward and ran my fingertips along his brow, then up near his scalp. His hair — thick, stiff, and straight as the fibers of a paintbrush, dark as a bar of bittersweet chocolate — fell over my fingers, his eyelids drowsing as if I were casting a spell over him, seducing him down into the peace of sleep.

I rolled over and slid off the bed. The carpet, damp as George's shirt, was sticky, its nap tugging at the soles of my feet as I walked across the room.

"Where are you going?"

"To close the window."

A middle-of-the-night urgency and desolation gave the air outside an edge, a chill that spoke to a loneliness in my bones. There was something melancholy in the coolness, an intimation of loss which seemed to turn the world beyond the window into a movie image, something stark, arresting, and incorporeal. A light like white nylon fell away from the building in static, seamless waves, then gave way, across the two-lane road, to a blackness as still as the face of a lake. I rolled the window along its track until it caught and locked. It made a small sucking sound when it did, as if drawing the last breath of air out of the room.

The bed cover was lying on the floor, tossed there in a heap. I picked up one end of it and laid it over George. "You're burning up," I said, feeling his forehead with my palm. "Are you sure you don't want me to call a doctor?" He nodded, tugging the edge of the quilt down around his shoulders. "I'll get you some aspirin then."

I rummaged through my road bag, pulling out jockstraps, fresh T-shirts, pairs of jockey shorts, jeans, and soft cotton pullovers. The clothing, freshly washed, gave off an almost tactile aura of health. The white cotton shirts and shorts nearly glowed in the dark, their bleached, laundry-detergent-bright presence luminous as unblemished souls. Even the aspirin bottle was reassuring. Its red and blue lettering, wrapped around a milk-white body, seemed to promise not only pain relief, but salvation.

I went into the bathroom for a glass. White towels, folded and stacked on gleaming stainless steel rungs, sat above the white toilet. Stitched into the center of each of them as if they were Easter vestments was a brilliant, gold, rising sun — the motel's corporate logo. Rays of light streamed from it in gold thread, the shafts of sunlight infused with Resurrection Day fervor. Complimentary ablutions — shampoo, soap, conditioners — stood beside the sink's polished chrome faucet, its smooth neck gleaming like the face of a chalice. The fluorescent bulbs above the mirror threw a light that seemed infinite and continuous, as if merely to stand in it was to be absolved. When I had filled a glass with water, I turned off the light and walked back to George. As I knelt in front of him, his breathing was rickety and erratic. It seemed out of place in the room, as if the point of the things we were surrounded by was to encourage a deflection of all thoughts which tended toward mortality.

"Here, take these."

I put one hand close to his mouth. With my fingertips I laid two immaculate white aspirin on his tongue. He took the glass, drank from it, then handed it back to me. When his head dropped back onto the bed, I slid the Bible and phone book to one side of the bedside table, then set the glass beside them. The detritus of George's pockets — keys, coins, the stray piece of lint, crumpled dollar bills, a rabbit's foot, a condom, stars-and-stripes-colored bubble gum wrappers advertising improbably high-tech para-phernalia: long-range binoculars, walkie-talkies, X-ray glasses that let you see through walls into girls' bedrooms — were heaped in one corner of the table like a junkyard sculpture. There was something sorrowful in their uselessness and dispossession. The entire pile had a forgotten aura about it, as if it would never be returned to, or reclaimed.

I rose and walked around the bed, then slid beneath the cover as a sudden chill rattled through me. George's breath was still coming in deep, staccato clutches, his legs shaking. I put my hand on his shoulder.

"Come on," I said. "Try to sleep."

He continued to shake. "Cold," he whispered.

"Just relax. It's all right."

I pulled myself close to him, wrapping the outline of his body within my own, one arm dropping past his breastbone as I drew him to me. The scent of his hair, smelling of bar smoke, shampoo, and almonds — woody, flat-edged as a ruler — filled my nostrils, mushrooming in the dark until its heated perfume drowned my senses and, with George's breathing easing into a tidal rhythm as time and darkness spun down around us, I fell through myself again into sleep.

Twenty-Eight

I FELT we were burying an era when we buried my father, laying aside an epoch of the republic's past which had been distinguished by militaristic arrogance, narrow-sightedness, and a barely veiled, unrepentant racism.

Born the year Ruth hit sixty homers and "talkies" hit the Art Deco movie palaces and black-faced Al Jolson, the Russian émigré, crooned "Mammy" in a nasal, minstrel-style legato, my father lost his baby teeth as the Depression wore on through New Deal prescriptions and failed financial remedies. He traipsed to public school along the streets of an Irish ghetto clad in knickers, socks the color of coal, and round-toed lace shoes with holes the size of quarters in each of their thick soles. During the 1930s, he swept out upper Broadway movie houses in exchange for a few nickels a week and free admission. He reached puberty the year Hitler invaded Poland and DiMaggio hit .381 and won the MVP award, began smoking when Ted Williams, our namesake, batted .406 and the Japanese bombed Pearl Harbor. He lost his own father, a stern, wayward figure, to bitterness, drink, and leukemia, and left school at the age of sixteen, working dead-end jobs until the war ended and a white-picket-fence image of prosperity returned with ballplayers from Reese to Rizzuto. He earned a high school equivalency diploma, enlisted in the Marines when he turned eighteen, was called back up briefly for Korea, then settled into an office job and a marriage during the rookie seasons of Mantle and Mays. He fathered me, his older son, during a spell of zero inflation, passbook savings, day games, and political witch hunts. Bennie followed four years later, on the heels of a move into a new home that came complete with bad pipes, rain-darkened shingles, and a 5 percent, thirty-year mortgage.

As a boy, he had worked for a Manhattan grocer and had delivered sacks of food to Babe Ruth's Riverside Drive apartment. He felt personally betrayed, as if the sanctity and importance of his past had been negated, when Maris hit sixty-one to break the single-season record and Aaron took the all-time lead. He belittled the achievements of not only Aaron, but Reggie Jackson — as if they were tainted, for some unspoken reason — despite the fact that by the midseventies Jackson had won the MVP award, a third World Series ring, and a $75,000 contract. My father's anger continued, unmitigated by the ceasefire in Vietnam, or the cardiologist's warning to bag the smoking and cut down on porterhouse steaks and salt-crusted eggs. After Elizabeth's birth and Carter's election, he grew comfortable and frustrated. The year I made a serious run at hitting .400, he wore a Reagan pin on the lapel of his cadet-blue suit, telling me over Christmas drinks that my generation of players was pampered, self-indulgent, and inferior.

The day before we buried him, a summer movie opened. It was a resuscitation of the thirties Saturday afternoon action serial, featuring cliff-hanging perils, evil, dark-skinned villains, and American derring-do. When it began shattering box office records, I wished my father had lived to see the fulfillment of his nostalgic longings. We had not gone forward as a nation, but back, retreating into aggressive insecurity and petulant, infantile self-indulgence. We had reached the end of an era, and yet, as we began a new one, little had changed in the nation's soul beyond the colors projected on its movie screens, the range of its missiles, and the playing of its national pastime within the bounds of a commercially dictated night.

Dressed in a dark blue suit, white shirt, and regimental tie striped like a barber's pole, my father was watched over by my mother, Bennie, Barbara, and me, each of us clad in black and seemingly locked within our own private grief and sense of dislocation. Elizabeth — her small, delicate legs each white as an ash bat — played hopscotch in the azalea-ringed parking lot of the funeral home, her tiny feet skipping over the pitted black asphalt in gleaming patent leather shoes. A sense of drift, of being unmoored in time, overtook me, the hours and days scudding past like clouds — insubstantial, shifting, dissipating — the rituals of the wake and burial failing to anchor me. It was as if I had been carried along by a river, swept through childhood, adolescence, and the green, confusing years of my career, collecting like twigs and branches along the way a wife, a daughter, an accumulation of griefs, pleasures, accomplishments, and possessions, one long-dead friend, now a dead father to go with him, a dead father and a black star floating inside my shoulder. Each of these things was less like an anchor than a cut line, a sheared-off centerboard or rudder, so that I was simply drifting now, listing, spinning in slow circles. At the VA cemetery, with my father's coffin backed by a row of cadets, their young faces as innocent as those of the kids who come up to A ball every spring, and the somber words of the eulogy echoing down to the center of my thoughts, I felt the blossoming of a bottomless remorse rush through me. A pressure built around my eyes and temples, the tears I was ineptly trying to hold back being driven by the memory of my father, young and full of hope all those years ago, as I imagined him stabbing a single hand into the air and plucking a foul ball out of the sky as if he had caught hold of a single moment in time; then, later, turning the grass-smudged trophy over to me, his easily awed son, making it mine. And this remorse unexpectedly — for there was no volition behind it, only surrender, which may, after all, be the way to step into responsibility — tempered my sense of drift. Although that continued even when my shoulder tightened around the black star inside it as I heaved my father's casket into the air with Bennie and four other pallbearers. It continued throughout the repeated claps of gunshots as my father was lowered into the ground, his coffin draped with a flag until the end. It continued when Barbara, unaware of the black spot, asked me for a separation, claiming that our love existed somewhere out of reach, tied inextricably, almost unexplainably, to the past. It continued even after a second MRI showed a reduction in the size of the black cloud, the moisture in it no more than fluid caused by the swelling of inflamed tendons. It continued — with nothing ahead to guide me, no landmarks or lights or compass points, only the faint, seductive, reassuring beacon of Mr. Percy's offer, his voice floating through my head like a siren's song, as it always had, nothing else whispering to me, except the faint, unformed stirrings of responsibility, some intimation of a way to exist beyond the end point of innocence, and beyond the fear of death, without succumbing to Mr. Percy's warped, power-mad nihilism — until, while I was on the road, in some indistinct major league city days after my father's funeral, the fathers of the game and the federal courts ordered our union either to play or strike, and the vote came back to walk. We removed our uniforms for perhaps the last time, packed and carried our own bags, and began to split up on the deserted streets outside the ballpark.

"Where you heading?" Otis said, his road bag sitting on the ground as he lighted first my cigarette, then his own.

"No idea. What about you?"

Otis shrugged. "I thought I'd try to go see my kid."

"Didn't know you had one."

He nodded, flicking the tip of the cigarette's ash away as if that were all that remained of the past. "Want to take a ride?" He studied me for a moment, then said, "Shit, I don't bite. What the fuck else you got to do?"

I stood there, the cigarette between my fingers feeling like the only solid, real thing in the world. Then flicked it into the gutter and said, "Let's go."

Downtown at the team's hotel, we collected our luggage, bolted a pair of drinks in the lobby bar, then charged a rental car to Otis's account.

"Why a Benz?"

"You know what a nigger in a Cadillac is?"

"What?"

"Under suspicion."

On the roof we hunted among the pillars, pipes, and parked cars for our vehicle. Beyond a graffiti-smeared parapet the city's skyscrapers rose beside the hotel like glittering, ice-flecked stalagmites, lighted office and apartment windows shining inside them like silver coins. The atrium atop a landmark commercial tower — celebrated as the symbol of the city's financial rebirth — sparkled like a fat jewel. In the distance, the lights of a bridge, draped like pearls from suspension wires, glowed above a black river, and beyond them the closely packed traffic thinned into single, antlike lines as it rolled into the fields of low-lying suburbs, great patches of dim, seamless light spreading out around the city like prairie grass, leaving the intoxicating, feminine sparkle of the city behind as it rolled on into horizonless plains of darkness.

"Yo, toast. Over here." Otis had found the car, an elegant machine, polished and black as a hearse. There was something invulnerable about it. In the trashed surroundings — oil-stained floor; smashed light bulbs and mangled electrical fixtures; candy bar wrappers and cardboard fast food containers lying crushed and windswept in corners; discarded newspapers and pasted-up flyers announcing health club openings, sessions with a visiting Maharishi, gay rights demonstrations, and bargain-priced flights to European capitals — the car appeared to rise above the detritus of the city like a moral law. The inside smelled like a new wallet, the leather upholstery seeming to breathe in the dim light. Otis slipped the key into the ignition and the dashboard lit up with a silent, reassuring alertness, the precision of the numbered gauges and the steadiness of the green and golden lights that illuminated them lending the panel an air of infallibility. In this car, the glowing needles seemed to say, you cannot break down, become lost, or die. Static burst from the car's speakers as the radio caught the first spark of electricity. Otis turned the tuning knob, searching for a station. Sheets of buzzing interference rolled through the cab, clearing when the needle passed over a strong signal. The nasal whining of a country and western–style, my-hair-hurts, my-feet-stink, and I-don't-love-Jesus ballad followed the trilling allegro of a classical piano solo and an ad for breath mints. Robotic, devolution rock bled into hurry, this-sale-ends-now hysteria. An irate talk show caller asked a question that hung in amplified silence. Faintly, below the slinky funk of a blues riff, I could detect the drone of an anchorman, his ticker tape voice reporting the number of dead found in a Central American church. Otis let the needle settle when he found a thick, booming bass line glazed with the sugar of a rough-edged male falsetto backed by fuck-me-slow, ice-cream-voiced female vocalists. He cranked the volume to brain death and the car shook, the speakers exploding with soft cannon shots of sound. Otis began grooving in his seat, hands swaying above the wheel, fingers snapping, million-dollar-a-year torso undulating, hips thrusting as if he were humping the steering column. He turned, glanced at me, leaned back limbo-style, and screeched, "Yow!" Then reached behind himself into his bag and pulled out a short, cherry-colored pipe and a clear plastic bag. "Doctor, doctor," he said, stuffing the end of a marijuana bud the size of a waterbug into the bowl of the pipe. Humming, he took out a disposable lighter, put the nipple of the pipe to his lips, then — reaching over and snapping the flame to life inches from my face — gyrated in a long, slow groove as he touched the heat to the nappy crown of weed. After three tokes, an orange glow began to creep down the faces of the bud. Otis took a deep, lung-filling hit, then extended the pipe to me. I hadn't smoked pot for ages, and as the perfume of the drug swirled into the cloud of music corkscrewing through the interior of the car, George seemed to be sitting behind me, leaning forward over my shoulder, his voice warm and moist near my ear. "Take a hit, for Christ's sake, and pass the fucking thing," his energy and lack of patience with my procrastination undiminished in death. The tip of the pipe was wet with Otis's saliva when I put it between my lips, the heat in the stem intensifying as I drew a stream of milky white smoke through it. Long, thin threads of smoke snaked down through my chest as I held my breath. Otis, head back, eyes closed, released a bouquet of smoke that spread across the doe-colored roof of the car, then fell down around us. Veiled by smoke, his face lit by the low light of the dashboard, Otis seemed less recognizable, darker and more impenetrable — until he passed into insubstantiality — with each exchange of the pipe.

His skin blended into the soft blackness between us, and he receded to a dreamlike distance, the space in the car telescoping as
the drug slithered over deep recesses in my brain. When I looked
at him, all his boyish reticence and insecurity were gone. In their
place was a mischievous glee. He flashed his large, white teeth as
he turned and offered me the pipe a final time. He laughed, at me
I thought, or at something else, something beyond me, from the
far end of what seemed to be a long, watery tunnel. Startled, I
turned and looked over my shoulder. George was gone, the seat
vacant and dark.

"Hey." Otis laid a hand on my thigh, and through the smoke
and the radio's light, a reggae cut playing in the background now,
I saw the hand's history, the way it looked on the handle of a bat,
a hoe, an oar, manacled, wrapped at the wrist by a sacred charm
bracelet made of animal bones. When I looked up, Otis's face was
there in the echo of his word. His strangeness had vanished; I no
longer felt I could reach out and pass my hand through him as if
he were a spirit or apparition. Instead, I felt an impulse to reach
over and touch the black skin covering his face.

'Yeah?"

"Chill out. We ain't gone nowhere yet, you're having a heart
attack." Otis looked at me, silent, waiting. And finally I nodded,
feeling, as I did, that I was unmoored — casting off the lines of
home, family, community, the game — but was not in danger of
becoming lost. Instead, I was pointed toward something.

On the street, we darted into a stream of charging, seemingly
heedless traffic, red taillights bobbing and sliding ahead of us like
a herd of floating, migrating souls. The shops and department
stores were closed, the tableaus in their windows lighted and vig-
ilant, as if to darken the products in the spaces would open a
window onto chaos. Here and there on the deserted sidewalks,
between mounds of glistening black trash bags, a lone figure, or
huddled couple, stood anxiously flagging a taxicab. With the city
washing by us, the pulsing, synthetic funk blaring from the speakers seemed to falsely animate the dead buildings, electric lights,
and gliding, disconnected flow of cars. The traffic thinned as we
cruised along the avenue, leaving behind the bright, gold-arched

windows, the wide, well-swept sidewalks, and festive curb-to-doorway awnings. Overstuffed dumpsters, garbage bubbling up through their open lids, stood in front of black-faced, lightless buildings, their ground-floor windows protected by accordian-style steel gates. A man dressed in a ratty raincoat and pants riding several inches above his shins limped up to a phone booth and fingered the change well before going on. Poster-splattered plywood boards ringed abandoned construction sites. Ahead, its brightness rising out of the night like an oasis, a twenty-four-hour cafeteria appeared, long-legged hookers smoking cigarettes on the sidewalk beneath its hot-coal-colored electric sign. The pot was turning the city into a dreamscape through which I floated from palaces to slums as smoothly and effortlessly as scanning the radio waves. As we stopped for a red light, I turned and, staring at Otis, I wasn't sure which was more intoxicating, the drug or the sense of movement, of being in motion, pointed, running.

Otis turned and looked at me. "Don't worry," he said. "I ain't gonna let nothing bad happen to you."

I looked back at him for a moment, then said, "Okay," watching his face sparkle in the passing beams of headlights.

And as he slammed the gearbox into first and we began to move, I heard the voices I was leaving behind, from my father's hoarse, distant, deathbed whisper and Mr. Percy's stern, seductive, diabolically ministerial tone of accusation and forgiveness, to Elizabeth's fleeting, small-voiced, forever-elusive innocence, the magic in it floating above the fields and the tarred strips of the interstates, beckoning, impalpable as O'Kane's ghost, outracing us as we rushed deeper into the republic's engulfing, seemingly limitless night, forever beyond the precincts of the sweet illusions of the game.